From Prisoner to Princess

Alana Dyer

Royal Rebellion Series

Dedication

Dedicated to all those feeling lost. One day you will find that you are a boss ass Queen or King and live your best life.

Prologue

"Hush, little one. They will hear you." The Maid shushes as she holds on tightly to the child Princess, her worry filled voice shaking as she does her best to keep the two of them hidden in the shadows. The Princess slowly stops crying, her lips quivering as she hides her face in her Maid's shoulder, letting the woman carry her down the hallway and into the hidden passage only servants use. The Maid's footsteps are barely audible as she carefully descends the stone steps knowing that if she were to make the smallest noise, the enemies will find them and kill the last remaining member of the Royal Family.

The sounds of swords clashing and gun shots being fired frightens the little Princess, making her cling to her Maid. She knows there are bad men in her home - that everyone is fighting - but no one has told her why. All she knows is that her Maid is taking her to safety.

The stairs finally come to an end with a small passage way leading straight to the way out ahead. The Maid sighs with relief, tightening her hold on the Princess and quickening her steps.

"Just a little further and we will be free." She whispers, the Princess nodding her little head. The Maid's arms are growing sore from carrying the Princess since she found the little girl huddled in her room full of fear, but she has a sworn duty to protect the little blonde girl and as she pushes the door open and the fresh air greets her, she feels a new found strength inside her. With the Princess so close to being safe, the Maid knows that the future of her country will be bright.

The Maid smiles as she rushes into the cold night, sticking to the shadows of the trees as she tightens the cloak on the Princess, doing her best to keep her warm. Finally, she rounds the corner to find who she is looking for - a black horse saddled and ready to take her Highness away from the war filled

Palace. A man in armour sits on top of the horse with a young boy in his lap – the Princess's playmate and a Knight in training. The Maid knows that this mode of escape is old fashion but if anyone were to take one of the vehicles they would be tracked down and killed by the rebels. In this high-tech world, the quiet escape on horseback is what will save their Princess.

"Listen to me Princess." The Maid begins, her pace nearly a trot at this point causing her voice to come out breathless.

"The Knight will take you to safety and when the time is right, we will return you home." She places the Princess on her feet, looking into her watery violet eyes as she too does her best not to cry in front of the little girl she watched grow since the day the Princess was born. Reaching into her pocket, the Maid retrieves the necklace that the late Queen entrusted her with, carefully placing it around the young girl's neck.

"This is from your parents. Know that they love you with all their heart." With these final words, the Maid lifts the girl into her arms for one last hug before passing the Princess to the Knight, tears in her eyes as she watches the young green eyed blonde boy wrap his arms around the Princess and hold her tightly.

"Protect her." The Maid pleads, before the Knight looks to the scared children before him. With a nod to the Maid as a silent promise, the Knight flicks the reigns and the horse takes off galloping away into the darkness with the Palace fading away.

♔[1]

The woman jolts awake in a cold sweat, her cell freezing in the winter night. The vivid dream that she has just awoken from begins to fade from her mind as she tries to recall more than just the feel of warm clothes and the sounds of metal clashing. She sighs, her breath coming out as a cloud in the cold air. Its been years since she lost her memory and she feels hopeless, as if she will never remember who she really is.

Looking out the small window of her cell, she shivers and realizes that dawn is hours away. If she wants to have any strength for the day ahead, she will need to get more rest.

Pulling the thin material that the prison calls a blanket around her body, she curls in on herself hoping to conserve warmth. Her hand clutches the

---

1. **https://coolsymbol.com/copy/White_Chess_King_Symbol_%E2%99%94**

small gold necklace that she has had since childhood and she wills herself to fall asleep.

♔²

Slamming his fist against the wall, the man screams in frustration. Fourteen long years he has been searching for Her. Everyone kept telling him that she was dead. That she had been killed in the Rebellion. But he knows that is not true. He personally helped her escape so how could she have just vanished into thin air without a trace.

Suddenly the screens light up in alarm and the man rushes to see what has happened, worried that the latest search for a trace of her might have come up empty again – but he is met with something he has dreamt of for years.

Fourteen years of searching has come to an end. Fourteen years of using the small trace of DNA left on her hair brushes finally yielded the results he has always wanted. But who would have thought that she would have ended in a prison of all places.

With a grin he prints the results and stalks out of the room. Who cares how she ended up *there* of all places. She is safe and its time to return her home.

---

2. https://coolsymbol.com/copy/White_Chess_King_Symbol_%E2%99%94

Chapter 1

The sounds of shuffling, banging and screaming coax me from my sleep, my body shivering from the cold air as I slowly become alert. Its morning time judging by the small amount of light that filters through my window and soon the Guards will be forcing me on my feet.

"Get up girly, its time for fun." Banging on the bars to my cell, the Guard takes one look at me as I push myself into a sitting up, trying my best to keep the thin blanket wrapped around my body to try and keep warm. My warm breath becomes fog in the air as I yawn, slipping my feet into the prison issued slippers and standing from my bed, if that's what you could call the thin mattress on a concrete slab.

My cell doors open and I throw the blanket onto my bed before slinking out to join the others. As I line up with the others that were caught as thieves, I think about how I ended up in Lady Pricilla's Prison for Troubled Women.

♔[1]

I race across the street heading to the alleyways that would take me to my hide out and to safety. I dodge the cars and bikes that drive by me, my bag slowing me down with the weight of the food inside. But I needed it if I wanted to survive the winter this year.

"Stop in the name of the Crown!" Ahead of me a man shouts while pointing in my direction. The Police Officer causes the pedestrians to look in my direction with fear and disgust as they part to the side and give him easier access to where I stand. Rolling my eyes, I turn right and head into the dark alley beside me.

I know these alleyways like the back of my hand, know them better than I know myself. Growing up in the Slums after loosing any memories I had

---

1. https://coolsymbol.com/copy/White_Chess_King_Symbol_%E2%99%94

before age six, I learned that the world is not for a lone child and that to survive I have to be fast and learn faster.

I keep to the shadows as I run through the back alleyways, always zigzagging in hopes of confusing the Police pursuing me. Past crumbling walls, under clothes hanging to dry that were washed earlier in the day by the ladies of the Slums, through backyards baren and ruined from years of neglect.

Finally, I stop and slink into a dark hollow door way and take a moment to catch my breath before checking to see if I have lost my pursuers. Thankfully, I find the coast is clear and decide to make the final stretch to my house, if that's what you could call the run down single room Shack with an attached bathroom I found at eight years old.

The way to my Shack is uneventful, my eyes and ears alert for any movement that indicates the Police have found me, luckily no one has. With a grin, I stop just before the current alleyway ends and look down both sides of the rundown street. Small bungalows make my little rundown Shack look out of place, but it is enough for me to know that no one would think to check the unassuming building that I have been putting work into making it a decent home. With the coast clear, I run the short distance towards the back door of the shack, slipping silently inside and shutting the door before locking it. I am safe now.

Smiling, I make my way to the small dining table and place my bag on top of it. The first thing I do is sort the food, placing the cans on the small shelf above the minifridge before removing the money and jewels I managed to secure from some rich woman in the shopping district. Taking a deep breath, I remind myself that I am one step closer to being able to leave the Capitol - Zalaris - and buying my own piece of land where I can live a good life. I just need to hang on just until spring next year.

Taking the money and jewels, I carry them to the bathroom where I lift the loose tile behind the toilet and take out the small tin cookie box. Placing it on the counter, I open the lid with my free hand and sigh at the money and jewelry that greets me. I add my haul to it before securing the lid and hid the cookie tin once more. Making sure the tile is secured in place, I head back to my food stash and take out a few piece of fruit I had stolen today, deciding a small fruit salad is a meal fit for celebrating a good haul. With the diced fruit in the bowl and the scraps in my small compost bin on the table, I make my way to the cot I call a bed and sit down, enjoying the sweet taste of the fruit. Suddenly the power goes out just as I finish the last bit of my meal, causing me to curse in the dark. I swear the weather here sucks.

Placing the bowl on the bed, I stand and make my way to the door. Storms are problematic in the Slums, always cutting out the power that we get here. I had thought I fixed this issue when I placed a solar panel on the roof of my hut, something I had stolen three years ago when I got sick and tired of the power cutting out for days, but clearly I need more to keep the power steady here.

a sigh, I exit my home and lock the door before I go to see what I can do to restore power. The fall rain pelts down on my body, causing me to shiver as I make my way to the right side of my shack where the power box is. Reaching it withing a minute, unease settles inside me when I notice the wire to the solar panel has been cut, its stored power that would usually work unable to connect to my power box.

Realizing that I am in trouble, I turn and try to run back inside to the safety of my shack but I am too late. Strong arms wrap around my neck forcing me back against a sturdy body, one I know I have no chance of fighting against.

"Allison of the Slums, you are under arrest for crimes against the citizens of the City Zalaris including larceny, theft and burglary." A man shouts in front of me, the Police Chief appearing from behind the large Oak tree beside my Shack. With that, I am forced onto my knees as a group of Police Officers surround me, their guns painted in my direction while another Officer comes to handcuff me. Secured and in their grasps, the Officers pat me down – more like groped me – checking me for any weapons before dragging me to the back of a transport van leaving me alone and left in the dark with my fate unknown.

♔[2]

That is how I become prisoner number four-zero -four-five. There was no trial. No Judge to decide my fate. To the law, I am an unwed fertile female in need of correcting. I needed a strict hand to guide me in becoming a proper female for society.

---

2. https://coolsymbol.com/copy/White_Chess_King_Symbol_%E2%99%94

With a sigh, I find that I am last to line up with the other and take a chance to look at the girls in the corridor. Many are like me, here for petty theft or burglary hoping to make a living and find some form of escape from the hell called the Capital Slums. After our meal, we will be sent to the many facilities to work either in the mines, the textile shops or the farms where we obtain the food we eat. But this is work only for thieves.

For prostitutes, their fates are worse.

If you were caught and arrested as a prostitute and sent here, you have one of two options. Accept the help to change right away and be sent to what we call the "Plush" room where you will be trained as a proper lady before being sold to the aristocrats as a mistress. Or be defiant and endure the Guards taking turns raping you until you break and are forced into submission. From there you are sent to the Palace and the Regent – Juden Trilavantas - decides your fate. Although I hear that the fate he chooses for you is worse than being sold as a mistress.

Rubbing my tired eyes, I count the number of prostitute in line up – four. These are the ones that were screaming last night, their first night in this prison. These are the ones that said no to being sent to the Plush room and after a night of the Guards treatment, were given a chance to reconsider their options and by the looks of their hunched over, wobbling figures, they choose to repent and be rehabilitated. They will be enjoying the plush room from now on until they are deemed worthy to leave.

With a sigh, I follow behind my line as the Guards order us to move, watching a primly dressed woman approach the four broken prisoners and guide them away. For some reason I find myself being thankful that I stole to survive instead of selling my body as I watch their listless bodies move towards another corridor.

Chapter 2

"Thanks Artie." I smile at Aurther the head chef of the prison, a gentle giant of a man who got stuck here after killing a man in self defense. Everyone loves him. He is friendly, polite and always helping those that don't cause him any trouble. The best part is if you are kind to him and help him in the kitchen, then you'll earn extra desert in this hell hole.

"Not a problem Alli Cat. Also, take this." Holding out a cupcake to me, I quickly reach over to receive the treat and place it onto my tray, my necklace slips out from under the collar of my shirt and catching the light as I do so.

"You better hide that or some one will try to steal it." Aurther states quietly, motioning to the simple chain with a locket. With his warning, I quickly reach for the necklace and tuck it back into its hiding spot, praying that no one else saw it as the insignia on it is the only clue to my past. That and a photo of me as a baby placed inside with the note 'my darling, my world, my princess' written by a feminine hand, one I believe to be my mother's. After confirming with Aurther that no one saw, I thank him and his staff once more before taking a large bottle of water at the end of the que and make my way to the lone table in the corner.

Not many like to sit here with the corner table being isolated from everyone else, but I prefer this table. It gives me the advantage of looking around the room to see who is left here in this Prison and who is new. Of course, not many have left since my last time in solitary confinement, but ten new girls have joined us this morning. The new ones are the hardest to deal with. They are either scared and jumpy, crying at the drop of a hat or arrogant and thinking they rule the Prison when really that will just earn them a beating or solitary confinement. And they always come for me since I sit alone.

I take a deep breath and close my eyes; three more months and I will be out of here if I stay on my best behavior. If I can stay our of solitary confinement this week, then I will not have to worry about another one being added to my sentence.

"Hey, bitch I like that necklace I saw earlier." Comes a snarky voice before me. The room goes silent, the clinking of silverware on plates stopping as everyone most likely turns to stare. A good show will begin for those watching on.

Slowly I open my eyes and look at the curly haired redhead in front of me and stop myself from sighing. *Prostitute* my mind registered, taking in her looks from her slightly bruised and messy body to the arms crossed under her large breasts that the shirt barely hides hickies under. Guards must have had fun trying to break her, so why is she here and not the plush room.

"The last girl who said that to me ended up in the hospital wing" *and I found myself in solitary confinement.* I retort with, thinking the last bit to myself. Taking a bite of my cupcake I size up the redhead and her two blonde goons on either side of her. Looking at the first one – a platinum blonde with pin straight hair and tanned skin - I notice similar bruising on her and just about rolled my eyes out of my head. After turning to look at the raven haired girl with pale skin I confirm my suspicions that all three sold their bodies, but it still doesn't tell me why they are here in front of me. I wonder if maybe they were being kept by a handler and that's why they were with my group and not in the plush room. The thought alone makes me chuckle as I finish my cup cake.

"What's so funny?" Platinum Blondie asks, giving me a glare as she sizes me up. I ignore her in favor of taking a bite of my sandwich, deciding that if these three bimbos try anything that will land me in solitary confinement, then I might as well go with a full stomach.

"Maybe she is a little slow." Raven girly answers, scoffing as she throws her hair over her shoulder. Red just stands there, trying to look intimidating as her hands move to her hips.

"I don't care what she finds so funny, I just want that damned necklace." Red growls out, surprising me. Who knew humans could growl like wild animals.

"Like I said earlier, the last girl who said that to me ended up in the hospital wing. Now go sit down and eat your food." I sigh out, feeling like I am talking to children. Actually scratch that, the children I used to keep an eye on in the Slums listened better than these three idiots. My words seem to be the trigger for their short fuse as if on que the three move to lunge at me over the table. With quick movements, the hand I kept under the table lifts it up, flipping it into their faces and creating a nice lovely crunching sound. It seems these three will need a nose job later today.

Before they can react, I push myself to my feet and move to the right, getting into a fighting stance in case they try anything else, but the sounds of boots on concrete catches my attention and I relax. Guards will be here soon to break up what ever fight has started. Frowning, I feel something touch my foot and jump, looking down to find my water bottle. I take a chance to pick up the bottle and chug the drink. With the Guards on the way, I want to finish the drink just in case I don't get anything for a while in solitary confinement.

"Can't say I didn't warn you." I shrug nonchalantly after wiping my mouth clean. Guards have entered the room by now, creating a circle around the three ladies and me. I quickly put my hands up, dropping my water bottle as I do and slowly get to my knees. Looks like my fun is ruined and I will be back in solitary confinement. Yippee.

The Guards order the three to their knees, Red seeming to defy them as her goons comply easily. I scoff, enjoying the Guards man handling Red out of the common area with her kicking and screaming while the other two are cuffed and escorted out with dignity for complying easily. Someone takes my arm and yanks it behind me none to gently, making me wince as cuffs are placed onto my wrists before I am hauled to my feet.

"Move you slut." The Guard behind me orders, pushing me towards the door. I wince, wanting to glare at the man but I know better. Glaring will get you a smack across the face. I know where I am being taken to though, it's the same place I am always taken to after getting into a fight I did not want to be in – solitary confinement.

With a sigh, I move towards the path that will lead me to the black room with little to no light inside. But something feels off, like a looming danger is just around the corner. With unease inside me, I look back to notice only one

Guard following behind me. Usually there are three, one to keep me in sight and two to shoot me if I fight back. My stomach churns and I am getting ready to run when strong arms grasp the cuffs keeping my wrists together, using the force to push me into the nearest wall.

"You always get into trouble missy." The Guard begins, pushing himself against me.

"So since you want to act like a tough girl, how about we see just how tough you really are." He continues, flicking his tongue along my earlobe and causing me to shudder with disgust. I try to struggle as his hands move from my wrist and snake around my body, slowly feeling along my waist as one moves to grope my breast while the other holds me closer to him. I keep trying to throw him off of me, to try my best to get free but the man presses his hips against my ass, and I feel the tell tale lump of his erection. I am doing nothing but turning him on further.

Fear takes hold of me as I slowly come to realize that my struggling is futile. That if this man wants to take my virginity, then he will. Nothing will stop him from hurting me and with a silent tear, I pray that some guardian angel sends help my way.

"Unhand her at once!"

Chapter 3

"**A**re you hard of hearing, stupid, or both." The voice that yelled earlier repeats as the Guard ignores him, his hands already moving to push at my shorts. This time I fight back, throwing my head against his in hopes of breaking his nose as well. The Guard curses as my head connects with his chin but he continues to the ignore the other person and the pain I caused him, his lust more important to deal with in this moment.

"I said unhand her you ignoramus." The deep male voice is close and right now he is my only hope in getting out of this mess. The Guard stops, giving me a chance to try and take a look at the man who is saving me but unfortunately for my luck the Guard is like a brick wall blocking my view of everything but the concrete wall before me.

"What I am doing doesn't concern a Palace Guard, now keep moving pretty boy." The Guard nearly yells back, causing me to flinch for a moment. What the hell is a Palace Guard doing here of all places. The Regent never cares about this place.

"This is the last warning." The Palace Guard warns, his voice growing closer. The Guard holding onto me scoffs, most likely deciding to ignore the man. Without warning, the Guard is off me and howling on the floor, his screams of pain making me wince but I am free of him. Shocked, I do nothing but stare at the sight and wish that I had something to record this moment. Never had I saw anyone take down the Guards here and it is pretty damn awesome in my books.

"Thank god I got lost in here or else I would have been to late to protect you." I turn to look at the man that just saved me, slowly taking in his attire. He wares black dress pants, a matching black leather Jacket, a navy blazer and a deep blue dress shirt under the blazer. A silver belt with a gold buckle holds his pants up and attached to the belt is a sword in its sheath and a gun holstered and kept in working condition. The only thing missing is the taser in his hands that he places in his pocket.

He looks to the Guard still on the floor before back at me, his eyes scanning my body before he lands on my arms. I frown, wanting to cover myself up but I can't. My arms are still bound behind my back.

"Can I help you take those off of you?" He asks, hands up in surrender. I hesitate before nodding, stepping towards the man and turning so that my back is facing him. He makes quick work in removing the cuffs, throwing them onto the ground and making me jump from the clattering sound.

"Sorry." He whispers sheepishly. With my hands free, I turn to face the man once more and rub my wrist that are sore from the mistreatment.

"Are you cold?" He asks and I nod, unsure if I should be talking to him. He sighs, stepping back and slowly takes off his jacket before stretching his hand out to me. I reach for the jacket, craving the warmth it can provide but hesitate. What if this is a trap.

The man waits patiently, giving me a friendly smile and I decide that trap or not, I want to be warm. Taking the jacket into my hands, I quickly put it on and sigh with relief. I haven't felt this warm in ages.

"Thank you." I whisper, getting a smile from the man. The scent of his cologne lingers, giving me a sense of déja vu as if I have smelt it somewhere before, some time long ago. Confuse, I reach for my necklace, finding some comfort as I rub my thumb along the crest.

"Were you hurt?" The man asks and I turn to look back at him, catching the insignia on his blazer – one that was the same as the crest on my necklace. Looking to his face, I feel like he is familiar. That deep down I know this man from his startling blue eyes to black as the night sky hair. I feel my heart begin racing as I try to figure out how I know this man, but a sharp pain in my head has my vision blurring and the world spinning.

"Are you alright? Did he hi-" The man begins to ask, worry etched in his voice. Before I can hear the rest of his words, my ears begin to ring and I soon find myself falling. Strong arms catch me before I can hit the hard floor, the scent that lingered on the jacket wraps around me as the world fades away.

Chapter 4

Groaning, I open my eyes long enough only to wince and shut them tightly, hiding my head under a soft plush pillow as a migraine wrecks my brain. *Just what happened to me after the Palace Guard saved me?* I wonder, allowing my body to sink deeper into what ever I lay on. The air feels clean and fresh as I take a deep breath and my body relaxed and warm.

Bolting up at the realization that this is *not* my prison cell, I wince again and regret the sudden movements. My head feels like an ax is splitting it in two, the only memory I have being that I passed out after seeing the insignia on the Palace Guard's blazer. From there I had dreams, or were they nightmares, that flew past my mind like a blur of colours I could barely see. With a groan I shut my eyes and run my fingers through my messy hair before massaging my temples, hoping to relieve the pressure.

"Where the hell am I?" I whisper, trying to piece together what happened after passing out. Deciding I need to take a look around, I take a deep breath and open my eyes, wincing and squinting when the bright light causes more pain to my already throbbing head. After adjusting to the light, I am finally able to open my eyes fully to take in the room.

I sit upon a large canopy bed -my guess is a king size frame and mattress- that is comfortable and soft. Large fluffy pillows are behind me, the scent of mint and vanilla wafting from them, calming my slightly racing heart. I've always loved those two scents mixed together.

Across from me is the source of the light, two large floor to ceiling windows only separated by columns that support the open double glass doors, fresh air filtering in from outside. There is no musty and damp scent that I have grown used too, only the scent of winter snow on the wind that is crisp. Thank God for the large fluffy duvet that covers me or I would be freezing right now.

Curtains on either ends of the windows are held open by a rope, allowing the sunlight to stream in and be the cause for worsening the migraine that I wish would just go away. It seems that the double doors lead to a balcony that is kept clean of snow and for some reason I feel the urge to curl up outside with a cup of hot chocolate while relaxing and reading a book.

Looking away from the window, my gaze travels to the right where I notice a study area. A desk is situated in the corner against the cream and gold wall with a book shelf directly beside that. Infront of the desk is a small sitting area with a glass coffee table and four arm chairs. It looks like the perfect place to study or – once again – curl up and read a book.

Continuing my gaze, I notice that between the first book shelf and the one closes to the bed is a large fireplace, a fire already crackling inside it and explaining why the room is so warm even with the doors open. In front of the fire place is a set of couches and lounges face the large grey brick centerpiece of the room, a flat screen television mounted just above it. Then we come to beside the bed, another thin floor to ceiling window letting in more light.

After examining the right side, I begin to explore the left. Beside me is an open door, one that leads to the bathroom by what I can see from my spot on the bed. Beside that is a vanity made of gold and something white - maybe marble – with a large jewelry box on the right of the vanity and some make up brushes and bottles on the left. I have the feeling that if I were to open the drawers I will find make up and skin care products. To the right of the vanity is another door, one that peaks my curiosity but I will have to explore it later.

Finally at the very end beside the first set of floor to ceiling windows is a set of double doors, these one made of what I assume to be solid wood. As if my staring called him, these doors open and in walks in the Palace Guard that saved me.

"Glad to see you are awake. You slept for two days." He greets, a large smile splitting his face and bringing a childish air to him. I smile back, motioning to the room I am in before opening my mouth.

"Where am I?" I ask, shocked that I slept for so long and needing to know answers as this room feels too familiar to me – like I have been here before. This leaves me feeling confused as all I have ever known are the Slums.

"You are where you should be, where you should have lived your whole life, Princess Allisara." He answers, his happy look slowly disappearing until there is nothing but a solemn expression left. Without warning, he stops beside the bed, getting down on one knee and bowing his head towards me.

"Welcome home, my Princess." The air in the room became thin and I find it growing harder to breath. This man must have the wrong girl as I am not Royalty. Everyone knows that the Rebellion killed the King and Queen fourteen years ago and that their daughter, the Lost Princess, has been missing for all these years. The Princess has another six years to appear before the Regent and his family can assume the title as the next Royal Family.

"Allisara, its okay please calm down." Strong arms pull me close and a gentle voice fills my ears as the man rushes to sit beside me, holding me like some fragile doll as if at any moment I am going to break. It helps though as the scent of his cologne fills my nose and I use that to focus. Deep breath in. Deep breath out. Repeat.

"Thats it, just breath." He sighs out with relief, his hand moving to rub my back. I pull away for a moment to look around the room as my breathing steadies and I find myself calming down.

Suddenly something flickers in the light by the balcony and a golden blonde little girl in a ruffled pink dress walks angrily towards the bed, tears running down her chubby little face. At first I think that she is a ghost, until I realize I know that dress and that little girl. It's the same dress I wore when I woke up in the Slums. That little girl is me.

"Alli I am sorry, come play please!" A voice calls out as another child appears; his features barely visible as he walks towards the little me.

"Go away Demi. I am mad at you!" Came the young me's reply. The boy grows closer, his exasperated look making me feel a little unease. No child should look like that when a friend is mad at them. Then I notice his eyes, a startling blue that stared into mine as he rescued me from the Prison Guard before he could rape me. What I can only assume to be a memory fades away as I take in what I just witnessed. What this man said is true. This room I am in is my room. Turning to face the man, I feel his name on the tip of his tongue. Deep down I know Demi is a nickname. Then like a light switch, it clicks.

"Demitrias?" I whisper, almost questioning if I am right as I lightly run my fingers across his stubbled jaw. He looks tired, the dark circles under his eyes telling me that it hasn't been easy for him the last fourteen years. Has he been searching for me all this time?

"So you are remembering." He whispers back with hope in his eyes, his face coming closer to mine. I feel his lips press softly against mine, his blue eyes closing as he pulls me closer. I freeze, unsure how I feel about him kissing me like this and unsure how I feel about him. The man before me is Demitrias – Demi – Trilavantas. Eldest son to Duke Juden Trilavantas and my... my what?

Your betrothed. Something inside me whispers, causing me to pull away in shock, surprising Demitrias as well. Closing my eyes I wince as memories flash through my mind of he and I playing together as children. Of my fifth birthday when my parents informed me that one day Demitrias and I will be married and rule the Kingdom of Nimairene.

But then flashes of that night pop in, of the night I was whisked away from my home because of a Rebellion. My Maid, Rainnah, had handed me to someone – to a knight – and told him to protect me. But no one protected me. In the end I found myself in the Slums alone, cold and hungry with no memories of my past until now, while Demitrias was able to enjoy the comforts as a future Duke, the warmth and luxuries in the Palace, in my home.

"Get away from me." I practically growl out as hate and disgust fills me. I was too blind as a child to see it, but with each memory that surfaces I can see the real Demitrias behind the fake mask he wears. He never cared for me, never wanted to be around me. He only catered to me because we are betrothed, because he had to put on a show.

"Alli I can ex-" He begins as I push him away and quickly climb out of the bed from the other side.

"Oh really?" I cut in sarcastically, glaring at him. Without hesitation, I remove his jacket from me, throwing it directly at his face as I try to widen the space between us.

"Explain to me why my memories were taken away? Why my life was spent in the Slums?" I quickly question. Watching as his shocked face soon becomes morphed with exasperation and anger I try not to show the disgust I feel towards him. It seems the mask is cracking.

"How about you tell me why I nearly died from hunger and hypothermia while you lived in my home safe and warm eating anything you desired?" I shout back, shaking as my anger turns to rage. Demitrias flinches, his blue eyes searching my face as I glare back at him. If he is looking for the same weak little Princess that used to want his undivided attention well too bad. She is gone and she is never coming back.

"My father said you had died after your Maid had taken you somewhere to be safe." He whispers, his eyes meeting mine with a pleading look. It's a good act he is putting on but I can see the slight annoyance hidden in the depth of his eyes. My parents were fools thinking he was a good match for me.

"Your father, the current Regent? The man responsible for the way my Kingdom is declining?" I question, studying his reaction. A look of confusion passes his face, but I notice the way his fists clench and how he slightly shifts to sit straighter. He is hiding something from me and it's probably the fact his father isn't happy to know I am alive. If in six years time I had not returned, his father would have become King and Demitrias would be the Crown Prince as twenty years would have passed deeming the Royal family eradicated and gone. But here I am perfectly healthy and alive ready to claim my birthright.

"Clearly whatever you have been through has made you a little hysterical. How about you go shower and relax and when you are ready we can talk." He sighs out, giving me a look like he is settling a child down from a tantrum. I scoff, walking towards the exit to my room and holding one of the doors open.

"Get the fuck out Demitrias." I order, watching as the mask falls once again and he stands to his feet, angrily stomping towards me.

"Alli-"

"It is Princess Allisara to you." I cut him off, squaring my shoulders and readying myself to fight if need me. I catch sight of two Guards watching from the hallway, hands on the pistols as they eye Demitrias. Looks like I have a few loyal men beside me, good.

"Princess Allisara." He grinds out, his body trembling. Seems like I am finally getting under his skin.

"I suggest you watch that attitude of yours if you know what's good for you." He continues before storming off. I roll my eyes, watching as one of the Guards – a blond haired, green eyed man - shoves him away from my door before nodding to me respectfully. I thank them before closing the door and locking it. I do not need anyone to come and bother me while I remove my prison uniform and shower off the grime.

Making my way to the open door by my bed, I am happy when my memory does not fail me and I find myself in a large bathroom. With a sigh of relief I step inside only to shiver from the cold tile floor. Usually I have my prison slippers on but someone must have taken them from me when I was asleep. Taking another step onto the cold tile, I try my best to get used to the feeling as I walk towards the mirror to see just what damage being in Lady Pricilla's Prison for Troubled Women has done. I keep my eyes down for a moment, taking time to calm down after dealing with Demitrias, before lifting my head and looking into my reflection.

My violet eyes – a trait of the Royal family – are filled with unshed tears. The skin underneath them is dark and sunken in and it will be a few more days of good sleep and food before my skin will look plump and healthy again.

Dirt covers my skin in splotches while my long golden hair is left in tangles. No one really cared for the looks of those that were made to do labor. We were there to work while we were prisoners and that was that.

Searching through the drawers of the bathroom vanity, I quickly find a brush and set to work on detangling my hair. After what feels like an eternity and a lot of wincing and cursing, the knots in my hair are gone and I finally feel ready for a shower.

Stepping away from the mirror, I pad across the cold tiles once more towards the shower but not before I look towards the claw foot bath tub with longing. I would love to have a bubble bath right now but this sense of urgency I feel after kicking Demitrias out has me walking away, deciding that a bath will be left for tonight. Stripping off the skimpy clothes that is my prison uniform and quickly throwing them in the trash I enjoy the freedom I feel washing over me as I stand naked in this large room. I will never return back to that place – to Lady Pricilla's Prison for Troubled Women – unless its to destroy it.

Stepping inside the high-tech shower, I take a moment to look at the handles wondering just how hard it is to turn a shower on until I finally manage to get the damned contraption working. Instantly, warm water sprays onto my body, surprising me before I find myself enjoying the warmth and relax.

My mind wanders to everything I have been through from waking up in the Slums, the many nights I spent searching for shelter and warmth while staving. How a man took me under his wing and taught me to steal to survive for two years before I found my shack. All of this to end up with me being the Princess of Nimairene whose memories have yet to all return.

My body starts to shake as I slide along the titled wall to my knees, my tears finally spilling as the emotions take over. I cry for the lost memories that are returning to me. Cry for my people that have suffered the last fourteen years since the Rebellion took the lives of my friends and parents. I cry for everything including myself. How I was abandoned by people who were sworn to protect me. I cry until my tears run dry and the pity that took hold of me starts to fade before I stand up and wash the grime from my hair and body.

I let the water wash away the remnants of the Slums and prison from my body, let it calm me as I begin to think of a plan. First, I will need to take back control from the Regent. Duke Juden Trilavantas has caused so much damage that I need to reverse starting with taking away his power. Second is finding people loyal to me and me only. From there I can sort out the Government and the Military before fixing my Kingdome.

With my mind set, I turn the shower off and step out to grab one of the many fluffy towels that I promptly wrap around my body. Thanks to the shower, my curls have returned to my golden hair and it takes some time for me to dry them, deciding to allow the locks to flow around me freely as I leave the washroom and head back into my bedroom then promptly to the only set of doors I have yet to explore.

Taking a deep breath, I send a silent prayer in hoping that this is indeed the closet from my memories before I open the doors, smiling as the lights above illuminates the wracks of clothes. Gone are the little princess dresses I used to have as a child, now the wracks are filled with clothes fit for a Queen. I decide to by pass the many dresses that hang on the left hand and instead focus on the right side where blouses, pants and business suits hang. I need something that screams power, a way to show that the rightful Heir is back and taking charge. Then I see it, a set of black leather pants.

Grinning, I throw the towel onto the bench in the middle of the room and grab a set of under garments before slipping into the leather pants. From there I find a knit silver turtleneck tank top. The final touch to my outfit is a cropped leather jacket and a pair of knee high boots. With one last look in the mirror I take a deep breath, something sparkling catching my attention just over my shoulder in the mirror's reflection. There, glittering under it's own light, is a tiara I remember my mother wearing made of white gold with violet coloured amethyst - the colour of my eyes. I grin and make my way to the display, carefully picking up the tiara before returning to the mirror and settling the tiara on top of my head. This is the final touch I need to show my rightful place here as future Queen.

Exiting the closet, I make my way to my room's exit and throw open the doors, smirking as the Guards jump from the heavy wood hitting the walls. With a step forward, I walk past the men and make my way through the main hall towards my destination. I know what I need to do and now it is time to show the world that Princess Allisara Nimair is back.

This is my home.

My birth right.

And it is time I take back what is mine once and for all and end the misery the Trilavantas has caused.

Chapter 5

My footsteps echo along the halls as the two Guards follow silently behind me. One is the blonde from earlier, the other is a short man with red hair shaved short. Along the way many of the residents of the Palace recognize me as I make my way through the halls, bowing and whispering about how the rightful Queen has finally been found. My strides grow in confidence with their whispered support even when my memories fail me when trying to find my destination. Thankfully the Guards stay silent, allowing me to walk the halls at my own pace.

It takes a few twist and turns before I eventually I find myself standing in front of large oak doors with my family's crest etched into them. The doors are slightly ajar and as the Guards that have accompanied me move to open them, I hold out my hand and shake my head no. I can hear the shouting of two men in there and I want to listen in for a moment.

"She is a child!" A man's voice angrily shouts, causing me to roll my eyes at this out burst.

"Allisara is not a child. She is twenty which is old enough to rule." Comes a reply. I recognize the voice belonging to Demitrias and chuckle. Who ever he is arguing with is not happy that I am back.

"I have sat on this Throne longer then most rulers. This is my Throne. A Throne I have worked hard for." Rage takes over as I recognize now who is arguing with Demitrias. How dare this man claim what belongs to me.

"No, it is MY Throne and MY kingdom. You are done screwing around with it Juden." Throwing open the doors I state these words as I walk into the Throne Room and march to the center of it. Shock fills the eyes of the Guards stationed around the room as well as the two men that I now despise with every fiber of my body as they take in my appearance. I ignore everyone in the room, my gaze glued to Duke Juden Trilavantas as I glare at him, allowing him to see the hatred and rage I have towards him shine through. He looks at me with a mixture of shock and horror before a mask of a smug smile takes its place. Now I know where Demitrias gets the skill from.

"Princess Allisara, we both know I own all the Guards here." Duke Juden Trilavantas begins, his voice dripping with condescension and greed. I grit my teeth and stand straighter, ready to fight if need be and kill the man that sits so comfortably on my Throne.

"So you will sit quietly like a good little doll and marry Demitrias as agreed upon by your parents and I while I run the Kingdom. How does that sound." He continues, his smirk growing as he leans back into the Throne – my Throne. My hands clench at my sides as I take in his words. They are filled with greed and I know now that there is no way in Hell that I could ever trust him or the Trilavantas family ever again.

"Mister Trilavantas." I begin, relishing when I watch his smirk falls as I address him as such. Point for me in getting under his skin.

"You must understand that you have royally fucked my life up for the last fourteen years. Do mind the pun." Continuing, I hear a few of the Guards snicker as I take a step closer to the Throne, no one dares to stop me and I can see that this visibly upsets the man that has yet to budge off of what is mine.

"Now, I will give you five seconds to get off from my Throne and leave my Palace for good." I finish, reaching my hand out quickly and taking the pistole from the holster of the Guard closest to me – the blond that has been guarding me since I left my room. I grin as I flick the safety off and cock the pistol, readying it to be fired before pointing it directly at Duke Trilavantas' head.

"One." I call out loud and clear.

"You don't want to do this Alli." Demitrias pleads

"That is Princess Allisara to you." The Guard whose gun I took corrects, pulling his sword out and pointing it at Demitrias' throat.

"Two." I continue counting, taking a step forward.

"N-now Princess, you don't have to do this." Duke Trilavantas calls out, his voice shaking as his smug face falls

"Three." My finger moves to the trigger and I stand smugly staring down the man that fucked my Kingdom over.

"Princess Allisara, this is my father." Demitrias calls out as if I didn't know. I just ignore him, already knowing that after today our betrothal will be voided.

"Four." I prepare myself to have to see blood and brain matter being splattered on the thrown and walls behind it. It seems this room will need to be renovated soon.

"I-I was joking okay." Duke Trilavantas whimpers out sitting up straighter. Too bad I am not.

"Five." I am about to pull the trigger when he jumps off of my Throne, throwing himself on his knees before me with tears falling from his face. It seems that the man my father called his best friend is nothing but a coward. Smirking, I strut towards the Throne, climbing the small set of stairs before taking my rightful place on the golden chair with cream cushions. I will need to have it cleaned after having filth sit on it for fourteen years but right now I will take this victory in regaining my Kingdom back from the Trilavantas.

"Guards, arrest Juden Trilavantas for treason and threats against the crown." I order, watching as four men step forward.

"He and his family are to be stripped of their titles and Juden Trilavantas is to be deemed a Traitor to the Kingdom. For now, his family may remain on the Estate until a new Duke can be conferred the tittle. I will send Guards to seize any and all assets that belong to the Royal family." I continue as the former Duke is seized and cuffed, the Guards not being gentle at all in their handling of the Traitor. Demitrias lets out a gasp of horror, causing me to look at him with a questioning gaze.

"Our engagement is off. It would be bad if I married a Traitor's son." I state, deciding to send another blow to the father son duo. Demitrias' face is one of pain and despair but I can see the seething rage in his eyes behind the mask, He isn't fooling anyone.

"You can't do this Alli, I love you." He shouts, causing me to laugh.

"If you love me like you claim I would have been raised as a princess, not a slum child." I retort with through my laughter, having to wipe away the tears from laughing so hard from my eyes. Demitrias and love is such a comical concept.

"The Allisara you knew as a child is gone. You have your father and your self to blame. Now leave, you are no longer Captain of my Guards." I continue after regaining composure. Demitrias goes to protest but the Guard who's sword is still pointed at him gives him a warning glare. Another two come to escort Demitrias out after his father had been taken away kicking and screaming. The Throne Room soon settles into a calming silence and I sigh, turning to look at the Guard that remained as he sheaths his sword.

"Mind if I keep it?" I asked, motioning to the gun that is set on the arm of the Throne and getting an amused chuckle.

"Not at all, you seem to know what you are doing." I laugh as well, smiling as I stand and hold my hand out towards the man. He takes it, his large calloused hand warm against my dainty one as we shake.

"Skylard BlackHawk, Your Highness." Skylard introduces himself, the name seeming so familiar to me.

"Call me Alli." I smile, deciding that right then and there I can trust this man as he had backed me when I was dealing with the Traitor, stopping Demitrias before he could come between his father and me.

"Then call me Sky." Sky answers, making me smile.

"Just to let you know Alli, I am glad you are back. I hated Juden Trilavantas. He is a power hungry tool." I giggle at his confession and take this time to examine Sky. He has deep emerald eyes that when the light reflects off of them feels like a warm pool you can dive into. A chiselled jaw that leads to an easy going smile, one that has me wanting to smile when ever I see it. His dark blonde hair falls to his shoulders while half of it is tied back and out of his eyes. He is tall and lean, his shoulders broad and judging by the way his uniform clings to him, he is made of muscles.

"Done staring at me?" He asked chuckling, causing me to blush and release his hand in embarrassment.

"Sorry, I was just deciding on if you would make a good Captain of the Guards. I need some one I can trust." I retort back with, looking towards the Throne. My words seem to be the thing to quiet him as a moment of silence passes between us. Looking out from the corner of my eyes, I smirk as I take in his bewildered expression.

"I-I-um." He stutters, trying to find the right words.

"What do I say?" This time I laugh, bending over and clutching my stomach while Sky stares at me.

"How about thank you." I manage to spit out, wiping tears from my eyes from laughing so hard. No sooner were the words out of my mouth that I feel myself being lifted into the air as strong arms hug me to an equally strong body.

"Thank you." Sky whispers, causing me to laugh even harder. I hug him back, relishing in the warmth that Sky brings as the two of us smile and laugh. This is what I need, a friend, someone I can trust, and someone I know I can rely on. Our laughter slowly dies down as we regain our composure and my feet are returned to solid ground. A slight blush creeps along Sky's face, but I choose to ignore it. No need to tease my new friend when I will be relying on him from this day forward. There will be plenty of opportunities to mess with him as we fix the mess Juden Trilavantas left for me.

"As my new Captain, we need to approve of my Palace Guards." I decide to bring up the first thing I want changed. With the Palace Guards being in charge of my safety, I will need to know I can trust the people sworn to protect me.

"Lets start with those loyal to the Crown, to me and you. We can slowly weed out those loyal Trilavantas and remove them from the Palace." Continuing my thought, I look out the window and sigh. There will be a lot that needs to be done with my Kingdom, but even more that I need to do inside the Palace.

"Thats something I can help with. There are a lot of good men who hated Trilavantas as much as I do." Sky muses, turning to face the window as well.

"They will bend the knee and follow you; I can guarantee it." I smile at Sky's words. If I can make sure that people are loyal to me, then I can help the Kingdom.

"Good, we start tomorrow. Tonight I need to do some...thing." My voice cracks as I reach for my necklace, my thumb rubbing against the crest.

"They are in the Royal Cemetery." Sky states, surprising me.

"The one thing he did right as Regent was give them a proper funeral. Although I am pretty sure he did it just for show." He continues, rolling his eyes at the mention of Trilavantas.

"How do you know this?" I whisper out, surprised by how he knows so much.

"My father was the gardener here. I helped him plant the roses that grow behind their graves just after your parents were buried." Sky answers, giving me a sad smile. I vaguely remember the gardener with dirty blonde hair always working rain or shine in the garden. He was a kind and gentle man from what I saw in my dreams, always teaching me about flowers and helping me when I wanted some as decorations for tea parties.

"Thank you." I whisper before making my way out of the Throne Room. Footsteps behind me has me turning to look back and see that Sky is following, the gun I had left on the Throne in his hand as he catches up to me.

"Do you know the way?" He asks, causing my steps to faulter until I stop. I want to say that I do, that I know my home like the back of my hand, but that would be a lie. Many of my memories are still missing and I know that if I am left alone, I will get lost. Turning to Sky, I give him a helpless smile and shake my head no, not knowing how to ask him for help.

"The quickest way is through the gardens. Let me lead you." He suggests, handing the gun to me. I thank him as I awkwardly let the hand that holds the pistol hang at my side, unsure of what to do.

"Do you think you can hold onto this until I can get my own holster?" I sheepishly ask, getting a chuckle from my new friend.

"How about tomorrow you come with me to the armoury to pick out a few weapons for yourself. Now come one, its this way." He takes back the pistol and places it into the holster before motioning me to follow him. After a few twist and turns we find ourselves in a sun room, the doors wide open letting in the crisp winter air. From here Sky lets me take the lead and I take my first steps into the garden. I can tell that it hasn't been maintained for a while as all the plants that usually stay green in winter are beginning to wilt, causing me to frown.

"What happened to your father?" I ask, turning to Sky.

"He was fired three months ago; you can guess by who." He answers, hatred seeping into his voice. I nod, turning to look at the scene before me before continuing down the stone path that could use a few rounds of maintenance.

"Call him, tell him I want him working here once again. He will be the head gardener and can choose his team." I order, leaving no room for discussion or protest. The sounds of footsteps no longer follow me and I turn to see Sky staring at me with a dumbfounded look. As amused as I am with constantly making this grown man speechless, I also know that the gardens need to be returned to their former glory if I am to show that I am the one true leader here.

"Not to sound rude but now would be a good time to call him." I state, watching as Sky nods in response. His hands fumble in his pocket until he triumphantly pulls out a cell phone. It isn't long until he is deep into a conversation, a large smile on his face as he excitedly talks to whom I assume is his father. The call ends quickly and with out warning, Sky pulls me into his arms for another hug.

"Dad will be here tomorrow with his team. He told me to thank you and that he is happy you are back where you belong." With his voice full of enthusiasm, Sky thanks me on behalf of his father bringing a smile to my face. With the issues of the garden settled, Sky leads me the rest of the way to the Royal Cemetery. The walk through the garden brings small memories to my mind and I find myself needing to stop for a moment to focus and sort through all the new information entering before my brain overloads. Thankfully Sky is patient, allowing me time to sit and rest when the splitting migraine from earlier today comes back. Its only when we reach the black wrought iron gates to the Royal Cemetery that the memories subside and the migraine settles.

"Would you like to go in first?" Sky asks, pushing the gate open. The metal has seen better days as the creaking sound echoes along the empty garden, causing me to shiver with slight hesitation. It seems this place has been neglected as well with the Trilavantas' sitting on my Throne.

"How will I know which graves are there's?" I ask, unsure whether or not I genuinely want to go in alone.

"Just keep walking on the path. The will be the ones under a willow tree. The roses will have wilted by now, but the scent should still linger." He answers, giving me a gentle smile. Taking a deep breath, I step past the gate and follow the path that Sky told me to stay on. Rows upon rows of graves pass me by as I continue walking, many of which have started to become over grown with weeds and vines. This place should have been a beautiful scenery as a final resting place for my family that have passed on, but now it has become a desolate and unwelcoming area.

Coming to the end of the path, my steps falter as I come to a stop noticing the willow tree a few meters away with its bare branches swaying in the breeze. Two black grave stones stand solemnly in front of it, the remnants of rose bushes planted just behind them. It looks so lonely and forlorn, as if no one has visited these graves in years. Fourteen years. I spent fourteen years wondering why I was left in the Slums all alone. Fourteen years of wanting to know if my parents were alive and why they gave me up. And here they are buried in the cold hard ground.

Tears fall from my eyes and I find myself unable to continue forward. All strength I had earlier leaves me and I fall to my knees. Wrapping my arms around myself, I cry for them, for their untimely death and for the love I should have grown up with. I cry for the little me that was left with no memory of them and who spent fourteen years wishing for her parents warmth. I cry and cry until my tears run dry and my body is left shaking and quivering.

"I'm sorry Alli." Sky whispers, scooping me into his arms and cradling me to his chest. He turns away from their graves, carrying me down the main pathway and out of the cemetery. He takes me past the garden and to the sunroom where he settles me onto the comfortable love seat before kneeling in front of me.

"Feel better?" He asks, brushing away a stray tear from my face.

"No." He laughs at my answer, tucking a loose strand of hair behind my ear and handing me a handkerchief from his pocket. I thank him and carefully wipe away any remaining traces of my tears. In the end, I find myself clenching the small fabric in my hand as I look out the windows of the sunroom.

"It gets easier Alli, so don't worry." I nod at his words and take a moment to breath in the floral scented air that still hung in the winter, taking in the earthy scent of Sky's cologne with it as well. I smile, knowing that with Sky helping me the Kingdom will flourish again. And to think just a few months ago I was readying myself to leave and live in the countryside.

"I just need this day for myself. Tomorrow I will be the Queen this Kingdom needs." I whisper, closing my eyes and taking another deep breath.

"That's understandable. It been a long day for you." Sky muses, sitting beside me on the love seat. Nothing is said between the two of us as we sit in silence left to our own thoughts. There is nothing to be said as we both have had a long and emotional day. I think about the work that will need to be done when I see his father tomorrow. One thing is for sure, it will take a while for the gardens and Royal Cemetery to be fixed.

Deciding that a relaxing bath is needed, I ask Sky if he can lead me back to my room. It will take a few days of learning to navigate my home once again but Sky promised me he will help me to learn the twisting and winding halls. As soon as I reach my room, I thank him for his help today, already noticing two Guards standing at attention ready to protect me at a moments notice.

"I will send a Maid with food for you Alli. For now, get some rest." Sky says as we say are farewell. I nod, accepting his help before I bid him good night and head inside. The first thing I notice is that my bed has been made with fresh bedding, a note from the Maids welcoming me home. This makes me happy and I set the note on the bedside table, deciding to keep it safe. I head into the bathroom, the clawfoot tub I saw earlier welcoming and inviting and – thankfully – is easier to operate than the shower was. It isn't long until I am soaking inside a hot bubble back, the water soaking away my pain. Today is my last day as Allison of the Slums. Tomorrow I am Allisara Nimair, future Queen of Nimairene.

Chapter 6

Staring at the list of names in front of me, I sigh and lean back in my chair rubbing my temple. This morning as promised, Sky had showed up to my room and lead me to the armoury, helping me pick out a few weapons that I can keep on my body at all times for self defense. After that, he lead me to my father's Study explaining that no one other than the assigned Maids were allowed inside. It was a burden lifted off my shoulders that I never knew I had in mind when I walked into the room and learned from Ellisia – the Head Maid in charge of this room – that nothing has been changed in the last fourteen years. From there Sky and I began to weed through the names of Guards now under his command.

Right away Sky had pointed out the ones that he knew for a fact were supporters of the Trilavantas, their promotions over the years being ones that made me question if they truly deserved their current rank. Of course I added them to the list of those who will be let go and groaned when I realize it was over a third of the Guards.

"We will need to go through enlisting new Guards soon." I muse just as Ellisia walks in, a cart full of snacks and steaming hot tea being pushed in front of her.

"Might as well throw in hiring new Maids. I kept a list of those I was suspicious of over the years and a few I feel like were more than just loyal to that Traitor if you know what I mean." She chimes in, a frown on her aging face. This piques my interest and I find myself sitting up straighter in my chair, motioning for Ellisia to take a seat on the other side of the desk.

"Do you have the list on you?" I ask as the Maid sits beside Sky, her frown deepening.

"No, it's in my room. I can go get it for you if you'd like your Highness." Straight to the point, Ellisia answers me with honesty; a trait I have grown to like about this forty year old woman. In the short time that I have met her, Ellisia has been frank when answering me, never holding back her words but always being polite. It lead to Sky and I discussing making her the Head Maid of the Palace. I could use her as an ally in my home managing the ones who work to maintain the Palace.

"Sky and I can come with you to retrieve it later so that no one tries to harm you. For now, I want you to keep an eye on the Maids working in the Palace and report back to either him or I if you hear anything in favor of Trilavantas." I shrug, watching as a look of relief crosses her face. It seems having the information that she does is a ticking time bomb, one that could lead to being killed over. As if sensing my thoughts, Sky stands and heads to the door way, motioning for someone outside. He soon returns with a young man I would say is about a year younger than me, his brown eyes and red hair a striking feature I would recognize easily in a crowd.

"Princess Allisara, Miss Ellisia, this is Adam. He is a newly knighted Guard of the Palace. He will be assigned to guard Ellisia and help be our eyes and ears if need be." Sky introduces Adam to us, causing me to really study the man before my desk.

"Who trained you?" I ask, deciding to test this man.

"Sir Skylard did your Highness." He answers instantly, no trace of nervousness or worry on his face. Surprised, I look to Sky who gives me a smug look and I in turn roll my eyes at him. Adam can be trusted which is good for us.

"Very well then. From this moment forward you will guard Ellisia. We are working on cleaning up those who support the Trilavantas from the Palace and only keeping those loyal to me." I sigh out, turning to look back at Adam who smiles with enthusiasm.

"I can help with that. Sir Demitrias loved coming to the barracks to brag to us new knights about the Maids he kept around to warm his bed. There are probably a few carrying his children as we speak." Frowning at Adam's words, I stand from my chair and walk to the window, visibly shaking with rage. We were betrothed and yet he messed around with others. I am glad I broke off our engagement.

"Did...did I say something wrong?" Adam whispers, his voice wavering with slight fear.

"No, on the contrary you said the right thing. You see our Princess here was once engaged to that piece of shit. She called it off yesterday but hasn't announced it yet." Sky answers, getting a chuckle from Ellisia.

"He was a piece of work too. Many of my Maids were harassed by him trying to enter here. Luckily he would back away as soon as I rounded the corner." Comes her retort, causing me to smirk. It seems my hunch is correct in wanting to make her my Palace Head Maid.

"Ellisia, I want you going about your day as usual. If anyone asks why Adam is with you, just say I ordered him to help you. Make up any excuse you want and I will support you." I order, Ellisia standing to curtsy before asking to leave. After granting her permission, she takes Adam by the hand and drags him out behind her, causing Sky to chuckle.

"I think we need a break. How does lunch sound?" My friend suggests. I go to protest, needing to get all this work done, but my stomach decides to grumble in that moment. I sigh, conceding that the snacks that Ellisia brought in will not be enough and agree to going for lunch as long as it is in the Dinning Hall.

Leaving my office, I make sure to lock the door with the key Ellisia had given me before following Sky down the corridors. Maids and Recruits were running about performing their daily duties but stopped to bow or curtsy when we would pass by - something I have not gotten used to yet. It doesn't take long for us to reach the Dinning Hall, the sounds of laughter and conversation floating out the door bringing a smile to my lips.

"I asked all the Guards and Knights to be here. The Recruits are still in training so we won't need to worry about them If it comes to it, we can just flunk them out of training and send them to the Military Barracks." Sky states as we keep just out of sight. I nod, deciding to observe the men in the hall and taking a chance to see if I can tell who are those we can trust and who we need to remove from the Palace. It doesn't take long to notice a divide in the room. On the left the tables were arranged in a way that made it seem like one big community, the men laughing and sharing food as they ask about each other's day and family. On the right is a little quieter with less people. The tables were in an orderly manner, a look of distain on the men's faces as they look on at those on the left.

"Can you tell which side is which?" Sky asks with a chuckle, making me smirk and give him a knowing look from the corner of my eyes.

"I can. It also doesn't help that many wear their rank and distain on their shoulders." I point out, receiving a low impressed whistle from Sky. Without giving him a chance to respond, I nod to the Recruit stationing in front of the doors, my smirk growing as I stand straighter.

"Her Highness, Princess Allisara Nimair." The Recruit calls out. Instantly all the men in the room rise from their chairs and stand at attention, the room becoming pin drop silent as I stride into the hall and towards the small stage set against the far wall. Sky follows behind me, his face emotionless as he stands at the bottom of the stage guarding me while I take my time to stare at each and every one of these men in their eyes. It seems those on the right hold distain for me. Good. It will make getting rid of them easier.

"At ease men. You may be seated." I call out, watching the one hundred and fifty men take their seats. With everyone's attention on me, I take a deep breath before continuing.

"As many of you already know, I am Allisara Nimair and your soon to be Queen. Starting today I will be taking control of my Kingdom and working towards fixing the mess caused by the traitorous Regent and the Rebellion that took place fourteen years ago." I address the room but my eyes scan the men on the right, watching as some of them frown at my words. I can tell that my presence here angers them. Good. This means it will be easier to remove these men from my home.

"Before I can fix my Kingdom, there are things I need to take care of here in the Palace. With that being said, I expect all of you to swear your loyalty to me. If you haven't by this time in three days, I will have to replace you." I finish my announcement, waiting to see what those on the right will do.

"I swear my loyalty to you Princess." Came a response from the left, making me turn and face that direction as a man with a slim build – one could even consider him to be an androgynous beauty - steps forward, his long black hair braided down his back held in place by a black ribbon. He comes to stand before Sky, nodding to him before dropping to his right knee, his right hand over his heart as he stares into my eyes, their grey colour captivating. I note his unwavering loyalty and nod, ready to thank him when the rest of the men who sat on the left side soon follow, forming rows of five behind the first man. When all have bent the knee -their right hand over their heart as they stare at me - I look to Sky who smiles at these men, his men.

"We swear our loyalty to you, Princess Allisara, future Queen of Nimairene." The group of one hundred men chorus together, causing me to jump slightly. Pride fills my heart as I take in each and ever one of their faces, deciding that there and then I will have Sky keep a look out for any outstanding men that will be perfect for a promotion. We will need a few high ranking Guards to help keep track of training and patrol.

"Rise men. I thank you for your loyalty and ask that if there is anything you required be it for health reason or work related, that you come to me or Skylard BlackHawk, the Captain of the Royal Guards." The slamming of silverware on plates causes me to turn towards the right as those who were previously promoted by the Traitor stand to their feet. We watch in silence as they all stand and stomp their way out of the Dinning Hall. It seems announcing Sky as my Captain of the Guards seem to be their breaking point as soon the right side clears. I scoff, giving Sky a pointed look and watch as he signals to a few men. Without any reply, four men that were kneeling before me stand, bow respectfully to Sky and me, then leave. No doubt they were ordered to spy on those still loyal to Juden Trilavantas.

"I have a feeling you all will be passing a few new Recruits soon." I muse, scoffing as the dining hall doors close. The remaining men before me chuckle as they rise to their feet and with their help, we rearrange the tables before Sky and I join them for lunch. With the fifty men gone, the atmosphere in the room becomes warm and cheery as I spend some time getting to know my Guards. I learn that the first man to bend the knee is names Arian and that he has been a member of my Guards since I was born, starting out as a Squire – the position that was soon replaced by Recruits. We soon become good friends when he tells me he came from the very Slums I was dumped in and we muse how we never ran into each other at all when he visited his friends and family.

"To think the Princess was just around the corner from me as a child." Arian chuckles out, passing me a bowl of salad and I pile the greens onto my plate.

"To be fair, I was terrified of interacting with anyone from there during my first year. I had no memories of my past and no clue who I was or how to survive." I shrug as I set the bowl down between Sky and I, the former watching Arian and I with a bemused smile.

"That makes sense. From the stories Arian told me, those Slums are dangerous." He chimes in as I take a bite of my salad, Arian and I looking to one another before I nod in agreement.

"They are. I watched many girls be taken after they had their first period. I made sure to never show any signs of weakness to avoid the human trafficking that takes place there." Sighing, I think back to the first time I watched a girl a few years older than me be taken away. Her name was Haily and she was a natural red head like Adam. It was only a few months after I was left to the Slums and her begging and pleading woke me from a hunger induced slumber. I remember how terrified she sounded. How a man had slapped her hard across the face until she was shoved into a car. Then she was gone.

"That must have been horrible." Sky whispers out, his smiling face becoming a grim frown.

"It was. Speaking of girls, why are there none in the Guards." I ask, motioning around the room. Arian chuckles, taking a sip of his water as his pale blue, almost clear, coloured eyes watch Sky fumble for an answer.

"Because no one wants a girl doing a man's-" He begins, his words trailing off as my curious gaze becomes a glare directed at him.

"I will get a few candidates for you to look at." He quickly adds, rubbing the back of his neck in embarrassment. Arian chuckles, causing Sky to glare at him in turn.

"That would be a good idea. Arian, I would like to offer you the position as Vice Captain of the Guards." I state, turning to face the tall man just in time watch as Arian does a spit take from the second half of my words.

"I...you...what?" He fumbles out as he wipes away the droplets that stuck to his chin. This time I smirk at the speechless man, the table growing quiet to watch the three of us closely.

"Sky needs a second in command, and since you were the first to swear your loyalty to me and judging by how he trusts you, I want you as Vice Captain." I state, leaving no room for arguments. Sky his shaking beside me, doing his best to stifle his chuckles as the rest of the men watch with amusement.

"I... thank you Princess." Arian stutters out, his eyes wide as he looks from me to sky then back to me. With a grin, I motion for us to continue eating as I take this meal time to get to know the men tasked to keeping me and the Palace safe. After finishing the meal, I bid farewell to the men and motion for Arian to follow Sky and I back to my Study. It doesn't take long for the three of us to reach it and soon I am facing my computer with Arian and Sky in front of me.

"I will need you two to keep an eye on Trilavantas' men. Make a list of who they try to contact and what they are up to these next three days. I expect a report at the end of the day." I begin, watching Arian and Sky look at one another before turning back to face me.

"What else should we do?" Arian asks, an amused smirk on his face.

"Schedule training sessions and recruit female Guards. It will be easier guarding me if we can disguise a few as ladies in waiting." I add, getting a nod as I bring up a list of Generals in command of the Royal Army. Frowning, I print out the list and hand a copy to each men.

"Schedule a meeting with all of them and make sure to mention that Juden Trilavantas exposed many of them embezzling funds in order to lesson his sentence. If we have a few men trained in espionage, assign one to each man to gather evidence." Sky lets out a low whistle at my words as Arian looks at me with a look of shock. I smirk, feeling proud of myself for impressing my Vice Captain.

"Do I want to know how you came to this conclusion?" Sky asks, folding the paper and placing it into his pocket.

"I noticed some irregularities in the financial records earlier this morning. When you grow up stealing in the Slums, you get surprisingly good at accounting and spotting any fraudulent dealings." I answer, pulling up the statements and turning the computer screen to show the records of Military and national security founding. I begin explaining the trend I noticed during the years when my parents ruled and how after their death and over the course of last fourteen years the funding went from being relatively the same to drastically decreasing.

"I can have someone blend into the barracks and speak with some of the Soldiers to see if there have been complaints made." Arian suggests, making me grin.

"Sounds like a plan. You and Sky can take the rest of the day to organize and plan everything. We have seven days to sort out the Military if we want to help better the lives of the citizens." Agreeing with Arian, I turn the screen back to its rightful position. The men take this as their que to leave with Sky promising to bring me a list of men he believes will be great for my personal Elite Guards. Arian volunteers to be one of them but is shot down when he is reminded that we will need him to help lead the Palace Guards. As they begin to walk towards I look up from the computer screen and call out to Sky.

"Can you fine Ellisia and gather the information of the Maids she believe to be traitorous?" I ask, getting a nod from my friend.

"Give me an hour and I will bring her and Adam here." With that, he and Arian leave my Study, the room growing quiet. I can feel a headache coming on and with a groan, I lean back on the chair and take a moment to just breathe. It is only my first day gaining back the control of my Palace and already it has taken a lot out of me.

Deciding that I have an hour until Sky returns, I figure now would be a good time to look into all laws created in the last fourteen years under Trilavantas' rule. If I want to change the Kingdom, I need to know what laws will help my people.

Chapter 7

Taking a bite of the fruit platter Ellisia brought in for me, I continue pulling up the files of the Maids that were confirmed to have slept with Demitrias. It been two days since announcing my intention to the Guards and only a handful of men who sided with Juden Trilavantas have pledged their loyalty to me. Without needing to be told, Sky had assigned men to keep an eye on this small group knowing that until we are one hundred percent certain of their loyalty, we will have to be careful around them.

"Have the three ladies who are confirmed to be pregnant agreed to a DNA test?" I ask Sky as he walks over and steals a strawberry from my plate.

"Yes they have. We already obtained a sample of Demitrias' saliva and if the test confirms he is the father, we will be firing those ladies and giving them enough compensation from the Trilavantas Estate to tide them over until the children are in school. The others suspected of sleeping with both Demitrias and Juden have been fired with appropriate compensation and Ellisia is in the midst of interviewing new Maids." I frown as Sky continues to steal fruit from my plate, taking a moment to move the plate to my right side and continue to enjoy my food in peace.

"Hey, I was eating those." He grumbles, trying to lean over my desk and swipe a cantaloupe. I once again move the plate, taking this chance to eat a few pieces while he glares at me.

"Go to the kitchen and get some more." I sigh out, handing him the half empty plate and watching as a smile lights up his face.

"After I eat these I will." I chuckle as he pops a piece of watermelon into his mouth, returning my attention to the screen and sighing. I start thinking about the little shack I used to live in and wonder what happened to it after months of no power. Did the Police find my stash of stolen money? has anyone taken it over with it being vacant for so long?

"What's wrong Ally?" Sky asks through a mouth full of grapes.

"Do you think we can sneak away for the rest of the day?" I ask instead, getting a suspicious look from my friend.

"Why?" I smile sheepishly at him, turning my chair to look out at the window as snow falls gently outside.

"I want to visit the Shack I lived in and retrieve my items. I haven't been there in a few months." Deciding to answer his question, I tell Sky about how I found the little shack and turned it into a home. How it was the one place I felt safe while surviving in the Slums.

"If this place meant so much to you, why haven't you been there in a few months?" I sigh, running a hand through my hair as I debate whether or not I should tell Sky the truth. I mean, who would want a Prisoner for a Princess. Deciding that these last few days Sky has done nothing but helped me, I turn and face him, a sad smile on my face.

"Its hard to go anywhere when you are a prisoner." I state, watching his eyes widen in shock.

"Wait, a prisoner!" He nearly shouts, causing me to shush him. After making Sky promise not to repeat what I just told him to anyone else, I relax back into my chair and swing it from side to side.

"Everyone assumes that I lived a life of luxury when I went missing or that I had died. But as I have said many times, I grew up in the Slums. I had to steal to stay alive and one day I got caught. After that, I was sent to Prison." Explaining my past to someone I can trust lifts a weight from my shoulder, causing me to feel lighter than before. The struggles I faced as a child forced me to grow up faster than most children and it is why taking control of the Palace is easy for me. Years of surviving has given me an edge over the men who have underestimated me these two days.

"I have to know, was it Alcraft that you were sent to?" Sky asks, keeping his voice low so as not to alert the Guards outside my office. I shake my head no, amused as he leans back into his chair to think.

"Forgress?" Another head shake no. He stops and stares at me in disbelief. There is only one prison left.

"Not that one?"

"Yep. I was sent to Lady Pricilla's Prison for Troubled Women. Trust me when I say reforming that Prison is top of my list with how horrible we are treated there." I state, running a hand through my hair once more. Sky sighs, turning to look out the window as the room grows silent.

"You got sent there for stealing." He muses quietly after some time passes, causing me to laugh.

"Yeah. Managed to hide my stash before I got caught too." I brag, proud of myself for securing my goodies.

"Well, show me how you stole." My eyes widen as I stare at him in disbelief. When most people learned I stole to survive, they stayed away from me not wanting to be the next victim.

"Are you serious?" I can't help but ask, trying not to chuckle at this absurd request.

"Very." His eyes stare into mine, causing any amusement at thinking Sky is joking to disappear. The man must be a total nut case if he finds this amusing.

"Everyone learned the hard way not to steal from a Guard. Sorry if I have a bit of misgivings about doing it." I point out, standing from my chair and making my way pout of my office. I need to stretch and maybe find a way out of the Palace for a bit. Familiar footsteps behind me alert me to Sky following behind. It doesn't take long for him to catch up with his long legs and I roll my eyes at him.

"I will help you out of the Palace if you can show me just how good you are." Laughing at his persistency, I turn to give Sky an amused smile as he takes my hand and leads me down a different hallway, one I have yet to explore. Here I was, thief turned Princess, and my first real friend in years wants me to steal from him. Just the absurdity of it all is really hard to take in.

"Deal. But I am going do it when you least expect it." I agree, allowing Sky to lead us towards what ever destination he has in mind.

"Fair enough. Anyways, we are here." He smirks, stopping before a plan looking door at the end of the third hallway we turned down. Confused, I turn to look at him and wonder if he is trying to prank me.

"This looks like a storage room." I state in a monotone voice, leaning against the opposite wall. If he expects me to open an unknown door, he is sourly mistaken. To my surprise, Sky lets out a deep laugh, shaking his head at me before he reaches for the handle and pushes the door open. There is nothing black darkness and this piques my interest. What sort of room is left pitch black?

"Ladies first." Sky declares, mock bowing while chuckling at me rolling my eyes at him. Deciding to humor my friend, I walk closer to the door and take a deep breath before carefully walking into the dark room. After walking ten steps, I stop and turn to face the open door where Sky's silhouette stands, his body shaking as he continues to laugh at me.

"There is nothing here." My voice echoes around the room as I voice my frustration, surprising me as I turn to look back at the blackness behind me. This room his huge. A clicking sound comes from behind me and without warning, the lights turn on row by row revealing neatly parked vehicles ranging from sports cars to practical S.U.Vs.

"Welcome to the Royal Garage. Your ride awaits you, your Highness." I hadn't heard Sky come up behind me, but suddenly his lips are close to my ear and my heart skips a beat at his deep voice. I blush at his closeness before stepping away, deciding that this is just him messing with me and focus on the vehicles in front of me.

"So I can pick any vehicle?" I ask, my eyes scanning each one until I find myself standing in front of a matt black Hummer.

"Yes. As long as it is winter worthy. No need to freeze ourselves to death for a quick outing." Sky answers, slowly walking towards me.

"Then lets take the Hummer." With a chuckle, Sky walks towards the passenger door and holds it open, waiting for me to climb inside. I smile, thanking him as I climb into the passenger seat.

"Just remember Alli, I need you to be navigator to your Shack." Sky adds, before closing my door. I watch as he rounds the front of the vehicle before the driver side door opens and he climbs in. With a push of a button, the Hummer starts and Sky carefully navigates out of the Royal Garage. I am shocked to learn that the entrance is hidden in plain sight as we soon drive out of a barn that sits on the farm to the West of the Palace.

"You own this farm by the way. Its how the Palace gains its supply of fruits and vegetables." Sky informs me as we pass rows on rows of bare fruit trees. I smile, excited to learn just what other surprise my home holds for me to discover.

Chapter 8

"Turn left right here. Its the last house – well shack - on the street." The Hummer turns at the next street with Sky effortlessly navigating the rough roads of the Slums with my help of course. The trip had been short, about an hour from the Palace with the Slums being on the South side of the Capitol, and this opportunity gave me a chance to see just how my city is divided from the Palace having the Northern most point that leads down to the rich district where many of the lesser Nobles live to the shopping district I always planned my heists in.

I could feel the transition from the smooth roads that were kept maintained to not hinder those in the lower-middle class and up to the bumpy and pot-hole ridden roads that were the Slums. The street I grew up in being the worst.

"Tough street." He sighs out, his knuckles on the steering wheel turning white as he holds it in a deathlike grip. After a minute of driving onto the road, the vehicle begins to slow as Sky navigates the many large pot-holes that threaten the livelihood of the Hummer.

"Its worse after a storm. One wrong step and you end up knee deep in a hole." Chuckling, I begin pointing out where the worst ones are until finally Sky pulls up beside the shack and shuts of the engine.

"No offense, but this place looks unsafe." He muses as we climb out of the Hummer. I shiver from the cold winter air and hurriedly make my way towards the back with Sky following behind me.

"It looks better inside." Assuring him through clenched teeth as pull my sweater around me tighter, I curse myself for not bringing a jacket.

"Sure it does." Sky shrugs, his eyes staring wearily at what I called home sweet home.

"Don't sound so judgy." Chastising, my friend I roll my eyes in annoyance at how he judges the shack. Is it beautiful, no. But it was the place that kept me safe here in the Slums after nights of sleeping in a dark corner shivering.

"Judgy?" Glaring at Sky as he scoffs at me, I stop momentarily to point my finger into his chest.

"Yes, judgy. It's a word."

"Is not."

"Is too."

"Says who?"

"Me, the Princess, duh." This earns me an eye roll and an exaggerated sigh from him as the two of us argue all the way to the back door about whether or not "judgy" is a word.

"Why not use the front door?" Mid argument Sky points to the front door that we walk past, his steps slowing as he falls behind me.

"Because I boarded it up when I found this place." Rolling my eyes at his attempt to change the subject, I decide to humor my friend as we reach the back door – Sky looking at me with confusion - and I take a moment to look around to see if anyone came to tamper with the outside of my Shack since my arrest. Satisfied with my search, I reach up over the door where the ledge is, reaching with cold fingertips until I find what I am looking for. I am happy I had gotten into the habit of locking the door before leaving and even happier to know the key is still in its hiding place.

"Oh. For safety reasons I am guessing." A statement and not a question.

"Yeah. As I stated earlier, the Slums are dangerous for a girl." I laugh as I turn the key and unlock the door. With a grin, I push the door open and step inside the dark room. I wonder if the power will work after having the cord that connects to the solar panels cut and let out a quiet curse. I should have checked to see if I could fix the cut cord or if Ron had, but I guess it's too late to regret it now.

Walking deeper into the room, I am happy to know I still remember the layout as I step closer to the direction of the bathroom. The sudden blinding light above has me wincing and closing my eyes for a moment, wondering what the heck just happened. It takes me a minute to realize that the lights were turned on when I managed to open my eyes without wincing and see

Sky with his hand beside the light switch as he takes in the inside of my shack with wide eyes.

"You were right, it is better inside." He is impressed and it causes me to smirk. I will have to go to the house across the street to see if Ron did fixed my power for me while I was away and thank him.

"I told you so, and yet you were still judgy." Gloating, I take in the condition of my shack. The doors and windows are still securely boarded up. The bed is still in its corner and so is the bowl I had ate from the day of my arrest with slight signs of mold on it. Other than a thin layer of dust and some garbage I need to put away, everything is still in place. In the spring I should be able to start focusing on fixing the Slums and helping the people get back on their feet and maybe I can turn this little shack into a home away from the Palace.

"You know, this place has potential." I hear the bed squeak slightly as Sky sits before the dust he disturbed causes him to cough and sneeze. Wondering if he ignored the dust on purpose, I continue making my way to the bathroom and to my hiding spot, quickly removing the loose tile and finding my little tin that is slightly dusty but thankfully was left undisturbed.

"I know, I plan on having this place fixed so that I can escape here for some peace a quiet." I call out. Taking the tin cookie box in my hand, I walk back into the main room and head towards the small dining table, Sky hoping from the bed and coming to stand beside me.

"What's that?" He asks, peering over my shoulder in the small space.

"My stash." Giving him a sly look, I set the tin down and pull off the lid. Sky's sharp breath is all I need to know that he is impressed.

"You stole all of that?" His deep voice is low and brushes past me, making me supress a shiver. Something must be wrong with me as I have never had this reaction before. Maybe I am coming down with something.

"I did. Its what I would have considered my life savings a few months ago." After confirming that everything is still in the tin, I place the lid back on before grabbing my bag from the lone dining chair and tell Sky to get comfortable. Busying myself, I begin packing away what little I owned in the shack from clothes to books to the small art supplies I have. The final item that I pick up is the small teddy bear that comforted me through the long nights since I moved into the shack.

"That bear looks like its seen better days." Jumping, I feel strong arms steady me from behind while my hands clutch at the teddy bear. I seriously need to put a bell on Sky.

"I know, but it was the only comfort I had as a child." I run my hand over the well love bear, a soft smile on my face as I hold it tight.

"You must have had it rough." His voice is filled with sadness, his concern for me making my smile grow and turn to reassure him.

"In the beginning it was. But one of the Slum Kings taught me for two years and the elderly couple across the street helped me a lot." Thinking about Liz and Ron Rinmer, I begin explaining to Sky how I stumbled into the shack twelve years ago when I was eight. How for the first two months after loosing my memory I went from place to place begging for food and warm place to sleep until Latham took me under his wing and taught me to steal. He trained me for two years before mysteriously vanishing, leaving me alone and roaming the streets once more barely able to survive.

The night I found this place it was in the middle of a storm and I hadn't been able to find shelter for the night. Apparently I had made a lot of noise trying to get into the shack when Ron had come outside looking to see where the noise was coming from. I don't remember much after seeing his face, but I woke up on their couch, for once feeling warm and rested. When Ron and Liz entered the room to see if I was hungry, I was apprehensive of them. After losing Latham I became weary of everyone due to watching girls like me being taken away.

I kept quiet when Ron and Liz asked me questions, not moving from my spot on their couch. My main goal was getting away from them until Liz brought me a bowl of warm oatmeal and told me I was safe, that no one would take me away like they do those other girls. That day, Ron and Liz un-officially adopted me as a granddaughter and after learning that the shack was abandoned, Ron helped me to fix it up and make it my own home since they did not have the room in their own home at the time. With out their kindness and Latham's mentoring, I probably would have died in the Slums.

"This teddy was the first gift Ron and Liz ever gave me. Ron didn't agree with me stealing to make ends meet, but he understood the Slums were tough. I also helped them by providing money when they needed it and when I stole the solar panels, they didn't ask any questions and helped me to instal them as long as I brought a set back for their house." Taking about them made the guilt inside me grow. They took care of me, helped me when I caught a cold and even treated me like family. And instead of writing them to let them know I was alive and okay, I got into trouble in prison and focused on trying to get out on time.

"They sound like wonderful people." Sky smiles at me, lightly poking the teddy bear and making me laugh.

"They are. So was Latham." Slowly I place the teddy into my bag and tie it shut because the last thing I need is for my things to fall out.

"Would you like to meet Ron and Liz?" I ask as Sky and I exit my shack and make our way to the Hummer after locking the door.

"Sure, but wouldn't you like to go alone?" Sky asks, opening the back door for me and using his body to shield me from the cold wind.

"I'm scared to face them alone. They watched me get arrested." I look away from him as I place the bag in the back of the Hummer. I am ashamed that when I was arrested, I spot Ron looking out of his house towards mine through his window. When Liz joined him, I held my head down in shame as the Police Men dragged me away.

"I will be your back up then, and you can tell them who you really are. They might understand that you had to do what you did to survive." I jump when I feel Sky take my hand, my head turning to see him staring at me with a gentle smile, his emerald eyes staring back with understanding. Before I know it, the door is shut and he is leading me away from the Hummer and to the only other house I can call home.

Chapter 9

Standing in front of the familiar wooden door with the paint chipping and pealing away, my hand is raised to knock, to let Liz and Ron know I am home, but the nerves inside me causes me to hesitate.

"You going to knock?" Sky asks, concern lacing his voice.

"Eventually" He sighs at my answer and steps beside me, knocking on the door. Instinct tells me to run and hide, but a strong grip on my wrist keeps me in place as Sky gives me a helpless sigh. I know he is doing this for my own good, but I don't think I am ready to face Ron and Liz. A muffled shuffle coming from the other side of the door tells me it is to late to back down now and in seconds the door is pulled open, Liz's smiling face morphing into one of shock.

"Allison?" Her voice cracks as tears slowly make their way down her wrinkled face before her surprisingly strong arms pull me into her for a hug. She smells like cinnamon and in moments my own tears fall from my eyes while I return her hug.

"Ron, come here!" She calls out over her shoulder when our hug ends, holding me at arms length as her hazel eyes stare into mine.

"Why? Is it the delivery guy." Laughing at the absurd answer, Liz rolls her eyes and mouths men to me. It's like no time has passed and I am glad she still treats me the same as always.

"Just get here now." The clicking of Ron's can on the old hard wood floors makes me fidget. I have no idea how Ron will react when he sees me after watching the Police arrest me months ago.

"Allison?" The clicking stops and I look past Liz's shoulder to see Ron staring at me, his own wrinkled face filled with shock and relief. There is no anger or pity, just relief to see me standing before them alive and well.

"Hi." My voice cracks as he makes his was towards us, his arms pulling Liz and I into his embrace. Their warmth is familiar, one I have grown to love these last twelve years. These two are the Grandparents I grew up to love. Maybe I can convince Ron and Liz to move into the Palace with me.

"Um...should I go?" Ron pulls away as Sky awkwardly calls out. The two men stare at one another and I realize that I have a lot to explain to Ron and Liz. One of these being Sky who stands on their front porch wearing the Captain of the Guards jacket over his casual clothes.

"Alli is he your... boyfriend?" Ron begins asking, making me blush and quickly want to explain my situation.

"No Ron its not like that." I begin, getting a quizzical look from Sky.

"Sky here is my friend and Captain of my Guards." The elderly couple stare at me with an unamused look, reminding me of the time I lied to them about where I got the money to help Ron get his cane. This prompted me to explain my past two years under Latham's tutelage and how I survived before meeting the elderly couple. They were disappointed that I had learned to steal from one of the Slum Lords but understood that there was only so much help they can provide me. That was when I explained that in order to survive, I needed to steal. I promised to only steal from the corrupt and rich and would be as safe as I can when going on a heist.

"Okay Allison, no more pranks. He isn't your Guard." Liz chastises me like a child, making me sigh and look to Sky for help.

"Actually I am, and this is Princess Allisara." Relieved when he answers, Sky steps forward and takes out his new identity badge from his pocket allowing Ron and Liz to hold and examine it. Ron looks from me to the badge and then to sky before taking a deep breath. I have a feeling this is going to be a long talk.

"How about we head inside and out of the cold. You can explain everything us over some tea and snacks." Handing back Sky his badge, Liz cuts off any questions Ron may have and takes my hand, leading me into the house with the men following behind us. It feels as if another weight has been lifted off my shoulder as I am led into the living room where I quickly claim my favourite armchair. Sky finds a comfortable spot on the love seat as Liz takes her time busying herself in the small adjacent kitchen. Soon, we are all sat around the coffee table filled with snacks and a mug of hot tea in our hands.

"So tell us how all this happened." Impatience lacing his voice, Ron motions for me to start explaining what has happened since the last time they saw me, and I oblige.

♔[1]

After some time of telling Ron and Liz everything I have been through since being arrested, my mouth feels dry and knowing that Liz keeps a stocked fridge I make my way to the kitchen and grab a glass of milk. I know everything is a lot to take in and so as soon as I return to my seat, I decide to just dunk a chocolate chip cookie into the milk while I wait for Ron and Liz to start their questions.

"So you really are the long lost Princess." Liz whispers out, her hands wringing the faded pink handkerchief I had given her as a child. Liz used to be a seamstress and on chilly winter knights she taught me to embroider. I can still see the tell tale signs of the rose I embroidered into the pink fabric.

"Yes. It feels surreal to me as up until a few days ago I had no memories before age six. But lately they have been coming back." Finishing the cookie, I look down at the nearly empty glass of milk in my hands and sigh.

"Technology these days can do anything Alli." Ron chimes in, giving me a small smile.

"Maybe your memories were meant to be sealed away until a specific time." Being reassured by Ron, I accept the cookie he hands to me and instantly shove it into my mouth, getting a chuckle from Ron and a disapproving sigh from Liz.

"At least you haven't changed missy." She mock scolds, causing Sky to laugh as I chew and swallow the treat.

"Why would I Liz? I like being me." This retort gains me a warm smile from her.

"So I take it that her table manners have always been like this?" Sky chimes in as he swipes the last Danish from the table, making me roll my eyes at him.

"Unfortunately, yes. Hopefully now that she is a Princess, she can learn to eat more civilized." Liz answers, making Ron and I look at each other in

---

1. https://coolsymbol.com/copy/White_Chess_King_Symbol_%E2%99%94

amusement. We both know that that will never happen and Liz is just voicing her wishful thinking.

"Liz, do you need help cooking dinner?" Doing my best to change the subject, I notice the time on the grandfather clock in the corner and take this opportunity to point out their dinner time is fast approaching and with the growling of Ron's stomach emphasizing my words, Liz hurriedly stands from the sofa she shares with her husband and beckons me to join her. In moments, the two of us have whipped up some fried pork cutlets and a salad, Liz surprising me with the fact she had many fresh vegetables available.

"I won some money on a lottery ticket." She explained when I was cutting some of the lettuce earlier. I guess she saw my surprised look.

The idea of asking them to move into the Palace with me comes up over dinner, but the two refuse, stating they love their quiet little home. Deciding not to push my luck, I give up on asking them but let the two know that they can come and live there any time they want. All they need to do is call the Palace and Sky will come with a few men to help Ron and Liz move. With dinner finished and everyone full, Sky helps to clean the dishes, Ron teasing me quietly about Sky being husband material leaving me blushing and Liz telling Ron to leave me be.

"You make sure to come visit us." Ron states as he and Liz walk Sky and I to the front door.

"I will, on the condition you allow me to bring you some money to help." I state, Liz giving me a sigh.

"Fine. I know you'll worry about us Alli, so we will accept your help." She agrees, making me smile. I hug the two tightly with Sky watching from the bottom steps of the porch before saying my farewells once more. The elderly couple watch as we walk towards the Hummer, waving goodbye to us as we drive away.

"We can come back in a few days if you'd like."

"I know Sky. Thanks for today."

Chapter 10

The ride back to the Palace is quiet. Sky focused on getting back safe and sound while I replay the nice night I had seeing Ron and Liz again and again. I wished they had agreed to move into the Palace but knowing that they still treat me the same is the best outcome for me. One of the things I know I will need to get done as soon as Winter ends is fix the roads leading to the Slums. With this, many of the residents there can easily leave to find better jobs and return safely without having to worry about the cracks and pot-holes in the road.

"So what do you think of my adopted Grandparents?" I finally ask Sky as he turns onto the road leading to the farm that will take us to the garage. The rows of empty farm plots and bare fruit trees pass us by as I wait for his answer patiently.

"They are nice people. I can see where you get your attitude from." I laugh at Sky's answer as he presses a button and the barn doors open. He drives slowly into the underground parking until the Hummer is returned to it's rightful spot.

"Either way, you're going to come with me every time I visit them right?" I ask while climbing out of the Hummer and grab my bag from the back seat.

"Of course, Ron is awesome and Liz's food rules." Sky agrees without hesitation.

"I also helped cooked!" I pout slightly at his words, giving Sky a glare.

"Your food rules too." He laughs at me as I huff and start speed walking away from Sky, disappointed when I realize that my speed walking is his normal speed.

"Are you done pouting?"

"No!" I snap back, ready to push open the door to exit the Garage.

"Well you should be, you're to cute to be pouting." I stop dead in my tracks and slowly turn to look at Sky, seeing him looking away from me and running a hand through his messy hair.

"I...I'm what?"

"Don't make me repeat it" He is blushing and I can't help but blush as well.

"But I want to hear you say it again." My voice is quiet, my hear fluttering as I think about what he just said. Maybe Ron is right. Maybe Sky is husband material for me.

"You're too cute to be pouting." He whispered the words this time, still looking anywhere but at me. I smile gently and turn around, pushing the door open and stepping into the halls. After exiting the Royal Garage with my bag in hand we soon notice the Maids running around in a frenzy. It turns out Ellisia had come into the Study to talk to me about something earlier today. When she couldn't find me, she soon asked around to see if anyone knew where I was, but no one had seen me for a while. Soon chaos erupted in the Palace as the Maids and Guards began searching the everywhere for me.

When I finally stopped a Maid to ask what is going on, new spread of my return and I found myself in the Dinning Hall standing before everyone and apologizing for my disappearance and how I needed to get some space with everything that has happened the last few days. After promising to tell Ellisia and Arian when I will be leaving the Palace, I was able to appease my staff before Sky and I made a quick getaway to the Library with two goals in mind – finding books on laws and politics and hiding away from Ellisia who scares me when angry.

"So why are we hiding in here?" Searching through the shelves, I find the books I am looking for and bring them to the sitting area by the large windows. The soft light of the Library makes the space feel cozy and judging by how Sky is stretched out on the sofa with a book on politics in hand, I have a feeling he feels the same way.

"I need to change a few laws and abolish a few others. Unfortunately for me, I am not sure how to go about it so I need to learn." I answer, getting comfortable on a love seat. Sky rolls his eyes but doesn't say anything else as the two of us become absorbed in our books.

Chapter 11

"See that girl?" A calming voice with a slight Southern accent calls out as he helps his son to weed the garden. With his Squire training, his son has grown faster, stronger, and more capable of helping the man in the Royal Gardens.

"The one singing to the roses?" The boy asks, his green eyes watching the little girl as she sings a lullaby to the flowers.

"Yes my boy."

"Isn't that just Allisara?" The young boy looks to his father wondering what this lesson is about. The girl is only three and he is eight. He is her sworn Squire and protector. Has been since the day she was born, the day he started his training.

"She is not just Allisara, Sky. She is our future Queen." The man states with a grin, ruffling his son's hair.

"And as her Knight in training, you must learn to protect the people and things that she loves. Do you understand?"

"Yes father..."

♔[1]

Jerking awake from my dream, I look around the unfamiliar dark room wondering just where I am. It takes a moment for me to realize that I spent the night reading in the Library while Allisara researched into law making and abolishing. A soft sound has me reaching for my gun ready to take down any threat but I soon realize that the sound is Allisara moving in her sleep, her breathing slow and even while the book she was reading before is loosely held in her hand. I chuckle, standing from my sofa and quietly padding to

---

1. https://coolsymbol.com/copy/White_Chess_King_Symbol_%E2%99%94

where she lays, gently taking the book from her hand and placing it on the table after using a bookmark so that she can pick up where she left off.

Turning back to look at her, I take in how peaceful she looks when asleep. It seems that her violet eyes carry a hint of unease when she is awake and I find her sighing and worrying more than a young woman should. I worry for her, knowing that her life before returning as the Princess was horrible from what she shared with me.

Carefully I graze my fingers across her jaw, her skin soft against my own. In my mind I see the adventurous girl that used to play in the garden and sing to the roses, who trained with swords beside me when she was four while Demitrias sat back and stared at us lazily. She has matured since I last saw her, but I will never forget the way she clung to me when her Maid handed her to the Knight and I on the night of the Rebellion.

Unfortunately she remembers me as the gardener's son, not as the boy who protected her from wild dogs and thieves. Not as the boy that held her tight when we escaped from the Palace on horse back. What even Juden did to cause her to loose her memories must have been traumatic. I just hope her memories return soon and that she will recognize me at last.

"I wonder what you dream about" I whisper gently, leaning forward to brush my lips on her temple in a light kiss. I was eleven when I realized I had a crush on my Princess, but she was engaged to Demitrias and I was just a commoner. No way would we have ever been married.

"Sky..." I freeze, thinking that she woke up and has found me standing over here. After a moment of silence, I final peak down to see that she is still fast asleep and that she dreams about me. This thought alone makes me smile. Spying a soft throw, I grab the blanket and carefully cover Allisara with is, watching a soft smile play on her lips as one of her hands clutches the corner. It seems that little habit hasn't changed.

My stomach decides to let it be known that I am starving and I curse, taking the opportunity to walk away from Allisara and sit on a lounge chair. I haven't eaten anything since Ellisia brought snacks in some time around ten last night and right now I could use something to eat, but I do not want to leave Allisara's side in case something or someone came to hurt my Queen.

My stomach growls again and I look to the door. If I don't get anything to eat then my growling stomach will wake Allisara and she will laugh at me.

Sighing once again, I make my way to the Library exit and open the door only to come face to face with a Maid, giving her a fright.

"Sorry Sir Skylard, I was doing my rounds of cleaning." She stutters out, her eyes wide as she presses a hand to her chest.

"It's my fault, I was about to head to the kitchen for something to eat. I am in the middle of doing some work for the Princess and lost track of time." The lie flows through my lips as I did not want the Palace to know Allisara is fast asleep in the room behind me. If word got out, it would be something for the Nobles to ridicule her about.

"Would it be too much to ask you if you can grab me some food to eat?"

"Not at all, if it's work for our soon to be Queen, then I will gladly get some food for you so that you can continue." She says cheerily, her soft brown eyes set in determination. I smile, happy to see loyalty towards Allisara from this Maid and make a mental note to talk to Ellisia about finding Maids specifically to take care of Allisara.

"Thank you, just knock when you have it and I will come to the door for the food." With that, the Maid leaves and I returned inside the library, sitting on a chair closest to the door where I can see Allisara and still be able to protect her while waiting for my food.

"Protect the things she loves, who she loves, and her as well." I whispered the chant I had memorised from those days long ago when I first saw her singing to the roses. She was only three at the time and I was not interested in her at all as a child, only wanting to practice swinging a sword and become a Knight that will protect her and also so that I could make my father proud. Looking back now though, I realize Allisara was born with a kind heart, one that made her perfect but would cause a lot of trouble. As unfortunate as it was, Allisara living in the Slums helped her to grow into a proper ruler without her realizing it.

A soft knock at the door startles me, and I grab my gun while slowly making my way quietly to the door.

"Sir Skylard, I brought you your food." It was the Maid from earlier, her voice muffled by the thick doors. Quickly I holstered my gun and opened the door, taking the basket of food from the Maid and thanking her. She smiles and gives me her name – Ciera – leaves again knowing that the Library is off limit for now. I closed the door, locking it and sitting back down in my sofa across from Allisara, taking the chance to make sure she is still sleeping peacefully.

After making sure that she is still asleep, I slowly searched through the basket and nearly cheer when I find bagels, chocolate chip muffins, grapes and a few bottles of water. I check for poison out of habit before taking out a cold bottle of water, a muffin and a plain bagel filled with cream cheese and settle into my night of keeping watch and enjoying the quiet night with my snacks.

Chapter 12

"Some one help me!" Pressing myself against the sturdy tree, I find the nearest branch and use it to swing at the wild dogs. Their barking and howling fill the air and their sharp teeth snap towards me, dripping with saliva. If help doesn't come soon, I will be their dinner.

"I'm coming!" A boyish voice calls out, over the sound of the dogs. I do my best to fend off the dogs until someone fights his way through the horde, slicing away until he reaches my side. He shields my small body from the wild dogs, his sword swinging and slicing as they lunge at us. I try to see who it is that saved me but his face is blurred.

"Are you okay, Princess Allisara?" I nod yes when he looks at me, doing my best to keep my tears from falling. I don't want this boy seeing me cry.

"Take my hand then. When I give the signal, we run." He instructs me, his right hand stretching out behind him as he stabs at a lunging wild dog, killing it before our eyes. I reach for it; my small hand being grasped in his.

"Now!" With another swing of his sword, he fends off a smaller wild dog giving us an opening. We run, weaving through trees and bushes. I know I am slowing the boy down as he is older than me, but he keeps pace with me and helps me when I trip. The wild dogs are hot on our trails but gun fire sounds and the tips of the tents come into view.

My parents are there, standing with the Palace Guards and I release the boy's hand, my little legs racing into my mother's outstretched arms where I finally cry.

"My little Princess, you were so brave..."

[1]

---

1. https://coolsymbol.com/copy/White_Chess_King_Symbol_%E2%99%94

I jolt awake throwing what ever was covering me off as I look around the room, disoriented from the dream. No, not a dream.

"A memory." I whisper sadly, running a hand through my messy hair. Early morning light filters through the windows, making me smile as I look around the Library. It is peaceful here. Quiet. I know with my love of reading I will find myself here many times as my escape while I get used to the idea of being a Princess.

Looking around the room, I find the book I was reading set aside and smile. Sky must have moved it for me. My smile faulters though as I think about the dream and wondering if Sky might know the boy that saved me. I know that I will eventually remember him, but I hate knowing that I have a friend out there who took care of me and I do not remember him.

The sound of what I can only describe as a chain saw causes me to jump and search the room for the source. When it sounds again, I realize that Sky is sleeping across from me and with his mouth slightly open. The sound comes again and I burst out laughing when I realize that the sound is Sky snoring.

"What's so funny?" His groggy question causes me to laugh harder as the sounds I make wake him.

"You snoring." I say through laughter, wiping my eyes as tears slip bye.

"You look so peaceful and cute although you sound like a chain saw."

"I am not cute; I am manly and brave." He mock gasps, pretending to clutch at non-existent pearls. Any attempt at calming down my laughter is gone as his action causes me into a laughing fit. He just rolls his eyes and throws a pillow at me.

"So what are we doing today Alli?" Rolling his eyes at me again as I catch the pillow, Sky pulls out a water bottle from a basket I did not know he had while my laughter comes to an end and throws it at me. Happy for my quick reflexes, I catch the bottle with ease and take a long drink from it.

"We need to evict all of Trilavantas' men." I sigh out, looking towards the window and catching a glimpse of snow falling. Today is the promised day, if the rest of the men loyal to Juden do not bend the knee to me today, they will be sent away.

"We can do that after a shower." His chuckle has me smiling as I finish the bottle of water. I have another four days to get my Palace in order before meeting with all the Royal Army Generals. Hopefully Arian will have all the necessary information gathered by then.

"I'll ask one of the Maids to have Arian gather all the Guards and Recruits in the Dinning Hall while we shower and prepare ourselves." Shrugging, I stretch my sore muscles and make a mental note to return to bed. Library couches are not the best place to sleep it seems.

"You okay?" Sky asks, his green eyes watching me with amusement.

"Yes. Just no more sleeping on couches." I answer, wincing slightly when I feel a pop from stretching.

"Amen to that. Next time I am carrying your ass to bed so I can sleep properly." Sky stands from his sofa as I reach for the nearest pillow, throwing it at his face and watching him fall back stunned.

"You did not just do that!" Shock covers his face and a feeling of unease runs through me. I have a feeling that if I don't leave now, I will be in for some form of payback. Without waiting to see what Sky will do; I race towards the Library doors and notice that they are locked. Cursing, I manage to unlock them just in time to doge Sky and rush into the hall ways.

"This isn't over Allisara!" He calls out behind me as I race down the halls towards my room, laughing and passing the Palace workers who chuckle and cheer me on.

♔²

Staring at myself in the mirror, I wait for Sky to finish showering so that we can make our way to the Dinning Hall where Arian has gathered the Guards.

My hair in a simple updo with loose curls framing my face and a simple white gold tiara upon my head. My attire is a white off the shoulder shirt that is fitted to my body, a red corset that hugs my frame and shows off my small waist, and a white shawl attached to two rings that I wear on each hand directly above the first knuckle on each of my middle fingers. I chose a pair of black jeans to go with the outfit and a pair of riding boots that end just below my knees.

This is the second time I will be addressing these men. The first was to demand their loyalty and thanks to Sky and Arian, eighty percent of these men have proved their loyalty to me. The other twenty will be sent to the

---

2. https://coolsymbol.com/copy/White_Chess_King_Symbol_%E2%99%94

Army, retired or imprisoned depending on the information Arian and his men have gathered.

Deciding to distract myself from my thoughts, I decide to look around the room. The first thing I notice are the many picture frames sitting on the fireplace mantel with a few on his dresser. I can see the story of his life from him helping in the Royal Garden with his father beside him to his first day of Squire training in the Royal Guards squad. I chuckle and continue looking at each individual framed photo. Displayed before me is a little history book about Sky's life as he displays an easy going smile in each picture. The same smile I get when we talk, laugh or when he sees me emerging into a room. But these eyes that I have grown used to always hold a deeper meaning when I see him, one I am not sure I am ready to learn about.

"Sorry for making you wait." Pine scented shower gel flows through the open bathroom door that Sky is leaning on. Turning to greet him, I take in his appearance as he focuses on buttoning his crisp white shirt with the Royal Guard insignia on it. His dark blonde hair is damp, the tendrils curling slightly as small droplets of water fall onto his exposed skin, skin that covers well defined muscles.

"I...um...its okay." I manage to stammer out, turning away quickly to hide my blush. I return my focus on his pictures, doing my best to get the image of his half naked body out of my mind. The last thing I need right now is to make a fool of myself in front of him.

I can hear Sky moving about his room while he finishes getting ready for our big confrontation. My mind wanders to the scene earlier and I find myself shaking my head to dislodge the thoughts. I need to get the image of water dripping down his muscles before I face the Guards I plan to kick out.

Studying the pictures, I notice that Sky is always staring at the camera, his eyes full of laughter and mischief. I find myself smiling, wondering what kind of child Sky was like until I find an image hidden behind two that show a stoic looking Sky. In this one he is standing beside a girl who can't be no older than five. She is wearing basic training clothes that I have noticed the Squires wearing in previous images. Her hair is braided back but due to her being covered head to toe in mud, I can't even tell what colour her hair is. Her eyes are closed as she laughs, a front tooth missing but it adds to her smile. Sky stands beside her equally muddy, their arms wrapped around each other.

Where the girl faces the person taking the picture, Sky is staring at the little girl with a soft smile and a tender look in his eyes.

"What are you looking at?" He calls out, his voice close.

"A picture of you with a girl." I can feel him behind me, his face just inches from mine as his scent fills the small area. He smells good.

"Is she your sister?" I ask, feeling like I know the girl in the photo.

"No. She is the first girl I fell in love with and the only one I stayed in love with." His voice is low and husky, brushing against my ear.

"Oh." Is my response. It feels like something is clenching my heart, a slight pain I didn't like feeling. A sigh escaped his lips after a few seconds of silence and he slowly backs away, running a hand through his damp hair.

"What happened to her?" I ask, curious to know if there is a happy ending between the two.

"She was taken from me by a power hungry bastard. Her memories taken away. I am still waiting for the day she remembers me." His voice is filled with hate and longing, one I envy.

"So she is like me then?" I ask, finding it hard to speak.

"Yes." He turns to look at me, his emerald eyes staring into my violet ones with such intensity I feel like my heart might crack. My mouth feels dry and for what seemed like eternity we just stare at each other until the clock on the wall chimes the time. Eleven in the morning. The Guards will be gathering soon as we asked Arian to have them in the Dinning Hall by this time.

"W...we better get moving." I say quietly as I turned to leave, catching Sky nod as I make my way through his door. I look across the hall to where my room is, taking a deep breath. Sky insisted he move into my wing to better protect me after my first time addressing the Guards. At first I agreed, but now knowing that there is a woman in his heart, I feel like it is inappropriate to have him so close at hand. When we train a few female Guards, I will have the ones chosen for my own Squad move into the vacant rooms meant for Ladies in Waiting. It will be easier to be protected by them.

With a small sigh, I walk towards the Dinning Hall, lost in my own thoughts. I know Sky is trailing behind me, protecting me like he has done the last four days. Once I have my own Squad it will give him free time to perform his duties as Captain of the Guards.

Chapter 13

Staring down at all the men standing in front of the stage, I notice the divide between the Guards that have sworn their loyalty to me versus those that are still loyal to Juden by the one foot gap made directly between the two groups. Inwardly sighing, I look to Sky and Arian who stand in front of the stage facing the men before I look down to the list of names in my hand that Arian gave to me before we entered the Dining Hall.

"You all probably know why you are here." I begin, looking each and every man in the eyes.

"As stated, it has been three days since I announced that I expect loyalty from my men. Many of you have bent the knee - including all of the Squires - but there is a small group who still refused to do so." My eyes move to those loyal to the Trilavantas, many looking at me with distain while others look uninterested. Unfortunately for them, many will be imprisoned for their crimes that Arian and his men have uncovered.

"When your name is called, step forward." I order, lifting the list to chest level for the men to see. Those who held distain fidget. Good. Unfortunately for them, it is too late.

"Mikael. Stephen. Gortle. Dewey..." I continue calling out the names, watching as twenty of the men step forward. Each one stare at me in fear making me smirk. They had their chances to bend the knee and be loyal to me. Had they done that, I would have given them a chance to repent and repay back the benefits they gained under Juden.

"Each one of you were closest to Demitrias and Juden Trilavantas. Each of you have gained many benefits – benefits that were caused by treason and fear." Sky motions to those that have claimed their loyalty to me and forty men move at once. My men split into teams of two, each team taking hold of one of these twenty Traitors before the Traitors could try and run away.

I watch each Traitor try to struggle but they are held too tightly and their struggles are futile.

"You will all be sent to the dungeons for questioning. Take them away." I state, feeling proud at how easily the first part of this confrontation has gone. Without wasting another moment, my men drag these Traitors away while the Traitors plead and beg for a second chance, that they are sorry. Unfortunately for them, their pleas fall on deaf ears and I turn to face the rest of the men waiting for their own fate to be told.

"The rest of you I have a feeling you will not bend the knee, and that is your choice." The unease their eyes from seeing their colleges dragged away disappear, making me smile slightly.

"So I will offer you a chance as none of you have committed any crimes." I continue, watching as they all begin to relax.

"If you promise to be loyal not to me but to the good of the people, then I will allow you to choose which army squadron you want to serve under. If you wish to return to a civilian lifestyle, then I will have Sky and Arian write letters of recommendations for you." Shock crosses their faces at my offer, one I know must seem too good to be true. The men begin to discus this amongst each other quietly, and I allow it. They had until today to bend the knee, to change sides and become loyal to me. Now they only have these two options left.

"Excuse me, your Highness, but if we choose either of these options will we be monitored?" A man steps forward with his hand raised. It is a good question, one that impresses me.

"Depends. If you stay on the path of being righteous and maintain neutrality, then no. The moment there are any traces of you turning Traitor to this country, then I will have your ass in the dungeons with the other Traitors." I answer honestly deciding that since they are not loyal to me, I shouldn't sugar coat my intentions to them. I can see their minds working as my words sink in. I will not tolerate any Traitors in my country and they know this. I already have one I thought as my Uncle sitting in a cell deep in the dungeon, I do not need any more that know the ins and outs of the Palace.

"You can come to Sky or Arian with your answer, but I will need to know what you each decide by the end of today." With that, I walk down the stage and hand the list back to Arian before Sky and I leave the Dinning Hall. As much as I want to eat with my Guards, I know it will be awkward until I know all my men are loyal to me. I need some fresh air no matter how cold that air is and so I make my way towards the sun room that takes us to the Royal Garden. Once outside, I take a deep breath and lean against the wall. Sky stands beside me, his eyes scanning the garden until a smile lights up his face. Looking in the direction he is staring at, I see a man working with a team and watch their skilled hands remove the dead branches and leaves from the garden beds before adding some mulch.

"Go say hi to him." Bumping my shoulder into his, I encourage Sky to go to his father. He hesitates, looking back at me but I shoo him away. He leaves me reluctantly before walking over to his father, tapping him on the shoulder. Watching the two hug brings a pang to my chest as I think about my own parents. Parents that were stolen from me in the Rebellion. I need to visit their graves again but I want to do it when I have changed our Kingdom for the better and can stand proudly before them.

"Dad says hi. He likes his new pay raise too." Lost in thought, I jump at Sky's voice before his words register inside my mind.

"He...he deserves it." Shrugging, I turn and walk into the sun room as the cold winter air becomes a little too unbearable to stand in. Deciding I should get some work done. I ask Sky if he can find Ellisia to bring us lunch while I make my way towards my office. I am almost done combing through the laws created in the last fourteen years and I want to get them done by tonight. Hopefully I can finish it today and call a meeting with my Cabinet to work on abolishing and creating better laws that will push Nimairene forward.

Chapter 14

"You sure you want to do this today Alli?" Staring at the door that will lead to the Dungeons, I debate on if I am ready or not for this. The last time I saw Juden was six days ago when I barged into the Throne Room to take back what's rightfully mine.

"No, but I need to. He has all the answers I need." Sky hums at my answer, his steady presence calming me. With a deep breath, I motion for the Guards to open the doors to the Dungeons and begin to descend the stairs. Five minutes of descending the long stair case and I find myself on the first floor of the Dungeons expecting to see a damp dingy hallway and not a place brightly lit with secured doors spaced evenly on either side.

"Which one is his?" I ask, looking towards Sky who takes the lead.

"Last one on the left." We walk in silence until we come to the cell, anxiety growing inside me. Something deep inside me tells me he is the reason why I grew up in the Slums. That he is the reason why the Rebellion took place fourteen years ago.

"Has he said anything since being imprisoned?" I ask the Guard Max, a tall man with ebony coloured skin built like a wrestler with a balding head and a short beard. I remember him from my first time dining with the Guards the other day. How max had been laughing and joking loudly at the other end of the room after introducing himself to me. I am happy that Max is the one tasked to guard Juden as I he gave me the impression that he is a trust worthy and loyal man.

"Other than he wants to see you, no." Nodding at his answer, I motion for Max to open the cell and step inside once the door has been opened. Sitting on the cot is Juden Trilavantas, his usually neat hair standing on end and a smidge of dirt covering his prison uniform. It seems the Dungeons don't suit his lavish lifestyle.

"Allisara, what a surprise." He calls out as if greeting a guest, his suave smile making me want to punch it off his face.

"You know why I am here Juden." I spat out, motioning for Sky and Max to handcuff the Traitor.

"We need to talk about the Rebellion and why you thought my Throne was yours." With that, I lead the way to the interrogation room. The one room by the stairs where the door was left open. With a mask of indifference, I watch as the men drag Juden into the room and cuff him to the metal interrogation chair. Sitting across from him, Max takes the spot just behind Juden while Sky stands behind me.

"Now lets get this started."

♔[1]

An hour has passed since we entered the interrogation room and I am getting annoyed with looking at the now dishevelled Juden Trilavantas who has done nothing but irritate me when a question was asked. Max has had a fun time punching Juden when he would refuse to answer my questions or would tell me what my smart mouth could do with his cock. I am fairly sure Sky is itching to lay into him as well but I won't allow him to dirty his hands with Juden. Max is more than capable of getting the answers we need.

"Tell me again why you thought that my Throne was yours?!" My eyes narrow as I state my demand impatiently, wanting nothing more than to kill this bastard.

"I told you; I thought you were dead." He drawls out with a shrug, wincing when he moves his shoulder the wrong way.

"You're lying." Sky shouts, stepping closer to Juden. Placing my hand out in front of him, I prevent Sky from landing a punch to Juden's smug smile and send a warning look to my friend. If anyone hates Juden more than me, it's Sky.

"How would you know?" Juden tries to edge him on, to goad Sky into punching him like I so want to.

"Because with out the body of any last living member of the Royal Family, the Regent can't become King or Queen until twenty years have passed." I answer instead, watching the muscle in Juden's jaw tighten. I had him.

---

1. https://coolsymbol.com/copy/White_Chess_King_Symbol_%E2%99%94

"Now tell me the truth." Leaning forward in my chair, I stare into Juden's eyes and allow my hatred to show. How I wish I can kill him right now, but I need answers.

"Make me." His grin infuriates me and with a look to Max, I snap my fingers. Max takes this as his que and the sound of Juden's pinky finger breaking and his screams of agon bring a sort of twisted satisfaction to me. This bastard deserves it.

"Tell me!" I continue leaning back into my chair and relaxing while watching pain flicker in Juden's eyes, eyes that glare at me with such hatred that I wonder if this is the true feelings of the man I called my Uncle.

"Fuck You!" He snarls back and I snap my fingers again as my answer. Max breaks another one of Juden's fingers and Juden releases another agonizing scream. Growing up in the Slums I grew used to violence and bone breaking. This is nothing from what I witnessed. His screams are nothing compared to those that betrayed the Slum Lords.

"You have two thumbs, six fingers and ten toes." Listing off the extremities, I watch Juden's face pale another level. He is scared. Good.

"If I have to ask again, not only will you have every finger and toe broken, you will have them butchered off. Now that's a total forty torturous moments. Refuse to answer me and you will regret it." I wait for a moment after my warning, watching Juden Trilavantas while he takes deep breaths and weigh his options. I take this time to study his chained hands and notice his two broken fingers. They were a clean break like I want. It will make it easier to set the bones and allow Juden to heal properly if I am satisfied with his answers.

Juden glares at me once again, his hatred making me want to shrink into the chair I sit on, but I decide against it. This is no longer the man I called Uncle. No longer the man my father called his best friend. He is a criminal.

"Fine, I'll tell you." It seems my threat worked as Juden concedes. I grin, nodding to Max and allowing him to back away from Juden. The threat still stands though. If he doesn't tell the truth, then the torture will continue.

"Good, get started." I order.

"But to tell you I have to start the night of the Rebellion." He shrugs and I pause, not sure if I am ready to hear about that night. That was the night my parents were slaughtered. The night that changed my life. If my Maid hadn't had saved me and taken me to the Knight and his Squire, I would have been killed alongside them. Taking a deep breath, I look to Sky who gives me an encouraging nod. Knowing I have him beside me, I turn my gaze to Juden and lean back in my chair.

"Continue then."

Chapter 15

S tanding in my Study I watch out the window as my men reach the Palace walls. It seems that planning this day on the Princess' sixth birthday was a smart move and soon this Kingdom will belong to me. I had planned everything correctly, found men that would side with me inside the Guards and Knights that will help take control from King Alexander and his wife Queen Evelyn. My son is safe at our Estate and will not be implicated in this mess. The Knight he Squired to had whisked him away by my command when signs of my Rebellion began as promised.

Suddenly the door to my Study bursts open and my personal Elite Guard Ronan barges in, a look of panic on his face. This isn't good.

"Lord Trilavantas, Princess Allisara and her Maid are missing!" He gasps for breath, his panic evident. Anger courses through my as I turn to face the window again, my fingers clenched into fists.

"She was supposed to be in her room!" The plan was fool proof. My men would sneak into the Palace with many disguised as Guards. They would slink their way to Allisara's room and slit her throat as she slept. An easy and clean kill. So how did they loose a little brat and her Maid.

"We went to personally kill her, but the room was empty and cold. Some one must have snitched to the Maid." Ronan explains, his breath coming easier. Screams of those dying can be heard clearly now as the rebels 'find' their way into the Palace. At least one part of the plan is going accordingly. Turning to face Ronan, I go to give him an order when the door bursts open once again, King Alexander and Queen Evelyn rushing inside.

"Juden, are you okay?" King Alexander asks as he does his best to barricade the door with an armoire that I use for storage.

"What's all the commotion Alex?" I feigned concern as I rushed to his side, Ronan helping Queen Evelyn to a chair as Alexander and I work to secure my Study. Little did they know that I was hoping for a chance like this.

"The rebels. They got into the Palace." Turning to look at the sobbing Queen, I give Ronan a silent signal to prepare for the next phase of the plan.

"I saw. What a horrible thing to happen on the Princess' birthday." Walking towards my desk, I pick up the sword that I had finished sharpening just hours before. With the door barricaded and the King and Queen in my grasp, I can't let this opportunity go.

"Juden, who do you think started this?" Queen Evelyn asks, turning her tear stained eyes to me. Such a lovely blue colour that should have been mine, but Alexander swooped in, taking her from me when we were all at the Royal College. Walking towards her I give her a sympathetic smile. I loved this woman, wanted to marry her, but she chose Alexander over me. She looks up at me as I stand before her, those blue eyes I would have gladly drowned in now disgust me.

"Oh, I did." I answer. With my confession, I plunge my sword deep into her chest, the shock and fear etched permanently onto her pretty little face as her heart is sliced in two like mine was that day ten years ago.

"Juden what are you doing?" King Alexander demands, trying to rush to his wife's side. Pulling my blood soaked sword from her chest, I swing it towards him, preventing him from doing anything for his now dead wife.

"Taking a Kingdom and making it my own." Chuckling, I glare at King Alexander, watching his violet eyes widen in shock and confusion. We grew up together, studied in the same Academy. But I was the son of a Duke and he the Crown Prince.

"Why would you do this!" He demands as I walk towards him, watching the man that called me his brother grow hopeless.

"Because you never deserved Evelyn or the Throne." With King Alexander backed into a corner, I plunge my sword into his abdomen, wanting him to die a slow and painful death.

"But our children would have been married. You would have been the next King's Father." Alexanders's voice grows slow as he falls to his knees, the sword swiftly being pulled out of him.

"But I want to be King." I state with a grin, relishing in the pain on Alexander's face and the realization that I, his best friend, betrayed him. Ronan comes forward and takes my sword from me. He will make sure that all traces of me being here has disappeared by tomorrow morning. No one will know what happened here tonight.

"It's a good thing my daughter, my Alli, escaped then." With his final breath, the King turns his head to look at his wife, a single tear slipping down his cheek. Finally he is dead.

"Lets go. We need to find the Princess and Kill her." With the King and Queen dead, Ronan and I unbarricade the door and knock the armoire onto the ground. I need it to look like the room was breeched. My men standing outside waiting for their orders and I sigh. Knowing that the next part is needed for my ascension to the Throne, I take a deep breath and allow my men to attack me. Everything needs to look real if people were to believe that I tried to protect the King and Queen. Looking to Ronan, he takes a sword from another man and stabs me in my abdomen. The pain is unbearable but necessary.

"It's not fatal you Majesty, but you will bleed a lot. Bear with it for now." Ronan helps me to the ground, allowing me to lay face first. Another man hands me a sword identical to the one I stabbed the King and Queen with, the blade looking as if its been in battle with some specks of blood on it.

As my vision blurs and the pain takes hold, I smile and know that as soon as we have Allisara in our grasps, the Kingdom will belong to me.

Chapter 16

With my body shaking with rage, I feel Sky place a hand on my shoulder to steady me. Hearing about the night of the Rebellion brought memories to my mind of that day, of my birthday. It was a simple party with my friends in attendance. My parents announcing that when I turned twenty I will be married to Demitrias.

"You killed my parents." Glaring at the man that betrayed my family, I watch as his eyes shine with amusement as he looks at me. A loud slap sounds around the room and I find myself being pulled away from Juden who now sports a red hand print on the left side of his face, my right hand stinging. Sky whispers into my ear, but the rage I feel burning inside me makes his voice sound muffled.

I want to kill the bastard sitting so smugly chained to that chair.

"Can't say I blame you for that slap. You are a lot stronger than you look Allisara." Juden taunts, his gaze meeting mine. It takes everything in me not to fight my way out of Sky's grasps when all I want to do is kill this man with my bare hands. Fuck knowing the truth, he deserves to die.

"Alli, take a deep breath. You can't let him get to you like this." Sky whispers into my ear, his words finally registering in my mind. Closing my eyes, I take in the scent of his pine shower gel and do my best to calm down. Sky is right. I can't allow Juden to get to me.

"Tell me why you thought I was dead then." I demand walking to the far wall and leaning against it. I feel that standing as far away from this criminal is the safest option for him. If my rage takes hold again I know Sky can intercept and stop me before I do anything that will mark me as an unfit Queen from this range.

Chapter 17

"We found her my lord!" Running into my Study, Ronan announces this news with a smile on his face, his brown eyes filled with excitement.

"By her, do you mean Allisara?" Placing my paperwork on the desk, I stare at my Guard with hopeful eyes. It has been three months since the Rebellion and in that time I had healed from my wounds and taken over the Kingdom. I thought everything was going smoothly and soon I would be crowned King, but news of that insufferable Princess being still alive spread like a wildfire across the Kingdom. All the Nobles demanded that I find her and bring her back as the rightful Heir to the Throne and so began the search for her. If I can get to her first, then I can rid the Kingdom of the Nimair line and take control of Nimairene for good.

"Yes! I just received the report. We only have an hour to get to her before the others do." Ronan confirms with a grin.

"Where is she." I demand, standing from my desk and making my way out the door. Five of my men are waiting in the hallway, their eyes flashing with murderous intent when I motion for them to follow Ronan and me.

"Out on the apple farm just outside of the city." He answers. Perfect. The family owes me a debt for helping them during the drought last year.

My men and I make our way to the Royal Garage, our group of seven climbing into two S.U.Vs. The drive is short, but one that makes me feel like a child on Christmas day. It is a miracle that Princess Allisara was found so soon. A miracle that I will get to her first. Hopefully no one else knows where she is.

Traveling through the Capitol City Zalaris, I take in the damage from the Rebellion that is still healing. Many businesses had taken a hit when riots broke out and it is now a slow process of rebuilding the City to my liking.

No one will know that I caused this to happen. No one will know that the Regent who took control and started the rebuilding process is the villain they all curse.

Soon the S.U.Vs drive out of the Capitol, the many building giving way to farm land until the driver makes a left turn and we pull onto a bumpy dirt path. It doesn't take long for us to reach the farm house where a little girl swings on a worn out tire swing tied to an old oak tree.

Climbing out of the vehicle, I look at the little girl and frown. It is indeed Allisara and the urge to strangle her right then and there is strong.

"Smile, your Majesty. She can't know something is wrong." Ronan reminds me, his face a mask filled with smiles. Taking a deep breath, I plaster on my own loving smile and slowly walk towards the tire swing.

"Allisara." She stiffens as I call out her name, her little legs stopping the tire swing. Allisara turns her little body to look at me, her violet eyes so much like her father's staring at me with shock.

"Uncle Juden you came for me!" She shouts, tears falling down her face as she jumps off the swing and runs towards me. Her little arms wrap around my waist as she sobs into me with relief. Playing the role of the dutiful Uncle, I pat her back and comfort her with my men watching on. The couple that owns the farm make their way towards us having heard the commotion and I nod to Ronan.

"Allisara, I am here to take you home. Go pack what ever items these nice folks gave you." Pulling away from her, I bend down to her eye level and place a hand on her shoulder. Her little face is covered in tears, but thankfully no snot. She nods obediently, promising to be right back before she runs to the couple, giving each of them a hug and thanking them for taking care of her before running into the house excitedly.

With her out of the way, I thank them for sending Ronan the tip of Allisara being placed in their care as Ronan hands them an envelope filled with cash. The couple promise to keep silent about this, knowing that soon the little Princess will be joining her parents.

When Allisara returns, a small tote in hand, I help her into my S.U.V. and we are off. Unfortunately for her, she will never see the Palace again.

Chapter 18

Listening to Juden explain how he found me, I close my eyes and try to envision the apple farm. I vaguely remember the tire swing he mentioned. But then again there was one in Ron and Liz's back yard that I always used. It seems that is something my body remembered even after losing my memories.

Taking a deep breath, I open my eyes and take in Juden looking at me with curiosity, as if trying to see into my mind.

"You don't remember them, do you?" He inquires unable to hide the surprise tone in his voice.

"I don't." Deciding to be honest, I inwardly sigh and wonder if – in time – I will remember the farmers that betrayed me.

"If your goal was the Throne, why didn't you just leave me with the couple instead. You say they owed you, so you could have had them keep me without anyone be the wiser." Feeling like I am stating the obvious, Juden lets out a deep chuckle, his laughter echoing in the room.

"It's not that simple Allisara. There are laws in place. Laws the prevents anyone from taking over the Throne." I know the laws he is talking about. The ones that state a surviving member of the Royal Family must show in twenty years time before the Crown is passed to the Regent or next highest Nobel. I even voiced that law to him half an hour ago.

"Continue explaining then." Feeling Sky place a hand on my shoulder, I relax into my chair waiting for the end on how I ended up in the Slums with no memories.

Chapter 19

Sitting in the S.U.V outside of a medical clinic, I look to Allisara who stares outside curiously.

"Uncle Juden, why are we here?" She asks, turning her gaze to me. My hand moves to the pistol at my waist and I think about how quick it would be to kill her, but that would leave a trail back to me.

"You've been gone for three months. I want to take you to a doctor so that he can give you a check up." Pulling my hand back and placing it on my lap, I give this annoying brat a gentle smile. I remind myself over and over again that after today I will become King. All I need to do is wait for the Doctor's job to be done and I will finally be rid of this brat.

Opening the door, I climb out of the S.U.V and help Allisara to exit it as well. She holds tightly to my hand and I allow it. The clinic is empty as we walk inside, the Doctor being given notice earlier today that I will be arriving with Allisara to get rid of her.

"Hi there, you must be Allisara." Walking out from the back room, Doctor Tomas greets Allisara. She timidly hides behind me, furthering my annoyance with her.

"Allisara, this is the Doctor I want to take a look at you." I coo to the little girl, watching as Doctor Tomas holds a hand out to her. Silence passes between us but finally she steps out from behind me, letting go of my hand and taking his.

"As your Uncle stated, I am Doctor Tomas. I hear you need a bit of a check up?" He is friendly to her; his soft gentle smile the perfect act I need to deal with the last of the Nimair blood line.

"Rory, take Allisara to the back while I talk with Duke Trilavantas. Allisara, Rory is a great helper. He has to leave soon so can you keep him company while he waits for his mom to pick him up?" After calling for the first of his many assistant, Doctor Tomas bends down to talk with Allisara. Her timidness is gone as she gives the Doctor a wide grin before agreeing to his request. Disappearing into the back with Rory, Doctor Tomas walks towards me, his friendly façade gone as he gives me a deep bow.

"What do you need me to do, your Majesty?" Happy for his change in demeanor, I help the aging doctor to stand.

"I want her dead, make it look like she was killed by the rebels." Giving him the order, Doctor Tomas nods. For years this man has been on my family's payroll, always helping my father and then me to get rid of those that stand in our way.

"Give me three hours. I need to make sure that it looks like she has been tortured then have someone drag her dead body somewhere to make it look believable." Happy with his answer, I hand him an envelope of the agreed upon payment. I know with his help nothing will go wrong, but his Assistants worry me. I heard he brought in a new man to help during the night and I hope that nothing goes wrong.

♔[1]

Returning to the Clinic at the agreed upon time, I walk into the waiting area with my men trailing behind me.

"You did what you fucking incompetent idiot!" The sound of Doctor Tomas screaming at someone draws my attention, making me want to learn what has happened. Walking into the back room with Ronan taking the lead, we round the corner to find Doctor Tomas beating a man I have never seen before. This man does not try to fight back or defend himself, his eyes dazed as he giggles.

"What is going on?" Shocked by the scene, I shout my demand. Doctor Tomas stops his beating, his face pale but the rage still simmering deep inside his hazel eyes.

"This fucking drug addict I hired fucked up." He shouts back, throwing the metal pole he was beating the man with earlier to the side.

"Instead of taking her body to the Slums like I told him to, He decided to sneak some Opium and put her body into the cremation oven while he got high." The man sits up as he lets out a giggle, blood dripping down his face

---

1. https://coolsymbol.com/copy/White_Chess_King_Symbol_%E2%99%94

from the beating. Disgusted by him, I order my Guard Clark to check the oven.

"There is a body in there, but its nearly Ash." His reply comes within minutes, my own rage simmering. Because of this Opium addict I have lost my chance at becoming King. Now I will need to wait for twenty years.

"Doctor Tomas, you have disappointed me this time. But your skills are still need." I watch the fear in the Doctor's eyes disappear as I address him. His only fault is hiring a drug addict. Looking to the man on the floor, disgust joins my fury and I look to my men.

"Put him into the oven with Allisara. Leave him alive." Not bothering to watch what is to unfold, I make my way out of the clinic with Ronan behind me. This little hiccup has cost me twenty years of waiting, but as Regent I still have control of the Kingdom. After twenty years I can be crowned King and when Demitrias marries and has his first child, I will pass the Throne to him.

Chapter 20

"So you see, I thought you were dead." Leaning back in his chair, Juden shrugs as he concludes his confession.

"And without your body as proof you were dead, I had to wait for twenty years to pass so that I could claim the Throne." Shocked by all this information, I run my fingers through my hair and try to make sense of all of this. The Rebellion fourteen years ago was caused by this man. My parents death was caused by him. But there is one thing I need to know.

"You never tampered with my memories, did you?" Looking into his eyes, Juden stares back at me with an unwavering stare.

"No, I just wanted you dead." I can sense his honesty in his words and sigh. The mystery of how I lost my memories remains.

"Your confession has been recorded. You will be executed in two months time and so will your co-conspirators. It will be public and televised and the people will know what you did." My decision is final. The people need to know what a monster Juden Trilavantas is and how he murdered innocent people for his own gain.

"Did your family know you did all this?" Sky asks, his emerald gaze filled with the same hatred I feel.

"No I kept it a secret from them." Another truthful answer. I take a moment to think before pushing off from the wall I leaned on. There is a lot I have to plan now with all this new information. Looking at Max, I notice how his keen brown gaze is kept on Juden, never wavering while he stands ready in case Juden tries anything.

"Make sure his hand is healed." I order Max, getting a quick look and a nod from the Guard before his gaze returns to staring at Juden.

"And Juden-" I call out.

"Yes." His gaze meets mine and I hesitate for a moment.

"- Your family will be spared. They will no longer be part of the Nobel families, but they will retain some land and their businesses as long as there is no Rebel ties. The land closest to Zalaris will be given to a new Duke of my choosing." Watching his eyes tear up knowing his family is safe, I take one last look at him before striding out of the interrogation room. Walking up the stairs, I find myself in need of some fresh air for my thoughts to stop running amuck in my head.

"Do you know a place where I can be alone in the Gardens?" I ask Sky, knowing he is following behind me.

"I do. My father and his team returned the Green House back to its former glory. We can go there." Taking my hand in his, Sky leads me down the familiar path that will take us to the Gardens.

Chapter 21

Looking at the lotuses floating on the pond, I allow my thoughts to wonder back to the information Juden gave me about the night of the Rebellion. I don't remember that day, remember the fear and pain caused by Juden and his men. But something inside me nags at me.

"Are you okay?" Taking the spot beside me on the bench, Sky wraps his arms around my shoulders and pulls me to his side. I sigh, resting my head against him and lean into his touch.

"No, but eventually I will be." I whisper, wrapping my arms around him. The green house is quiet and calm, the perfect place to be alone without worry.

"We need to find that doctor Trilavantas mentioned. See if he can give us answers on your memory loss as well as what sort of business he had with that man." It feels like Sky is inside my mind as I was thinking the same thing. This Doctor Tomas seems to be the link to my missing memories and how I ended up in the Slums. After agreeing with him, Sky and I return to looking at the pond in silence as the soothing sound of trickling water from a man made water fall calms my thoughts. The scent of the many flowers brought in by Thorin, Sky's father, floats around the air.

"Have you gotten any memories back lately?" Breaking the Silence, Sky pulls away to look at me, his emerald eyes filled with worry.

"Just one." I admit, giving him a small reassuring smile.

"I was in a forest being chased by wild dogs and a boy came to save me. I know it wasn't Demitrias but at the same time I couldn't see who this boy was. His face was blurred, as if my brain is stopping me from remembering him." Sky stiffens at my words, something I find strange but maybe he might know about this incident. He was a Squire by this point from what I saw in his pictures.

"I wish I could remember him, the boy I mean. I would tell him thank you for protecting me and helping me. I actually think he is the one who brought me to that Apple Farm." Admitting this to Sky feels good. I remember having vague dreams when back in the prison cell, how there was sounds of fighting, a man and a child in front of him and what sounds like a horse. But that's all I can remember. Sometimes I feel like it was just my imagination, my mind trying to help me deal with being in prison, but now knowing what I do because of what Juden told us makes me believe that my dreams were actually memories. Memories that were fighting to make themselves known to me.

"I bet he already knows how you feel." Sky muses, running his fingers in my hair and pulling me closer to him again. Resting my head against his chest, I can hear the steady beating of his heart. It is soothing, calming me more than relaxing with all these flowers ever can. Since Demitrias took me away from the prison, my life has become chaotic. Every day is a fight to prove to people that I am the rightful ruler Nimairene needs. Tomorrow I need to confront my Generals. To reorganize my Military. From there I will need to have hire tutors. I will need to prepare for my ascension to Queen in a few months.

"You seem to have a lot on your mind." Chuckling, I pull away to look into Sky's eyes, feeling my heart skip a beat.

"I do. The worst part is I only have a little time to sort it all out." Admitting this out loud makes it feel all to real. All to crazy.

"Well I can take one worry off your mind." His fingers draw small circles on my back, distracting me for a moment.

"Arian has started training new Royal Guards and your Personal Elite Guards have been chosen. You can meet them Tomorrow after dealing with all the old coots at the Generals meeting." Closing my eyes, I let out a soft sigh of relief and rest my forehead against his shoulder, feeling tears of relief slipping down my cheeks.

"Thank you." Knowing that my Guards are now fully loyal to me and my country is the best feeling. I no longer need to worry about sleeping with one eye open. No threat of having a knife being stabbed into my back by one of Juden's men.

"Its my job as your Captain and friend." He whispers back. My stomach decides in this moment to let my hunger be known, making both Sky and I laugh.

"Hungry Alli?" Pulling away from me, Sky pokes my nose, followed by his own stomach growling as well.

"Seems like you are too." A blush covers his cheeks as I poke my finger into the small dimple on his left cheek, getting an eye roll as my response.

"I am. We should ask the staff to make us something to eat." He suggests, making me scoff.

"Screw that. I can whip us something up pretty quickly."

"You do know there is a full staff waiting to feed you right?"

"You do know that I know how to cook right?" Giving him a pointed look, I stand from the bench and stretch.

"Okay, but I get to help since I want macaroni and cheese." Smiling at his idea, I hold my hand out to Sky and watch as he takes it. Soon he is standing beside me, his emerald gaze warm and welcoming as he looks into my eyes.

"Sounds good to me then. I could use some help in the kitchen." With that, we make our way out of the Green House and towards the Palace. Hopefully the Kitchen staff can be understanding with me wanting to cook. Maybe I should redesign my wing of the Palace and include a kitchen and dining area for mine and my Elite's personal use.

Chapter 22

"Alli, veggies do not go into a mac and cheese." Looking up from cutting the red bell peppers in front of me, I roll my eyes as Sky glares at the small amount of vegetables in front of my cutting board. You would think I just said I killed a puppy with how he is looking at the bell peppers.

"Mine does. You need something to counter the meat and copious amounts of cheese." Returning to chopping the bell peppers, I make sure to keep them small and bite sized.

"Wait there is going to be meat in it?" Stopping my cutting once again, I look up at Sky who raises his hands in surrender. I guess he finally took the hint he is starting to annoy me. Around us the chefs and cooks are chuckling, leaving Sky and I in the small corner while they prepare meals for the rest of the Palace staff.

"Yes. So grab the pack of ground beef in the fridge and start cooking it off. Make sure to strain the fat when its done so the mac and cheese isn't too greasy." Ordering Sky about, I return to finishing my task at hand. Some of the Cooks watch on, one coming to question why I am saving the seeds to the bell peppers instead of throwing them out. After explaining that we can grow more vegetables with the seeds, the Cook runs off excitedly to tell the head Chef.

"So you want us to save the seeds of vegetables and fruits if we can?" Looking up at the new voice, I notice a man with gray hair under a chef hat standing on the opposite side of my table.

"Yes please. I believe it will be good for our kitchen staff to learn how to grow our produce so that there is less waste." Answering his question, I finish dicing the vegetables and place them inside of a clean bowl before setting my knife down.

"Good. I was trained in knowing where our food comes from and being able to grow some of our own will cut down food costs in the kitchen. You think the head Gardener will help set some land aside close to the kitchen to grow some vegetables?" Smiling at his enthusiasm, I instantly agree that lowering food costs with so many to feed will be helpful and mention the farm land next to the Palace. The Chef, Theon, helps me find a pot as I set about getting the noodles ready to boil. We talk about adding a few fruit trees into the gardens closest to the Kitchen and what vegetables will be perfect to plant for our use as well as how to cycle the gardens as the seasons come and go.

"Talk to Thorin BlackHawk when you get a chance. He is the Head Gardener and can help set about creating a vegetable garden and hire people to take care of them with the Kitchen staff." I mention this to Theon as I pour a healthy amount of salt into the pot of water, Sky bringing the now cooked and strained ground beef over.

"Why did you add salt to the water?" He asks, setting the bowl on the counter as Theon is called away to help with a dish that will be served to the Guards for dinner.

"It helps to heat the water and flavour the noodles." Rolling my eyes, I turn away from the pot to focus on grating cheese, Sky deciding to find another grater and help get the task done faster.

"That seems redundant and stupid." He shrugs, taking a chunk of cheese and popping it into his mouth.

"To those who don't cook, it seems stupid. To those that can cook, it is magic. Add the noodles when the water boils." After my explanation, I gather all the cheese into a bowl and find another pot, setting about making a thick cheese sauce. Sky watches me, his gaze following my every movement with interest from pouring milk into the pot to slowly adding the cheese once it boils. Reminding him to keep an eye on the pasta once he pours it into the pot of boiling water, we make quick work of finishing the mac and cheese. After placing it into the over to bake for a bit, I start the clean up process.

"You really do seem to know what you are doing in a kitchen." Sky muses, drying the dishes as I wash them.

"Thanks. Liz taught me everything I know." I muse, thinking back to the days I would bake and cook with Liz after getting to know her and Ron.

"To be honest with you, I was going to leave Zalaris and find a small town to move to. Maybe even open up a small restaurant." I admit, a soft smile taking over my face as I think about my plans for leaving the Capitol.

"Then I was arrested and later learned my true identity." Wiping down the counter now that all the dishes are done, I disinfect the table Sky and I worked at before throwing the rags into the laundry bin and moving towards the oven to check on the mac and cheese deciding it needs another few minutes to finish baking once I notice the colour of it.

"You really do have a talent for cooking. I can see you owning a restaurant if you weren't a Princess." Smiling at Sky's praise, I join him in leaning against the wall while we wait for the mac and cheese to be ready.

"That's why I am the chef in the relationship and you just stand there and look pretty." I state with a chuckle, bumping my shoulder against his.

"So we are in a relationship now." I turn and see his eyebrows raised, a glint of mischief and something else in his eyes. Blushing, I look away and try to come up with something to rebut with.

"You know what I mean." Trying to diffuse the situation I got myself into, I try to walk towards the oven only to have Sky gently grab my hand and stopping me in my escape. Watching nervously as he steps closer to me, our bodies only inches apart, I find myself holding my breath and feel my heart beat quicken. He leans forward, his lips inches away from my ear and the scent of his pine shower gel wrapping around me.

"If we are in a relationship, does this mean we can go on dates?" He whispers, his warm breath brushing against the side of my face. Suppressing a shiver, I try to come up with an answer but the timer thankfully goes off. Backing away from Sky and freeing myself from his grasp, I take the pair of oven mitts from the hook on the wall and make my way to the oven, turning off the timer to check the mac and cheese.

"It's ready." I proclaim thankful for the change of subject before taking the pan out of the oven and placing it onto the counter to cool. Sky busies himself with finding plates, a serving spoon and some cutlery, Theon thankfully helping him as Sky nearly caused a few items to fall before he returns to my side.

"What else do we need with out meal?" He asks, his easy going smile back on his face.

"Two glasses and orange juice." You can put everything in a basket and then just follow me. Thankfully Sky grabs what I suggest, placing the items he gathered into a basket while I use the mitts once again and carry the pan out of the Kitchen after thanking the staff for allowing us to use the small prep station. Sky follows me diligently, the two of us making our way to my Study. Once inside, I place the mac and cheese onto my desk and removes one of the oven mitts before I begin searching the book shelf to the right of my desk.

"What are you doing?" Getting a puzzled look from Sky, I ignore his questioning gaze.

"You'll see." Finding what I am looking for, I pull out a book titled "Hidden Secrets" and smirk as the shelf slowly moves to the right side. Sky lets out a low whistle as I place the mitt on once again before picking up the pan and climbing the stairs in the hidden passage way.

"Wow." Is Sky's only response.

"Hurry up before the door closes." I call out over my shoulder, hearing the shelf moving once again. Sky's hurried footsteps tells me he is following me and I grin. It takes a bit of time for us to climb to the top but soon the stairs come to an end and we find ourselves on a landing, the small area quickly opening up to a large room hidden in a tower.

"How the heck did you find this?" Sky asks as he slowly steps into the room, his emerald green eyes wide with excitement.

"I was searching the books for something to read a few days ago. One book caught my eye and when I went to pull it out, the shelf moved." Walking towards the little table in the middle of the room, I place the pan onto it and motion for Sky to join me. He places the basket beside me and I get to work taking the items out.

"I think I used to come here as a child when my father was in the Study as there are children's toys meant for a little girl. I have been slowly cleaning the room up in hopes of renovating it." Dishing out the mac and cheese, Sky walks around the room exploring it, his emerald eyes taking in everything from the balcony to the little table set meant for a child.

"This would make the best spot to protect you." He states, coming to sit opposite of me and taking the offered bowl of food.

"Or a great hiding spot when we need a place to go. There is a way to get here from my room surprisingly." I counter, taking a bite of my mac and cheese.

"That too. What do you want to add into here?"

"A bed, maybe a two person chair and table set for both inside the room and the balcony. Definitely a mini fridge for snacks." Shrugging, I continue eating the meal, with Sky and I talking about what we could do to make this hidden tower room homier for us.

"I have been tasked with asking you when do you want to have the "Debut into Society" Ball every royal gets." It was a question I had been dreading. Every Nobel in Nimairene will host a Ball for their child welcoming them into society at the age of fifteen. Seeing as I was living in the Slums with many thinking I was dead, I never had the opportunity to plan one.

"If I say never would that be a good answer?" I ask, looking at my now empty bowl and wondering how I can get out of this predicament.

"Sorry Alli but you need to see your Nobles and be welcomed into Society." Sky sighs out, giving me an apologetic look. Sighing again, I lay on the cold wooden floor and turn my face to look out of the balcony, the snow gently falling in the sky.

"I know, but they all want one thing." I agree reluctantly.

"To gain some fort of favor or worse, a marriage alliance?" Sky adds with a chuckle, nudging my foot with his.

"Exactly. Now that my Betrothal to Demitrias is gone, I am free real-estate in their minds. They will want to pair me with either their son, grandson or nephew." Groaning, I start to think of ways to get out of this Ball. Maybe I can use working on rebuilding Nimairene as a way to avoid a Ball.

"How about we throw the Ball after you've settled all the matters with Juden. I know you want to change some laws and tomorrow you have the meetings with your Army Generals." His idea is perfect, and I tell him as much as I push myself up on my elbows. Sky and I begin to plan how we will handle the meeting tomorrow and what I will need to do with all the information that was gathered. Sky takes this time to inform me of who will be on our side during the meeting and I am happy to know Arian will be there with his stack of evidence against the Generals that will need to be replaced.

Deciding that we will need to have a thorough plan, Sky and I gather the remnants from our meal and head down the stairs. When we reach the book shelf wall, I show Sky how to open the door by pushing a button and we step into my Study. He goes to fetch Arian while I take the time to shuffle through my notes for tomorrow. It will be a long day and many people will be arrested.

Chapter 23

"Now sweetie, that man who brought you here wants to kill you." Looking up at Doctor Tomas, I wonder what he means. Uncle Juden came to find me, to take me home. So why would he want to kill me.

"Why would he want to do that? He is my Uncle!" I ask after trying to wrap my mind around this idea. The Doctor lets out a sigh and pulls me into his arms, hugging me as I begin to cry. I did not want to die. I want to go home to my mother and father. I want to see Rainnah.

"Because he doesn't like you. He wants to be King and you are in his way." Doctor Tomas does not make sense but I can tell he is being honest with me. Something about him screams that I can trust him.

"But Demitrias will be King when we get married. Why does Uncle Juden want to be King?" Unable to wrap my mind around this, I ask the Doctor this question as I sob. My father is King so how can Uncle Juden be King.

"Because he is a bad man, Princess. I am sorry but I need to help protect you so he doesn't ruin Nimairene." The Doctor pulls away from me, resting his hands on my shoulders and looking me in the eyes.

"How will you protect me?" I ask, lips quivering. Will I ever see mother and father again? Will I be able to return home? SO many questions race in my mind, questions I want answers to.

"I have to lock your memories away. It is the only way for you to escape Juden Trilavantas until you come of age." He explains. Looking down at my lap, I think about it for a moment. If Uncle Juden really wants me dead, then he will find me and kill me. I have seen him kill bandits before to protect Demitrias and I, I know he will do it.

"Will it hurt?" I ask, scared of the pain.

"No, but you won't remember things until you turn twenty years old; the age you can claim your birthright." I nod slowly. Mother and father told me that at twenty I will be preparing to take the Throne and marry Demitrias. At twenty one I will be crowned Queen and Demitrias crowned King.

"Close your eyes Allisara. It won't take long." Trusting Doctor Tomas, I lean back in the chair and close my eyes. A needle pricks my skin and soon I find myself falling asleep as the beeping of a machine begins.

♔[1]

"Wake up sweetie." A calm voice calls out to me. My eyes feel heavy and my body feels like someone has been hitting me. Everything hurts. Finally being able to open my eyes, I take in the strange room I am in and the word Clinic comes to mind. But that is about it. I try to think about why I am here, but a pain in my head makes me wince.

"Who...who am I?" I wonder.

"You're Allison." The calm voice from earlier calls out. Looking at the elderly man – a Doctor – I nod and test the name he gave me. It feels right.

"How old am I?" I ask, the Doctor coming to kneel in front of me, shining a light in each eye.

"Six. You are a patient here." The Doctor explains, a sad smile on his face.

"I am sorry to say but the accident you were in killed everyone." Confused, I try to think about the accident but the pain returns, making me whimper and wince.

"Careful there Allison. You might have some memory loss." He explains, quickly hugging me. I stop thinking, the pain going away as soon as I do.

"Will my memories return?" I whimper out, feeling tears fall down my face. I am confused because I remember things like tears, body parts and what a Doctor is, but I can't remember anything about me.

"I believe in time they will." He sighs, pulling away to look at me, his sad smile still on his face.

"I am going to guess you don't know where you live. I have a friend that runs a shelter for girls and will take you in till you can find your way in life." As if on que, a pudgy women walks in, her purple dress flowing around her plump body.

---

1. https://coolsymbol.com/copy/White_Chess_King_Symbol_%E2%99%94

"Is this the girl you told me about?" The woman asks in a sickly sweet voice. The Doctor nods but something about the woman worries me. She looks nice but something is wrong.

"Good. I have a room for her ready to go." She takes my hand and helps me off the bed. I look to the Doctor for help but he shoos me to follow her. His eyes look to the door behind him as the woman drags me towards another direction. Something doesn't feel right.

"Tomas says that you can't see customers, but if I am raising you, you will do what I tell you." The woman states as she drags me out the door into a back alley. I shiver with her cold tone, the sickly sweet voice gone. Instinct tells me to fight and without thinking, I bite the hand that holds onto me. The woman screams and releases me and without a second though I run away. I know the Doctor was helping me, but I will not go with that woman...

$$♔^2$$

Bolting Awake from my dream, I look around disoriented until I realize I am safe and in my room. I shiver for a moment, wondering why I am so cold until I notice that my body is drenched in a cold sweat. The dream was so real, so vivid and it takes a moment for me to realize that it was not a dream, but a memory. The memory of how I lost my memories. With a groan, I stand from my bed and walk towards my balcony, wrapping a soft throw blanket that I grabbed from the lounge chair around my body. The cold air is just what I need to clear my mind, the freshly fallen snow glowing under the full moon. It is quiet and peaceful and just what I need to sort through my thoughts.

"At least I know why I am alive." I whisper into the air, wiping away a stray tear. The woman I saw in my dream was one I had seen around the Slums one too many times. I learned quickly she was the Madam of the brothel, a place for lost girls who were victimized at a young age. I would have been one of those girls taking customers for her greed if I had not ran away that day.

Deciding that I need to help those girls, I walk into my room and find a notebook, quickly taking a seat at the desk and working on a plan. Those girls will need therapy and doctors. God only knows how many diseases they contracted being forced to take customers for their pleasure as long as they paid the Madam. After that they will need career options. Maybe I can take

2. https://coolsymbol.com/copy/White_Chess_King_Symbol_%E2%99%94

what the Prison did and help them learn to read and write, maybe even find jobs for them that pay well.

With my thoughts sorted and a plan to help the women of the brothel, I find myself yawning and make my way back to my bed. It will be a long day tomorrow dealing with the Generals of my army and I need sleep.

Sadly for me, sleep does not come easy and I find myself tossing and turning. With a groan of frustration, I throw the blankets off of me and stalk towards the door. Hopefully Sky is awake because right now I could use his comfort.

Chapter 24

I lay awake in my bed thinking about today. From The interrogation and how heartless Allisara was when Max was torturing Juden. She never flinched, just stared on with a blank expression. He had it coming, but even I flinched when he screamed in pain from his fingers being broken. At first I was worried with her reaction, but then when we left the dungeon and made our way to the green house I saw the girl that always sang to the flowers. The soft kind hearted smile that she gives to those who are kind to her.

"I wish I could remember him, the boy I mean. I would tell him thank you for protecting me and helping me..." Those words - her voice - float through my mind. I wish I could tell her everything, let her know the truth of who that boy is and how long I have been waiting to see her again. How leaving her that day at the apple farm broke me. Demitrias never deserved her, never deserved to go retrieve her from Lady Pricilla's Prison for Troubled Women after I was the one that found her. With a groan, I sit up and look at the pictures on my dresser.

"At least she is remembering me." I whisper with a sad smile, my eyes moving to look at the image of the two of us covered in mud. She was so young, five years old to be exact, and the picture was taken two weeks before she turned six. I had just turned eleven that year and after training as a Squire, I grew fond of Allisara as the Knight that trained me was the one in charge of her protection, a role I was training to take over completely when I finished my training.

Sighing, I decide to check on her, to see how she is handling the news that her parents were murdered in cold blood. I know her, know that Allisara will have nightmares soon enough. Maybe what we learned from Juden will trigger more memories, helping her to learn about her past.

With a smile taking over my face, I make my way to my door and open it just in time for her to open her own door shocking both of us. She is wearing a pink tank top over a pair of shorts. I know that she runs in the morning through the Garden, something that surprised me the first day I caught her since not many royals like to stay fit, but even I found it to early to run right now.

"Um...hi." Her voice is quiet as she looks at me, a blush on her face as she takes in my bare chest. It is now that I realize I am only wearing a pair of pajama pants hung low on my hips. Shit.

"Hey." I smile out awkwardly, running a hand through my long hair.

"Can't sleep?" I ask. She shakes her head and walks towards me, wrapping her arms around my bare waist and resting her cheek against my peck. Instinctively my arms wrap around her, holding her close. God she feels so good in my arms.

"I saw how I lost my memories." Allisara mutters out quietly, her breath fanning against my skin. She doesn't understand how her touch affects me.

"Want to talk about it?" She nods and lets go of me and I reluctantly release her. She walks into my room, surprising me as she walks past my couch and towards my bed where she crawls under the covers. I have to remind myself that she is my friend no matter how much I want her to be more. But I have to wait. I waited fourteen years; I can wait a little longer.

Closing my door, I smile at the sight of her yawning while curled in my bed. I dreamt of what she would look like as an adult, what she would be like and now I finally get to see it. With only being five years older than her, the only thing that would stand in the way of me asking her out is the fact that I am a commoner. The Nobles wouldn't want to see their future Queen with a commoner.

"You okay Alli?" I ask climbing into bed, wrapping my arms around her as she shuffles closer to me and rests her head against my chest. Distracting my thoughts from going down the gutter, I find myself playing with her golden hair as I wait for her answer.

"I hate being alone." She whispers, my heart breaking slightly at the sadness in her voice. She's been alone for fourteen years. Scratch that, she had Latham, Ron and Liz but she still lived in that shack all alone.

"You're not alone." Reassuring her, I pull her closer to me, taking in the vanilla scent of her body wash.

"You also have Ron and Liz we can visit. There is also Ellisia, Adam and Arian." I continue, feeling her smile against my skin. I really should have worn a shirt. She yawns, her body relaxing as she presses closer to me and I decide to ask her what brought her to my room. She begins with talking about the Doctor that Juden mentioned and how she gained the name Allison. It was close to her true name, Allisara, but it was also the one that hid her. The Doctor was smart, knowing that Juden is an evil man, but I am shocked to learn that Allisara almost ended up in a brothel. It explains why she was alone in the Slums for a while until she met Latham then Ron and Liz.

"I have a feeling that my memories will come back stronger. I might even space out when it happens." She explains through a yawn, her violet eyes watering. I chuckle, going back to playing with her hair and finding her adorable as she fights to keep her eyes open.

"I will be by your side the whole time then." She chuckles, reminding me that I am the Captain of her Guards and I tell her to hand it to Arian. I'd rather protect her than order men about anyways. After promising to talk more about it in the morning she gives me a soft smile, one that causes my heart to skip a few beats.

Her eyes start to close until finally she falls asleep, looking so peaceful and adorable wrapped in my arms. One of these days I will tell her how I feel and work towards a possible future of being her one and only. Demitrias never deserved her. He didn't care whether she was found or not or if he married her or some other woman. He was just like his father, only wanting power and riches. I am glad he is a normal citizen now. He can find a woman who will use him the way he tried to use Allisara.

"Sky..." I hear my name and look down at the sleeping girl, a serene smile on her lips. I smile as well, placing a gentle kiss against the top of her head and watch her as I fell asleep.

Chapter 25

Waking up in a warm comfortable bed that smells like pine, I find myself melting into the bed. I remember waking from my dream, of wanting to talk to Sky, but then nothing. Confused, I slowly open my eyes and notice that I am not in my room at all. This seems to be happening a lot lately. Groaning, I close my eyes and try to remember what happened the night before. Someone wraps their arms around me, pulling me closer and making me turn around to swat at them.

"I get it, you are not a morning person." A deep husky voice calls out with a chuckle. Suddenly the events of last night flashes through my mind and I remember that after waking from my dream, my memory, I walked into Sky's room to talk to him. I must have fallen asleep on his bed and now I am pressed to his side.

"Um...morning." I say sheepishly as my hands feel the hard naked muscle under me. Yep, I am not living this one down for a while.

"Good morning." He says back, running his fingers through my hair. Leaning into his touch, I find myself enjoying this moment and feeling that this is the perfect place to be right now. If only my parents had betrothed me to Sky.

"What time do we need to meet the Generals?" I ask, pulling away from him and sitting up. The blanket pools around our waist, revealing his well defined muscles to me once again.

"The meeting is at one in the afternoon. Arian is already working and just getting our men into place for what is to come today." Nodding, I look at fireplace mantal with all of his pictures, my eyes zeroing on the one with the girl covered in mud. He loves her, so why am I in bed with him?

"What time is it now?" I ask, turning away from the pictures to look at Sky.

"Ten in the morning. We can relax for now unless you want to do something else." Sky answers, Sitting up beside me and giving me his easy going smile.

"Can we meet with my Elite Guards today?" I know Sky mentioned he would like to pass his position to Arian and be in charge of my personal Elite Guards, but I feel safer with him in charge.

"Sure. Your Study or the Dinning Hall?"

"Dinning Hall. It's been a while since I dinned with everyone and with new Recruits, including female Guards, I need to dine and meet them." I slowly get up and climb out of bed, stretching and turning to look at Sky. His smile is still on his face, but his eyes shine with something I can't place my finger on.

"I am going to get changed. Meet me in ten in the hall way so that we can get breakfast? "

"Sure Alli." I smile and lean down, kissing his cheek, surprising me and him. Before he can say anything, I quickly walk out of his room and into my own, leaning against the closed door. My heart beats fast, the realization that I kissed Sky making my skin heat up. With a sigh, I think about what a future of dating Sky might look like and find myself smiling. There is something I will have to do to stop tongues from wagging if or when he and I do decide to date, but that is a problem I will need to deal with at a later date.

With a long day ahead of me, I walk into my closet and dress, pulling on a pair of black jeans, a simple blouse and an indigo blazer. I will need to look the part of a strong leader when dealing with the generals today. Finding a pair of wedges, I slip them onto my feet and walk out of the closet in time for Ellisia to walk into my room with Adam trailing behind her, a smile on her face.

"Something tells me you will need help with your makeup and hair, so I am here to help. Go wash your face and brush your teeth while I prepare everything." She states, shooing me into my bathroom. Rolling my eyes, I thank her for her help before doing what she told me to, coming out with a clean face and even cleaner teeth. She sits me down at my vanity, the top holding makeup, a brush and a few hair ties.

"I have a feeling less is more with you missy." She chuckles out, her hands expertly working my hair into an elegant French braid. With a smile, I enjoy how the small strands that frame my face matches the braid before my vision is blocked by Ellisia.

"Close your eyes." She orders, making me chuckle as I comply. Soft brush strokes graze my skin, the scent of make-up reaching my nose. This takes less time than my hair did and soon Ellisia says I can look in the mirror.

With a deep breath, I open my eyes to see my reflection staring back at me. Ellisia kept it light, only placing a shimmery nude shadow on my eyelids with a dark liner framing my large violet eyes. My lashes were darkened with the mascara she used moments earlier making my lashes appear longer than they are. It takes everything in me not to cry as I see my mother in my reflection. Her golden curls and button nose the same ones I have. The only difference are the violet eyes I gained from my father.

"Thank you." I whisper in awe, trying my best no to cry.

"You're welcome Allisara." Nodding to Adam, Ellisia takes the tiara that he held on his hand and helps to settle it on top of my head. With that final touch done, She helps me to my feet and the three of us walk out of my room. Sky is waiting in the hall, dressed in his uniform and leaning against the wall. His hair is tied into a bun, his cheeks carrying the morning stubble.

"Ready to eat?" He asks when he spots me, his emerald green eyes scanning me from head to toe. That shimmer in his eyes return, causing me to blush as I walk towards him. Ellisia and Adam scurry away, stating they have business to attend to, and I wave them good bye.

"Yes I am." I answer cheerily, the two of us walking down the hallway. The walk is quiet, not knowing what I should say to him. Thankfully we reach the Dining Hall in no time. I pause in the door way, taking in the table set up. As usual, those that bent the knee to me are in their usual seats, but the seats that used to be filled by Juden's men are now filled with women. Shocked by the divide, I pull aside a Maid that was bringing food to the table and ask her to remove all the food from the men's table. She complies, the men protesting when more Maids and Butlers come to help until one of the Guards notices Sky and me standing in the door way.

"I never thought my Guards would be so rude to women." I call out when the room quiets, the men looking down in shame.

"I want this room to be rearranged how my father had it in the past within ten minutes. In this Palace we are a family and that means I want each and every one of you to get to know one another." With a resounding 'Yes Ma'am' the men stand from their chairs and begin to rearrange the tables. They start with an outer line, the tables forming a square with one table missing from the center of the North and South side. After apologizing to the women, the men take the food off of their table and onto the newly arranged ones before moving the tables they sat on and making two lines inside the square. With the tables now arranged, the chairs were moved, spacing them evenly on both sides of the table until all the chairs were placed.

"Thank you gentlemen. Now that the room has been rearranged, I would like to have two buffest sections on either side of the room where we can easily access food. From now on we are one unit, one team. We will switch seats until we have all gotten to know one another." With my point made, Maids and Butlers bring in more tables, getting to work with placing the cooked food onto them and removing the served food from the tables that have been rearranged. The final touches being a beverage station at the end of each table and a stack of clean plates and cutlery at the beginning. Making my way to the left buffet table, I grab a plate and cutlery set and begin to portion my food, smiling when the others follow suit.

With Sky and I having full plates, I make my way to the tables, walking into the middle and sitting down. Sky places his plate beside mine, promising to be right back and leaving quickly only to return with a glass of orange juice for the two of us.

The tables begin to fill up, both men and women introducing themselves to one another bringing a smile to my face. Soon the room begins to fill with conversation and laughter until the line of tables that Sky and I sit at fill up. Max sits in front of me, a grin on his face as he nods a greeting.

"How is he doing?" I ask, watching his smile grow wider.

"Good and taken care of. He will be healthy when its time." He answers quickly before taking a bite of his bacon. I chuckle, looking to the others that join us.

"I have never seen a Royal or Nobel sit with us grunts and enjoy the same food as me!" Someone exclaims as he takes a seat to my left, his bald head shining from the light above.

"Kian Grant, your Highness." He introduces himself, holding his hand out to me.

"Well if it is good for my Guards, then its good for me too. Besides I hate being alone." I answer back, reaching out to take his hand and giving it a firm shake.

"And call me Alli."

"I like her already." Kian chuckles out elbowing a woman beside him. She rolls her eyes at him before looking towards me, a smile on her face. Her blue eyes are clear and calm, something I like in a person.

"Alice Grant and Kian's sister." I chuckle as she swipes a sausage from his plate, realizing that I am going to enjoy having these two around. Soon the others begin to introduce themselves. The twins Lia and Mia Crossroan are skilled in disguise having come straight from cosmetic college before joining the Palace Guards when they heard females were finally being recruited and Alec Blighte, a new recruit fresh from the Military who decided guarding the rightful Queen sounded better than retiring with honors.

"These bright Guards are also your Elite, Alli." Sky chimes in with a grin, his emerald eyes sparkling. Shocked, I look at each and every one of them, seeing the five people nod in confirmation. To think my Elite would be easy to get along with.

"I thought we agreed upon six. Three men and three women." Confused, I look back to Sky who gives me a shrug, looking away from me for a moment before turning to face me once more.

"I want Arian to become Captain of the Guards. He has been here five years longer than me and had been trained under Sir Carlos, your father's Captain of the Guard." He admits, shocking me once again. Taking a moment to collect my thoughts, I look down at my hand and try to calm my quickly beating heart.

"Then what will you do?" I ask, scared to know the answer.

"Be the Captain of the Elite Guards."

Chapter 26

Sitting in front of my computer, I look at the screen and try to focus on emailing my Cabinet members, needing to set a date for a meeting before I head over to the meeting with the Generals. Sky had shocked me when he confessed he wanted to be the Captain of my Elite Guards. I wanted to refuse, to ignore his request, but instead I asked for some time to think and ran to hide away in here before the Guards went about their day either patrolling or training. My Elite were given a tour of the Palace thanks to Ellisia and Adam while Sky and Arian went to finalize the plan for arresting those in cahoots with Juden.

And I went to hide with the intention of doing work.

The door to my Study opens and Adam walks in, Ellisia following right away with a tray of snacks and sweet tea.

"You okay Alli?" He asks, coming to sit in the armchair in front of my desk while Ellisia sets the tray down.

"No. Sky wants to be a part of my Elite." I admit honestly, Adam letting out a low whistle.

"I mean, it makes sense. He is always by your side protecting you and Arian usually performs the duty of Captain of the Guards." Ellisia chimes in, handing me a glass of sweet tea.

"Do you think he would be better as Captain of my Elite?" I ask the two, Adam and Ellisia looking to one another before facing me.

"Honestly, yes. Arian has been a part of the Guards since he was ten and under Sir Carlos Remone tutelage. He is twenty nine now with more experience than most men." Ellisia answers, taking a seat on the other arm chair and biting into a chocolate chip cookie. I sigh, leaning back into my chair and taking a moment to think.

"I will need to make these changes after the meeting then and instate them tomorrow." I finally concede, realising that Ellisia and Adam are correct. Sky will be better by my side and I his and Arian has proven more then capable of leading the Palace Guards. These two will still need to work together when it comes to planning my safety, but the Elite will remain separate from the regular Guards.

"Well, we have work to do. Adam is helping me train the Maids and Butlers in self defense today." Ellisia stands from her chair, Adam quickly helping her to her feet.

"Wait, before you leave can you have some Maids prepare these room in my wing of the Palace." I call out, handing a small folder to Adam who then hands it to Ellisia.

"What is this for?" She asks, giving me a smile.

"My Elite Guards. I met them earlier today and finally was able to finalize who will take what room." I explain, getting a chuckle from Adam.

"Man, I wish I could be an Elite." He sighs out, looking over Ellisia's shoulder as she examines the plans.

"Who is to say you weren't the first member." Shock crosses Adam's face and I chuckle, reaching into my drawer and taking out a small pin made of amethyst.

"Everyone thinks you are guarding Ellisia, but the reality is you are the communication between her and I. Anything that happens with my Palace staff, you relay back to me. You are an unknown spy that everyone is happy to talk to." His face lights up as he places the pin on the inside pocket of his blazer out of sight and my smile grows. I am glad Sky brought Adam to me, he is indeed a great friend and Guard.

"You help protect me from the shadows. When we have a meeting with the Elite and I, you and Ellisia will be there." This seems to boost their spirit as Ellisia is also handed a pin, her smile so wide it emphasizes her smile lines.

"Violet Guards." Adam whispers, catching my attention.

"What was that?" Curious to know his thinking, watch his face turn red for a moment.

"We can't just call it the Elite Guards. We need a name." Smiling at this suggestion, I agree that it is fitting and decide to call my Elite the Violet Guards. After their help, I wish Adam and Ellisia luck in training everyone as they leave my Study. I find myself able to focus once again when they leave and turn to face my computer. I pull up the draft for the Cabinet meeting on my email, double checking that the list of Politicians and Nobels are correct on the recipient line before sending the email. I have it set for five days from now, needing to correct all these laws for the good of Nimairene.

Looking to the binder on my desk, I frown. After seven days of going through the laws made in the last fourteen years, I found fifty that hinder the success of the citizens but boost those of the already rich. With a sigh, I take the binder and lock it away in my desk. The last thing I need is someone sneaking in and stealing it before I bring these to the attention of my Cabinet meeting.

"Alli, meeting is in thirty minutes." My Study door opens once again and in walks Sky and Arian, the two contrasting one another. Arian's black hair is tied at the top if his head, the long strands flowing freely from the ribbon that keeps them together. His height is just slightly shorter than Sky's, but both men scream "Soldiers" in their uniforms with their guns holstered to the right and swords on the left.

"I guess we should head on over to the Throne Room then." I shrug, picking up the binder set aside for todays meeting and rising from my chair. I pause for a moment before reaching for the remaining pins in the drawer and place them in my pocket. I will need to hand these to my team when I see them. Leading the way out of my Study, I stop when I notice outside the five Guards I met earlier are waiting along the far wall. The girls are dressed in a similar style to me but the colours help them blend into the background. The men are dressed in the usual Guard uniform, their posture screaming protector.

"Captain Sky told us we need to dress the part of Ladies in waiting." Alice steps forward, taking the blue binder from my hand with a smile on her friendly face. Thanking her, I lead the way to the Throne Room, my heels clicking on the floor. Today will be another momentous day in claiming my country back as the rightful heir.

Arian and Sky stand on either side of me, Arian holding out a list of men attending the meeting. Each name is listed under a picture. If they have a star next to their name, they are loyal and trust worthy. Anyone without a star is set to be arrested today.

"This is yours for the meeting. There is one new General that is not listed." Handing me the list, Arian lets out a sigh as he finishes explaining about this new General. Surprised, I look to the last name and try to decide what I should do with this information.

"Taylor Knight. Sounds like a strong person." I joke, handing the list to Alice for her and the others to memorize, explaining the star detail to them. As we reach the doors to the Throne Room, two Guards salute us and Alice asks me what to do with the list. After telling her to place it in the binder so that I can glace at it when needed, I nod to the Guards Mathew and John to open the doors.

With a deep breath and reassurance from those with me, I walk into the room with my head health high. These old fools waiting for me will have no idea what is about to hit them.

Chapter 27

Marching past the long table set in the middle of the Throne Room, I carefully observe the few men that watch me with contempt in their eyes. My stride is even, my back straight and shoulders back. With my head held high, I do my best to show these men that they do not scare me. If anything, they should fear me.

I nearly faulter when a mass of curly red hair crosses my gaze and I spot a woman sitting there, her own back straight and head held high. Her picture was not on the list of names and an idea of who she must be intrigues me. Suppressing a chuckle, I make it to the temporary Throne that was placed at the end of the table. The Butlers did an amazing job setting this room for the meeting.

Taking my seat, I thank Alice as she hands me my binder, Sky and Arian taking the two seats positioned on my left and right while Lia, Mia and Alice stand behind me. Max, Kian and Alec take their position with one of them standing behind Sky, Arian and me respectively. Flipping open the binder, I look at the list of names and move to the last one. Taylor Knight.

"Is it safe to assume you are Taylor Knight?" I turn to face the woman, a smile on my face as I take in her appearance. She wears the uniform of a General, the dark blue -almost black- fabric fitted to her body. Her overcoat is pressed to perfection, covering the white dress shirt underneath. Her insignia on the left shoulder states she is a Brigadier-General, the lowers rank of all Generals. Although this is a semi-formal meeting, she does not wear a beret on her head, instead it sits on the table to the left of her neatly clasped hands. The hash marks on her sleeves tells me she has been in the Military for ten years, making her the youngest General at this table. I am intrigued, ready to hear how she came to this rank.

"Yes, your Highness." She answers, her voice clear and firm filled with the authoritative tone fit for her rank. I nod, deciding not to give her too much attention for now as there are more pressing matter at hand.

"Well, thank you for your service in the Royal Nimairene Armed Forces. Now, if you can all turn your attention to the binders in front of all of you, I would like to start today's meeting." I thank Taylor, excitement of getting to know her eventually bubbling inside me.

"You mean a meeting about nothing." Someone scoffs as soon as I finish speaking. Looking to the far right of the table, a man with a balding head and closely shaven beard leans back in his chair, glaring at me. Frowning, I glance at the list of Generals and nearly grinned like the Cheshire cat. He is one of Juden's men.

"General Penn Gibson, leader of my Military." I call out, watching his eyes widen.

"If you have a problem with this meeting, state it now." I order, watching him slowly sit straighter in his chair.

"Oh I have a problem all right. You come in demanding a meeting when we have more pressing matters to deal with!" Slamming his fist on the table, General Gibson lets known his frustrations until his voice is nearly shouting at me. Sky and Arian move to defend me, but I stop them. I do not need them to fight my battles, especially since this battle is taking place in my Throne Room.

"What pressing matters do you have that is more important than meeting your Princess who is soon to be your Queen?" I ask, giving him a friendly smile. I need to draw him into my trap, get him to tie the noose I plan to hang him with.

"How about relief to the poor in the outer provinces. Or maintaining the borders with the Crorus Kingdom to the South of us." He continues ranting on how he had to rush here on a last minute flight due to a fight caused by the civilians where his men are stationed, how they came demanding food and medical care. Listening to him continue his rant, a few men agree with him while others stay quiet two of the younger men rolling their eyes. His rant finally ends, his yelling and screaming finally over as he takes a long sip of his water. The trap is set and now it is the final blow.

"I know all about the fight caused by the people in Roten City. How they experienced a flood by the unusual rain fall this summer and many of their crops were destroyed. What I also know is that relief funds were sent and would have been enough to sustain them and the surrounding villages and farmlands. I also know that just after the money reached your area of command, your family received many new items from clothing to jewelry to even vehicles." I state, my voice even as I pull out a list from my binder and set it onto the table.

"If all of you please take a look at the paperwork under "Juden Trilavantas men" you will see a list of names from Privets all the way up to General." I watch as the few men set to be arrested pale, their expressions changing from one of agreement to one of fear.

"You'll be happy to know that my Army is being cleaned up just like how my Royal Guards were cleaned up as we speak." With this line, the doors to the Throne Room are thrown open and fifty Guards run in, guns in fifteen of their hands while the others work on capturing and arresting twelve of the twenty seven attending Generals.

"Those now cuffed are under arrest for crimes against the Crown including theft and embezzlement of relief funds, unlawful torture of civilians, accepting bribes within Military ranks, conspiring with a Traitor, conspiring treason to dethrone the rightful monarch. And many other charges." Many of the Generals still seated look at me with awe and fear, making me wonder what they are thinking witnessing this spectacle.

"Arian has already collected evidence against all of you and your families. Lieutenant-General Kolten Elliot and his men have helped co-ordinate the arrest of Military personal that conspired with you and will be sent to Military Prison while awaiting their trial. All of you will be executed alongside Juden Trilavantas. Take them away men." The room slowly clears, leaving me standing at the end of the table looking at the remaining Generals in front of me.

"That was bad ass." Taylor chimes in from her seat, her face lighting up as she begins to laugh. I find myself smiling along side her before I too begin to laugh. Sitting on my chair, I lean back and accept the glass of water from Alice, taking a long drink.

"If it makes you all feel better, Lieutenant-General Elliot had to be vetted and interrogated for twenty four hours before he was allowed in on the plan." Sky chimes in.

"And unable to sleep during that time." Lieutenant-General Elliot calls out with a bit of mock anger in his voice.

"Blame me for that. I had to make sure I had someone I can trust to be the leader of my Army." I sigh out, motioning to the binder.

"Sorry about the commotion but this meeting was a farce to perform a coup d'état in the Military and take back control over it. Juden's men are like fleas. You think you got them all but then a few show up unannounced. You are all free to take the binders and read what they are all being charged with but know that I have also thoroughly investigated every last one of you and your men." I continue explaining before my eyes lock in on Brigadier-General Taylor Knight.

"All except for you. You are a wild card." She laughs, standing from her chair and performing a salute, her green eyes filled with warms and laughter.

"I am honoured to be a part of your Military Ma'am and promise to be loyal and just as a General in the Royal Nimairene Armed Forces." She states.

"At ease. Today is informal between all of us now that the Traitors are gone." I wave her off, chuckling as she lets out a sigh of relief before plopping herself in her chair. With the large scale arrest made, I feel more at ease talking to the remaining fifteen Generals in the room. Brigadier-General Ryu Riordan suggests we go through the binder and come up with a plan to weed out any more Traitors that might have been missed and any men they believe should be promoted to help maintain the order in our Military.

"One of the things we should do is cross training with the Navel, Armed and Air forces." Taylor suggests, a smile on her face.

"That is a good suggestion, Alice write it down." Sky agrees instantly. An hour into our talk, Alice became the scribe in keeping track of ideas we could perform to increase efficiency in the Military. One of them being sending everyone from Privet to General for retraining at base located two hours away from Zalaris. From there we can see who deserves a promotion and who will be demoted.

After two hours, Ellisia brought in dinner for us, the room filling with a buffet style meal. What I thought would be a quick thirty minute meeting turned into a three hour one as we went to work in restructuring how our recruitment and training process will change to better Nimairene's defence.

We were all just sitting around the table, formalities thrown away with drinks in our hands. We agreed that this will need more than one day of discussion and with an agreement to implement the easiest changes of training and recruitment, we agreed to take a month of restructuring the Military before we gather once again.

"Taylor and Kolten stay back please." I call out as my Generals stand, ready to retire for the night in the rooms prepared for the night.

"Kolten in five days time my Cabinet will meet to discuss laws, some are Military laws." With the room cleared of everyone but my Elite, I begin to explain why I held Kolten back.

"Okay, so what do you need from me?" Confused, Kolten takes a seat beside Arian on the left, Taylor sitting beside him.

"Well, with Gibson now imprisoned, I will be promoting you as my General, leader of the Royal Nimairene Armed Forces. You will be stationed in the Capitol and so will your men." Shock crosses Kolten's face, his grey eyes shimmering with unshed tears.

"So why was I held back?" Taylor cuts in after I ask for Kolten to stay behind for the next week as I will need his help with these ideas we all came up with.

"You will be helping me train an all female team. You will become Kolton's Lieutenant-General and will help with creating a strong task force of women that can be used for espionage and relaying information throughout the Royal Nimairene Armed Forces. We will find a location for them to be trained in and I want you to pick out women you know from the Naval and Air forces to bring in." Her green eyes lights up and within seconds Taylor is saluting me once more, sincerity towards me for this opportunity shown in every ounce of her being.

"Thank you, your Highness. This is a life changing opportunity." She gushes, tears falling from her eyes. I smile, telling her to remain here for a week so that we all may converse about this arrangement before I dismiss them to bed. They must be tired from their flight here and the time differences between Zalaris and where they are stationed must have given them some form of jetlag. Tomorrow I can meet with these two and discus plans moving forward.

"So that was a longer meeting than expected." Arian sighs out, leaning against his chair and letting down his hair. Sky reaches for the bourbon on the table, pouring a healthy amount into his glass before throwing his head back and gulping it in one go. Arian takes the bottle and directly drinks from it as Alice, Mia, Lia, Kian, Max and Alec join us at the table, bringing the food from the side table and placing it between all of us.

"You know, I did not expect the future Queen to be so laid back." Mia muses, throwing a grape at me. Chuckling, I throw one back at her and cheer when she catches it in her mouth.

"That's because like me, Alli grew up in the Slums." Arian states with a smirk, handing the bottle of bourbon to me. I happily take a swig from the bottle. Enjoying this moment with people I am slowly considering my friends.

"And some how we both ended up in the Palace." Scrunching my face from the spiciness of the bourbon, I place the bottle back on the table and reach for some water. I think I will stick with wine.

"Anyways, there are going to be some changes coming in the next few days." Everyone around the table quiets as I look between Sky and Arian. Adam and Ellisia were right when they said Arian would make a good Captain of the Guards.

"I did some thinking when I was working in my Study." Taking a deep breath, I face Arian. He is reliable, organized and a strong leader. With him in command, I know my Guards are in good hands with him.

"Arian, in the next few days you will be promoted to Captain of the Guards." I state, watching his grey eyes widen. With a smile, I turn to look at Sky catching him watching me with a gentle gaze.

"Am I fired?" He asks, reaching out and taking my hand.

"No. You are still a Captain, its just your team only has five other people." Clasping his hand in mine, I look to the five other people at the table, Alice giving me a knowing smirk.

"Everyone, please congratulate Sky in being promoted to Captain of the Violet Guards." I state, the table erupting into cheers.

"Why Violet Guards. Why not the Elite?" Kian asks, pouring juice into is glass.

"Because the only people in the world to have violet eyes are members of the Royal family. And you six are Guards for only me and any future family I may have." Voicing my thoughts, I lean back in my chair after releasing Sky's hand. It feels nice having a table full of people to talk to. People I can trust with my life and in return have them trust me with theirs. The only people missing are Ellisia, Adam, Ron and Liz.

"Arian, you and Sky will need to work together planning the security for future events as well as the general security of the Palace." Accepting a glass of orange juice from Sky, I explain what I expect from them.

"That can be done." With an agreement made, I reach into my pocket and stand, passing around the pins I brought earlier.

"I had these made for everyone to wear in the Violet Guards. You actually have Adam to thank for the name." Watching as everyone stares at their pin, I return to my spot.

"He works closely beside Ellisia as her Guard but is also our spy within the Palace. Both are members of the Violet Guards but we will not disclose this to anyone outside this room." Turning to Sky, I hand a pin to him before turning to hand the last one to Arian.

"And with Arian as Captain of the Guards, he will wear one on the inside of his blazer attached to the inside pocket. I trust you all, even if I met a few of you today." Everyone begins to silently put their pin on, the amethyst shining in the light.

"Now, it is currently five at night and it has been a long day. Ellisia should have gotten your rooms ready by now so go pack what ever belongings you have and make your way to my wing of the Palace." With that, I stand and leave the Throne Room, deciding that I need a snack and maybe some time to relax. Familiar footsteps behind me lets me know that Sky is catching up and I slow my pace.

"Where to Alli?" He asks, coming to stand beside me and bumping my shoulder playfully with his.

"The kitchen. I want to get some cookies and milk and a nap." Resuming my walk, I take Sky's hand in mine and drag him alongside me. He chuckles, allowing me to take the lead until we make our way to the royal kitchen where I happily get to work ransacking the dessert side and fill a basket with freshly baked chocolate chip cookies as Sky grabs a carton of milk and two glasses. I wave to Theon on our way out before Sky and I head to my bedroom. Maybe I can convince him to watch a movie with me and take the rest of the night off.

Chapter 28

Dipping a chocolate chip cookie into my glass of milk, I am glad I asked one of the Maids if she could run to the kitchen and grab as many of the freshly baked treats as she can with a couple of cartons of milk as once everyone settled their things into their rooms, they all ended up in my room with each one of us wearing pajamas.

"These are delicious." Lia states as she shoves a whole cookie into her mouth, getting an eye role from her twin. I laugh, taking a bite of my own as Sky sits beside me on the love seat, his left arm resting along the back of the furniture.

"I think Alli can make better cookies." He chimes in from beside me, winking at me when I roll my eyes at him.

"You can bake?" Max asks excitedly, making me sigh.

"And cook. Sky hates that I put bell peppers in my mac and cheese -"

"That's because vegetables don't belong in a mac and cheese." He cuts me off, giving me a dramatic eye roll as he takes a sip from his glass of milk. Everyone chuckles at Sky and I, Alice giving me the same knowing look from earlier that I decide to ignore.

"Is it safe to say we should look forward to you cooking then?" Max asks, his brown eyes lighting up at the prospect of food. I laugh, nearly spilling my glass of milk in the process.

"Yes it is." I final manage to answer, wiping away tears of joy from the corner of my eyes.

"You all have rooms spaced out in this wing of the Palace, but there are many still empty that I need to design. I plan to turn one into a room for us to be able to relax and cook in when ever we want." I continue, reaching for another cookie from the giant pile on the coffee table.

"I like that idea. When do you want to start the process?" Alec asks, pushing the plate closer to me before he too grabs a few more cookies.

"Soon, maybe within the next few days." I shrug, dipping one of the cookies into the milk and cursing when I accidentally break it and watch as the half that was dunked slowly sink to the bottom of my glass. Sighing, I face my fate and begin to chug my milk until the soggy half of the cookie reaches my lips and I manage to tap the glass and get it into my mouth.

"Need a refill?" Max asks laughing, handing Sky a still cold open carton of milk who then hands it to me.

"Thanks." Taking the carton, I refill my glass and continue to dunk the dry half of my cookie into it, careful not to over saturate it in the liquid.

"So what's the plan for tomorrow?" Alice asks as she sets her glass down on the end table beside her.

"Relax and rest for the morning, then meet with Taylor and Kolten in the afternoon." Groaning, I set my own glass down and lean back into the love seat, Sky wrapping his arm around my shoulder and pulling me close to him as I yawn.

"Its been a long week for me since finding out I am a Princess and I think I need a moment to relax." Continuing, I relax into Sky's side and close my eyes. Maybe I should reschedule the meeting with my new General and Lieutenant-General till the day after tomorrow.

"Maybe you need more than a moment." Alec chimes in as if reading my thoughts. Looking at the man, I nod and decide that if someone I just met today agrees that I need more than a moment, then maybe I should just take the day off tomorrow. Sky and I could sneak off to see Ron and Liz again.

"I'll tell Kolten and Taylor you are taking the day off. Not many people can pull off what you have done in a month, let alone eight days." Pressing his head on top of mine, Sky chimes in and I feel myself nod in agreement. He is right. In eight days I went from a child with no memories thrown into the Slums to a Princess regaining control over her Palace and Kingdom. What I have done would have taken some weeks, if not months, to do. And in five days time I plan to do more that will improve the lives of my Kingdom's people.

Noticing my exhaustion, Alice wrangles everyone from my room, telling them I need to rest. I thank her as she and the others divide the remaining cookies into seven equal piles before they leave my room, leaving only Sky and I sitting on the love seat.

"She would make a good Second in command." Sky muses, scooping me into his arms and carrying me from the love seat. I am too tired to protest and allow him to carry me to my bed, my hand clasping his wrist when he settles me down and tries to back away.

"Stay the night please." I plead, not wanting to be alone in case more memories surface in the form of dreams.

"I will. Just let me turn off the lights." I nod and slowly loosen my grasp on him, watching as Sky walks to the light switch and flicks it, the room becoming dark instantly. Snuggled under the covers, I wait until the left side of the bed dips and I am pulled into his arms. This time he wears a cotton shirt thankfully, sparing me from becoming a blushing mess.

"You should make her your second." I yawn out as I get comfortable, my head resting against Sky's shoulder.

"Alice?" He asks, fingers drawing small circles on my back.

"Yes."

"I will tomorrow morning. You should get some sleep Alli. You've earned it." I hum in agreement. Sleep comes quick between being exhausted and the slow circles Sky draws and I welcome it. I look forward to a much needed day off tomorrow.

Chapter 29

Walking in the garden I notice how unusually warm it has become. It has been three days since meeting with my Generals and the early March air is starting to hold hints of Spring coming earlier than forecasted. In two more days I will be facing off with my Cabinet and Nobles deciding how we will implement abolishing laws that Juden made in favor of the rich. Taylor and Kolten have been extremely helpful, the three of us with Sky and Arian have come up with a method to implement changes in both the Military and the Palace Guards within the next year that will slowly move towards the Police Force hopefully in two years time.

I have yet to have any memories pop up, but I am okay with that. Yesterday after having a Baron barge in to my Study demanding I do a DNA test to prove that I am really Princess Allisara Nimair with a crowd of citizens and lesser Nobles was the excuse I needed to have a well loved news crew come in and document the whole process live. After two hours or testing and waiting, it was deemed that I am the rightful heir and those that came to cause a scene quickly apologized and pledged their loyalty to the Crown live on television.

"Penny for your thoughts." Jumping in surprise, I find Thorin BlackHawk standing beside me, his greying hair the only indication for his age as he gives me a warm smile. The same smile Sky gives me.

"Sorry, I was just..." I trail off, not knowing what I was doing in the gardens. Today was a hectic day with finalizing the Cabinet meeting that will take place in the Parliament tower East of the Palace and I am not ready to face more scrutiny from these old fools. I need to find ways to bring more women to power to have a wider range of support.

"Looking for a break. I notice you come here when you are overwhelmed. You did that as a child too." Thorin finishes turning to stare out at the garden.

"I watched you grow up when I was a new gardener here. Your parents although fair, were blind to the things you put up with because of your cousin Lady Lilith. The gardens were your hide away and every time you came here, your brought a smile to everyone's face." He continues, motioning me to follow him as we walk around the large garden some more.

"I have a cousin?" I ask, confused by this news. Thorin nods, giving me a sympathetic smile as we stop in front of a pond. The water held ice around the edges, but the middle had thawed out with the warm weather coming in. It's mesmerizing how the weather can change at the drop of a hat when you least expect it.

"You had a cousin. Your father was an only child, but he had a cousin on his Aunt's side. They were close, like brothers, and he cherished Prince Philip's daughter Lillith until you came along. His whole family was killed the night of the Rebellion fourteen years ago in their Estate." Shocked by this, I try my hardest to remember them, to remember my cousin and Uncle, but nothing comes. My mind is blank and I sigh, feeling defeated.

"Sky told me about your memory being locked away. When the time is right, you will remember everything." He reassure me, placing his hand on my shoulder gently. I feel a sense of fatherly love from this man and find myself agreeing with his sentiment.

"Is there anyway I can learn more about them?" I ask, feeling like Thorin would be able to give me help in looking for more answers of my past.

"I know there are archives of the Royal Family in the library, try there when you get a chance." He smiles, removing his hand from my shoulder before turning to look down the path we came from.

"Spring is coming and there is a lot of work to do. If you ever need a break, come to the garden and I will teach you how to take care of the roses you love so much." With that, he walks away leaving me in front of the pond and to my own thoughts. I know if I head to the path on the right it will take me to the Royal Cemetery. I haven't been there since my first day back to the Palace and so much has happened since then, but I am not ready to face my parents graves once more. Deciding on strolling around the gardens until someone comes looking for me, I take in the fresh air and look around, spying signs of life from the little green grass that fights to thrive in the snow, to the buds on trees. Soon this place will be full of life and the bleak Palace I returned to will be the vibrant place I remember living in before my life was destroyed by Juden.

"Alli!" Turning in the direction my voice is being called from, I notice Alice coming towards me, a smile on her face.

"Sky sent me to find you. Apparently there is a Noble waiting for you in your Study." She explains as soon as she reaches me, her blue eyes holding contempt as she talks about this Noble. Feeling like something is wrong, I follow her back into the Palace and through the halls. She explains that a Marquis came to visit, demanding to speak to me at once without a formal invite. Arian was ready to throw him in the dungeons for the night for his rude behavior but Sky came to recognize him and invited him into my Study to wait, sending Alice to find me.

Entering my study through the already opened door, I notice a man sitting in front of my desk facing away from me as Sky leans against the wall beside the window that I usually sit in front of. He smiles at me, his emerald eyes lighting up as I grow closer and as if sensing the presence of Alice and me, the man stands from his chair. He is an elderly man, his face filled with wrinkles that shows he has lived a long life. His hair is full but completely white and kept neatly on top of his head. His eyes seem familiar, like I have seen them many times before, but I can't place where.

"Little Sara." He calls out, his pale blue eyes filling with tears.

"Do...do you know me?" I ask hesitantly, looking to Sky for answers. He only gives me a smile before I return my gaze to the Marquis before me, realizing I will not get answers from my friend.

"Know you? I was the first one to hold you after your mother and father did." The man explains, taking a step closer to me as tears slide down his face.

"You look so much like her, like my Evelyn. Except your eyes. You have the Nimair eyes." My eyes widen at this confession, the image of the man blurring until a younger version of himself with golden hair that began to grey shinning in the light.

"You're..." I whisper out, feeling my voice catch on the lump in my throat.

"Your Grandfather. Yes." He sobs out, reaching for my hand and clasping them in his. Tears fall from my face as memories of this man begins to flood my mind. Of him teaching me how to ride a horse for the first time with my mother yelling at him to be careful, to him holding me in his arms by the fireplace reading a story to me before bed.

"I gave up hope thinking you had died that night but when rumors of you being alive began two weeks ago, I started hoping again." My Grandfather begins to explain, pulling me gently into his arms and hugging me tightly to him. I smell the scent of mint and cigars on his clothes, the scent soothing as I close my eyes and picture a hot summer day by a lake, him smoking a cigar while a woman that looks like an older version of my mother hands me a slice of watermelon.

"Then the news mentioned of confirming that day the woman in the Palace was indeed you, it caught my attention. Then I saw you. Your golden curls and violet eyes. I knew instantly it was you Little Sara even before the results confirmed it was you." Little Sara, the nickname he gave me when everyone else called me Alli as a child. Only he and my Grandmama were allowed to call me it, no one else.

"Is Grandmama here?" I ask, relishing in the warmth of a living family member.

"No, she is back at the Estate. She had a Function planned but will be arriving tonight to see you." I nod, pulling away to look at my Grandfather and seeing the unconditional love in his eyes. For years I thought I was alone, that I had no living relative. But here I am standing in my Grandfather, Marquis Everette Blanchard's, arms.

"Have you been told why I was missing?" I ask, wondering just how much he has been told.

"Unfortunately no. I tried to reach out to Juden, but the whole Trilavantas' Estate has been placed under house arrest." Sighing, I guide my Grandfather to the sitting area, deciding that if he is going to learn the truth about the Rebellion fourteen years ago, then it will be because I told him.

"Do you want me to explain what happened fourteen years ago or from how I returned to the Palace?" I ask, Sky giving me a smile before he and Alice leave my Study to give my Grandfather and I some privacy.

"From that night fourteen years ago." I nod, accepting this decision from my Grandfather and being to explain what Juden did. I left out no detail, watching as grief fills my Grandfather's eyes as I mention how my parents were murdered. Anger radiates off of him, but he stays silent as I move on from the Rebellion to how I lost my memories and how I lived in the Slums under the name Allison. I left no detail out about my life. How I learned to steal and con people of Nobility. How I would pick locks and break into houses. Most importantly I told him about Latham, the man that taught me to survive as a thief in the Slums, and Liz and Ron and how they took care of me, treating me like a granddaughter for most of my life and how they were there for me when I needed help. This caused him to ask to meet those two and I happily agreed as I wanted my grandparent to meet my adoptive Grandparents.

Then I reached the one part I am still not proud of and explain how I ended up in prison. I pause for a moment when Ellisia comes in, brining ice cold water and snacks for us before I continue explaining my life as a prisoner before I take a much needed sip of water.

Finally I explain how Demitrias found me and brought me home, recounting what happened when I took back control of my Palace from Juden and all that has happened until now. When I finally finish explaining everything I am clutching a glass of ice water waiting for my Grandfather to speak.

"You have been through so much Little Sara." He whispers out, sounding defeated.

"And I trusted that snake as Regent thinking Juden was a victim as well." Reaching out and placing my hand onto his, I reassure my Grandfather that it was not his fault. That I had no memories up until now and even I he knew, Juden would have killed him, Grandmama and anyone else part of the Blanchard family.

"What is important now Grandfather is that I am here, that I am alive and bringing justice for those who died because of Juden." I reassure him, placing my glass onto the coffee table and leaning into my grandfather's arm. He sighs, agreeing with me that knowing I am alive and well is the best thing for our family.

"If there is anything I and your Grandmama can do to help, let me know." He states, the two of us watching the crackling of the fire in the fireplace.

"There is one thing. Tomorrow is a Cabinet meeting to reform and abolish many laws. I could use your help with this and any help from those that support you." Finally feeling like I have found a life line in this messy life of mine; I find myself feeling like another weight is lifted off my shoulders. I knew the Blanchard family was a long standing Noble family in Nimairene. That their weight in politics could sway the favor of many. Knowing that I am the granddaughter of this family makes me happy because it means I am one step closer to undoing what Juden Trilavantas and his supported did to my Kingdom.

"What ever it is Little Sara, I will help. I promise you that." Hearing my Grandfather make this promise, I pull away from him and make my way to my desk. Pulling the binder from one of the drawers meant for tomorrow, I bring it to where he patiently waits. Explaining my plan for tomorrow, I allow my Grandfather to riffle through it as I show the laws I want to abolish and ones that need modifications.

"Sounds like you have a solid plan." A voice calls from the door, causing me to jump in surprise. No one is allowed into my Study without strict permission but there in the doorway stands an elderly woman with bright blue eyes and raven black hair streaked with white.

"Darling you made it!" My Grandfather calls out cheerfully as he places the binder onto the table before standing to his feet and greeting the woman. An image of her in my mind comes back, the day she handed me watermelon by the lake. Grandfather hugs the woman, placing a quick kiss on her lips before he guides her to where I sit. Nervous, I stand and take in the woman, my Grandmama, and sheepishly hold my hand out for her. With surprising strength she pulls me into her arms holding me tight.

"Welcome home Little Sara." She mumbles, her voice breaking. Closing my eyes, I hug her back as sobs rip through me. I cry in her arms like I was a little girl again. Letting all the loneliness and pain I have felt for fourteen years out. My grandmama, Lillian Blanchard, holds me tight, telling me to let it all out and so I do. I cry for the little me who was stolen from her home. For the little me whose parents were killed too soon when she needed them the most. For the little me who had her memories taken to protect her.

I cry for the years spent in the Slums fighting to survive every day and wondering if that day would be my last. For the long tiring week I have had since being brought home and working to reclaim what is rightfully mine. I cry until I can no longer cry and I come to realize that I am sitting on the floor laying in my Grandmama's lap as she runs her fingers through my hair soothingly.

"Feel better?" She asks as I slowly sit up, my Grandfather taking out a handkerchief to wipe the tears from my face.

"Yes and no." Letting out a sigh, I rest my head on her shoulder and take in her floral perfume -a mix of roses and vanilla- before looking around to see Sky sitting on the arm chair watching me with a worry filled face.

"You knew they were still alive." I question, getting a small nod from him.

"I told them about you the day you imprisoned Juden but they asked me not to say anything until one- you were confirmed to be you or two- you remembered them. They lost so much already and I couldn't hurt them because you would hurt me if I did." He explains, reaching out and taking my hand. I smile, accepting his answer knowing Sky would never lie to me.

"Thank you." Squeezing his hand I let a comfortable silence settle between us. I thought about pushing the Cabinet meeting to the day after tomorrow and even voiced this thought to everyone, but my Grandfather tells me to keep the schedule. The faster we change everything, the faster Nimairene grows.

Ellisia comes in announcing dinner is prepared and that a room was set just for us. With the help of Sky, I rise from the ground and watch as he helps my Grandmama up. I will have to discus my plans for him with my Grandfather as Sky will need a backer for what I have planned in the future.

With Ellisia and Adam guiding the way, we leave my Study and make our way to a room just down the hall, my Grandmama refusing to let go of my hand until we are seated at the small dining table. Before dinner begins, Ellisia announces a room was prepared for my Grandparents in my wing of the Palace and then leaves us. Our dinner is spent with my Grandparents telling me about my Aunts and Uncle and how they are waiting for when I am ready to meet them. How some of my cousins have gone into the Military working their way up the ranks with one being close to becoming a General, while others have married and started families. When the night is late, Sky and I show them to their room which is directly beside mine before we bid goodnight.

Sleep comes easily, my heart full of happiness and love and for once I look forward to the future.

Chapter 30

Sitting in the carriage on the way to the Parliament Building, I look outside at the scene. Snow still clings to some places but you can tell by the way the people dress that the warmer weather will soon take over. Children run around on the side walk, their parents chiding them to be careful while shop keepers show their wears. It is such a peaceful scene, one you would not see in the Slums, and it makes my resolve in changing the Slums for the better.

"Is this your first time in a carriage?" Sky asks as he watches me, a bemused smile on his face.

"From what I remember so far, yes." Turning away from the window, I let the curtain fall and relax into the plush seat. My Grandmama chuckles, handing me a cookies from the basket Ellisia packed for us while my Grandfather flips through the binder.

"Your cousins and some of my friends were given a heads up for today's meeting this morning by me. They are ready to support you." Closing the binder, my Grandfather takes the treat from his wife, leaning in to give her a quick kiss on the cheek before taking a small bite of the cookie.

"That's a relief. If you hadn't had come yesterday, I would be a nervous wreck worrying about how this meeting will go down." I admit. For fourteen years the members of my Cabinet and the Nobles were under Juden's reign. This meant that me coming into the picture would be hard for these old fools to accept and I know there will be some - if not a lot - of resistance to the changes I want to make.

"Even if that news hadn't broadcasted you were our Little Sara, we would have instantly recognized you the moment we laid eyes on you at todays meeting." My Grandmama reassures, reaching over to squeeze my hand. I smile at her, accepting her show of affection. The carriage is then filled with preparations for today's plan starting from how to introduce myself and the agenda at hand to how I will deal with certain Cabinet members that will be arrested today.

It turns out Arian had sent many spies to gather information on those the support Juden. I did not know this until this morning when he and Sky appeared at my bedroom door after I finished getting ready for the day asking to have a short meeting in my Study over breakfast. Of course my Grandparents were already there waiting for us and with reassurance from Sky and I, Arian gave me the small folder with information on potential Traitors and those who are confirmed Traitors. Within an hour we came up with a plan and with the help of Kolten and his men, we have begun another mass arrest in secrecy. Many will be arrested after the meeting today so that when the votes are counted, theirs will be voided and hopefully thing will end in our favor.

The carriage slowly comes to a stop, the sounds of people chattering outside catching my attention. The door is opened and the driver pokes his head inside, a friendly smile on his face.

"We are here." He declares before stepping back. After setting the binder aside, my Grandfather and Sky exit the carriage first, both men helping my Grandmama then myself as we exit after them. Behind the Royal carriage, Kian and Alec sit on horse back scanning our surroundings. These two won the luck of the draw by drawing the two shortest straws this morning and were chosen to accompany us in order to protect my Grandparents and me during the meeting. We may be in a Government controlled building, but even I know this does not guarantee my safety.

Turning to face the building I am shocked by how large it is. Being a two story building with a basement, the Parliament Building is half the size of the Palace. No other buildings are near it with it being in the center of a large nature park, giving the Cabinets and Nobles a peaceful atmosphere to wander when dealing with their stressful jobs. Kian and Alec climb down from their saddles, handing the reigns to the driver before coming to stand on either side of me and Sky.

Being as I am single and still a Princess, I will need an escort when I make a public appearance and with approval and support from the Blanchard family, Sky was nominated as my escort this morning. Instead of the usual

Guard Uniform, he wears an exquisite navy blue suit and freshly pressed cotton dress shirt. His gun is holstered at his hip and the amethyst pin is glittering proudly on his lapel.

His outfit matches the navy A-line asymmetrical chiffon and lace dress my Grandmama chose for me to wear. It is elegant and regal, paired with a silver belt, silver heals and the white gold and amethyst tiara that I cherish as one of the few items that belonged to my mother. Strapped to my thigh is my own gun, my Grandmama chiding me for wanting a weapon but my Grandfather agreeing that a little extra protection is a good idea.

With the driver taking care of the four horses and the carriage and our group ready to enter the building, I follow my Grandparents down the large path lined with flower beds and benches with ponds and fountains in the background. I have a feeling that I will not get used to the scenery for a while with how beautiful this place is. Poshly dressed men and women nod to my Grandparents, their curious gaze landing on me until realization hits them and they bow and curtsy as I pass them by. Deciding that acting like a tourist is a bad idea, I straighten my posture and keep my gaze staring ahead. I am their future Queen that has only returned twelve days ago. I need to be as regal as possible if I am to succeed.

Our group reaches the entrance in no time, the front of the building made of glass allowing in as much natural light as possible. Built ten years after the founding of Nimairene, the Parliament Building is the second oldest building in the kingdom next to the Palace, this being the hub of politics and law creation. Two men wearing Military uniform open the doors for us silently, the patch on their right shoulder telling me they are Kolten's men, good. It seems he has taken control of the security of the Parliament Building without anyone being the wiser in the last five days. Nodding to the men in thanks, we enter the main hall and from there I look to my Grandparents for guidance. They know this building like their own Estate and with their help, our group navigates the winding halls towards the Cabinet Room. Many men and a few women are beginning to file in, making their way to their designated seats.

Being related to the Royal Family, my Grandparents will be seated to my right at the head table. As my escort, Sky will be seated behind me to the left. Kian and Alec will be left to stand directly behind him and I feel sorry knowing that they will be spending hours on their feet until we leave to go home. Although Sky will not be beside me, Kolten and Taylor will be seated to my left as General and Commander and Chief and Lieutenant-General to the Royal Nimairene Armed Forces. Their input when we reach restructuring laws for the Military will be imperative today after three days of discussing which laws to keep and which to abolish for our Military.

Carefully climbing down the stairs, I follow my Grandparents to the stage where the head table is set, noticing smaller tables set to the back behind specific chairs.

"For Sky and other escorts." My Grandfather explains as he helps my Grandmama up the stairs. Sky takes my hand, carefully helping me to climb after them and leads me to the seat of honor. A brand new Throne shines under the lights, the plush seats covered in a dark violet fabric. Running my hand along the top of it, I smile before taking my seat with Sky's help before he bows respectfully and takes his own seat. Kolten and Taylor arrive shortly after, their friendly smiles one I return as I greet them. With my seat having an advantage point, I look around the room and notice freshly placed binders in front of each seat, my own included. It seems the preparation staff managed to print everything I sent to them two days ago. Happy that I left my own binder in the carriage, I run my fingers along the smooth plastic of this new binder before opening it to the front page that holds today's agenda. We have another twenty minutes left before the start of today's meeting, giving me time to study those entering the room while pretending to read over the information once more.

"Little Sara." My Grandfather whispers, catching my attention.

"Yes?" Closing the binder, I turn slightly to face him, wondering what it is he want to tell me.

"Third row the first five seats from the left. Those are your cousins. Above them on the fourth row for the first ten seats are people that will support us." He nods his head in their direction, my own eyes moving to see the people that my Grandfather points out. In the first five seats of the third row sit three men and two women, their pale blue eyes and golden curls a trait of the Blanchard family. They notice my staring and nod at me and I return their greeting with a smile. The man in the middle turns to the row behind him, conversing with a middle aged man in a red suit that instantly turns to look at me, a smile blooming on his face.

"That is my grandson Eathan's father-in-law Count Rodrigo Kaitelle. He went to school with your mother and his family are long term friends of ours." My Grandmama explains, leaning closer to Grandfather and me. I smile back at Count Kaitelle, getting a sense of familiarity with him. If my family trusts him, then I trust him as well. My Grandparents begin to take turns pointing out our allies in this meeting after I motion for Kolten, Taylor and Sky to come closer. I can tell those finding their seats are watching us, wondering what the six of us are discussing, but we keep our voices low.

Finally the doors to the Cabinet Room closes and everyone finds their seat. Conversations come to an end and a hushed silence settles over everyone.

It's show time.

Chapter 31

Standing from my Throne, I take a deep breath to steady my nerves before addressing the room. I have practiced this all morning with my Grandparents, I know I must be the one to start the proceedings first with an introduction.

"Good morning Cabinet Members and those of the Nobility." I begin, feeling all eyes focus on me.

"I am Princess Allisara Nimair, heir to the Nimairene Throne, and I have called this meeting today to discuss the creation and abolishing of laws." My voice is clear and strong, carrying around the semi-circle room and bouncing against the walls. I can hear the slight whispers as some open their binders, shock written on their face. It is rare for laws to be abolished, or so my Grandmama told me. I can see why many would be shocked.

"I know this is so sudden with my return only happening twelve days before, but you all watched the news. I am the rightful heir and now I am undoing all the damaged that Juden Trilavantas caused while I was in hiding for my own safety. To prove to you all that the laws he created were In his favor, I have a short video to play." Nodding to the Guard to the right of the stage, I take my seat as the screens above me turn on and Juden's confession plays for all to see. Hiding my hands under the table, I clench my fists to calm the rage that builds just from hearing his voice. I know the Kingdom deserves to watch his public execution, but part of me wished I had killed him in that interrogation room after his confession.

The video ends and the room is filled with many discussing this revelation. I can hear some individual words how they knew they never should have supported Juden, but with over one hundred people in this room, everyone's voices merge together into on cacophony of sounds.

"Silence!" My Grandfather yells from his seat, the room quickly becoming so quiet that I can hear someone accidentally drop their pen. Stifling a laughter, I compose myself while my Grandfather stares out at the people before us.

"We have all be played by that bastard for fourteen years. Because of him, my family believed our granddaughter was dead. If he had had his way, she would have been murdered alongside her parents and paternal family." He continues, his voice shaking with anger. Reaching towards him I take my Grandfather's hand in mine and give it a squeeze, letting my presence reassure him that I am here. That all the pain him and the Blanchard family faced has come to an end.

"We all know that many laws were created in the last fourteen years, laws that I believe are unfair and unjust to the people of Nimairene." I voice once I am sure that Grandfather has calmed down.

"So with all of your help, I wish to discuss them in great detail and as we decide how to change or abolish them completely. My hope for the end of this meeting is to come out with a stronger law system for the people of Nimairene be they residents of the Slums or Provinces, to the Nobility and Politicians that help maintain the law of the Kingdom." My words seem to calm the anxious faces of many, but I notice a few that keep looking to one another. Tapping my binder five times – a signal we came up with – I confirm with Kolten that these four men and one women are indeed confirmed Traitors. Good. The best way to catch a rat is to smoke them out, and this meeting is the perfect place for it.

"If I may, your highness." A woman with black hair cut into a pixie style raises her hand and stands, her pale green dress making her stand out amongst the males that wore dark suits.

"You may, Miss..."

"Baroness Olivia Kenzington. This is only my fourth meeting your highness." Nodding my head, I allow Baroness Olivia to speak as she is the first brave soul to stand out when others are too cowardice to ask.

"What brought about the need to change?" She asks, her tone even and steady.

"What brought about the need for change was my first day back in my Palace with Juden threatened me, stating my Throne was his. I had a gut feeling that there was more to this interaction and I was correct when I read the laws passed in the last fourteen years." Taking a breath to collect my thoughts for a brief second, I hold up the binder for all to see.

"Many laws were created in his and his men's favor and as we all know, once a law has been in circulation for twenty years, it will take another ten to change it." Baroness Olivia nods, stating that she accepts my answer and is excited for change. Many also voice their favor for change and I inwardly fist bump the air. This is the first step on the long journey is a success.

"Are their any other questions?" I ask, placing the binder in front of me, watching for any signs of hesitation from those in attendance. One man raises his hand before I motion for him to stand.

"Cabinet member Marquas Hanz, your highness." Marquas Hanz introduces himself.

"When do you expect to begin the process for these changes?" He asks before sitting down again.

"As soon as possible. There are many that I have noticed can be abolished or changed within the next month, but there are many that will take some time to implement. My goal is to have everything changed within the next two years." The room grows louder with mummers from those discussing my answer. I manage to hear some stating they are relived that there is a bit of a grace period and can get their affairs in order, while others voice their concern that two years might be too soon.

"If you have a problem with this, you may leave. But know that the moment you stand to leave, I will have your position removed and you will become a normal citizen." Standing from my Throne, I let my voice carry over the displeased people before me. They all seem to settle with my threat, some regaining their uneasy looks again while others sit quietly, their smiles hiding their true thoughts.

"I know you all may think that I am just an immature child and your thoughts are valid. I grew up in the Slums of this city fighting every day to survive and so I know first hand just what this Kingdom needs to change for the better." Taking a deep breath, I begin to play to those who seem empathetic. If I can turn majority of the room in my favor not for the reason of being the true heir, but for growing up in horrible conditions, then the changes I want will be able to happen faster.

"I want a future where the Kingdom prospers and everyone is able to live in peace but I can't do it alone. So I ask you all today, will you help me?" With my small speech done, I wait patiently as they discus their options. Whether they like it or not, the change will happen because I will fight each and every nay sayer with all my might. It will be easier for everyone if they were with me though and not against me.

Time ticks by and as the four minute mark hits, the hushed conversations slowly come to an end before Baroness Olivia stands, a smile on her face.

"We are with you, Princess Allisara." She states before returning to her seat. Filled with relief, I smile at her before addressing the room.

"Let begin with the Military Laws." Returning to my seat, the meeting begins with Kolten and I taking the lead after I introduced him as my General and Commander and Chief to the Royal Nimairene Armed Forces. It is clear that many of those present do not understand the importance to the six laws we are looking to abolish and the three we wish to place as this section of today's agenda passes smoothly with majority in favor. What they do not understand is that they have agreed that only the Royal Nimairene Armed Forces is considered the one and only army of this Kingdom and that any smaller armies created and maintained in the provinces and territories managed by Nobles are considered militia and will be treated as Traitors.

They may have Guards that protect their Estate, but that is it. Anyone one with their own armies will have to disband them or place them into the many units that will be led by those trained under Kolten. It will be easier to keep an eye on these men this way and notices will be sent next month when these laws are instated.

Our next discussion are for the laws created in favor of Nobility. This stage takes the longest as many that were created were for the benefit of the rich. The one I wanted to get rid of the most was the way Nobility were taxed in their businesses. Currently, those of higher ranked are taxed the least and I can tell that this law is the favourite amongst the men here today. I state that although their wealth is theirs, being taxed unjustly leads to their households being targets for those living in the Slums, citing my own upbringing and vaguely hinting that I watched many children of the Slums steal from the businesses of these men on multiple occasions. I counter that with them being taxed fairly, we can use the money to increase the livelihood of where their businesses are located and help reduce the crimes caused. That the money will not go to fill my pockets but better the lives of everyone.

This seems to work as only a handful are apposed to abolishing this law but these people are already on our watch list with many set to be arrested by the end of this meeting. The only other benefit I find to hosting this meeting other than to abolish the laws Juden created is that unless it is a dire emergency, no one will be allowed to enter this room until we have adjourned for a lunch break or until we are done with the agenda for the day. None of those close to Juden will know their families have been arrested and assets seized as Kolten and his men have control over the security here until they too are arrested.

Two hours pass and we have finally come to an agreement on these laws. By now it is lunch time and we adjourn the meeting for a quick lunch break. The doors are opened and with the help of Kolten's soldiers, everyone is led to the luncheon where a buffet awaits us. It is there that I am greeted by my five cousins and the friends of my maternal family and we spend the short hour getting to know one another. I am happy to learn that my cousins did not name their children after my parents, wanting to leave the option for me as they had believed that without my body as proof, I was still alive. Touched by this, I find myself wiping away some stray tears and before lunch comes to an end, I promise to visit the Blanchard Estate in Zalaris as soon as I can.

Returning to the Cabinet Room, Sky informs me that Arian and Kolten's unit have finished the mass arrest, making me happy in knowing that this part of the agenda went smoothly. If all goes well, the Royal Coffers will be increasing meaning the plans to help my people will be able to happen sooner than planned. Thanking Sky for passing on the message, I move to sit in my Throne ready to finish this meeting and return home for some much needed rest.

Chapter 32

Letting out a sigh of relief, I close the binder and scan the crowd. The laws that I found to be supressing the commoners of my Kingdom took the longest to go through light I thought would happen and I am glad I set them to be discussed after lunch when many would be complacent and drowsy after eating their fill of food. Thorin Blackhawk was right the last time he and I talk. To make a man complacent, feed them a grand meal.

"Remember, you have thirty days grace period before the first laws go into effect. Please get your affairs in order and be an example for the people of Nimairene." I remind everyone as they stand and stretch, their bodies not used to sitting on their semi-comfortable seats. Kolten catches my attention as he stands, his face a blank mask as he calls everyone's attention onto him. Keeping my own emotions in check, I sit straighter in my chair as he takes a deep breath.

"Ladies and gentle men." His voice echoes around the room, silencing the conversations that buzzed in the air.

"As you were told earlier today, Juden was a Traitor to the Crown and murdered countless of innocent people including our late King and Queen." Sky moves closer to stand behind me, his hand ready to draw his gun if need be as Kian and Alec move to stand behind my Grandparents, ready to protect them at a moments notice as discussed before we departed the Palace.

"That being said, we have learned that he was not alone and has help." On que, the doors to the room are thrown open and men in our Army uniform com pouring in with guns held ready to shoot. The room erupts into screams and panic, but the ones that expressed being one-hundred percent behind me calmly return to their seat as if nothing is happening at all.

"Today we made a mass arrest on many Noble houses and Cabinet members that helped to conspire with the Traitor in the first Rebellion fourteen years ago. Now all that is left is to arrest those in attendance today." With the room secured by Guards standing at either end of each row, another group of Soldiers walk in and calmly make their way to specific people. I watch as Marquas Hanz tries but fails to fight off two of the Guards, his slightly pudgy body being tackled to the ground before he is cuffed and hauled away. It sinks in that everyone has been tricked, that there was a second reason to this meeting and many willingly step forward accepting their fate. All that they ask is that we perform a thorough inspection and release those innocent in their family.

I know better than to make promises in front of a room of people and instead stay quiet, allowing Kolten and Taylor to do their job. Those that realize they are innocent copy what my cousins and our allies did, taking a seat and waiting things out. It must have clicked that I already knew who to target today as I nod my approval at their actions and promise them that I will answer any questions they have once all the arrests have been made.

Amongst these people are a few that opposed me, their whispered conversations wondering if I will punish them for voting against me. I say nothing, not wanting to distract the Army unit and decide to address this when the room has cleared and it is just those that attended the meeting remaining.

The mass arrest takes another thirty minutes to complete and with confirmation from Kolten that all those placed under arrest are waiting in a secured room for me to address them as one and that Taylor is guarding them, I finally place my focus on those waiting patiently for me to explain what just happened.

"First, let me apologize for the secrecy." I begin once the doors have closed once again, Sky taking Kolten's seat as he had left to over sea the care of our new prisoners.

"This meeting was originally supposed to be one to address the unfair laws created by Juden but unfortunately it was brought to my attention that many of those in this room were also his supporters and helped his coup in taking the Throne from my family fourteen years ago."

"Are we suspected of this as well?" Baroness Olivia asks, cutting me off. Someone chastises her for interrupting me and being rude, but I quickly reassure everyone that it is okay to interrupt me if the question benefits everyone, getting a confused look.

"So you're not mad Liv cut you off?" A man to the right asks, his curly orange hair and beer belly two features I notice right away.

"No. It is human nature to be worried and that's what Baroness Olivia is, worried." I reassure him, watching as a sigh of relief escapes everyone before me. I chuckle at their reaction but instinct tells me Juden struck fear into these poor people.

"I will say you all were investigated but it was confirmed you were just and lawful people, always being exemplary examples to those around you and I thank you for this. I promise you that none of you are in harms way as long as you follow the laws we write together." Answering the Baroness' question, she thanks me, her eyes becoming misty with unshed tears.

"And for those who wonder if opposing me was a bad thing, it isn't. Here we all have a voice and our voice matters. If there is a law you do not agree with, I want to hear your reason and your proposal for change. We are the people the run this Kingdom. We guide everyone to a better future and I promise that even if I have an opposing view, I will consider every word you say and bring a vote to a Cabinet meeting." I watch as their eyes light up, the slight fear that the arrest caused disappear in each and every one of them. The door opens and Kolten slips inside, giving me a nod. It seems everything has gone smoothly.

After reassuring everyone that nothing will happen to them, I dismiss them and watch as the room clears. There are many people I trust, like Baroness Olivia, but there are some that I still need to investigate further. I was as honest as I could be with everyone given the situation after the mass arrest but I left out the fact that some of the people among us are suspected of being acquainted with the Traitors taken away. Unfortunately telling them this would ruin the trap set to expose those that still secretly support Juden and I couldn't have that if I want to make sure my Kingdom stays safe from their grasps.

"You okay Alli?" A glass is placed in front of me by Sky, his green eyes filled with worry. Kolton comes to join us now that the room is cleared, his face full of smiles. I am glad I made him my General.

"I am not sure, but I will be when we return home." Being honest with him, I take the glass and sip on the cold water. Looking to Kolten, I ask if I can be led to the room the Traitors are being held in and with him taking the lead, our group consisting of Sky, Kian, Alec, my Grandparents and I follow behind him in the confusing hallways of the Parliament Building. It doesn't take long for us to reach a room with the plaque "Conference Room B" written on the doors and two Soldiers standing guard. They salute us before opening the doors and allowing us entry.

Entering the conference room, I notice the noise proofing boards long the wall, noting that this will keep what happens in this room secret from the rest of the world. I am not here to interrogate anyone, that can happen when they are transferred to either the Palace Dungeons or a High Security Prison. Right now I am here to give them a chance at making a deal.

"I see you all have been treated well." I greet, looking at the men and women seated on the comfortable office chairs, their hands cuffed behind their back.

"Go to hell you stupid bitch!" Marquas Hans shouts back, his hatred clear for all to see. I ignore his little tantrum, motioning for a Soldier to gag him so that there are no other interruptions before I address why I came to see them.

"We all know that you all conspired with the Traitor, Juden Trilavantas. We also know that many of you helped with the Rebellion fourteen years ago." I begin, satisfied to know I have everyone's undivided attentions.

"What we don't know is who in each of your families were privy to this knowledge. As such, we are doing a thorough investigation. The innocent will be spared but those who are found guilty of conspiring with Juden will face consequences. How you co-operate going forward will determine the severity of these consequences." Relief fills many of the men in this rooms eyes, but they stay silent. Some of these men pleaded for me to investigate and spare their families as they were dragged away from the Cabinet room so hearing my words must be like an unanswered prayer.

"That being said, every member of your family will be stripped of their titles and their wealth will be audited. Anything not recorded through the proper channels will be seized and placed into the Royal Coffers to help with reforming the Kingdom into a stronger nation. I will not keep a single cent of it. I will also be confiscating ten percent of each of your businesses as compensation for your crimes. The rest your family can keep so that they can rebuild their lives after you have all ruined them." With my intentions stated, I turn around and leave. It has been a long day and I finished what needed to be done. If these Traitors want to speak to me, they can do so after thinking about the choices the made for a few days.

Kolten's voice sounds from the open doors as I walk into the hallway and he gives out orders. My Grandparents waiting for me as they decided not to face the men and women they thought were friends of theirs. I understand their anger and hatred knowing that many of them caused the death of my mother – their daughter – so I don't push them on this topic. Instead, I walk into my Grandmama's open arms, accepting her warm hug as Sky and the others join us.

"You make a good Queen." Alec praises, playfully punching my shoulder after I step away from my Grandmama's embrace. I laugh, swatting his hand away and thanking him, telling him he makes a good Guard and that I am proud of him and Kian for how they handled themselves today.

"It was either behave for face a pissed of Sky." Kian dead pans, causing Sky to roll his eyes as my Grandfather lets out a hearty laugh. Looking to my friend, I wonder if Sky is as scary as Kian makes him out to be. Since meeting him, he has been nothing but kind and friendly. With the Guards, he treats them like family. My Grandmama cuts through my thoughts as she suggests we all make our way to home to the Palace. It has been a long day – hell, its been a long two weeks. I really need some rest.

Chapter 33

"Do you need help?" Someone whispers, making me want to find the mute button.

"No. You'll be surprised to know how much of a normal thing this is for us." A deep voice replies equally as quiet as the first whisper. Something wraps around my body, scooping me close to someone warm and the scent of pine wraps around me.

"Sky." I mumble out with a yawn, opening my eyes to see Sky looking down at me.

"Hey sleeping beauty. We're home." He greets, giving me his easy going smile. Home. For so long I thought I would have to keep stealing, conning and lying until I saved up enough to buy my own place. That I would build a place of my own deep in the country wilderness far away from Zalaris, the Capitol city that I lived my whole life in. That I would have a restaurant some time in the future and make a life of my own. But here I am, in the arms of someone I am sure I am falling in love with, being carried up the steps of the Royal Palace.

"I can walk." I yawn out, hoping Sky doesn't see the slight blush tinging my face.

"I know." Although he says that, Sky doesn't put me down one bit. Instead he holds me tighter.

"I have a question." My Grandfather chimes in from beside Sky. Lifting my head to look at him, I see an amused smile on his face as he watches Sky and I.

"For me or Sky?" I ask back.

"For you Little Sara." Nodding, we pass through the large doors into the entry way of the Palace. Maids and Butler bustle about, smiles on their faces as the watch Sky and I pass by.

"Is it true you broke up with Demitrias?" He asks, Sky letting out a chuckle.

"She did. Did it while I held my sword to his throat." He carries me to a small sitting room on the left, one that would house visiting dignitaries for me to entertain for the day. My Grandfather stops just inside the room as Sky sets me on the couch, pressing a kiss on my forehead that causes us to both pause for a moment.

"A sword?! Like a bloody stab it through your enemies, sharper than a kitchen blade sort of sword?" My Grandfather shouts, shuffling to the nearest chair and plopping down on it. I laugh, thinking back to when I took back my Throne. Of arresting Juden Trilavantas and kicking his son out from my Palace.

"Pretty sure if Demitrias had tried anything, it would have been stabbed through his neck." I shrug, thanking the Maid as she hands me a mug of tea.

"Pretty sure had you even indicated to Sky to do anything, Demitrias would have ended up as a shish-ka-bob" My Grandmama states, coming to sit beside me and thanking the Maid as she places another mug of tea in front of her with snacks between us.

"So that makes you single." My Grandmama mused, looking at me from over the rim of her mug as she sips on her tea. Looking over to Sky who sits on the armchair beside my Grandfather, part of me wants to say 'For now' but instead I nod and reach for a cookie.

'The first girl I fell in love with and the only one I stayed in love with...' Those words echo around my mind. He is in love with someone, probably waiting for her. No mater how many times I bring it up, he gives me a small smile before changing the subject.

"Maybe you and Sky should go on a date. He's always kept us in the loop of things when that bastard and his son were in charge. I trust him with you." Nearly choking on my team, I look to my Grandfather and see him staring at me with an unwavering gaze. He is serious.

"I mean, you do need a date for your debutant Ball." My Grandmama chimes in with a giggle.

"I don't need a Ball." I cut in, looking to my Grandmama as Sky tries to hold back his chuckles.

"Hush Little Sara. The moment we learned it was really you, I started planning a Ball at the Blanchard Estate. Your Aunts and Uncles are already helping me." Looking to Sky for help, he gives me a helpless shrug which causes me to groan in defeat. We had talked about this just days ago, how I did not want a Ball until after my memories returned. But it seems like any protesting I may have will be ignored by my Grandparents.

"When?" I ask, giving in and watching as my Grandmama beams, her smile growing wide as child-like excitements twinkles in her eyes.

"Three days from now. I already talked to Sky about people to invite and he gave me a list. I will have outfits sent to these Ron and Liz. To thank them for caring for you. After the Ball, we will need to plan the Spring Parade as that will be your first appearance to your citizens." She continues to prattle on about social events that I will need to attend, a headache forming from the thought of having to dress up like a doll and fake a smile for all to see. The thought of being judged by people who do not know me makes me frown, but my Grandmama seems so happy.

"I will do the Ball and the parade." I cut in on her rambling, watching my Grandmama take a breath ready to continue. Holding my hand up, I take a breath of my own. She spent fourteen years thinking I was dead. I know she is excited to throw me into the Noble's spotlight, but she needs to wait. I need to do things my way.

"After those two events, I need to plan for my coronation and focus on fixing my Kingdom. Social events can come after I am sure my people have a stable life. I am not a doll Grandmama; I am a Queen and I need to make sure my people are taken care of." The excitement in her eyes dim and her straight as a pin posture deflates a little. It hurts me to have to tell her no.

"She is right Lillian. Our Little Sara is no longer a child and we need to respect her wishes." Grandfather agrees, giving me a proud nod.

"But Everette -"

"There are no buts. There will be plenty of Balls and Functions but Allisara just returned to us. She did not grow up in the Palace nor in the Noble circle. We need to ease her into it and help her along the way." Grandmama huffs out a breath, stating she just wanted to help me while turning her body away with a pout, and I reassure her that she will help me, just at my own pace. This seems to placate her and she agrees that she will go at my pace. With this settled, we finish our tea before my Grandparents retire to bed. Tomorrow they will return to their Estate.

Sky and I decide that bed is a great idea and make our way to our wing. He informs me that Kian and Alec took the horses to the stables with the carriage driver, promising to make sure all four animals are taken care of before they too retire for the night.

"So a date to your Ball?" He asks, nudging my shoulder. Blushing, I look down at the floor, not sure what to say.

"Maybe after that we can plan a date that's a little more intimate." I sheepishly suggest. It takes a few seconds for me to realize that Sky has stopped walking. Turning to face him, I feel my blush grow with how hot my face feels as he stares at me wide eyed, mouth opening and closing like a fish.

"I mean, if that's-" Before I can finish trying to salvage my embarrassment, Sky marches towards me pulling me into his arms. His lips crash down onto mine, and I find myself kissing him back.

"Yes." He states as he pulls away, leaving me breathless.

"What?" A little disoriented from the kiss, I try to catch my breath and focus on what he is saying.

"Yes. After the Ball we can do something intimate for our second date." His lips are back on mine before I can say anything, this kiss both strong and gentle. He doesn't force anything, doesn't try for more, and I am thankful for that. Cheers cause us to break away as we realize we are still in view of all the Palace staff. Two Maids scurry away with giggles, and for the umpteenth time today, I groan in frustration and burry my face into Sky's chest. Come tomorrow morning every one will know Sky and I made out like a bunch of teenagers in the hall-way.

"Why don't we keep walking. I have a surprise for you." Taking my hand in his, Sky leads me away from public eye and to the safety of the Princess wing. In a few months it will be renamed to the Royal Wing.

"Um, this isn't mine or your room." Rounding the corner, Sky and I bypass our rooms and continues down the hallway until we pause at the second to last set of double doors.

"I know. But its your surprise." He shrugs, motioning me to open the doors. Sceptical, I slowly turn the handle and push open one of the two doors.

"Surprise!" Jumping back, I see Kian, Alec, Max, Lia, Mia, Alice, Adam and Ellisia standing just inside the door, their smiling faces holding in their laughter. Sky places his hand against the small of my back, encouraging me to continue into the room explaining that Arian went to visit family for the night but will be back by dinner tomorrow.

To the right is a high-end kitchen with state of the art appliances the black marble countertop on dark oak wood cupboards excite me the most. It is a dream kitchen if I ever saw one.

In the middle of the room sat a long dining table with enough seats to sit twelve people. At each end were regular soft cushioned seats and long benches on either side of the table. All of it was made of the same dark oak wood.

Finally, to the left of the room, a wall had been taken down connecting to the room next door to this one and in it was a sectional shaped into a large rectangle in front of a large flat screen television built into the wall. Shelves were also places on either side of the television also built into the wall. I could see some older equipment like a Nintendo Sixty-Four and a Blue-Ray-DVD combo sitting on the right shelf while movies and games filled the left shelf.

On the left side of the sectional along the wall between two of the large windows sat a popcorn machine and a cotton candy machine. Behind the sectional were a few desks, places people could work at if need be while the rest of us enjoyed the room. What made me smile were the two tables, a billiards table set and ready with all the needed equipment and an old air hockey table that someone must have gotten from an antique store. Suddenly, a memory flashes in my mind of my father teaching me, Demitrias and that faceless boy how to play on both tables. Before I could see anything else, it is gone just as quickly as it came. These tables must have been my father's.

"Sky mentioned to us a few days ago you wanted a room for us to relax in. A place to get to know one another and where you can be you, Alli." Ellisia states as I walk further into the room, doing my best to hold back tears.

"When did he mention this?" I ask, accepting the hug from my Head Maid and smiling at my friends.

"The day after the meeting with the Generals. I came to you asking if I could renovate a few rooms and you signed the paperwork while half asleep." She answers laughing, making me roll my eyes. Note to self, don't sign anything on rest days when trying to sleep.

"I have all the paper work for budget and materials. Most of the items came from storage though." I nod, finally letting the tears fall while I thank everyone, asking them to wait for me to take a shower and get out of this gown before we decide on what to do for the night. Alice takes my hand leading my emotional ass out of the room and to my own. She tells me that the group decided on a movie night with dinner and while Sky and I shower and change into a set of pajamas to match the rest of them, the twins will cook us something simple to eat.

Chapter 34

"So movie night!" Mia calls out as we gather onto the sectional with Sky and I taking the comfortable right corner so we can both stretch out. The twins had not cooked us a simple dinner like Alice had stated. Instead the room smelt like lemon chicken, fried rice and Asian mixed vegetables with a pile of spring rolls waiting for our return after a shower and a change of clothes. They also made the men do the dishes which amused me the most. Watching Max and Adam – two men built close to body builders – hunch over the sink cleaning the diner dishes was the most amusing thing to have happened since my return to the Palace.

"What are the options?" I ask, stealing a spring roll off of Sky's plate and quickly shoving the whole thing into my mouth. It is hard to chew it as I try my best to smile innocently at Sky who sighs and pokes my full cheeks, commenting that I look like a chipmunk.

"Option one from about two hundred and fifty years ago, the Harry Potter Series." Lia chimes in, motioning the pile of seven movie sitting on the edge of the coffee table. I laugh, watching as Lia begins to take the first movie – Harry Potter and the Philosopher Stone. I movie full of magic and a revolution at the end. Seems fitting to what I am dealing with right now.

"What the other option?" Sky asks, wrapping his arm around my shoulder and pressing a kiss on my forehead.

"Did we miss something?" Adam asks from the floor, deciding that sitting on a cushion at Alice's feet was a comfortable Idea. Someone has a crush.

"Alli and I are going on a date after the Ball her Grandparents are throwing." Sky shrugs, making me blush.

"Saw it coming, you all owe me ten dollars each." Alice yells, the rest of the group groaning.

"Except me. We are splitting that." Ellisia smugly laughs out.

"Back on topic please." I call back, motioning for Lia who stares between Sky and I for a moment before returning back to the movie selection

"Mister heart throb Damen Mathews staring in Darlings of the Forest." Lia hands me a tablet with the movie already opened up. Sky reads out the synopsis of the movies, a love feud between a Werewolf Pack and a Fae clan where the Daughter of the Fae Queen is mated to the Son of the Alpha of the Pack. My face scrunches at the cliché story line, thinking about how it reminds me of something else, something I can't place my finger on.

"No." Ellisia and I both groan out, getting what sounds like a literal growl of frustration from Mia.

"I prefer the timeless tale of Harry Potter." Ellisia takes a sip of her tea after throwing in her vote.

"Oh come on! It's a classic Romeo and Juliet type romance. The Moon Goddess takes pity on them and they are reborn in the end as new creatures." She protests, trying to convince us all into watching the love sick movie.

"I vote the wizarding world." I shrug, handing back the tablet to Lia who gives me a high five. Three for Harry Potter, one for Darlings of the Forest.

"Kinda got to go with Mia. D.o.F. for me." Alice places her vote, getting a cheer from Mia. Lia sticks her tongue out at her as the movie vote comes to a three to two.

"I want Harry Potter. We have seven movies we can watch with this series." Sky chuckles out, grabbing a blanket from the back of the couch and throwing it over us. Alec and Max throw in their own votes to Harry Potter. Even with Adam and Kian voting with Alice and Mia, the vote was in our favor and Mia reluctantly put on Harry Potter and the Philosopher Stone.

The lights dim as the movie begins, causing me to look around the room in shock.

"A function with televisions." Sky reassure me, pulling me closer to him. Something in my mind seems to click with this new information as my vision blurs for a moment.

"Tomorrow is your birthday Allisara, why do you want to watch a movie so late at night?" It was that boy again as we snuck through the halls in our pajamas, my hand clutched in his. We have to be quiet as we make our way to

the cinema room or risk being caught. My parent's and his Knight would not approve of us being out of our room so late at night.

"I don't want a party. They are all about being a doll and I don't get to have any fun." My small child voice replies. I hate parties. Everyone invited wans to fawn over me or my parents. If they can't get to me, they visit my cousin and she adores the attention as a Princess. She is third in line for the Throne if something happens to me and my parents.

"The parties do suck. You have to behave and that Nanny yells at you if you complain." He agrees with a laugh, an easy going smile on his lips. We manage to quietly sneak into the cinema room where we make popcorn and see what candy we can find before my friend carefully helps me to the nearest seat, the tablet to choose a movie in his hand.

"What movie do you want to watch?" The boy asks, throwing a blanket over us to stay warm.

"Cinderella!" He smiles at my response and puts the movie on before we cuddle under the blanket together...

The memory fades and I find the world returning to normal. Looking around the room a little disoriented, I find Sky looking at me, his worry filled eyes filling with relief when I look back at him.

"Memories?" He whispers as I rest my head onto his shoulder. I nod, realizing that this time I had saw more of the boy. His smile seems so familiar to me, like I have seen it recently, but I can't place it.

"It was of the boy. He and I, we watched Cinderella the night before the Rebellion." Sky's response to this is to pull me tighter to him, reassuring me that one day I will remember everyone and all I can do is take each day in strides before we return our focus to the movie. We were just at the part where Harry and that blonde kid from the snake house are walking in the forest. Sky catches me up on what I missed when I zoned into memory lane as we call it and it turns out they had gotten detention. Fun.

I find my mind wandering as I think about that boy. With every new memory unlocked, his feature become clearer and clearer. It's like my brain is trying to protect him. From what, I don't know.

The movie comes to an end and the lights slowly turning back on. Adam and Mia argue over putting on another movie but I cut them off, stating Sky, Kian, Alec and I have has a long day and need sleep. If they want to choose another movie, they can, but the Harry Potter series will be finished as a group. After getting those two to stop fighting, Sky and I say our good nights and leave the Amethyst Lounge as I call it, making our way to our own rooms.

"Do you want me to stay the night in case you have nightmares?" Sky asks, pulling me into his arms when we make it in front of our doors.

"I think tonight I will be fine. But if not, I know where to find you." I listen to him let out a quiet sigh. I know this answer is disappointing after agreeing to date, but tonight I need to be alone. I need to dream of my memories and if Sky is there, I wont remember anything.

"Okay. I am just across the hall if you need me." His fingers gently press against my chin, his lips finding mine as a sweet and gentle kiss is pressed onto them. My heart skips a beat as I kiss him back and with reluctance, we pull away. He watches me go into my room, his green eyes shining with affection as I close the door with a shy smile.

I know that I need to talk to my Grandparents now, to get things in motion if I want to make sure the Nobles can't disapprove of mine and Sky's relationship. Climbing into bed, I instantly miss the scent of Sky's body wash and realize that I am hopelessly falling for him; and falling hard at that.

Chapter 35

Sitting on the balcony in my hidden tower, I enjoy the view from up here as I work on my laptop. Five days have passed since the Cabinet meeting and Arian has been collecting confessions from those that were in cahoots with Juden with the help of his men. True to my word, their innocent family members were released from prison with only specific assets seized. With each new confession, the Royal Coffers grew and with this, I have been setting a plan into motion of revitalizing the Slums. The first thing I want to do is fix the roads.

"I thought I would find you up here." Sky's voice calls out from the door way. Looking up from my screen, I smile at him as he comes to sit beside me on the cold concrete, a plate of sandwiches in one hand and a bottle of apple juice in the other.

"Ellisia told me to bring you food if I could find you." He hands me the plate of food, taking my laptop much to my protest, but my stomach growls reminding me that I haven't eaten anything since breakfast - and that was about five hours ago. I mumble out a thank you before digging in, the taste of turkey, bacon, avocados and spicy mayo filling my mouth as I chew the delicious meal.

"So you are hiding from Lillian to work on the Slums project." He laughs out, scanning the documents I have been typing away at all morning.

"It is a really important project." I counter before taking a long drink of the much needed apple juice.

"And the Ball is a very important Ball for your image as the heiress to the Throne." Damnit, he has a point and he knows it. Sighing, I look towards the direction where the Slums are, the place I grew up too far away to see from here. As dangerous as they were, the Slums were my home and I want to see my home thrive. To become a great area to live like I know it can be.

"I know the Ball is important. That I need to go and flounce around like some debutant." Putting my half finished sandwich aside, I bring my knees to my chest and wrap my arms around myself. I want to be able to party and be a normal young adult. To be able to relax. But that night fourteen years ago took that option from me.

"But I have so much I need to take care of with Nimairene." I continue, closing my eyes for a moment.

"You will get it done Allisara, but you also need to relax and let loose, to let the Nobles know you're not just some dictator like Juden was." Sky is once again right. I hate that he is right. What's worse is he called my by my full name. This means he is being serious and I need to listen.

"Lillian wants to bond with you too. So why don't we put this aside and go try on the dresses she has for you in the sitting room."

"Can I eat my lunch first?"

"Of course Alli. Ellisia would skin me alive if you didn't eat." I laugh at that, watching Sky save my work before closing the laptop and putting it into the case to protect it from the cold concrete. He pulls me to his side as I eat my lunch, the two of us discussing what we should do to make this place a little more habitable for us before he helps me to my feet after I finish my meal and we make our way down the staircase and past the shelf doorway into my Study. Sky places my laptop bag onto the desk before we leave the room, a Maid taking my empty plate and bottle from me when she walks by pushing a cart.

Reluctantly, I follow him down the hallway and towards the stairs, knowing that my Grandmama will be waiting in the front sitting room with the designer she chose for the ballgown. To think in two days time I will be stepping into the Blanchard Estate dressed like a doll for all to see.

"There she is!" Stepping into the room, my Grandmama is the first to greet me, pulling me into her arms and hugging me tight. Sky chooses this time to back away, closing the door behind him and leaving me to my Grandmama's mercy. Traitor.

"It is a pleasure to meet you, your highness." A middle aged women comes to stop before me, giving a deep bow before she straightens herself. She is a short women with long black hair braided behind her back. Judging by the almond shape of her eyes and the paleness of her skin, I would say she is part Asian mixed with something else.

"Lidia Chao, owner and head designer of Hidden Treasures." Lidia introduces herself, giving me a bright and friendly smile. My Grandmama begins to describe how Lidia and her family have dressed the Blanchard family for generations, how my mother wore one of Lidia's designs for her wedding to my father. I smile as I think about the video I found of my mother walking down the aisle to my father, her golden hair just as curly as mine put into an updo. The dress was a gorgeous A-line neckline ballgown with a four foot train and as I had found and watched the video, Ellisia explained to me what the wedding day was like as she was a new Maid in the Place twenty three years ago.

"Lillian says that you look good in any dress, but I think you fit in pastels and jewel tones." Lidia takes my hand from my Grandmama and leads me deeper into the room where rows on rows of clothing racks filled with gowns are waiting to be tried on and a make shift changing room sits in the back corner away from the windows and doors.

Two other women wait by the first row situated by a tri-folded mirror and they introduce themselves to me as Daisy and Harper, Lidia's assistants. With introductions out of the way, the ladies get to work pulling dresses from the racks and shooing me towards the changing room. Pasting on a smile, I decide to enjoy the moment and let these women help dress me up. If I am to be attending a Ball in my honor, then I need the best dress to wear and Lidia seems to be the best person for the job.

"Try the red dress next." Handing me a red ballgown full of tulle, Harper sends me towards the changing room once more after stripping me of a fit and flair pink mermaid gown filled with sequins. We all agreed the mermaid dress is one that I cannot walk in after nearly falling face first into a table and with all the mermaid gowns put onto empty racks and put to the side, we began to focus on tulle gowns. I can already tell with how itchy and uncomfortable the gown is that tulle is not my thing.

"You look like a loofa." Lidia dead pans as soon as I walk out, making me burst out laughing. I though I would hate this experience, hate being treated like a little doll. Instead the five of us have been sipping on champaign and sorting through the gowns that do not suit me.

"I feel like a loofa to be honest." I agree, taking a slice of cantaloupe from the snack table and munching on it.

"So full tulle gowns and mermaid gowns are definitely not your style." Daisy sighs out, a frown on her otherwise unblemished face.

"Well we know A-line and sweet heart necklines suit her. Now we need to find the right silhouette and fabrics." Harper passes me my glass of champaign while my Grandmama browses the remaining wracks of dresses. I watch her intently for a moment until a triumphant smile lights her face and she pulls out a dress. One that has all of us intrigued by.

"Try this on." She shuffles over enthusiastically, taking my champaign from me before forcing the dress into my hands. I humor her, returning to the changing room and quickly switching the gowns. Staring at the single mirror in the change room, my eyes widen for a moment as I take in my reflection. Stepping out of the make-shift room, everyone gasps as the fabric flows with every movement.

"This. This is the one!"

Chapter 36

Today is the day I enter Noble Society. I think as the Blanchard Estate Maids work diligently on my hair and make-up. I told them I want a natural look for my face, not wanting to deal with a layer of make-up that my clumsiness will easily wipe away. Grandmama even agreed that simple and elegant is better for me. I am to be portrayed as a strong approachable leader, not a glitzed up Noble here to find a wealthy husband.

The dress we decided on was sent back with Lidia after my measurements were taken in order to finalize the details for tonight. We agreed that day that for formal events Hidden Treasures will be my only suppliers of gowns and dresses. Lidia's work was stylish, elegant and she had all of my measurements so all I need to do is call her for a gown – or any outfit as I soon later learned that her dresses already adorned me the day of the Cabinet meeting – when I need one.

"Time for the dress." Clarice, the Maid in charge of helping me get ready exclaims in excitement, helping me to stand from my chair after another Maid slipped my silver strappy heals - curtesy of Hidden Treasure - onto my feet. The silk slip I am wearing is removed from my body and Millia, Clarice's sister and another Maid of the Estate – holds the dress open for me to step into as Clarice holds onto my hands so that I do not fall. The Maids are quick to help bring the dress up my body, letting me slip my arms into the sleeves before they begin to tie it in the back. With the corset back tied and secured, Clarice tells me to close my eyes before her and Millia lead me to what I guess is in front of the tri-fold mirror.

"You can look now." Millia whispers out, the young Maid doing her best to hold in her excitement. My own smile must reflect her own as I open my eyes and find myself staring at my reflection once again. My smile morphs into shock as I step closer to inspect my makeup, my large violet eyes framed by light cream and silver eyeshadow with deep brown eyeliner – less striking but brings out the colour of my eyes. My brows were abused earlier this morning, being plucked and shaped to Clarice's satisfaction, much to my cursing and grumbling, but the dainty work is one that adds to my regal features.

My hair was cut yesterday, Grandmama saying I needed to trim my curly golden locks to bring out the bounce in them and she was right. This led to the stylist giving me wolf bangs that framed my face and blended into my curls. We all agreed that a half-updo will be perfect for tonight and Clarice used silver pins with twinkling little diamonds to keep half of my curls in place. Moving down, I notice a simple tear drop pendant placed around my neck, the pendant matching the earrings on my lobes while small studs line my cartilage. Tilting my head, I watch as the skin alone my shoulders and collar bone shimmer with what ever the Maids put onto my skin.

Captivated by this, my eyes move down to the boddice of my dress. Swirling beading, crystals and sequin shimmers on the embroidered lace applique against a foundation of sheer mesh. The silver and white gems are sewn delicately onto it mesh and lie against my skin perfectly. You would think the top would be uncomfortable with all these details but an additional mesh inset provide support to the plunging neckline bodice with the off-shoulder straps that delicately hand around my arms.

To me though, the best part is the bottom of the dress. Gathered at the natural waist, the flowy A-line chiffon skirt falls to a formal floor length to complete the elegant look. The whole gown is made of silver fabric and material, something we all agreed fit perfectly with my skin tone. Grandmama really did choose an amazing gown.

"You all did an amazing job." I praise the two ladies in the room, getting squeals of delight from them. I can't help but look down at my wrist, my gaze softening when I spot the simple silver bracelet Sky had given me before I left the Palace. My nails catch the light when I bring my hand up to look at the bracelet, happy I went with a simple French tip.

"We are happy to help Princess." Millia shrugs, handing me a champaign flute. Taking a sip, I return to stare at my reflection. The room I am using was my mothers and it is evident by the pictures left where she put them. In each one she is smiling and laughing, always stylishly dressed. Looking at the one of her on her wedding day taped to the mirror I smile and run my finger along the edge of the photo. Her dress was also off the shoulder like mine, but she was an explosion of lace and tulle.

Clearly I did not get her love of tulle.

The shocking thing is how much I looked like her when she was in her early twenties. The same slim build with curves in all the right places, the same curly golden locks and big bright eyes. The only difference will always be my violet eyes that I received from my father. Violet eyes that will be passed down to children of my own one day.

"Wow, Alli." A gasp calls out. Smiling at the familiar voice, I turn to see Sky staring wide eyed at me, his gaze unable to stay still as he takes me in from head to toe and back up to my head. He wears a black tuxedo, the amethyst pin pinned to his lapel with his hair combed into a simple man bun. This makes me chuckle as I think about all the prim and proper Nobles that will look on in disgust at this but screw them. This is the man I want.

"You look amazing as well." I smirk, carefully stepping towards Sky and using his speechlessness to press a soft kiss to his lips. The Maids in the room giggle and whisper at this scene which seems to reboot Sky as he thanks the ladies for getting me ready before whisking me away from what is soon to become the Estate gossip. Its bad enough I have to deal with giggles and whispers from the Maids of the Palace, now I will need to deal with it here.

"I say we never come back after tonight." Sky whispers into my ear when we descend the spiralling stair case. I snort out a laughter, wanting to agree with him but this is my home too now. It is where my only remaining family comes from.

"That will be a no. We deal with the Maids at home, we can deal with the ones here." He groans in defeat, placing a kiss on my cheek as we reach the main floor. Butlers move about the mansion, trays of Hors d'oeuvre in hand as they rush from the kitchen to the Ballroom.

"I think the party is in full swing and we are late." Tugging Sky towards the main entrance to the Ballroom, I nod to the workers of the Blanchard Estate before they disappear to the side door. Sky takes a deep breath, asking me to help adjust his bow tie before we face the doors together. It seems neither of us like this kind of social gatherings.

The large double doors open inward, the sounds of music and chatter filtering through. With a smile on my face, I loop my hand through the crook of Sky's arm and as a Butler calls out our name. The music stops and the guests turn to face us as we descend the small staircase of about ten steps. They bow and curtsy in turn, their eyes gazing at me with awe and scrutiny. It seems I am the only one in silver, most likely my Grandmama's doing. It makes me smile, thinking about how hard she has worked to make it so I stand out on what is to be my debutant Ball.

"You may all rise." I call out as confidently as I can, squeezing onto Sky's elbow as nerves take over. I can face the Cabinet, take control of the Generals, but the Nobles scare me.

"I just want to thank you all for coming to tonight. I look forward to getting to know all of you and have a night of dancing. You may not know this, but fixing a Kingdom is a lot of work and I can use a break." The guest laugh at this, many coming to step forward and welcome me back home. Any fear I felt earlier is gone as the music resumes and Sky and I make rounds along the Ballroom, talking to a few Dukes and Dutchesses, debating with a Marquis and learning about a new idea to help our farmers as the land he oversees is a large farming community. I am pleasantly surprised at how easy these Nobles are to get along with until I realize they are all friends of my family when I spot Count Rodrigo Kaitelle talking to a man I know as my cousin Eathan. Sky and I decide to greet the two, my cousin pulling me into a hug before shaking Sky's hand.

"Do you know how hard it is to meet you." Eathan jokes as he pokes my cheek, making me swat it away.

"I am a busy person, cousin. I have a Kingdom to run." I shrug, leaning into Sky's side as he wraps an arm around me.

"And a boyfriend I see." Count Kaitelle chuckles out, toasting Sky and me. He goes on to explain how many times he had to chase Demitrias away from the women of his family, the Ex-Heir to the Trilavantas Dukedom being described as a skirt chaser looking to find his next notch in his belt. He praises me for canceling the engagement to him before someone calls out to him and Count Kaitelle bids us a good night of dancing.

"I like your father-in-law." I state, taking a Hors d'oeuvre plate full of tomato bruschetta and prosciutto shaped into roses on top.

"I also like the food." I add, taking a bite of the bruschetta. Eathan laughs, attracting attention from those around us before they resume their conversations. I role my eyes for a moment and move to hand the plate to a passing Butler when the world starts to spin.

"Alli, are you okay?" Sky asks, his voice muffled and distorted. I go to answer, to reassure him but suddenly pain shoots through me and the Ballroom tilts. Before I know it, the Ballroom floor rushes towards me without warning.

Chapter 37

"Allisara!" I shout, catching her before she can hit the ground. Her eyes are closed, hand clenching the plate that had her Hors d'oeuvres on. Her breathing is shallow, her chest barely able to take a breath.

"Shut all the doors, no one leaves!" Eathan shouts as I slowly lay her onto her back. Guards rush to do what he says as I focus on Allisara. She is pale, too pale, and I realize someone managed to poison her.

"Secure the kitchen and all the food. Someone find me a poison test and the vials of antidotes!" I call out, watching as Allisara stops breathing. Panicked, I begin C.P.R. praying that my chest compressions are helping to keep her alive. A Maid rushes towards me with Everette and Lillian behind her, the two elderly shaking with fear and rage. The Maid carefully works to draw her blood before she test it, the machine beeping as it analyzes the poison that she ingested. Thankfully it doesn't take too long when the machine beeps loudly to a different tune and the light turns green.

"Prepare the blue vial!" The Maid orders her partner after reading the screen. A woman who looks similar to her obeys and soon a needle is filled with a blue liquid then quickly inserted into Allisara's inner elbow.

"Commander Skylard, stop the chest compressions." The Maid orders. I want to scream at her, to tell her to go fuck herself but Eathan gives me a look, my long time friend making me step back. The next few seconds are hell as they tick by and memories of Allisara and I as children, then as adults, fly through my mind until finally she gasps for air.

"Sky?" She moans with pain.

"I'm here Alli." I reassure her, scooping her cold body into my arms. She is shivering and I have a feeling it is the antidote working its way through her.

"You're safe now Baby." Tears slip past my eyes as Eathan begins to take control of the situation. Guests are led away by the Estate Guards but I know soon Arian will be here with our own men. Today is a reminder that Juden and his men can get to Allisara no matter how much we prepare for her safety.

"I am Clarice, that is my sister Millia. We helped Princess Allisara get ready for tonight." The Maid, Clarice, introduces herself to me as Guards roll a gurney towards us.

"Lets get the Princess to her room while the Marquis and Marquess work to find the culprit." Millia suggests. I nod, unable to trust myself not to curse at anyone until a Doctor has come to see Allisara. Placing her onto the gurney, we leave the Ballroom through a side exit and make our way to an elevator. Moments later we are rushing down the hall and into Allisara's room – the room that belonged to her mother.

Doctors are already waiting for us – female Doctors thankfully – and Alice is there in uniform.

"Kian and Max are securing the grounds with Arian; they have already done a background check on the Doctors." She informs me, pushing me out the door. I fight her, wanting to be there with Allisara but Alice stops me.

"Sky, we need to remove her clothes and put her into something more comfortable. When she is decent again, I will get a Maid to bring you in. I promise not to leave her side." With Alice's reassurance, I slowly back away until my back reaches a wall and the bedroom doors are shut. Once again I feel like the world is falling. Like everything is slipping through my fingers and there is nothing I can do to stop it.

She was right there. Right beside me. And those bastards got to her in a place she should have been completely safe in.

"How is she?" Jumping, I turn and pin the person who called out beside me to the wall, my fore-arm pressed to their throat. It takes a moment for me to notice the voice belongs to Christopher, the future Marquis of the Blanchard Estate. Releasing him, I mumble an apology to Allisara's Uncle and turn to look at the closed doors.

"Stable last time I saw her. I got kicked out when they needed to change her from the gown and into some clean clothes." Running a hand through my hair, I sigh and turn back to the man before me. Fourteen years ago he helped me through the news that Allisara was dead. He found me crying as guilt wracked my eleven-year-old brain thinking that it was my fault she was dead. That I left her at that apple farm thinking she would be safe.

"Sky, she is still alive." He had stated as if it was a prayer.

"If Allisara was dead, we would have a body." This is what broke me from my spiral. What made me stop to think.

"What do I do?" I had asked through sobs, looking to the man that held just as much hope and determination as I wanted.

"We find her, Sky. We find her and bring her home." And I did just that.

"She is still alive." Christopher states. I laugh, feeling relieved to hear those words once again.

"Those bastards tried again, but she is alive." He continues, his eyes set in anger.

"And she is going to wake up pissed and ready to find every last one of the men associated with Juden." I chime in, smiling as I think about what she is going to do when she finds out she was poisoned. She will be pissed that she couldn't drink and dance like we wanted. Then she will be on the hunt for the person who poisoned her and make sure they pay for it. I have a feeling she might even torture the idiot that poisoned her.

"I feel like she is no longer the little girl who used to call me Uncle Toph." Christopher chuckles, leaning beside me on the wall.

"She is definitely not. The Slums were hard on her." I agree, smiling as I think back to the first time I watched her burst out of her room and march towards the Throne Room. How she took the gun from my holster and pointed it at Juden. I was both shocked and happy for her strength.

"Is it true she held him at gun point?" He asks, making me laugh again.

"Yep. My gun to be exact." Before I can get into the details, the door opens and the Maid Clarice comes out, a relived look on her face.

"She is in bed and the Doctors are working on her, but you can come in." With these words, Christopher and I rush into the room, making our way to the foot of the bed while the three Doctors work on healing Allisara. Lines of I.V. are hooked to her right hand, the clear fluids dripping steadily into her.

"I was told you were the one who noticed she was poisoned." A Doctor calls out to me as she begins to cover Allisara with a warm blanket.

"Yes. We were standing beside each other and the last thing she did was eat some food." I answer, my eyes on Allisara's face. Her makeup is gone and her hair combed out of the updo she had earlier. I remember asking her why she used a wide tooth comb and not a brush and she explained a brush would make her hair poofy like a poodle. The comb keeps her curls in tact. Her face is still pale, but not deathly like earlier. There is thankfully some pink to her cheeks.

"Well, you did good in noticing it. You saved her life." The Lead Doctor praises me and after some instructions and after care, the three Doctors leave, promising to check in on Allisara in three days. It seems we aren't leaving the Estate any time soon. I ask Millia and Clarice to be her Maids for our stay and they promise that they aren't going anywhere. Clarice informs me that they both have medical training being ex-nurses and promise to help take care of Allisara until the Doctors give her the all clear.

"Ellisia packed a bag for both of you. Go have a shower." Alice hands me a black duffle bag, my name embroidered into it. I want to protest this, but she stops me saying Allisara needs me to be clean before I can take care of her. I wonder if Allisara feels as frustrated as I do right now when someone is repeatedly right.

Taking the bag, I make my way to the bathroom and quickly shower. In ten minutes I am cleaned and dried and in a fresh set of pajamas. Entering the bed room, I spy Alice sitting in an arm chair, a book in her hand about how to be a proper lady in waiting.

"Where are you staying?" I ask, watching my friend jump and drop the book. She glares at me, bending down and picking the book back up before deciding to answer me.

"The Marquis and Marquess have rooms for all of us on this floor. We will be here when ever you need us to watch Alli." I nod, thanking her as Alice stands and walks away. She wishes me a good night before closing the door. With her gone, the room is silent. Gone is the laughter from earlier when the Maids were helping Allisara dress for the Ball. The dress is hanging on a mannequin now, probably never to be worn again. Sighing, I decide I need to sleep, that no one will touch my Allisara as long as she is beside me. Poison is one thing; I can't control that even with all the preventative measures installed. But a physical attack is one no one will be able to do.

Climbing into the left side of the bed on the opposite side where the medical equipment connects to Allisara's right hand, I reach out and take her hand in mine.

"I will keep you safe, Alli." I mumble, bringing her hand to mine and kissing it.

Chapter 38

My body feels like every inch of it has hit a brick wall. It reminds me of the time when I was eighteen and had just finished looting some rich store owner and decided taking the roof tops was a great idea. That great idea soon became regret when I slipped jumping towards my next roof top and missed by an inch. The ground thankfully was covered in garbage bags and I did not break any bones, but I was bruised and sore for a few weeks and decided to never take roof tops again.

"Alli?" Opening my eyes at the sound of his deep voice, I notice I am not in my room. What happened to me?

"Alli, I am right here." Turning in the direction of Sky's voice, I notice him staring at me with concern but also relief. My brain feels groggy, like that time I had drank too much vodka.

"What happened?" Lifting my free hand, I wince when the movement tugs on the I.V. in my hand.

"Careful." Sky moves, his hand supporting the one with the I.V. and helps me lower it onto my stomach.

"You were poisoned last night. The Doctors say you will be sore." He continues with a sigh.

"Poisoned...Doctors?" Closing my eyes, the events of the Ball crash into me like a slideshow. I had finished talking to my cousin and his father in law. Had grab something to snack on. The pain. The dizziness. It all happened so fast.

"I am going to kill those bastards." I have never felt such rage and hatred till now. How the hell did they manage to get poison into a secured event. Everything was taken care of from the Guards to the catering. Background checks were done with both the Royal Guards and the Blanchard Estate. The only people who weren't scrutinized were...

"The Guests. What happened to the guests?" I ask, eyes opening as I stared at Sky. Someone in the guest list had to have been the one to do it.

"We only have a few left to interrogate and have already found five Traitors." Taking my hand in his, Sky places a kiss on it before giving me a reassuring smile.

"Two managed to slip the same poison they got you with into their own mouths, one died but the other is kept under watch while in a coma. The other three had everything removed from them but their undergarments. Even those were scrutinized before returned to them." Sky sighs as he explains what has been done.

"What about the staff?" Wondering how they managed to place poison onto the food, I want to know if the staff were involved. I hope that's not the case. Some of the people working here have been here since my mother was a child.

"It seems so far the Blanchard Estate staff are all innocent. Arian and his men are making sure they are thoroughly investigated. He even has his Shadow Squad involved." Relieved, a small smile forms on my lips. All of the staff here are friendly. They are like family here in the Estate. Sky then tells me I have been asleep for over fourteen hours, that the poison was fast acting but everyone else were faster in getting the antidote into me and the Doctors here right away. It seems that their goal was to kill me, but they made the fatal mistake with attacking me at my maternal family's Estate.

News of me waking spread like wildfire in the Estate when Clarice came to check on me with a few Maids I have yet to meet. One ran out as soon as I said hello and soon my Grandparents were rushing inside my room with my cousins, Aunts and Uncles. They gushed over me, making sure I was comfortable and fed while explaining what the Blanchards were doing in order to help with the poison investigation. Many were pissed their own trusted friends were Traitors, my cousin Eathan explaining how his father-in-law was working hard creating a list of Nobles he worries about to send to Arian to investigate.

"How long will I need to rest?" I ask as I watch the last of my family leave my room so that I can rest. Arian informed me that when the poisoning happened, he had the communication system shut down as soon as he was informed so that no news leaked from the Estate. No one outside the guests, the Guards and the workers knows what happened to me in order to keep the citizens calm. If people found out their Princess who just returned was poisoned at an event meant for her, there would be chaos.

"Doctors say three days, but we can bring your work here to work from the bed." Changing over my I.V. bag, Clarice gives me an apologetic smile as Millia sets the food she brought in for Sky and me to eat, claiming it was already tested for poison in a sing-song voice and making me laugh. The sisters were the ones who came to my rescue with the antidote kit. They worked fast and without them I probably would have died. My Grandmama told them they were to be my Maids for the next few days but I have a feeling that she will insist I take them with me to the Palace.

"Alli is supposed to rest, not work." Sky protests at Clarice's words, the Maid rolling her eyes and muttering something about over protective men.

"I can do both, Sky. Last night is proof enough that I am still not safe and I need to put a stop to Juden and his men before their next attempts succeed." Staring into his eyes, I can see Sky wanting to protest, to fight me on this. Thankfully he doesn't and instead looks away, defeated and deflated. We both know that I am not safe at all, not until Juden and his men are caught and executed and I sit comfortably on the Throne with my crown atop of my head.

"Fine. But you work only for two hours a day for the next few days." His terms are no shock to me and I know that it is my turn to back off. If he and I are going to be a couple, then we both need to compromise.

"Deal." With the compromise made and my medicine changed, Sky and Clarice help me to walk to the small table to eat, Clarice letting me know that she had sent Alice to get my work equipment for me an hour ago much to Sky's protest. Apparently she did this without informing him and it makes me like the Maid even more. Maybe I might ask them to be my full time personal Maids before my Grandmama can suggest it.

After a light lunch of soup, sliced fruit and bread, Alice returns with my laptop bag in hand and a lap-desk in another. I thank her while yawning, asking Millia to put it on the dresser and told them all after a nap I will do some work. Sky is right, I need to rest. With their help, I climb back into bed, the comforter being pulled up to my shoulders.

As soon as everyone clears the room, I find myself in Sky's arms and he and I begin talking about what protocols we will need to add to the Palace to prevent another poisoning. We already have the Amethyst Lounge where I can safely cook my food if need be or have Ellisia cook for me if I am busy. Sky reassures me that the Palace is secured after the work he, Arian and I put into cleaning it up, that the Palace Workers would be suicidal to try anything and with his reassurance, I decide to put this topic aside for now. We will need to discus this with Arian, Ellisia and my Head Chef Theon when I return home.

I yawn again, Sky tucking my head under his chin and telling me to sleep and so I do. Work can wait until after my nap.

Chapter 39

"How many people are we sending to prison out of the two-hundred and four people?" Taking the file from Arian, I sigh as I think about the many people being kept in the Dungeons and holding cells of the City Prison. It has been two weeks since the failed attempted assassination on me at the Ball my Grandparents hosted and in those two weeks Arian and his Shadow Guards managed to find information on more Traitors. This time, these people were part of the working class and many had been employed by the Nobles that supported Juden. This brought the total number of Traitors from one-hundred and fifty-seven to the current total. The only good news to all of this mess is the fact that there will be many jobs available throughout the Kingdom.

"A good one-hundred and twelve men and women will be sent to different prisons giving the severity of their crimes. After that, the rest with less sever charges will be sent to the outer Province to live out their lives under Military control and working in the fields." Arian answers, making me sigh with relief. It seems that even though they helped Juden, most of these listed crimes were new or very minor. Many will be in prison for five years; the rest will be there between ten to fifteen years. None of them seemed to deserve death. Yet.

There is still time before the public execution for more information to be gathered before transferring these prisoners.

"So where is mother hen at?" Arian teases, looking around for Sky. Groaning, I lean back in my chair and run my fingers through my hair.

"I told him either he resumed his duties and training or I am sending him five hours away to serve in the Army for a month." Arian bursts out laughing at my frustrated confession, the man hunched over clutching his stomach. Five days after the failed assassination we returned to the Palace.

Like I thought, Grandmama sent Millia and Clarice with me and the two Maids took control of my every day essentials while focusing on regaining my strength. Sky being the worry-wart he is, kept getting in Clarice's way every time she would try to check my blood pressure and temperature, making sure no lasting side effects settled in from the poison.

On more than one occasion the feisty woman cussed Sky out, her prim and proper look seeming out of place with how she called Sky every curse word under the... well... sky. At one point, she pushed him out of the room and locked the door just as Max and Alice were walking by, their laughter heard past the closed door to where I sat at my bedroom desk.

Millia and I were left both dumbfounded and amused by this and once she was sure Sky learned his lesson in getting in the way and overly worrying about me after five hours of being locked out, Clarice let him back in and made him swear he would - as she put it- sit down and shut while she does her damned job.

Later that night Sky asked me if I could fire the sisters and send them back to my Grandmama but I shut that down, stating that not only are they great Maids, but also great assistants when working. Both ladies refused to leave my side unless one of the Violet Guards were with me and it made it easier to have someone with me at all times while the other went to run an errand for me within the Palace.

Right now Clarice is sitting on the sofa reading a book about herbal medicine while Millia left to grab us lunch and Sky thankfully was not hovering around me like a mother hen as the others call him. He reluctantly agreed to train with the Violet Guards while I stay put in my study working on finishing up plans for revitalizing the Slums and bringing the people there out of poverty. The meant the Slum Lords there will need to be arrested and sent away some how. Just this thought alone brings me a headache.

"Start transferring the prisoners that are facing the smallest of minor charges to their respectful prisons as well as those who are to be relocated to the outer Provinces." Tucking the sheets of paper he gave me into a file folder, I place it into a drawer of my desk before taking out another one. This one labelled *Lady Pricilla's Prison for Troubled Women*. A few days ago I had sent Alice dressed as a wealthy Lady looking to sponsor the prison with Alec and Adam, the latter happy to be on a recon mission while Ellisia had a few days off, to learn information of the prison. I also sent two of the Shadow Guards with her knowing this would be the only way to get them in and out without being noticed.

"Do we have any more information on who runs this hell hole?" I ask, handing the folder to Arian who takes a look and groans.

"Sadly, yes. One of the men tied to Juden owned it but we seized the deed and have transferred it into your name. Kolten and I were talking about ways to take control over it and stop the mistreatment of the Ladies of the Night." I nearly spit out the sip of cola I took when Arian used the pseudonym for prostitute, eyeing the Guard before me with amusement. He had grown up in the Slums like me so hearing someone from there describe sex workers as Ladies of the Night is something new and amusing, and I tell him so.

"Look, that word is vulgar." He defends himself, arms raised in mock surrender. This sends me into a laughing fit as I take in the uncomfortable look on his face.

"We can schedule an inspection and set a plan in motion for ten days from now." I suggest, pulling up my calendar on my tablet, a new device my Grandparents thought would be great to help me with scheduling meetings. So far it has been helpful.

"From there We can remove all the Prison Guards I remember being power hungry assholes and remove any and all of Juden's influence from there. The concept of the prison is a good one, but it needs a lot of improvement if it is to really help women." Arian agrees instantly and we spend another ten minutes planning before Millia returns pushing a cart in front of her. The smell of food causes my stomach to grumble and I decide right then and there to end the meeting. I need to eat then meet with an events co-ordinator as the Spring Parade is right around the corner and as the only royal left, I need to attend on a carriage and wave to the masses.

Arian stays for lunch, the four of us talking about the parade and how it has lost its luster over the last fourteen years. Juden was too stingy to put money into creating a fun event for the people as the Spring Parade kicked off the farming season for Nimairene. This year I plan to make it fun and memorable for the people, working with vendors who wish to sponsor the event and offer fun activities for families and children of the capitol city. I made sure they knew this would include everyone. Not just the Nobility, the rich and the upper and middle class, but also the poor and the poverty stricken people of the Slums.

They accepted this which made me look highly on the ten businesses that came forward two days ago when the parade planning began. Word spread that this year would include a fair for all to enjoy free of charge curtesy of the Royal Family and honestly it really did not make a dent in the coffers considering the mass amounts of wealth I have taken from those associated with Juden.

After lunch, Arian leaves and within an hour the Even planner enters my Study, a smile on her round face. Her name is Laura Ross and she was the Spring Parade planner before the Rebellion. Juden fired her and hired one of his goons to do the job over the next fourteen years and I realized that if I wanted this parade to go well, I would need Laura.

We decide on the colour scheme this year, deciding to go with lavender, white, silver and pastel green, and focus on what would be great to add into the parade. One thing I plan to have are the farmers being part of the parade like they were before, each float a representation what they grow and provide the Kingdom. Laura loves the idea, agreeing that having them would show our appreciation to them, something that has been lost since Juden's control. Of course, there are some things we consider like which animal farmers could bring live animals due to public safety and if they would participate in the fair as well.

After a few hours of planning, my Grandmama appears with Lidia, Daisy and Harper, the three ladies rushing to my side and pulling me from my chair into hugs. Laura chuckles, greeting Lidia and my Grandmama and the planning for my role in the parade begins. I would be the last to run the parade route, dressed in a ballgown and wearing the amethyst tiara that I love so much. The carriage will be an open carriage driven by the two large Clydesdale horses, both a beautiful white with flowing manes. They belong to my Grandparents promptly named Romeo and Juliet, the play the two performed in together when they were in school and fell in love with one another. I loved these horses the moment I saw them and when the I.V. was removed, my cousin Eathen started teaching me how to ride them.

"Just so you know, the gown has to have pockets so I can sneak sugar cubes to Romeo and Juliet and to have children feed to them too." I shrug as I sip on my tea, Laura chuckling as she playfully push the bowl of sugar cubes to me, telling me to save them for the Clydesdale pair. Lidia makes a face but agrees right away, making me promise not to ruin her gown, which I promptly agree to.

My Grandmama tells us she plans to breed the two once more, saying that I can take this foal once they are weened and can train the foal to be my partner as all princess's should own a horse. As the planning comes to an end, I walk the ladies to the Palace entrance with Clarice and Millia trailing behind us.

After everyone is gone, I look out towards the city of Zalaris and wonder what would have happened had I not been caught and moved to the country side like I wanted. What would the people go through. Sadness settles in me at the realization that as much as I love fighting for my birthright and reclaiming my memories, I will miss the life I had planned, a life of peace and quiet that I wanted so badly growing up in the Slums.

"Are you okay Princess?" Clarice asks, her concern shinning in those light brown eyes of hers.

"I am not sure." I whisper back, giving her what I hope is a reassuring smile. I rushed into this life as Princess Allisara Nimair of the Kingdom of Nimairene without thinking twice. I was angry at what I had lost that I did not stop to think what I would loose. Taking a deep breath, I turn to head back into the Palace and pause. Sky stands in the door way, his emerald eyes boring into my violet ones. Without a second thought, I walk into his arms and cry.

If there is one place I know I can be safe and let out what I am feeling inside, it is in his arms.

Chapter 40

"Do you want to tell me what that was all about Alli?" Curled up in Sky's lap, the two of us sit in the green house surrounded by flowers. During my small breakdown, Sky scooped me into his arms and rushed me to the safety of the Royal Gardens and right to the green house. I cried as he did this, finally grieving for the life I lost when Demitrias came and took me from that prison. How I stole and conned to survive and save up enough to leave the City Zalaris and move to the country. I cried and cried for God knows how long before I was left trying to catch my breath and Sky comforted me until I could breath normally again.

"I guess everything finally hit me all at once." Closing my eyes, I listen to the steady beating of his heart, feeling exhausted after my break down.

"I went from a Princess to an amnesiac child in the Slums then back to a Princess with a Kingdom in shambles all because of a greedy man." My lips quiver as the pain I feel deep inside my soul washes over me again and I take a deep breath, focusing my mind on the sounds of a fountain nearby.

"I had a plan. I was ready to leave this place for good and not care about anything in this City. Its why I stole. Those jewels and money were my ticket out." Sky listens as his hold on me tightens, his comforting silence all I need right now.

"Do you regret it? Regret coming back here?" After some time passes, Sky asks his questions. I can hear the slight hint of fear in his voice as if asking these questions are something he did not want to ask. Sighing, I think about my answer for a moment and wonder if I regret coming back here. If I regret taking control of my birth right and fixing this Kingdom.

"No. I will never regret coming back." Pulling away to look into his eyes, I feel my answer and resolve solidify. Coming back meant meeting Sky and finding answers to questions I have been asking myself for fourteen years.

"It might have been against my will when Demitrias took me from that prison, but everything after wards was my decision."

"I am glad you don't regret it Alli." Placing a kiss on my forehead, Sky tucks my head under his chin and lets out a sigh. We enjoy the silence, my heart feeling lighter since talking to him. As much as I miss my old life as Allison of the Slums, I will not regret taking back my life as Princess Allisara. The people need me. They need the changes that I have always dreamt of happening. Without me, Nimairene would collapse under Juden's rule.

"Can we go to bed?" I ask, pulling away from Sky and yawning.

"Yes, we can go to bed." Chuckling, I slowly climb off his lap and stand, stretching as I do so. Sky takes my hand when I am done and we make our way back towards the Palace. What ever is about to be thrown at me because of Juden and his me, I will take it in strides. I survived his assassination attempt fourteen years ago, survived the Slums and Prison. Hell, I just survived being poisoned. I am a survivor and if there is one thing I know how to do it's fight to survive.

And that is what I will do.

Chapter 41

Sitting on the porch of Ron and Liz's house, I watch as the construction crew begin to tear up the rundown and old road. It has been three days since my small break down in Sky's arms and with a new resolve to do right by my people, I called around the construction company I planned to hire and asked what is the earliest day they can start their work. The owner of the company was excited to work with me as the future Queen and said within two days as long as the plans were sent to him so he can sort out a crew. During that call, I emailed the file to him and explained that I wanted to start with the Slums in the South and work my way out.

"It's so nice to see a change for once." Ron comments as he takes a seat beside me. I hum in agreement, taking a sip of hot chocolate. Yesterday morning I sent a group of Guards to go door to door with construction notices that would begin today, the people were hesitant at first to see my Guards, but when they read the notices and learned of the changes that will follow within the year, their hesitations faded away.

"I always wanted to see changes made here as a child. To know that many of those living in shambling houses are being sent to a hotel while their houses are rebuilt feels nice." Smiling, I lean my head against Ron's shoulder, happy to know that I can relax while the work goes on. Many of the Guards and Kolten's Soldiers were tasked with helping those whose houses were one storm away from collapsing pack and send them to a hotel. In each group, a Butler took note of how many rooms were in each house to rebuild it to the same specifications. Ron and Liz's house is one of the few that are still in pristine condition thanks to it being passed down in Ron's side of the family so I agreed to not have anything done to their house without their permission.

"Well now you are making those changes. I heard there were many jobs opening up deeper into the city by the way, was that your doing?" He nudges me gently, his tone a mock sternness. Ron's playfulness while asking the question has me laughing and I admit that technically it was. I told him about the attempt on my life and explained that I went on a hunt tracking down more Traitors.

"You live an eventful life now." He muses, pulling me in for a hug. We sit on the porch in silence after that, overseeing the new road being put in while my Violet Guards help with picking up trash around the place. With so many Guards and people around, it will be hard to try an attempt on my life here. Besides, Sky is inside with Liz working on snacks for all of us.

The smell of cookies and scones come wafting towards me as the front door opens and Sky walks out with a full tray in his hands, Liz following after with a pitcher of lemonade for us. They place it on the small table in front of Ron and I before taking a seat, Sky placing a kiss on my cheek.

"It seems like you have something to tell us missy." Liz states, her left brow raised as she stares at me. Deciding to play dumb I smile and take a white-chocolate-raspberry scone from the plate.

"My Grandparents asked if you and Liz would like to come for dinner the night before the Spring Parade. They want to thank you for taking care of me." I shrug, taking a bite of the scone as Sky and Ron chuckles, the two men deciding to stay quiet.

"We can do that, but you know well enough that that is not what I meant." She chides me, hands on her hips. I sheepishly smile, looking to Sky for a moment before facing Liz.

"Sky and I are dating." A wide smile spreads across Liz's face as she sits down, happy that I gave her the correct answer this time.

"Welcome to the family Sky." Ron jokes, nudging Sky's arm with his elbow playfully.

"Thank you but Alli and I only had one date." Reaching for a scone – a multi-berry one – Sky thanks Ron.

"And that ended in me being poisoned." I deadpan, Sky humming in agreement as he takes a bite of the scone.

"Well, did you catch the bastards that did it?" Liz asks, concern and anger on her aging face.

"We did. It's why there are so many jobs now in Zalaris and probably why so many from the Slums are working now." Sky answers this one, my mouth full of the sweet and tart scone. I nod, turning to look at the construction and noticing that the bulldozer was coming to tear down a few houses. It will take a few days for these to be completed and fences to be placed around each property, but knowing there is change makes me happy.

"Your Highness?" A voice calls out as the foreman – Jacob – walks up the porch steps, a friendly smile on his face with his dreadlocks pulled back to keep it from getting in the way while he works.

"We noticed that small shack over there, do you want us to tear it down and rebuild it?" He asks, pointing to what I called my home for years.

"No, not yet. That used to be my home and I still need to pack it up." I admit, watching as shock cross the Jamaican's face.

"No wonder you want to help these people. You were one of them as well." He muses out of shock and not of disgust. I smile, explaining to Jacob what happened to have me end up here and he takes in the brief history of my life. After asking if he wants my men to clear it out and provide a bigger home for me to use, I hesitate and look to Sky. There are only a few items left in there and the plan was to always come back and fix it up, but to tear it down feels wrong.

"It's your call Alli. We can get the others to come and clean out the shack. We will just need to store everything somewhere." Sky takes my hand in his, reassuring me that I make the decisions. I hesitate, looking back to the shack and think back to the life I lived there. If we tear it down, I will lose the last remaining thing to my past as Allison.

"You can store the furniture in our basement." Ron chimes in, giving me a soft smile. I hesitate again, wanting to accept this idea, but part of me wants to redo the shack my way.

"Leave it be, please. When you and your men start with rebuilding the other houses, I will work on the shack." Jacob takes the answer with a smile, offering to lend a few men to help me when the time comes. I thank him, watching as he returns to work as Sky, Ron and Liz give me a questioning gaze.

"It's the last piece of my childhood. A place that kept me safe. I am not ready to give it up." I state to the three, giving them a sad smile. The work on revitalizing the Slums continue and after planning to have Ron and Liz come to the Palace in three days, Sky and I leave to head home, leaving the Violet Guards to watch over the construction for the rest of the day with the exception of Max and Alice. Those two came home with us to help prepare for the Parade. Max will be doubling security to keep Juden and his men in line in the Palace Dungeons and Alice will be preparing my safety procedures with Sky.

Chapter 42

"So how was dinner last night?" Lia asks as Clarice and Millia helps to dress me for the Parade, a cream princess off the shoulder court train lace tulle ballgown with sequins. The bodice is made of intricate lace, the sweetheart neckline cut lower than I would like but the train is what surprised me. We agreed tulle did not look good on me weeks ago, but this full ballgown made of tulle with slight lace detailing really did look good on me.

"It went well. Ron and Liz hit it off with my Grandparents and they agreed to coming for more events my Grandmama hosts. I think Liz and Grandmama are going to be spending more time together." Millia carefully curls my hair into a cascading updo, the amethyst tipped hair pins shining in the light as she rearranges my hair. I asked her why she is curling my already curly hair and she stated to neaten them and add a regal flare to my look.

"Sounds like Liz needs it." Millia chuckles out, making me smile.

"She does. Liz and Ron are the only elderly couple in the Slums. She needs a friend her age and Grandmama enjoys getting to know Liz. I think Liz is going to teach her to bake." I agree as Clarice walks into the room with a pillow in hand, my amethyst tiara on top.

"You have so many tiara's in that closet of yours, why do you always choose this one?" She asks, setting the pillow on the table and carefully lifting the tiara.

"Because it was my mother's. My crown for my coronation crown will be a replicated mix of both her's and my father's crowns." I explain, the sisters looking surprised for a moment. With my hair finished by Millia, Clarice carefully places the tiara on top of my head, her eyes scanning me from head to toe as she backs away.

"We understand. Our mother died when we were little and both Clarice and I wear a necklace each that we inherited from her." Millia smiles as she stands beside her sister, her eyes also scanning me from head to toe.

"You're ready." With their approval, I tell them to go enjoy the fair today and follow Lia out of my dressing room. Currently we are in a warehouse just outside of the parade route that has been used for years. Sky and the rest of the elite are dressed in black slacks, black boots a cream coloured dress shirt and a blazer in the colour dark orchid – if I call it dark purple I am sure Lidia will give me another lecture about colour theory.

Each one wears the pin I gave them on their blazers, a smile on their faces as they help those in the parade with last minute touches before we prepare to leave. I watch as the farmers and volunteers mingle with one another, smiles on all their faces at the excitement of today. It has been a long time since the Spring Parade was this festive and I am beginning to grow nervous. Today will be my first formal appearance to my people, what if they hate me?

"I can't do this." I state as I start to pace beside the white carriage, Romeo and Juliet already connected to the front watching me with their large brown eyes.

"Yes you can Alli!" Sky reassures, stopping me in my tracks with one hand on my cheek and the other on my shoulder.

"You grew up in these streets, you know the people better than most royals do. You got this." He pulls me into a hug, his pine scented shower gel helping to calm my nerves. I hate when Sky is right because right now he is right. I know the streets of Zalaris better than most and know the Slums of Zalaris even more.

"Better?" He asks, pulling away to look me in the eye.

"A little. Maybe I need a little animal therapy." Sky chuckles at my reply, watching me as I step towards the horses and scratch both of them behind the ear. I look to the massive horses and reach into my pocket as I continue to scratch Juliet, handing her a sugar cube before Romeo buts his head towards the pocket of my dress where I produce a sugar cube for him as well. Just being near these gorgeous creatures lightens my worries.

Parade floats begin to leave the warehouse one at a time, following the instructions of Laura and her crew. I sigh waking towards Sky as he waits by the side of the carriage. Careful of my dress, Sky helps me into the carriage where I promptly take a seat. Sky climbs onto the driver seat beside the driver, the man dressed in a black tuxedo. Alice smiles as she joins me on the carriage in a light cream dress, the only Guard to portray herself as my Lady in Waiting.

"Do you have your gun?" She asks, giving me a once over. It seems she too had Clarice and Millia help her prepare for today. She places a bag on the floor of the carriage and I spy a change of clothes for her and I.

"I do. One of the pockets is fake and gives me access to it." She nods, relief on her face at my answer. We all know today is risky with Juden's men out there. I know deep down we haven't captured all of them but I will not give Juden the satisfaction of knowing I am hidden in my Palace. My people need to see me.

Lia and Mia wave to us as they join beside the carriage, both on top of black Friesian horses stationing themselves behind the carriage after making sure I was okay. Alec and Kian are riding in front of the carriage on their own black Friesians, the two joking around. Max was left at the Palace with a squadron of Guards he choose to make sure Juden and the other Traitors in the dungeons behaved today.

Our turn to exit the warehouse comes next and I take a deep breath before smiling as the carriage turns a corner and a crowd comes into view. I begin to wave at the people, spying a few little girls in puffy dresses as they call out to me. I wave at them, watching as their small faces light up. The parade is long, about an hour as the route brings us through most of the city. We will be ending at the center of the city where the Fair is placed inside a large park.

I continue to wave and say hello to the people, noticing more and more people from the Slums. Every so often flowers are thrown into the street, many from women and children. My heart warms at how loving and kind my people are and I begin to think that taking back my birthright as Heir to the Throne was the best decision I made.

As the carriage follows the parade down another street, I can see the edges of the park where the Fair is. We are nearing the end of the parade and I can't wait. I will have an hour of walking around in this gown before I can change into some comfortable clothes and join the festivities.

Suddenly gun shots ring out, the loud bang causing many people to scream.

"Long live King Juden Trilavantas!" Someone shouts, a bullet ricocheting off the carriage wheels spooking Romeo and Juliet.

"Allisara, get down!" Sky hops over the carriage as Alice kneels by the entrance, gun ready while she scans the crowd for the shooter. Sky pulls my body off the seat and onto the floor of the carriage, his own gun out as he keeps close in case he needs to shield me from another bullet.

Guards begin to rush the crowd, searching for the shooter, or shooters, as more shot ring out from various directions, the crowd screaming from the attack. I pull out a sundress from the bag of clothes Alice brought and pull it over my head before shimmying out of my ballgown. I am shielded from the carriage walls and Alice and Sky are keeping watch so I know changing now is my only chance.

"We need to get out of here." I shout over the chaos as I pull my own gun out, ready to shoot if need be. I know the area, have ran away from the Police many times from here. I know where to go to get to safety.

"No one knows this area." Mia climbs into the carriage from the back, stating a Guard took her horse to chase down one of the gun men.

"I do. I grew up on the streets remember." Mia nods as she looks to Sky to see what he says. I can tell he is hesitating, knowing that if we run now, the gun men will chase us away from the innocent people.

"Sky its your call, we can blend into the crowd if you take off your blazers." I continue. Sky finally nods, taking his pin off of his blazer and sticking it into his pocket. Kian and Alec are on the outside of the carriage already taking off their own pin and blazers before throwing them into the carriage. I hesitate as I feel my tiara, the conflict of leaving it behind knowing how important it is to me. Alice notices my hesitation and removes a purse from the bag of clothes.

"Give it to me. I will keep it safe." I thank her and carefully remove my tiara from my head, passing the delicate jewelry to her and watch as she puts it into the purse before placing it over her shoulder. Sky looks around one last time before directing his gaze to the driver huddled on the floor off the driving area.

"Make sure the carriage gets back to the Palace." Sky orders, the driver nodding hesitantly. Taking this as my que, I open the right side door of the carriage and carefully crawl out making sure not be seen as I look around and spot an alleyway directly across from me. I grin, making sure the cost is clear before I run into the alleyway, watching as Mia and Lia follow me before Sky and Alice joins us. With Kian and Alec being last, I look at everyone. They look too formal but it will have to do for now.

"Okay lets go." Taking the lead I begin to run through the alleyway, making sure to stop and check around the corners before moving on. This is the same rout I took on the day I was caught and sent to Prison. I know this rout and this time I will make sure I am not caught by anyone.

My shack will be the obvious place people look for me and I know I can't go there. Too many people now know that is my property because of the Slums revitalization program. Instead I think about the area around my shack and smile. There is a large tree house we can run to and hide out in until night fall. It is close to Ron and Liz's house so when night comes, we can rush there and call my Grandparents for help.

I make sure not to tell anyone where we are going, not wanting anyone to hear and ambush us. I am even more careful when rounding corners, me or one of the Violet Guards checking to see if the coast is clear. Of course they try to keep me from checking, wanting to keep me out of harms way, but I remind them that I know the back roads better than them and they relent when I take the lead.

"Hello Allisara." A deep voice calls from the shadows, my steps pausing as I turn to an alleyway with my gun held up. Three men step forward just as Sky and the others surround me, their own guns pointed at these men.

"Who are you?" I demand, eyeing them with contempt. They seem familiar, but I can't place where.

"Friends of Juden." The man in the middle states, his blonde hair greasy and unkempt. I bristle at the name of that Traitor and glare at them. How dare they show themselves to me after everything he's done.

"We thought that today would be a great day to kill you. I mean you did leave us with out a job." The man on the right chuckles, a scar covering half his face over is right eye.

"I thought you all agreed to behave with and signed a contract with Princess Allisara." Sky calls out, getting a chuckle from the men.

"We left before that happened. We weren't going to be like those pansies that give up when a new Bitch is in charge." Blonde guy chuckles out darkly, his own gun raised.

"I see you are still playing Knight in Shining armor to the Princess. How does it feel to be her bitch?" This time it is the person on the right talking, trying to taunt Sky into doing something rash. I frown, sending a warning shot and shooting his ear off. He screams, his gun dropping as he holds his bloody ear.

"As you can tell, I don't need to protect our Princess." Sky answers briskly with a chuckle, my own smirk on my face. Everyone else chuckles as the man with the scar rises his gun, arm shaking as I look him in the eye.

"You'll be surprised what you learn in the Slums." I deadpan, winking at the men as I raise my gun once more.

"Well then I guess you'll be just another Slums statistic when we kill you." Blondie yells furiously, finger on the trigger. Unfortunately for them, they don't get a chance to make good on that threat as Sky, Lia and Mia let bullets fly, killing each men with a shot to the heat for scar face, a shot to the head for blondie and a shot to the groin – which I believe is Sky's shot – before I end the guy who's ear I shot off with a shot to the head when he covers his now exploded groin.

"We should call this in later." Pushing the body of the blondie with my toe, Sky chuckles as I scrunch up my face. To think Juden still had power while in the dungeons.

"We also need to learn who these men had contact with." Kian adds, searching through their pockets and pulling out their wallet, taking their I.Ds and handing them to Sky. I agree before we leave these men in the streets, making our way through the back alleyways again, this time being more careful not to run into any more of Juden's men. It takes some time, but soon we reach the end of the final street coming face to face with the Slums I grew up in. We need to sneak around using the construction sights to keep under cover and when I mention that Sky takes the lead with me behind him.

"There." I point out to the grove of oak trees and to the largest tree with a treehouse hidden deep in the leaves. We are hidden in the half finish house of one of the residents staying in the hotels, the shadows keeping us safe while we wait to see if anyone is watching for us.

"You go first Alli, we'll cover you." Alec states, Sky agreeing as his eyes scan the surroundings. I nod, gun at the ready before I bolt from the cover of the half finished walls and race towards the ladder of the tree house. Once at the base, I place the gun into my thigh holster before scrambling up the ladder and into the safety of the tree house.

Lia and Mia are the first to Join me, followed by Alice. Sky is next, his emerald eyes full of exhaustion as he pulls me into a hug and kisses me softly.

"Remind me to never do parades again." I chuckle out as the kiss ends, Alec and Kian climbing into the tree house next and chuckling at my response.

"I think we are all done with parades." Mia groans, laying on the floor of the tree house.

"We need to stay here for tonight, make our way to the castle tomorrow." Sky says after a moment of our group trying not to laugh at Mia.

"No, we wait till night fall, which is in a few hours, then head to Liz and Ron's house." I correct. Sky stares at me and I smirk.

"You didn't notice the neighborhood I brought us too?" He curses and makes his way to the only window of the treehouse and I smile knowing that he could see my adoptive Grandparents house just across the street.

"The parade was broadcasted throughout the nation; they are probably worried sick. I was supposed to call them when I got back to the Palace tonight." I continue, closing my eyes and laying back against the wall. Sky joins me, wrapping his arm around my shoulders and pulling me to his side. We got lucky that the treehouse is large enough to fit all six of us comfortably.

"Okay, we go with what Alli says." Everyone nods and we wait for night to fall. I pray that it comes quick because if news gets out that I am missing, the Kingdom will be thrown into chaos and any of Juden's men left hidden will do their best to keep the chaos going

Chapter 43

We watched as the afternoon turns to night, the air gaining a slight chill with the sun disappearing. No one had followed us after that incident with the three men in the back alleyways thankfully and we all took turns resting. After we were sure it was completely dark outside, Lia left the safety of the tree house to scout the area. We all waited in the tense silence until the agreed upon signal – the call of an owl – was heard.

I was the first to hop down from the tree house, not bothering with the ladder as I have jumped out of here many times as a child. I landed silently beside Lia who jumps, eyeing me with surprise and I shrug. Sky it next, my boyfriend climbing down the ladder and giving me a disapproving look before he takes the lead and we make our way to the front porch of Ron and Liz's house. One by one my friends join us on the porch and when everyone is safely hidden in the shadows caused by the porch, I ring the door bell.

"Coming!" Liz's voice is muffled by the door but I can still hear the annoyance in her tone. I think the news must have broad casted the shooting at the parade as not much can annoy Liz except for mine and Ron's safety. The door opens and I can tell that Liz is about to yell when she stops, her eyes widening as she takes me in for a moment before she reaches for me.

"Alli! The news said there was a shoot out, are you alright? Did you get hurt? Are you hungry?" The elderly woman fusses, pulling me into a hug. Her body sags, probably with relief at seeing me before her, and I take a deep breath, smelling her apple scented perfumes and the scent of freshly backed cookies.

"I am fine, I did not get hurt, and we are all hungry." I take a shaky breath, holding back my own tears as I answer Liz's questions. I know she must have been so worried for me and I hate that what should have been a fun day turned into a disaster.

"Liz, we really need to get Alli inside." Sky urges gently, his eyes scanning the dark for any signs of danger. Liz pulls away to take in Sky and the others behind me. She nods, pulling me into the house as Sky motions for the others to enter after me before he enters the house last where he promptly shuts and lock the front door.

"Ron, put the kettle on and come to the living room" Liz yells as we pass the kitchen, Alec and Lia snickering behind us making me roll my eyes. As soon as we reach the living room, I go to sit in my usual chair but Sky beats me to it, pulling me into his lap and wrapping his arms around me. I know this whole ordeal has shaken him up and I don't fight it. Instead I lean into his touch, needing to be close to him just as much as he needs to be close to me.

"Do we have company hun?" Ron calls out before turning the corner, his foot steps pausing as he takes in me and my friends.

"Thank the Lord you're alright." He rushes with relief, shuffling over to look at me, the click of his cane loud and clear. I let Ron do a once over on Sky and I, the old man sighing as he takes a seat beside Liz on the love seat.

"We were watching the parade during their live broadcasting. We saw everything and when we didn't hear from you we thought-" Ron's voice ends as he chokes up with emotions, tears running down his face. Liz comforts him and I reach my hand out, squeezing his when he takes it.

"We are all fine." I reassure, smiling at my adopted Grandfather. I explain what happened from the start of the shooting to us ending up here. How we hid out in the tree house and Sky asks to use the phone to call my Grandparents. Ron tells us its in the kitchen and I climb off Sky as he goes to call them for me while I introduce Lia, Mia, Alec, Alice and Kian to them. Liz smiles, thanking them for keeping me safe and mentions how they all better come by and visit the two as they are now honorary grandkids, which Kian promises right away. I roll my eyes just as Sky returns, scooping me into his arms and returning to our seat.

"Everette and Lillian are happy to know we are safe. Arian was with them trying to locate us and I informed him about the three Ex-Guards. He sent a group of men to retrieve their bodies and told us to sit tight for the night." Sky informs us, groaning as he rests his head against my shoulders.

"After tonight there is going to be a lot to do. Lillian already set in motion a press conference." This has me groaning as well, not excited at all for the up coming press conference. I have yet to make another one since the D.N.A. testing as taking back my Throne and fixing my Kingdom has taken priority. I have a feeling the one my Grandmama is planning will entail another frilly dress and makeup.

"Who wants tea and something to eat?" As if sensing my discomfort, Liz distracts us with this suggestion and we all silently raise our hands, too drained to answer. Within minutes everyone has a steaming mug of tea with a plate of shepherds pie in our hands. The coffee table is filled with plates of sliced fruit and cookies. With our bellies full and bodies relaxed, exhaustion creeps in and I can see it on all of my friend's faces.

"I think we should get you all to bed." Liz sighs out giving us all a motherly smile.

"Alli, your room is still there for you. I know Sky isn't going to leave your side so take him with you." Liz starts, looking at Sky and I as I sleepily nod, too tired to speak.

"We have a guest room you three girls can share if you'd like." Ron adds, Lia, Mia and Alice thanking them as Ron gets up to lead the girls to the guest room.

"Kian and I will stay down here in the living room. Someone has to keep watch in case more Traitors come looking." Alec stated before Liz could offer anything else. She accepts this answer, telling them to use the shower down the hall to freshen up and that Ron will bring them some shorts and a t-shirt to wear to bed. Climbing off of Sky's lap, I waddle my way to my bedroom here in their house, Sky trailing after me with a chuckle. The room used to be used for storage but after meeting me Liz insisted to Ron that I needed a room on cold nights or when I was sick and needed to be cared for.

I by-pass the bed and go right to the closet, grabbing a tank top and pajama pants from the wrack before heading to the small bathroom. I shower quickly, the excitement of the day wearing off with the warm spray. Feeling clean, I turn off the water and dry off, dressing quickly and entering the bedroom to find Sky towel drying his hair, already dressed in a pair of pajamas from Ron. He pulls me into his lap when I get close, taking the towel from my hand and helps me to dry my hair. The gentle movements lull me to sleep and with my chin resting on his shoulder, I close my eyes.

Chapter 44

Huddled in the corner of my room clutching my teddy bear, I listen as swords clash and guns fire. I knew those sounds, my father making sure I knew how to wield both even. Today was my sixth birthday and the party ended hours ago. So why are people fighting?

"Mama?" I whimper out, clutching my teddy tighter while shivering. No one answers but the silence.

"Princess Allisara?" Someone whispers my name as light footsteps come my way. It takes a moment to recognize the voice in the darkness but soon I realize it is my Maid Rainnah. Throwing my teddy to the side, I rush to Rainnah's open arms and cry. She soothes me, begging me to quiet down as she rushes to help me dress. She chooses a long sleeve dress with a cape wrapped around my shoulders. It is late spring and I wonder why she is dressing me so warm but she told me I need to stay quiet because there are bad men about, so I stay quiet. Once dressed, Rainnah carries me into her arms and rushes to the secret door hidden in my closet. It is the servant door; one I was told never to use without Rainnah.

"Hush, little one. They will hear you." Rainnah shushes as she holds on tightly to me, her worry filled voice shaking as she does her best to keep us hidden in the shadows.

"I want my mama and papa." I whimper out, clutching Rainnah's shirt.

"I know Allisara. But we need to get you to safety." Rainnah coos, pulling me closer to her. I try my best to stop crying, my lips quivering as I burry my face into her shoulder. Rainnah's footsteps are barely audible on the stone steps and something tells me I can't make any noise with all the gun shots, screaming and fighting in the Palace.

The stairs finally come to an end with a small passage way leading to the way out ahead. Rainnah sighs with relief, tightening her hold on me and quickening her steps.

"Just a little further and we will be free." She whispers, I nod, turning my head slightly to look at her. I see Rainnah smiling as she rushes into the cold night, sticking to the shadows of the trees as she tightens the cloak on me and doing her best to keep me warm. Finally she rounds the corner to find who she is looking for, a black horse saddled and ready to run. A man in armour sits on top of the horse with a young boy in his lap – my playmate and personal Knight in training.

"Listen to me Princess." Rainnah begins, her tone urgent and making me pull away to look at her.

"The Knight will take you to safety and when the time is right, we will return you home." She places me on my feet, looking into my tear filled eyes I know she is trying not to cry, trying to be strong for me, but something tells me I will never see her again. Reaching into her pocket, Rainnah retrieves a necklace and carefully places it around my neck.

"This is from your parents. Know that they love you with all their heart." With these final words, she lifts me into her arms for one last hug before passing me to the Knight, tears in her eyes as she watches the young boy wrap his arms around me. The scent of pine is relaxing and I know with my friend holding me, I will be safe.

"Protect her." Rainnah pleads to the Knight. He looks down at us, patting my head gently before giving Rainnah a nod as a silent promise. He flicks the reigns and the horse takes off, galloping away into the darkness. I look back to see Rainnah crying, waving good bye to me before she runs into the Palace, my home fading away.

♔[1]

Jolting awake drenched in sweat, I look around the room as the sounds of fighting fades away with the dream... nightmare...

"Memory." I whisper. My hand reaches for the necklace around my neck, but then I remember I left it in my jewelry box in my bedroom. I had turned six that day. Had just celebrated with my family and friends. And it was all taken away from me.

---

1. https://coolsymbol.com/copy/White_Chess_King_Symbol_%E2%99%94

The bed shifts beside me and I know that I must have woken Sky up.

"You okay?" He mumbles, slowly sitting beside me. I nod, not sure what to say as I take in the memory and replay it over and over again in my mind.

"Alli, you're crying." Sky pulls me into his arms, hands rubbing my back as he soothes me. I hadn't realized I was crying until he pointed it out and now it seems I can't stop. I sob, allowing myself to feel the pain of loosing my family, of loosing Rainnah. She ran back into the Palace after getting me to safety and I know from the way people avoid talking about her that she died that same night. I am not sure how long I cried, but my tears finally stop and I hiccup for breath while Sky helps to calm me down, placing light kisses on top of my head and reassuring me that everything will be fine. Slowly I pull away when I feel like I have no more tears to cry and I feel his hands cup my face, his thumbs moving to wipe away the last few tears.

"Was it a nightmare?" He asks, his emerald eyes filled with worry. I shake my head no, taking a deep breath as I think about the last scene of watching Rainnah run into the Palace.

"No, a memory from the night of the Rebellion." I whimper out. He pulls me to his chest again, rubbing my back gently as my arms snake round his waist. His steady heart beat calms me and I close my eyes to listen to it. He doesn't smell like pine like he usually does and right now I really miss that scent.

"What do you remember?" He asks quietly, running his finger through my hair.

"How I woke up feeling something was wrong and how quiet the night was." I take a deep breath.

"My Maid, Rainnah, had found me in my room and had helped me out of the Palace. She brought me into the waiting arms of a Knight. He was the apple farmers' son if I remember correctly." I continue to explain, a smile on my face as I think about the boy that was with him.

"That same boy was there too, the one I keep seeing in my memories." I finish. The room stays silent after my confession. Sky asks if I have remembered that boy yet, but I tell him no I haven't. He hums, and I get the feeling he is slightly disappointed. The early spring air is chilly like it was that night and I begin to worry when I realize how quiet the street is. It's never been this quiet before.

"Something's wrong." I whisper, pulling away from Sky and looking towards the window. The door opens slowly, causing Sky to push me behind him on the bed as a silhouette appears in the doorway.

"Its me, we need to go." Lia's voice rang out. I quickly grab a pair of shoes I left in the closet and shove them on as Sky and I make our way towards her, our guns in hand in case something happens.

"Ron and Liz?" I ask.

"Right here." Came Liz's voice and I sighed with relief.

"Where are the others?" Sky asked as we make our way through the house and out the back door.

"Here. We grabbed supplies." Came Alice's reply as she appears behind us, Kian and Alec staring out the front window.

"Five men, all carrying what we think to be explosives." Alec explains grimly as the two men back away from the window and make their way towards us. Sky nods, looking to Liz and Ron who carry bags in their hands. The bare minimum that they can carry.

"Ron, Liz we need to leave. I know you love this house but it is not safe here." I explain to the two, catching tears glistening in Liz's eyes.

"We know Alli. We packed what we could with Lia's help." Ron explains grimly, taking my hand in his and giving it a reassuring squeeze. I nod, not sure what to say to the two. Silently we creep out of the side door that is connected to the garage. I know the two own an old van, one that is rarely used but kept in good condition. Stepping into the garage, Sky and Kian help everyone climb into the van, before they quietly open the garage door and climb into the front seats. Sky having driven here many times is the one behind the wheel while Kian lowers his window, gun ready to shoot if need be.

Silently the car turns on and creeps slowly out of the garage. We all hold our breaths as we look for signs of the assassins before Sky turns on the lights and drives off. Suddenly a loud explosion sounds behind us, shaking the car and the many half-built houses on the street.

"My house." Liz cries out, turning back to look at the now burning structure. Ron takes his wife in his arms, comforting her as Sky drives away. I close my eyes as a few silent tears fall. All the memories I had spending my days with Ron and Liz in that house flash through my mind. Without them, I would have never survived for as long as I had.

The drive to the Palace is tense but as we arrive to the main entrance I spy Ellisia, Adam, Grandmama, Grandfather and Arian standing there waiting for us.

"Mia called us, are you okay?" My Grandmama asks as we climb out of the old van, pulling me into her arms after giving me a once over.

"We are fine, just overwhelmed." I answer, resting my head on her shoulder. Ellisia steps forward with four Maids, introducing herself to Ron and Liz and explaining that a room had been prepared for the two. They look to me, Liz's face wet from tears, and I nod, telling them to go rest. That I will see them in the morning to talk about what happened and where we will go from here. My Grandfather suggests we all should head to bed and talk about what happened today in the morning. Sky agrees and after being reassured by Arian that security has been doubled around the Palace after today, we all make our way to our respective rooms. I don't argue with Sky when he follows me into my room, the doors closing behind us. Before I can say anything I am in his arms, his lips pressed to mine in a heated kiss.

"What-what was that for?" I ask breathlessly when we pull away looking into his eyes, the deep emerald green seeming darker, more feral.

"Just because." He mumbles, his voice husky. Confused, I allow him to lead me to bed where I find myself once again in his arms once we are under the covers. Sky is quick to fall asleep but I find myself wide awake listening to his steady heart beat and even breath.

Chapter 45

A knocking on my door wakes me from my sleep and with a sigh, I turn to look at the door. I have had a long night and honestly I do not want to deal with anyone right now. The door begins to open and I groan, I pull the duvet closer to my body, every muscle in me protesting. My head aches as I try to sleep a little longer knowing that once I leave my bed, a shit storm awaits me.

"Good morning Alli." The bed dips beside me as Sky gently pulls back the duvet, giving me an amused smile as I blink at him, frowning at the fact that he decided to disturb me.

"How do you feel?" He asks, brushing my hair from my face before bending down and placing a kiss on my forehead.

"Like I've been through hell and back." I yawn, giving him a small smile. He chuckles, running his hands through my hair. My eyes close involuntarily, the gentle movements making me want to fall asleep again.

"After yesterday, I would say we've been through hell and back." He muses, his deep voice making me open my eyes once more. He pulls the duvet off of me, silently signalling that it is time to get up. I groan again, not wanting to leave my bed.

"Lillian and Liz want to talk to you. Apparently the News has been going all day about the attack yesterday, some even claiming that you died in the attack." He explains as I slowly sit up. The doors suddenly burst open and Alice strides in, Clarice and Millia behind her as Clarice pushes a cart full of food towards the bed.

"Glad to see you are awake." Clarice calls out, rushing to my side and hugging me tightly. I hug her back, happy to see my friend.

"You slept the whole morning away and it's currently one in the afternoon." Alice smiles as she hands me a glass of water, the cool refreshing liquid being just what I need to cope with the headache as I down the glass in seconds.

"You mean I slept the whole day away?" I ask, handing the glass to Alice. Sky nods, pulling me onto his lap and pressing his lips to my shoulder. I shiver, my mind wandering back to last night, to the kiss he gave me.

"Yes, you slept the day away." Clarice confirms, pushing the cart closer to me and handing me a plate with a sandwich on it. I thank her, my stomach growling as I take a bite of the turkey club. Sky holds me tight, his chin resting on my shoulder. I can hear each breath he takes and it is very distracting.

"So I am guessing my Grandmama and Liz sent you in to grab me." I state after a few bites of the turkey club.

"Yes. They have a plan for a News broad cast." Alice turns the vanity seat around, sitting down and letting out a sigh. She thanks Millia as the Maid hands her a glass of juice while Clarice disappears into my closet. I sigh, deciding to finish my sandwich before I need to deal with anything else today. Alice then goes into an explanation that when Grandmama woke up, Uncle Christopher had come into the Palace to see if she knew what was happening with me and if she had heard from Sky or me. She reassured him that I was in bed safe at the time and he left to prepare the Broadcasting Room on the second floor just down the hall from my Study.

"So if my Uncle is preparing the Broadcasting Room, why do Liz and Grandmama need me?" I ask, getting a sigh from Alice.

"They need you in your Study to brief you on the situation out in the Kingdom and you need to go over the notes of what to say to reassure the people of Nimairene." Alice gives me a small smile as Clarice walks into the room with an outfit in hand. It seems this is something that as the next rule I have to do. The attack yesterday afternoon didn't just affect me, but also the people that were meant to enjoy the parade and fair. Instead there was chaos and gun shots. Who knew just how many casualties there are from the frantic crowd.

"So go for a shower after you finish eating. Millia, Clarice and I will wait for you here." She continues, taking a pastry. Sky doesn't eat, even when I offer him a bit of my sandwich. He just holds me while Alice takes my tablet from the bedside table and Millia and Clarice mill about my room tidying it up for me. When I finished my sandwich, I hesitate to get off from Sky's lap. Getting up means I have to dress and face my nation. To warn them that it isn't safe.

"Come on Alli. Time for a shower." I squeal in surprise as Sky tucks an arm under my knees, lifting me into his arms bridal style and carrying me to the bathroom.

"What are you doing!" I hiss out, wrapping my arms around his neck and hanging on for dear life. I do not want to fall to the ground.

"Getting a bit of alone time with you." With a chuckle , Sky pushes the bathroom closed with his foot before setting me down on my feet. I want to protest but before I can say anything, his lips are on mine and I am pressed between the bathroom wall and his lean body. His left hand snakes around my waist, pulling me flushed against him while his right tangles into my hair. The kiss is feral, his lips claiming me. His teeth nips my bottom lip making me moan a noise I did not know I could make. Sky takes this opportunity to slip his tongue into my mouth, claiming me further.

Just as quickly as the kiss started, it ends, and I find myself gasping for breath. My body feels warm and my mind slightly hazy as Sky continues to pepper kisses on my cheeks and forehead before pulling me closer to his body and tucking my head under his chin.

"Sorry Alli, I...I just needed to kiss you like that." He mumbles into my hair. I feel myself smiling as my fingers grip his now wrinkled shirt. He smells like pine again.

"I... I liked it." My admittance earns me a chuckle as Sky pulls away and places a finger under my chin, forcing me to look into his eyes.

"You liked it?" His voice is deep and husky, his emerald green eyes darker than ever. I nod, unable to trust my voice for a moment before his lips are on mine once more. This kiss is slow and gentle and I kiss him back, closing my eyes and leaning into his touch. This time I am the one to pull away needing to breath, and shyly hide my face into his chest.

"I...I need to shower." I mumble, catching my reflection in the mirror. My face is flushed red.

"I know. I have some things to take care of so I will meet you in the Broadcasting Room." I nod as Sky pulls away, looking at me with reluctance before he leaves the bathroom, closing the door behind him. Taking a moment to compose myself, I lean against the wall behind me and place a hand on my chest over the spot of my beating heart. Since agreeing to date, mine and Sky's relationship has grown. It has become something I never thought possible and I am falling hard and fast for him. I just hope that he is falling just as hard for me too.

Sighing, I push myself off from the wall and move towards the shower. Maybe if I can get this day out of the way quickly then I can ask Sky to go on a date with me tonight, even if it is sitting in our tower eating a meal we cooked.

Chapter 46

I waited in front of the bathroom door, Alice giving me a knowing smirk as she goes back to reading Allisara's schedule for the next two weeks, making notes in her own tablet of what she will need to do as my second in command of the Violet Guards. I know she is waiting for the day I have to step down and she can take my spot as Commander of the Violet Guards one day but I still don't know how I should feel about it. I love Allisara and I want to be with her. If things go our way I will one day be King beside her, but it will be hard when I am not a Noble.

The sound of the water is finally heard from behind the muffled door and my mind decides now is the time to imagine what she might look like as the water cascades down her naked body.

"Stop that." I grumble, shaking my head before running my fingers through my hair. That kiss from earlier is definitely one I have been dying to do and my body definitely agrees with my heart and brain that I want more. But I won't rush Allisara into it. She has most of her memories back, even remembers more about that night fourteen years ago when I helped rushed her to safety, but she doesn't remember me as the boy that protected her. The boy that was there for her and would do anything for her.

She wants me, that I know for sure, but I can see the hesitation in her eyes and I curse myself for being so stupid that day when I confessed about loving the girl in the photo on my fireplace mantle even though she is the girl in that photo.

"You look like you could use a cold shower." Alice's voice chimes clearly in the quiet room, Clarice and Millia looking over at me and giggling. I groan in frustration, sending a glare at Alice for pointing out the obvious but she just sticks her tongue at me before returning to what she is doing.

"I need something to keep my mind off of Allisara." I mumble, getting a chuckle from Alice.

"You only call her by her full name when she isn't around. Why don't you call her that when she is?" Fuck. Alice is seriously becoming the annoying little sister I never wanted.

"She told me to call her Alli, so I do." I answer, getting an eye roll from the blonde woman.

"Well maybe next time you kiss her senseless, moan her full name. That will make her change her mind." Clarice teases. Deciding that I am not going to win with these three women in the room, I mumble something about needing to check on the prisoners in the Dungeons and stride out of the room, their laughter following me even after closing the doors. I think I need to get Allisara new Guards and maybe a few new Maids.

Making my way through the Palace and down to the Dungeons, I check on Juden and make sure he is in his room. It seems he has decided to behave today and honestly, part of me wished he would have tried something to give me a reason to punch him. Max is sitting in the interrogation room now turned office, a few other Guards he personally picked helping him go through a list of who will be transferred to one of the nearest prisons.

"Any problem today?" I ask, leaning against the door and watching the four men work.

"No. Juden is being docile surprisingly, but something tells me he is up to something." Max answers, getting up from his chair and joining me by the door. He looks like he's aged a few years since I saw him yesterday.

"I have a bad feeling Sky, like something big is about to happen." He whispers, pulling me towards the stairs and out of earshot of the other Guards. He then goes on to explain some files are missing from the cabinets but thankfully he had digitized them into our files meant for Arian, him and I. I frown, when he goes on to tell me some footage from the cameras are missing during the night and asked if he could put up a few hidden cameras without anyone else but the two of us knowing. I agree, explaining that keeping Juden secured is our top priority and a look of relief fills Max's face.

"How are the others handling the situation since yesterday?" We are sitting on the stairs, the two of us looking down the long corridor of cell doors and I wonder just when was the last time the Dungeons were this full.

"Pretty good. Liz and Ron are coming to terms with their home being destroyed but Lillian and Everette are trying to convince them to move into the Palace with Allisara." Max nods, accepting my answer and the two of us begin to talk about what to expect with Juden. After last night's attack, I tell him that Lillian and Everette had a conference via video call with the Cabinet members and they all agreed to executing Juden and his men sooner than planned. That he and his influence needed to end now for Nimairene to prosper. Max agrees and promises to keep his eye out for any Traitors coming to see Juden at night. I leave the Dungeons with a feeling of unease before walking back up the stairs. If what Max said is true, I need to talk to Arian and make sure the security cameras are working in the Palace.

"Sky!" Turning to the person who calls my name, I spot Ron and Everette walking towards me, the two old men looking like long time friends. Ron has a new cane; his old one being left at his now destroyed house in our rush to leave.

"Afternoon." I greet the two, catching the weariness in Ron's face. He's been through so much in the last twenty four hours and I feel for him.

"We were heading to grab a snack while the women talk with Little Sara." Everette explains when they reach me, making me smile.

"Yeah, Allisara wasn't happy about waking up today. I think she blames herself for Liz and Ron loosing their home." I state, giving Ron an apologetic smile.

"Well it's not her fault." The old man states, slamming his cane on the floor. I agree with him, stating it's Juden's fault for everything and how I can't wait for him to be executed soon.

"Honestly, I blamed myself for Allisara disappearing for fourteen years and made it my mission to find her." Walking with the two men towards the kitchen, I let out the guilt I have felt for such a long time. Ron stops walking, causing me and Everette to turn back and that is when I see the shocked face of Ron staring back at me.

"You knew her before she ended up in the Slums?" He asks quietly. I look to Everette, the Marquis being there for me since child hood when

I promised the late King I would protect his daughter the day of her Christening. He nods, a silent permission to tell Ron the truth. I take a deep breath and look to the man Allisara calls her adopted Grandfather and decide I can trust him not to tell her. Allisara needs to remember everything on her own.

"I was the first person outside of her family to hold her when she was born. At the time I was five and had grown up in the Palace as the gardener's son" I begin, taking a moment to collect my thoughts as memories flash by my mind.

"That was the same day I took the Squire apprenticeship when Knights were still around. Juden got rid of them eight years ago." I continue, a light smile on my face.

"Her father told me that she is going to need a Knight to care for her and protect her and without realizing it, I blurted out that I will be her Knight. Her father was shocked, then smiled and laughed and told me I had six months to prove myself to him to be her protector. So I worked hard." My smile grows as I think about kneeling in front of the six month old princess, swearing to train hard be the protector she needs.

"In the end, we grew up together and on the day of the Rebellion, the Knight I squired under and I took her to the apple farm his family owned. That bastard gave up Allisara's location without a second thought and Juden got to her." I can feel anger rise in my as I think about that confession Juden gave. How he retrieved Allisara from the apple farm with intent to kill her. If it weren't for that doctor, Allisara would have died.

"Sky blamed himself for years even with Lillian, Christopher and I reassuring him that he did nothing wrong. He was to be Knighted eight years ago but Knights were disbanded the day of his Knighting. I think now it was Juden's way of protecting his men. Little Sara has no idea who Sky is, her memories of him are still sealed, but we all pray she remembers him. It's clear she is already in love with Sky and I think we can both agree we want him as our grandson-in-law." Everette pats me on the shoulder, leaving his hand there as he has done so many time in the past. I smile at the Marquis, feeling the grandfatherly love he has shown me since childhood radiating off of him. This is one thing I have always had over Demitrias, the love and respect of Allisara's maternal family, something he would never have.

"Well, hang in there Sky. Its the ones we love most that are some times harder to remember when we loose our minds." Ron steps closer to me, resting his hand on my free shoulder and giving me a smile.

"My Elizabeth was in an accident three years after we were married. We lost our unborn baby and Liz lost the ability to have any more. I think it was the pain and grief that caused her to loose memories of our eight year relationship but I stood by her until one day she woke up crying, telling me how sorry she was and that she remembered everything." He sighs as he turns to look at the window. A sad smile on his wrinkled face.

"It took another year of healing for Liz to be able to return to normal again." Shocked by his confession, I pull Ron into a hug and promise him that if Allisara and I were to get married and have kids, he and Liz would be a part of their lives as Grandparents. Everette agrees with me, calling Ron family for how he took care of Allisara. The three of us continue to the kitchen, me feeling closer to the two men and I wonder if with Everette's and the rest of the Blanchard's Estate family members support, maybe I can have a future as Allisara's husband.

Chapter 47

"You almost done Alli?" Alice calls out from the door way just as I turn off the shower. I sigh, sticking my head our of the door to see my friend looking at me.

"Give me a minute to dry off." I call back, getting an okay from her before the bathroom door closes. Taking a deep breath, I step out of the shower and grab the fluffy towel from the rack beside it, wrapping it around my body. I have a few more minutes left to myself before I need to prepare for the broadcast. Leaning against the counter, I use a smaller towel to dry my hair as my thoughts wander to that kiss with Sky – and how I wanted more as soon as he left.

My hands stop moving and I drop the towel onto the counter. I know the Nobels will push back if I try to marry Sky, so I need to set the plan in motion. Maybe I should talk to my Grandmama about throwing a Ball here, to do what needs to be done so that Sky and I can have a future together.

Smiling, I leave the bathroom and am instantly bombarded by Clarice and Millia whisking me to change into the outfit that Clarice choose – a cream blouse over black dress slacks and a pair of black strappy wedges. Once dressed, Clarice shoos Alice from the vanity chair and I am promptly plunked into it, the sisters getting to work with drying and styling my curly golden hair before dusting my face in light makeup.

"Where is Sky?" I ask once declared ready and Alice and I are on our way to meeting Liz and Grandmama who wait in my Study.

"Doing some work." Alice answers as we walk down a flight of stairs and pass a few Maids that curtsey as I walk past them.

"Probably had to have a cold shower after leaving the bathroom." She continues, teasing me. I blush, looking away from the keen eyed blonde and focus on making my way to my Study. Thankfully Alice stops her teasing and we make it to my Study in silence.

Stepping inside, I spot Liz and Grandmama on the sofa, the two ladies drinking tea by the fire while Liz explains that Guards had come back with items not destroyed in the explosion. I smile, asking Alice to call Arian for me so that I can thank him, only to be told that the Captain of my Guards will be in the Broadcasting Room later for safety protocol as new reporters will be in attendance. I have already escaped three assassination attempts in the last few weeks and Arian is worried something might happen during my broadcasting. I nod and decide to make my presence known by stepping off the carpet and onto the hard wood of the Study.

"Oh, Alli you're here!" Liz exclaims, getting up from her seat and waddling over pulling me into her arms. I hug her back, asking how she is doing as my eyes scan her from head to toe. She is wearing a dress, one similar to what she would wear in her house, but this one I can tell is made of finer material. Her feet are slipped inside a sturdy pair of black kitten heels, the same kind Liz always wore when going out for errands, and I smile. These ones aren't worn out like the pair she used daily and they seem to be even more comfortable too by the way she walks without a slight wince. The clothes look new and I have a feeling my Grandmama had a hand in this. The only thing that worries me are the dark bags under her eyes and the exhaustion that her body radiates.

"I am doing okay. Lillian here is helping me get used to Palace life." She waves me off as my Grandmama comes to hug me, the two little old ladies look thick as thieves as they look at one another with smiles. I accept her answer, knowing that I can't do much for her other then offer her a home here in the Palace the way her and Ron offered me a home twelve years ago.

"Come sit with us, we have a lot to discus." Grandmama takes my hand in hers, pulling me towards the sofa. With a mug of tea in each of our hands, the two look to one another before looking to me, a look of unease in their eyes.

"News reporters have been to our house." Liz begins, sighing as she looks down at her fresh mug of tea.

"They started reporting about my house being blown up with you inside. That the Palace Guards were combing the ruins for our – your – remains." She continues, a tear falling down her face.

"No one corrected them, wanting the world to know what has happened. We even slipped a few anonymous tips stating how Juden tried to kill you in the past and how he is still trying while imprisoned. We also mentioned how a Doctor helped to erase your memory to protect you in the past." My Grandmama picks up where Liz stops, giving me a small smile as she placed a hand on Liz's shoulder.

"We are also searching for that Doctor that Juden took you to. Hopefully we can find and keep him safe from Juden's men." Shocked, I place my mug on the table, needing a moment to process this information.

"So you let the news slip on why I was missing and how it happened?" I ask quietly.

"Yes but not all the information was given. Just enough to cause a stir in our favour. We want to paint the narrative that Juden's men are trying to start another Rebellion." Grandmama confirms. Standing, I begin pacing the floor in front of the fireplace, unable to sit still for the moment.

"With this news, how do you think the people are reacting?" I ask, pausing for a moment to take a deep breath.

"They are furious. Your act in cleaning the Slums and creating job opportunities for those around Zalaris has made them love you. Even abolishing specific laws has helped the people." Liz is the one to answer, a smile on her wrinkling face as she picks up a remote from the side table. She turns on the T.V., shocking me as the picture that hangs above the fireplace mantel flickers and a news broadcasting appears. The woman is standing in the Slums - specifically my street - standing across the road from the remains of Liz and Ron's house. My mouth opens in shock at the remains of the building with burnt wood. Palace Guards roam around the property while construction workers help to remove the debris into a dumpster. It is clear that someone ordered them to clean up and I have a feeling it was Arian.

"Sky and Arian asked for our house to be rebuilt, but Ron and I don't know if we will be moving back." I hum a noise of acknowledgment while I focus on the news reporter. She is talking to a woman I met when her and her family moved into the slums five years ago. Her husband had left her for some woman he met at work and this was the only home she could buy after selling everything her husband left behind. The woman, Beatrice, gushes on about how I helped her and her family move in while explaining the dangerous parts of the Slums and areas to watch out for. She talked about how I watched her sons on the nights she worked late and even cooked meals for them when Beatrice ended up sick. She even explained how the Slums rejuvenation project helped her family into gaining employment with the hotel they are staying in, giving her a better position as a cook for the day time and better hours to be with her kids.

"Allison... I mean Princess Allisara is a godsend. She is a Princess by the people, for the people." Beatrice ends, wiping tears from her eyes.

"You called her Allison, why is that?" The reporter asks, her blue eyes filled with confusion.

"Because that was the name the Princess went by in the Slums. She told everyone that that was the name told to her by a Doctor after she lost her memories. Everyone knew she was an amnesiac; she never hid it." Beatrice answers with a wistful smile. The reporter finishes her questions and Beatrice moves off screen. With Beatrice gone, the reporter moves on to explain that there is still no news from the Palace about my well being and safety then ends her speech wishing for my safe return.

Liz turns off the T.V. and silence encompasses the Study. Turning to face the three ladies in the room, I catch Alice looking at me with admiration in her eyes. She came into the Palace as a Guard and became one of my closest friends. Turning to look at Liz and Grandmama, I see them looking at me patiently and take a deep breath. I can see why addressing the press and the Kingdom is so important now.

"What do you need me to do?"

Chapter 48

Standing in the dressing room, I peak out from the behind the curtain to see an array of reporters from news crews to social media bloggers to those looking for a scoop for the Zalaris Star - the Capitol City's news paper. It seems that my Uncle spared no corners when it came to inviting anyone and everyone who could get the word out.

"Are you okay?" Sky's voice is just beside my ear, making me jump as I turn to face him. He chuckles, tucking a strand of hair behind my ear and making me smile.

"Nervous, but I can do it." I answer, taking his free hand in mine and relishing in his touch. Alice had told me that Sky went to check on Juden and the security in the Dungeons before he ran into Ron and my Grandfather. She had sent a Maid to find the three men to come meet us in the Broadcasting Room, which they thankfully did. I don't think I could face all those people waiting in the crowd for me without Sky beside me.

"Well, you get through this and then we can go on a much needed date." He leans down and presses a soft kiss to my lips, preventing me from saying anything for a moment. Date. He said date. I smile into the kiss as I think about what we could do for our date before the kiss ends and he straightens, staring down at me with a smirk.

"Where are we going for our date?" I question, the anxiety of facing the room full of people forgotten.

"Where ever you want to go, Allisara." He whispers my name, my full name, the sound of it coming of his tongue making me shiver in delight. I know I should say something, correct Sky into calling me Alli like always but I can't help and like the way he says my name. Its like he is claiming me as his. The truth is, I am his. At least, I hope I am. Maybe this long awaited date can be the one we clear up who we are to each other.

"I have a place in mind we can go, Skylard ." My voice is also a whisper, not wanting to disturb this small moment between us. His smirk drops in surprise before another bright smile shines on his face, my own lips curving into one that I know matches his. Our moment comes to an end though as Ellisia walks towards me, telling me it is almost time for the broadcast and that I need the final touch ups before I face the crowd.

Ellisia had come to help with preparations for today, helping Uncle Christopher with everything from welcoming the press to bringing refreshments. When the reporters, bloggers and press were sat in the room just beyond the curtains I stood behind, she came to the dressing room to help all of us that will be standing on the stage look presentable.

"Sorry Sky but I need her now." Ellisia shrugs, taking my hand and pulling me towards the small vanity where she retouches my makeup. Liz comes up behind us, her face filled with admiration and grandmotherly love as we look at each other through the mirror's reflection.

"Would you like to do the finishing touch, my Lady?" Ellisia asks Liz, backing away and motioning to the tiara that sits on the vanity. It isn't the usual amethyst one I wear but a decorative rose gold with diamonds and a ruby statement piece.

"Just call me Liz, dear." Liz calls out, making me laugh as Ellisia looks at her with a look of confusion.

"I am sorry my Lady, but seeing as your are the Princess' grandmother, you will be addressed as such." I can see Liz wanting to argue with her, but she decides not to as Ellisia lifts the pillow the tiara rests on and holds it out to Liz. The elderly woman sighs and with shaky hands, she lifts the tiara from the pillow and places it gently onto my head. She carefully rearranges my curly locks around the tiara before backing away.

"Beautiful." She mumbles, her smile filled with pride.

"I agree." My Grandmama muses as she comes to stand beside Liz, placing a hand on the other woman's shoulder.

"Now lets head onto the stage before Christopher has a conniption." She adds with a laugh, motioning for Liz to follow her as she walks towards my Grandfather and Ron. Sky comes to stand beside me, offering his hand to me which I take, standing to my feet and joining the others at the entrance. I think about what Ellisia said, of Liz being my grandmother, and she is right. Liz and Ron are my Grandparents just as much as Lillian and Everette are.

"Presenting Marquis and Marquess Blanchard, Lady and Lord Rinmer, Sir Skylard Blackhawk and her Royal Highness, Princess Allisara Nimair of the Kingdom of Nimairene." A Butler calls out as the curtains part. My Grandparents are the first to walk out, the two taking a seat on the stage. Next, Liz and Ron take a seat, Liz blushing at the attention as people call for Ron and her to look their way but they too take a seat. Sky leads me to the last two remaining seat that are situated between Liz and Grandmama, the two of us walking to our destination with our heads held high. We both take our seat, Sky giving my hand one last reassuring squeeze before we have to behave in front of the cameras with the red lights indicating they are on and live.

My Uncle walks onto the stage, his body clothed in a well tailored designer suit and I recognize Lidia's handiwork instantly by the cufflinks on his cuffs. He takes a stand at the podium, his face an emotionless mask as he looks towards the crowd of reporters and press.

"Welcome people of the press, reporters and those seeking the truth." He begins, speaking into the mic attached to the podium.

"I am Lord Christopher Blanchard, Uncle to Princess Allisara and I would like to let you all know that after a third assassination attempt, my niece is safe and Sound." He continues, the press asking multiple questions as he pauses. He holds out his hand, the crowd pausing for a moment giving my Uncle a chance to speak once again.

"If you have questions, please hold them till the end after Princess Allisara has spoken." My Uncle exclaims, the flashes of cameras peppering the air in front of us and capturing his image.

"Now, I welcome my niece, Princess Allisara, to take the podium as this is her press conference." He introduces me, stepping to the side of the Podium and holding his hand out to me. I stand from my chair and walk towards him, placing my hand in his and watch as he lifts it and places a kiss on the back. I thank him for putting this conference together so fast and watch as he walks to his own chair that is placed beside my Grandfather before I turn to face the crowd.

"Good evening the people of Zalaris. I am Allisara Crestal Nimair, Princess of Nimairene and soon to be Queen." I start and take a deep breath. Grandmama and Liz prepared me with what to say but I need to state everything in my own words.

"Yesterday during the parade I was attacked for the second time since returning to my rightful place, the first attempt was that I was poisoned at a privet event I was invited to weeks ago." I begin, watching horror fill the eyes of those before me.

"After the first attack, my Guards and I managed to escape using the back alleyways of the Slums and sought shelter with my adoptive Grandparents. Unfortunately that night their house was broken into and explosives destroyed their home. This was the third attempt on my life just hours after the shooting at the parade." I watch as a look of unease settles across the people before me and I wonder just what the people watching the broadcast are thinking.

"Your Highness, do you know who is behind this attack?" A man calls out, holding his microphone towards me. I smile in his direction before answering.

"The culprits are a part of Juden Trilavantas' faction. The ex-regent has confessed that the Rebellion that took place fourteen years ago killing many innocent lives, including my parents, was caused by him. His people want to see me dead with Juden back on the Throne." A collection of gasps and disbelief resonates around the room. I wait for them to settle down and ask the one question I am waiting for. Finally a woman stands up with her hand raised timidly in the air. I nod at her and she takes a deep breath. She looks like a blogger with how the man behind her films this interaction on a small device, but the unmistakable red light tells me she is live as well.

"Do you have any proof of this confession, your Highness?" She asks, her voice shaking slightly.

"I do, actually." Happy that someone asked the question I have been waiting for, I pick up the remote on the podium and turn to the screen behind my family, pressing play. The screen turns on and the video recording of Juden's confession plays out. The room is pin-drop silent, the crowd before me captivated by the video as my interrogation with Juden continues. When he gets to the point of how he was going to kill me, someone shouts out in outrage and a resounding *"shhhh"* sounds around the room. Finally the video comes to an end and I turn back to address everyone.

"Juden Trilavantas was like family to me. For the first six years of my life I called him my Uncle and was set to marry his son Demitrias." I begin, closing my eyes as the memories of Juden and my father laughing and talking flashes through my mind.

"But due to his greed, he betrayed my family in order to take the Throne. Had he waited till my twenty first birthday, Demitrias and I would have married and his family would have become royalty in the end. Instead, he wanted to be King." I feel tears falling down my face and I refuse to wipe them away. My people need to see the pain this caused me. That even through my tears I stand tall ready to fight.

"As he mentioned in his confession, Jude took me to a Doctor and it is because of this doctor that I am still alive. He sealed my memories and sent me into the Slums of Zalaris so that I had a fighting chance at living and could make it to the age of twenty – the age I am now – so that my memories could return to me and I can return as your rightful Queen." I paused, taking a deep shaky breath before smiling into the cameras.

"I promise to be the Queen the people of Nimairene deserve. I have already started by reforming the Military, removing those in power that took Juden's side. I have started abolishing the laws that Traitor created the last fourteen years and replacing them with laws that will benefit the people. But most importantly I have started rejuvenating the Slums and helping those find proper jobs that will help support their families. All of this is happing in Zalaris, but soon my plans will spread to the outer Provinces so that everyone can live a good life." Someone, a man with a recording device pointed towards me, asks what steps I have taken for the Slums and I happily explain that I am helping to rebuild many of the broken and run down homes, documenting ownership with those that have lived in said buildings for years. That I have helped others find jobs within and outside Zalaris. This answer placates him as he returns to his seat and I am able to continue speaking.

"Yesterday the fair planned for the Spring Parade was ruined by the shooters. As such I want to apologize to the people for this and in three days time I will have fairs around and outside the city take place. At the same time a Ball will take place for the Nobles to come to the Palace so that I may get to know the Nobles that help run the Kingdom." No one interrupts me this time and I am thankful for that as the last part is something I dread saying. It's been fourteen years since the last Rebellion and right now I need to stop any chances of another one occurring. For that, I need to do one thing that I have been looking forward to for the last few weeks since putting that man into the dungeons.

"Although we have fun times ahead of us, there are some unfortunate actions I need to take to prevent another rebellion that may lead into a civil war." The crowd starts firing question after question about what these actions are and I have to wait for them to settle once more before I can continue. The frown on my face must have been the signal that I was growing impatient and someone begins shushing the crowd until they all return to their seats with embarrassed looks.

"My people have interrogated many of Juden's men, including Juden himself. We have found that many of their family members had no clue of them turning Traitors as well as many that also turned Traitors. You may have noticed land being seized in the name of the Crown and the Trilavantas are no exception." I take another deep breath before continuing, my hands clenching into fists as I brace myself for another onslaught of questions I don't want to answer.

"I have canceled the engagement between Demitrias Trilavantas and I. Have taken back many of the land that belonged to all the Traitors but left some to those that are innocent so that they may rebuild their life after their spouses, children and relatives left them destitute by turning their backs to the Crown. I have removed people from rank and made them normal citizens and have taken shops and business that were used to fund Juden and his Rebellion. I hate that I have to do this, hate to know that people my family have trusted for generations would turn their backs on us just for money and power, but I hate that in a weeks time I will have to publicly execute many of these men and women because of the choices they made." The crowd gasps and shouts in dismay at this announcement. A public execution hasn't happened in over sixty years. I catch sight of my reflection in the glasses of some man in the crowd. I stand tall, my face a mask of pain and determination with tear streaks along my cheeks. This is the person I want to portray to my people, a Queen who has compassion for those she rules over but is determined to do what is right for the good of her Kingdom.

"My Uncle, Lord Christopher Blanchard will read a list of who is to be executed when I am done and answer questions related to this but I want to end with this warning for my people. As much as this may scare you all, please prepare yourselves for a Rebellion and a possible civil war. We have yet to find all of those associated with Juden Trilavantas but we are doing the best we can to hunt each and every Traitor down. I, as your soon to be Queen, will do everything in my power to prevent a civil war, but I cannot guarantee my preventions will work. That is all I have to say." With that, I return to my seat and my Uncle takes the podium. He begins with reading out a list of well known Traitors, starting with the ones who's minor involvement sent them to the Provinces or prison and demoted their whole family to commoner status. Some of the reporters in the crowd asks questions and he patiently answers them. I am thankful that he is able to take charge as this whole conference has left me feeling exhausted and sad. So many people want me dead for no other reason than because I am Royalty standing in the way of their greed.

Uncle Christopher continues the list, this time announcing the names of those to be executed and what punishment their family received due to their actions. The last name to be read is Juden's stating he will be the first to be executed for the crimes he committed fourteen years ago and over the course of his regency. No one protests to this, as the shock from the truth has worn off. Finally the conference comes to an end and Sky helps escort me from the stage. Guards will escort the reporters off the Palace grounds thankfully and I am happy to be done with everything.

"When did we decide on a ball?" My Grandmama asks when we enter the dressing room, giving me a pointed look.

"When I was addressing the press." I shrug, thanking Ellisia as she hands me a glass of water and greedily drink the cool liquid.

"Well, at least you gave use three days to prepare." She grumbles, but I can see the excitement in my Grandmama's eyes. I have learned since reuniting with her that she lives for Balls and Functions and to have free reign to plan one in the Palace must be making her giddy like a child on Christmas morning. My Grandfather chuckles, wrapping his arm around my shoulders and pulling me to his side for a small hug.

"You do know you'll have to wear a ballgown again, right." He states, making me roll my eyes.

"I know. But I have a few announcements I want to make in front of the Nobels, and what better place than at a Ball." I shrug as my Grandfather smirks, his eyes darting to look at Sky who is talking with Liz and Ron.

"Do those announcements have anything to do with those three?" He whispers into my ear and I nod, my lips curving into a soft smile.

"They do."

Chapter 49

"You did great, Allisara." Entering the Palace hallways, Sky pulls me to his side and kisses the top of my head. I blush, still liking the way my name sounds on his lips.

"Thank you." I whisper quietly, reaching up and pulling the tiara from my head. Sky chuckles, taking the dainty jewelry from my hand and passing it to Clarice as she comes beside me, asking her to take it to my room. She complies and then is gone in a flash. Sky and I walk quietly down the halls, aimlessly wandering for a moment until we find ourselves in the kitchen.

"Where are you taking me for our date?" Sky asks as he watches me from where he stands leaning against the counter, an amused smirk on his face watching me run around the kitchen and trying to not get in the way of the staff. An idea came to mind as and soon I found myself getting a picnic basket together as I know it will be perfect for our date.

"You'll see." I shrug, giving Sky a wink as I place the last items into the basket. He rolls his eyes, coming to wrap his arms around me and placing a swift kiss on my lips. Before I can protest, he takes the basket into his right hand. With a blush on my face, I take his left hand in mine and drag him towards the garage.

"Does where we are going require a vehicle?" He tries guessing, making me shrug in response.

"I wouldn't say a vehicle, but a motorcycle would do." He laughs at my response as we walk into the room, the lights flicking on. I already know what motorcycle I want to take; I had seen it the first time Sky brought me into here. Sky follows behind me, keeping a few steps back until we come to a stop in front of a teal Harley Davidson FLTRXST Road Glide ST made just over two hundred years ago in the year two-thousand and twenty-three. I look to Sky with a grin, wanting so badly to get on the motorcycle and ride away.

"We need helmets before we can go anywhere." He grins as he looks down at me. I smirk, moving towards the saddle bags and pulling out a helmet from each one, Sky shaking his head as I hand the larger size to him while I take the picnic basket from his hand and maneuver it into the saddle bag on the right side of the motorcycle

"Where are we going?" He asks, helmet in hand as he watches me with an amused smile.

"Out of the city. There is a lake just to the South I used to sneak to when the summer was unbearable." I answer.

"I know where that is. Dad used to take me there all the time." I smile, happy to know that Sky knows the way. Stepping closer to him, I stand on my tip toes and press a kiss to his lips before backing up and putting on my own helmet. Sky rolls his eyes, lightly rapping his knuckles against my helmet and dodges my hand as I try to slap his hand away with a chuckle. I want to stick my tongue out at him but he wont be able to see it with the helmet blocking all but my view. Thankfully Sky decides now is the right time to put his helmet on and now with both of us ready, it is time to go. Sky is the first to move, climbing onto the bike before I climb in behind him, wrapping my arms around his waist.

"Hang on!" He calls out, voice muffled by the helmet. With that warning, the bike roars to life and without a minute longer, we are off. The motorcycle zooms out of the garage and through the hidden entrance. The barn doors open and we once again drive past the farm beside the Palace. The wind is still chilly from the early Spring air and I am thankful that I cling onto Sky, the warmth from his body seeping into me. The ride is uneventful and I watch the city pass by through the tint of the helmet. The people I see walk with a weariness to them, the events of yesterday plus the broadcast from earlier must have been hard on them as well. I cling tighter to Sky and close my eyes. I don't want to see my people like this and hopefully their lives will get easier with Juden's execution.

I feel the bike beneath me speed up after a few moments making me open my eyes where I see that we have left the city. Farmland pass us by and I notice a few cows and sheep enjoying the small bit of fresh grass grown where snow has melted. I shiver, realizing I should have grabbed a jacket before leaving the Palace, but I had to get away after going through so much in such a short time.

Sky turns onto a small side road, the country landscape turning into a forest with many tall trees reaching towards the sky. I smile, slowly sitting straighter to get a better view. The lake isn't far now.

The motorcycle is smoothly navigated through the twist and turns of the road, Sky controlling the bike with ease. The trees block out the wind but the shade causes the area to be a little chillier now that the sun has a hard time reaching us. I expect Sky to go straight to the lake, but he by-passes it, turning left instead and surprising me. After another stretch of forest lined road, Sky steers the motorcycle to the right coming to a stop in front of small log cabin with a path to the lake that I can see just in the background.

With the motorcycle turned off, Sky flips the kickstand and I carefully climb off, taking my helmet off and enjoying the view.

"Who owns the cabin?" I ask, turning back to watch Sky take his helmet off and shake out his hair.

"I do. It used to belong to my mother and when she passed, I inherited it." He bends down, carefully removing the picnic basket from the saddle bag. I hand Sky my helmet and take the basket from him to put away and once the helmets are in the saddle bags, he takes my hand and leads me into the small cabin.

"We should have a few blankets we can use to keep warm for our picnic by the water." Sky muses, letting go of my hand to search for said blankets. I take this time to look around, placing the basket on the bench in the entrance way as Sky disappears behind a door on the right side of the back wall. Infront of me is a small sitting area, the couches facing a large fireplace that has logs waiting to be lit.

To the right of me is a small kitchen, the large window letting in lots of sunlight that manage to slip past the trees. To the left is a small table under another large window. I can see flower boxes on the outside and I can't help but wonder just what flowers used to grow there.

"I found a few blankets." Sky calls out, entering the main living space. Looking towards him I see the corner of a bed inside the room he came from. A pile of blankets are in his arms and as he comes closer to me, he sets the blankets down before wrapping the top one around my shoulders. It smells like him, like pine, and I wonder if he uses a pine scented laundry soap as well.

"Thank you." I whisper, watching Sky pick up the second blanket.

"You're welcome Allisara." He smiles, bending down and pressing a quick soft kiss to my lips.

"Now come on, I have a perfect spot for a picnic." With that, he opens the door and lets me walk through first after I grab the picnic basket before he takes my hand and leads me down a small path. The forest is slowly coming to life after the long winter and I spot a few early spring flowers already blooming. It makes me happy seeing the small purple blooms and green leaves surrounding it. I think these flowers are called trilliums. The walk takes all of five minutes and soon we find ourselves standing by the banks of the lake, the water rippling with soft waves. He takes me to a dry corner just under the sun and shakes out the blanket.

"My mother used to love having picnics here when I was little. My dad and I continued the tradition of coming here for a picnic every summer after she was gone." He explains, taking the basket from my hand and plopping himself onto the blanket. I step out of my heels and onto the blanket, sitting beside him.

"My dad is getting to old to continue the tradition but I want to continue it when I have my own kids." He continues, turning to look at me. Our eyes meet and I swear my heart skips a beat as I see the love and lust in the depths of his emerald green eyes. I blush, my mind wondering what a family with Sky might look like.

"What are you thinking about?" Sky whispers, leaning closer to me.

"N-nothing." I stutter out, my voice a whisper.

"I don't think its nothing." He chuckles, his voice deep and husky. His lips connect to mine once again. This kiss is fast and demanding and I am pulled onto his lap, his hands move to wrap around my waist. The kiss deepens when he bites my bottom lip, asking to be let in. I moan, parting my lips and feeling his tongue slip inside, the two of us not holding back. I can feel myself growing lightheaded and soon I pull away gasping for breath. Sky continues to kiss me though, his lips pressing along my jaw, my neck and even my collar bone. I shiver, my body growing hot for a moment.

"Allisara." He moans my name, making me shiver again, my hands fisting his hair and lightly tugging.

"Sky, I think we are moving to fast." The kisses slow down to a stop, Sky pulling away to look at me after taking a few deep breaths to calm himself.

"Sorry, I got carried away." He blushes, resting his forehead against mine.

"I...I did too." I admit with a giggle. Sky chuckles, pressing a kiss to my forehead.

"Tell me to stop when you need us to stop. When you are ready, you let me know." I grin at his acceptance and rest my head on his shoulder. I am happy that Sky is willing to wait for me, willing to stop whatever heated moment we are in if I don't feel comfortable. It makes me feel safer with him.

We listen to the waves as they roll against the shore, the two of us just enjoying the silence in each other's embrace. The quiet moment ends though as my stomach grumbles and I laugh. Sky lifts me off his lap, shaking his head in amusement as he pulls the basket closer to us and helps me unload the food I packed.

We decide to enjoy our date, allowing us a moment to be just two normal adults without the worry of a possible Rebellion and an execution looming over our shoulder.

Chapter 50

Looking at my reflection in the full length mirror, I do my best to make sure the hickey Sky had given me yesterday is hidden. Today is the day of my first Ball in the Palace and I do not need tongues wagging within the Nobles gossip circles. Lidia had done a good job choosing the gown I would wear today, a dusty rose coloured gown made from organza and lace with a slit up the left side of the gown. The sleeves were full length that started flaring out at my elbow and thankfully the material hid the mark on my shoulder. My hair was kept in loose curls with a decorative clip keeping the strands out of my face while my bangs were styled with a small flat iron.

Millia and Clarice wanted me to wear stilettos but I opted for a pair of rose gold peep-toed kitten heels. It will be a long night tonight and I want comfortable shoes that I can dance the night away in or fight if something happens.

Since the broadcasting three days ago I have been feeling uneasy. Max and his men promised to stay in the dungeon until the date of the execution but when Sky told me about Max's concerns the day after our date I have been feeling anxious. Like something will happen if I am not cautious.

"Will you be wearing any jewelry Princess?" Millia's voice calls me from my thoughts and I turn to face her. My hand instinctively reaches for the necklace with my crest on it. Ever since returning from the cabin with Sky I have constantly worn the necklace again, needing the comfort it brought me as a child now more than ever. Something inside me screams for me to keep it close and I need to figure out why.

"A gold tiara that matches this necklace please." I answer my Maid, getting a small bow before she returns to my closet and returns moments later with a simple tiara with small crystals twinkling under the light. She helps secure it on top of my head before producing two dainty hoops. I chuckle, carefully removing the silver studs from my earlobe and bend down for Millia to place the hoops in. She takes my studs and shuffles into the closet once more, most likely returning the jewelry to their rightful place.

"Allisara, are you ready?" I blush as my bedroom door opens, turning just in time to watch Sky step inside my room. He is dressed in a dark grey suit, the amethyst pin pinned to his breast pocket where a dusty rose handkerchief pokes out. His hair is slicked back into a half up pony-tail held together by a matching dark grey ribbon. His steps faulter as he takes in my appearance. His smile fading as a look of awe and adoration takes its place.

"Wow." He whispers out, his eyes scanning me from head to toe. I burst out laughing as his lack of words and step down from the platform, carefully lifting the long gown so as not to step on the hem.

"I am so getting you a dictionary – and maybe a thesaurus - for your birthday." I tease while making my way towards him. He takes my left hand in his, bringing it to his lips and pressing a soft kiss to the back of my hand.

"It's not my fault you're so breathtaking that I forget how to speak properly." He teases, making me blush.

"Well you don't see me loosing my ability to speak even though you are extremely handsome." An amused smile takes over my lips as I tease him back, Millia and Clarice giggling behind me as Sky blushes.

"Is everything ready for tonight?" I ask, my tone turning serious. I need this Ball to go off without a hitch.

"Yes, security is in place and your guests are arriving." Sky reassures me, letting go of my hand. He reaches into the back pocket of his pants, causing me to tilt my head to see what he is doing.

"I have something that will go great with your outfit." He states, pulling out a small box and giving me my favourite easy going smile.

"Sky you shouldn't have." I mumble, looking down at the black box in his hands. He just smiles at me, taking my hand once more and gently placing the box inside it.

"I wanted to give you something because I love you." He whispers. My head snaps up at this statement, our eyes meeting. I can feel tears welling in them and do my best to not let them spill. He loves me. Sky loves me.

Looking back down to the box, I open it to reveal a gold bracelet, a rose charm evenly spaced around it with dainty chains holding it all together. I gasp at how beautiful it is, watching as small crystals glitter in the middle of each rose.

"Please don't take this the wrong way, but I did have a craftsman place a tracker inside one of the roses." He mutters out, rubbing the back of his neck.

"Why? I never leave your side." I ask, letting Sky take the bracelet out and place it onto my left wrist.

"I don't want to loose you again. But know I will always find you." He whispers, pulling me against his body and placing a kiss on my forehead.

"I see." I whisper, resting my head against him. I did not miss the word *again* and wonder what he means by it. Sometimes I get the feeling Sky is hiding things from me, but I never push him for answers because I know deep down he will never hurt me.

"We should get going." Pulling away from Sky, I loop my left arm through his right holding on tight to him. The bracelet catches the lights overhead and the crystals sparkle as we move. Millia and Clarice send us off, telling us to have a fun time tonight before they turn to go to their own rooms. I gave them the night off, telling them to go do something fun since the Ball will be going on well past midnight tonight.

Sky helps me to descend the stairs so that I do not trip over the hem of my dress. He remarks that Lidia should have given me something shorter, but I remind him that the dress code for women are ballgowns. He mutter something about dress codes being stupid and I laugh, nearly tripping over the hem of my gown because of the distraction. Sky takes this as a reason to scoop me into his arms and carrying me down the rest of the stairs.

"We should change the dress code when you are Queen." He states once we reach the bottom of the stairs.

"And why is that?" I question as he sets me on my feet, making sure I am steady before letting go of me.

"Because that dress is heavy and bulky and it's hard to carry you when you wear it." I blush at his words and decide to stay silent as I loop my arm around his again, this time I am more conscious of the hem and carefully use my right hand to lift part of the skirt so that I can walk. Sky is right, these dresses are heavy but at least I decided to wear a pair of comfortable shoes.

We make our way to the Ballroom, the large solid wood double doors closed indicating all of the guests have arrived. The Guards stationed there bow as Sky and I approach them, a smile on their face as they look between Sky and me.

"Are you ready to face everyone?" Sky asks, turning me to face him. I look back at the double doors and take a deep breath. Am I ready? No, absolutely not. But I do need to face the Nobes. I have a few announcements I need to make so that Liz and Ron will be safe and so that Sky and I can one day marry each other.

"I am." I state, turning to give Sky a reassuring smile. He grins back at me, pressing a quick kiss to my lips before we turn to the Guards. I nod, and they grin back at me, telling Sky and I to have fun before they slowly push open the doors. One walks inside, most likely informing the Butler of our arrival, before he returns.

"They are ready for you two." The man states, giving Sky a fist bump.

"Thank you Derik. Make sure you two rotate shifts in three hours so you can both go home and rest." Sky thanks Derik, and I am happy to learn the name of another Guard under my employment. I thank them both before Sky escorts me into the Ballroom.

"Presenting Her Royal Highness, Princess Allisara Nimair and her escort, Captain Skylard BlackHawk of the Violet Guards." The Butler announces our arrival and the music comes to a stop. The guest turn to face Sky and I at the top of the staircase, bowing and curtsying in greeting. I spy my family standing at the foot of the stairs and I smile at them. Ron and Liz are with my Grandparents, the two dressed in a lovely gown and a black suit. I nearly laugh when I see that Ron wore a bow-tie and not a regular tie.

Taking a deep breath, I turn to face the crowd. Before the Ball can begin, I need to announce a few things.

"Good evening ladies and gentlemen of the Nobility." I begin, taking a step forward.

"I welcome you to my Palace for the first Ball since my return. I know we would all like to get right into the festivities and I would love to get to know each and every one of you, but I have a few things I need to announce." The crowd begin to whisper after my words and I do my best not to smirk. I knew this would cause a bit of a stir but I don't care. I want to be with Sky. I want Ron and Liz to be safe.

"As you all know, many people have been striped of their titles due to their family members being in cahoots with Juden Trilavantas. It has been a bit of a hassle trying to figure out who I can trust to be in control of the lands closest to the capitol city Zalaris and I come to the decision that Skylark Blackhawk and his family deserve them." I turn to see Sky stiffen at my announcement, his head snapping towards me and our gazes meet.

"He has been a loyal friend and protector since my return and nobody deserves the title of Duke more than him and his father." I continue, holding out my hand towards Sky. He hesitates for a moment, but then Sky steps forward and takes it, his face filled with smiles as he looks at me.

"I present you all to Duke Skylard BlackHawk. Sky, please tell everyone what you wish to name your lands." He takes a deep breath before he turns to face the crowd. I can see from the corner of my eye their hesitation at me proclaiming a new Duke.

"Considering the lands there are known for growing the most beautiful of flowers, Blume Dukedom." Sky announces to the crowd.

"It is settled then. May I present the Duke of Blume." I state happily, watching Sky smile widely as the crowd cheers for him.

"My final announcement before we dance the night away is I would like to welcome Elizabeth and Ronald Rinmer as Lord and Lady of the Castilla Estate." I watch as Ron and Liz look at me with shock. I let go of Sky's hand and carefully walk down the ten steps towards them, taking Liz's hands in mine as I look at both her and Ron.

"These two brave citizens took me in when I had no memory of my life as Allisara. They protected and raised me without hesitation when we met twelve years ago." I spy a tear slip from Liz's face and quickly wipe it away for her, feeling my own eyes fill with tears.

"They are my adoptive Grandparents and will be added to the Royal Genealogy as such. They deserve everything and more for being there and teaching me."

"Alli, we don't know what to say." Ron places his hand on my shoulder, his own eyes filled with unshed tears.

"You don't have to thank me. You're my family." I state, stepping forward and hugging the elderly couple. I feel a few tears slip past my eyes and I pull away. A hand quickly wipes my tears away and I notice Sky has join us, his smile wider than ever.

"With the announcements out of the way, lets enjoy our evening!" The band hired for the night begin to play, my Grandparents and their friends the first to come and congratulate Sky, Ron and Liz. I greet Count Kaitelle when Eathan comes to join us, a woman with raven black hair linked to his arm. Her gown is a deep navy, the sleeveless dress flowing around her.

"Its nice to finally meet you cousin in law. My name is Blaine Blanchard, I am Eathan's wife." The woman, Blaine, holds out her hand and I shake it, finally happy to put a face to the name. Blaine was missing from the last Ball, busy helping her sister with her first pregnancy.

"The feeling is mutual Blaine. Please, call me Alli-"

"Or Little Sara like the rest of us do." Eathan cuts me off. I playfully stick my tongue out at him, Sky chuckling beside us.

"I prefer just calling you Alli then." Blaine chuckles out. Her deep blue, eyes twinkle with mischief and I can tell right away the two of us are going to get along perfectly. Sky and Eathan decide to fetch us drinks, so Blaine and I leave the older generation to talk while we find a quiet place. I quickly learn that Blaine is one of the few women that is not a fan of Balls, but still came to finally meet me in person. We both start talking about our interest and she tells me she owns two Clydesdale – Thorn and Roza – and loves riding. I grin, telling her that my Grandparents are going to gift me the next foal of Romeo and Juliet and she goes into a tirade about how fun raising her two horses was. She invites me to come riding soon and I accept.

I tell her about how I secretly draw in my free time, my favourite medium being oil pastels. Her face scrunches up at the idea of drawing and I laugh. It seems she is more of a tomboy and I am okay with that. Eathan returns with two drinks in hand, but no Sky, and he gives me an apologetic smile.

"I think you need to save your boyfriend Little Sara." He chuckles out, handing a glass of champaign to Blaine.

"And why is that Eathan?" I inquire, narrowing my eyes at my cousin.

"Because he is surrounded by a group of vultures." Curious by what my cousin means, I excuse myself and go in search of Sky, spotting him easily with a group of women surrounding him. I can see he is trying to keep his distance, a drink in each hand. Pissed that these vultures would try and flirt with my boyfriend, I march my way towards them and push past the ladies. One went to confront me but quickly realized who I am. She whispers something to the girl beside her and soon the crowd of courtesans part. With no one blocking my way, I make it to Sky's side and take one of the glasses from his hand before wrapping my arm around his waist.

"I have been looking for you everywhere. I thought you were bringing me a drink." I pout as I take a sip of the champaign, catching a few women glaring at me. I make note of what they are wearing and plan to ask my cousin about them later.

"Sorry Allisara. I was on my way when these girls cornered me." Sky apologizes, wrapping his arm around me. His head dips and his lips connect with mine, his kiss filled with love as he claims me in front of all these people. I can hear those closest to us whisper and I try not to smirk into the kiss. They can whisper all they want. Sky is a Duke now and us being together is meant to be.

The music changes from the slow melody to a quick waltz and Sky pulls away from me. He passes his empty glass to a passing waiter before taking mine and handing it to the waiter as well. I smile, watching him glare at a woman as she tries to step close before directing his attention back to me.

"Shall we dance, beautiful?" He asks and I nod, pulling away from Sky and placing my hand in his.

"We shall." I agree, Sky placing a quick kiss to the back of my hand before leading me to the dance floor. He pulls me close, his hand on my hip as he leads me in time to the waltz. I can feel eyes on us as we dance to the music, our eyes never straying from each other. As the song comes to an end, another one plays and Blaine and Eathan joins us. Half way through the song, both sets of my Grandparents join us, Ron and Liz sticking to the outside where they can avoid the other dancing pairs due to their mobility issues. My Grandfather twirls my Grandmama around, her letting out a carefree laugh.

The third song plays and the dance floor fills with more people I laugh as this song is different and Sky twirls me around, careful not to let go of my hand at all times. By the end of the song I am ready for a break and pull him away, watching Blaine do the same with Eathan and drag him towards her father and a woman that I assume is her mother considering how similar Blaine and her look.

"That was fun." I grin, taking a sip of water as Sky and I cool off by an open window.

"It was. We should dance like this more often." He agrees, bending down and capturing my lips in a chaste kiss as soon as I put the empty cup down. A waiter walks up to us, offering a snack of fruit on skewers and I thank him, taking two. The sweet fruit are just what I needed to re-energize me and Sky takes his handkerchief out, dabbing at the corner of my mouth.

"I'd kiss you again, but the young Nobles here might get mad at me for stealing your time." He whispers in my ear, nodding his head in the direction of a group of Nobles. I sigh, realizing that I will have to dance with a few of them out of courtesy.

"Three dances with three other nobles and I am yours the rest of the night." I whisper to Sky while the Nobles edge each other on. I chuckle as one is pushed from the group, a bashful look on his face as he sheepishly walks towards Sky and me.

"I understand. Part of you being the Princess." He tucks a strand behind my ear as he looks at me lovingly, placing a kiss on my cheek.

"Go. I will find Eathan and Blaine and wait for you. Three dances and you are mine." He nudges me gently and I smile, my heart feeling full as I lean on the tips of my toes and place a kiss on his lips.

"I love you." I whisper before walking towards the timid redhead who was forced to come seek me out. I offer him a dance and he takes it with a triumphant smile on his face. The song thankfully is fast paced, but so were his hands as the one on my waist kept roaming South. I warned him twice but when he twirled me and replaced his hand, it lands on my ass with a squeeze. I pull away, slapping the redhead across the face and calling the Guards to come kick him out of my Palace for disrespecting me. The crowd watches as he begs for forgiveness and a man steps forward, a Lord, asking me to forgive his son. I warn him to get him lessons in how to not be a predator and how to treat a lady right before I go to the crowd of young Noblemen.

I tell them I have only two more dances left and one steps forward, his lanky frame screaming to me that he has two left feet when it comes to dancing and sadly I am right. He leads at first, stepping on my toes until I take charge and lead the dance instead. He apologizes about the first guy, saying that I did not deserve the treatment after the dance ends and I thank him before another of the young Nobles steps forward.

The third guy thankfully knew how to lead a dance, his hand never straying as he introduces himself as a Baron Cedric VonLicht. That he recently took the title from his father who retired two months ago.

"So what brought you to the Ball other than my invitation?" I ask as Cedric spins me around the dance floor.

"A bride. I am hoping to meet someone to fall in love with and marry them." He chuckles out. My eyes widen at his honesty. To think someone would use this event as a way to fall in love.

"Well, there are some vultures you should stay away from." He twirls me as I say this and I spy the women in the red dress that glared at me first when I found Sky. Of course the other girls would be with her, their eyes staring at me with contempt.

"Like that woman in red with the other four surrounding her." I continue, getting a scoff from Cedric.

"Patricia and her minions are on my do not date list. I know they wont make good wives." Cedric reassures me as the song comes to an end.

"Well, I will try to host more events so you can find love. I just ask for a wedding invite." I shrug, getting a chuckle from Cedric.

"Deal, Princess. Thank you for the dance but I think your Duke Blume is waiting for you." He nudges his head in the direction behind me. Turning, my eyes meets Sky's and I feel my heart skip a beat. He talks with Eathan, Blain and a woman I have met at the Blanchard Estate – my cousin Annalise. I smirk, looking back at Cedric and wondering if I can play match maker.

"Cedric, would you like to meet someone I know is single?" I ask, watching his eye widen in shock.

"A person my Princess knows personally, I feel honored." He gasps playfully. I roll my eyes, telling him to follow me if he wants as I make my way towards Sky, leaving Cedric where he stand. I miss being in Sky's arms already. Cedic quickly catches up to me when the lights flicker off. Something crashes to the ground and a few women scream in fear.

"Allisara, where are you?" Sky shouts, worry and fear in his voice. I rush towards the sound of his voice, calling out his name and hoping to find him in the dark.

"Sky, I am here!" I call out, hoping he would find me. Someone grabs my arm causing me to turn and send a punch towards them. I feel my fist connects with what I feel is their nose and I grin as they back away cursing. Before I can run away, both of my arms are captured by two more people, their rough hands locking my arms in place. I go to scream, to alert the guests of my predicament, but a sharp prick to my neck silences me as a cold liquid is injected in to my veins. Dizziness quickly dissociates me, causing my legs to give out.

"Allisara, answer me!" Sky's voice is close but I find myself unable to say anything. Tears well in my eyes as on of my captors lifts me into their arms like I weigh nothing to them.

"I have her lets go." One of my captor states quietly. I fight the sudden exhaustion that fill me, trying to say anything to attract attention to me but what ever they injected into me wins and I feel myself slip away into unconsciousness.

Chapter 51

"Allisara!" I call out into the dark. It had been a while since I heard her call out my name and I am beginning to grow frantic. The lights flickered on suddenly, the Ballroom filled with cowering Nobles clinging to one another. I look everywhere for her, spying the man she danced with on the floor with a bloodied nose. Rushing over to the man, I kneel beside him and look over his injuries.

"Where is she?" I demand after making sure that his nose isn't broken.

"I don't know where she is. I went to grab her to keep her safe and the next thing I know I have a fist flying into me and a bloodied nose." The man answers. Standing to my feet, I look around the Ballroom once more. Three songs. Three dances. She promised me that and then the rest of the night she would be mine. Now she was gone.

"Sky!" Turning to the sound of my name, I catch Alice and Kian rush towards me through the crowd.

"Alice. She's gone." I mutter out, panicking.

"Sky, it was Juden's men. They knocked the power out. Arian has the army surrounding the city. No one else has power but us." She reaches me, grabbing onto my arm and forcing me to stop pacing. I take a deep breath as her words sink in and take a moment to calm my panicking mind.

"Zalaris is out of power?" I ask, confused. How could the city loose their power.

"Yes. The generators for the Palace turned on as soon as we made it to the Ballroom. We have Guards securing the Palace as we speak now." I nod, feeling my thoughts calm down as I look around the room. If the power was out, this meant this was an inside job.

233

"Alice, you are in charge while I am gone. Everette and Lillian will help you. Kian, grab Alec and the twins. We are going after Allisara." I order. Alice nods, going in search of Allisara's Grandparents.

"Where should we meet you?" Kian asks as we march out of the Ballroom, the two of us nodding to a set of Guards as they let us out.

"Stables. This is a stealth mission and horses are the only option. Meet me there in ten minutes and I want all of you dressed in black and armed." Reaching the stairs I pause to look at Kian, seeing a grim look in his eyes.

"We will get her back, Sky." He reassures me. I say nothing. This is the third time someone took Allisara from me and I will make sure it is the last. I rush up the stairs and race towards my room, the Maids and Butlers jumping out of my way and I send an apology over my shoulder. Reaching my door, I enter my room and grab the closest black outfit I have from the closet. My phone rings as I pull the vest over my shoulder and I reach for it.

"This is Captain Sky of the Violet Guards." I answer, my phone snugged between my ear and shoulder as I grab my weapons and place them into their holsters.

"It's Max. The prisoners are secured but the security cameras aren't working properly right now. It will take some time rebooting them." I nearly throw my phone in anger as I take a deep breath. Fucking great. Allisara is missing, cameras are down and our men are already stretched thin.

"Call Alice and ask her to send you as many men as you need. Keep us posted on the situation in the dungeons." I state before hanging up. Right now I can't have any distractions. I need to find my girlfriend. Walking to my dresser, I grab the black box and open it, taking out the watch that will help me find her. Turning it on, a small light appears and I sigh with relief. She still has the bracelet on.

"Hang on Allisara, I'll find you." I whisper. Leaving my room, I take the servant's stair way as a short cut to the stables. This was like her fifth birthday all over again when bandits had taken her for ransom. She had been smart though and had taken off the beaded necklace I gave her and used the beads as a clue. No one noticed it. No one but me. I tried to get people to follow me, to find her but they all were busy searching the Palace. So I snuck away. I found her, shivering with fear in a shack up in the Northern woods. I had a small phone and called the King directly, telling him I had found Allisara and he sent three men. When they arrived I had managed to get her back home safely without help. We were soaking wet from the rain but she was safe. It turned out her cousin and her friends has pushed Allisara outside after the King and Queen announced her betrothal to Demitrias.

Lost in thoughts of the past, I reach the stables just as Kian comes out with Noir's - my black Arabian - reigns in his grip. He silently hands them to me as Alec, Lia and Mia mount their horses, each one of the Violet Guards dressed in black with guns strapped to their legs.

"Where too?" Kian asks as I mount Noir, Kian doing the same and climbing onto his own horse.

"East." I hold up my hand to show the tracker on the watch, Kian letting out a low whistle impressed by the technology.

"How much did that cost you?" Alec asks, steering his horse beside mine.

"Nearly all of my savings." I admit.

"But it was worth it now that we can find her. So lets go get Allisara." I nudge my horse into a gallop, taking the lead as we rush towards the eastern side of Zalaris. The Palace grounds are lit, acting like a beacon in the dark city. Alice was right, Zalaris has no power. The streets are thankfully empty, the Army, City Police and Guards doing their best to help the citizens find their way home.

We race past the city limits and into the eastern forest, the dot on the tracker is still moving, and moving fast, and it makes me wonder just where Juden's men are taking her. I am glad I decided to take the horses as the dot changes course and we follow deep into the woods and off the usual hiking trail. I can tell with how big the dot grows that we are getting closer and soon Allisara will be saved. Suddenly the dot stops moving and I motion to everyone to stop as well.

"What is it?" Mia asks, bringing Opal - her horse - next to mine.

"They stopped moving." I show the watch to her and she stares at it for a moment before motioning for Lia to join us.

"Dad used to take us hunting in this are. Isn't there a shack just up ahead?" She asks her twin. I turn to show Lia the watch and after studying it, she turns to Mia.

"We need to scout the area. She must be at the shack." I sigh with relief at Lia's words and tell them to be careful. The twins climb off of their horses and hand their reigns to Alec before they slink off into the shadows up ahead. Now we wait.

Chapter 52

"Sky." Lia appears from the shadows, a smile on her face as she appears beside Noir.

"Mia is watching the shack but she is there. Alli is there." Relief fills me as I slump in Noir's saddle. We are so close to saving her now.

"How many people?" I ask, climbing from Noir. I let his reigns fall to the ground.

"Four men. The shack only has one main room and one bath room. Hunters use it to camp out during hunting season." She takes out a dagger from her boot and motions for Kian to come join us. We all agreed Alec will stay with our horses so that we have an easy getaway.

"Alli is close to bathroom door. She is passed out on a mattress. It seems only one man is guarding the door, like he is waiting for someone." She draws the shack as best as possible in the ground, using a circle to show Allisara and triangles for the kidnappers.

"Three are inside playing a card game and drinking. I have a feeling they are drunk. It's the guy guarding the door we need to worry about." Lia continues. I study the drawing, asking about what the four bigger dashes are and learning from Lia that they are windows, one of which Allisara is sleeping under. A plan begins to form as I think about what needs to be done.

"Kian and I will go to the window to grab Allisara. Since you and Mia know this forest, I want you two to take down the man at the door." I begin explaining the plan to the others, telling Alec to move closer to the shack. We will need a quick get away and for that, we will need our horses closer. Kian hands the reigns to our horses to Alec before the three of us slink through the shadows, Lia pointing me towards the window where Allisara is. I thank her, motioning for Kian to follow me as Lia moves to find her sister.

Reaching the side of the shack, my fists clench when I realize the window Allisara sleeps under has no glass or curtains over it. Even I can see that the cold air is seeping inside. I want to kill these bastards that took her. Kian peers into the room for a moment, quietly cursing as he motions for me to follow him away from the shack.

"What?" I hissed out angrily, not liking being pulled away when Allisara is just in our reach.

"They wear our uniforms." I curse, punching the nearest tree. It seems that I was right. This was an inside job and we have Traitors in our rank still.

"Go find the twins and let them know plans have changed. They need to capture the man by the door before we storm the room and kill the other three." This time Kian punches a tree in frustration before he runs off. I return to the window and peer over the ledge, stopping myself from cursing when I realize that these men do indeed wear the Royal Guard uniform. Taking out my phone, I send a quick text to Alice about this, telling her to keep an eye on Max in the dungeons as a sinking feeling overcomes me.

A sound from the front of the shack causes the three Traitors to stand, weapons drawn as they creep towards the door.

"Someone go check in on Derik." One of the Traitors states and I once again find myself holding back a curse. Derik was guarding the door to the Ballroom when Allisara and I entered it.

"Why don't you check on him. He's your cousin Lucas." Another one pushes Lucas, the first Traitor that spoke. The two men begin to argue about who should check on Derik and while they do I hear a low whistle. Lia is signalling that they captured Derik easily. I smirk, taking my gun from it's holster and carefully aim it. We had one of the Traitors, the others can die for all I care.

A slight movement from the window across from me catches my attention and I notice Mia. Our eyes lock for a second and I nod before we both pop up and shoot. Lucas turns as our guns lets out a loud bang, his companions falling to the ground dead. He aims his gun in my direction but he is too slow as the door slams open and Lia fires a shot. Blood sprays out from the man's chest as the bullet pierces his heart. Lucas is dead long before his body hits the dirty floor.

Climbing through the window, I holster my gun and bend down to check on Allisara. She is still breathing but the noise should have woken her up. Scooping her into my arms, I rush out of the door with the twins hot on my heals, telling Mia to call Alice and have a Doctor ready for our arrival. She takes out her own phone and I hear her bark out the request of finding a Doctor as we reach our horses. Kian has Derik tied to his stallion and offers to hold Allisara for me while I mount Noir. Once seated, he carefully hands her unconscious body back to me and after making sure I have a secure hold on her, I race back to the Palace.

I know the others will be fine on their own, their priority being making sure Derik arrives alive to the Palace because I plan to interrogate the fucking Traitor myself. He stole the love of my life, used something to keep her unconscious and is working with Juden and his men. I will make sure he squeals like a pig about who he is working with since Juden is locked away still and flush out the rest of the Traitors hiding in the Royal Guards.

Some of the power has returned to Zalaris and I am grateful for that, it makes seeing obstacles easier as I race through the streets.

"Hang in there Allisara." I plead as I pushed my horse faster. Her breathing is light and I am worried that any moment now it will stop forever. Finally the Palace comes into view and the gates are wide open. Kolten and Taylor are waiting for me on their own horses, the two looking at Allisara in my arms with worry.

"Alice told us to wait for you." Taylor shouts as I race past them. I nod, not bothering to answer as the two nudge their horses behind me, the three of us racing towards the main entrance of the Palace. A crowd is already waiting and Eathan is the one to greet me at the base of the Palace steps. I hand Allisara to him before dismounting, the two of us racing towards the open doors while a Butler takes the reigns of Noir. I want to take Allisara back, but after riding like the devil was chasing me with her in my arms, I know my body can't handle carrying her right now.

Blaine is waiting for us on the third floor where our wing of the Palace is, her ballgown switched into a pair of jeans and a sweater I have seen in Allisara's closet.

"The Doctor is in her room with Millia and Clarice." She explains, running with Eathan and I towards Allisara's room. True to her word, an elderly man in a lab coat is preparing a table full of medical equipment as we rush in. He turns to face us as Eathan carries Allisara to her bed, Millia and Clarice quickly jumping in to remove her jewelry, all but the necklace she has had for fourteen years and the bracelet I gave her.

"I never thought I would see her again." The old man mutters out in awe as he comes to her side.

"You're Doctor Tomas, the-"

"The one who took her memories for her safety? Yes." Doctor Tomas confirms, placing his stethoscope onto Allisara's chest.

"Now what happened to her?" He demands. I bristle at his attitude but none the less he is the man that will save her, so I begin recounting what happened from the moment I realized she was abducted to when I found her. My eyes stayed glued onto the Doctor, watching each and every one of his movements. He is thorough in his examination and does not try anything that could harm Allisara further.

"Looks like she was injected with a sedative." He sighs out, his body slumping as he moves a lock of hair from Allisara's neck, pointing out a pin mark.

"Clarice, hand me a syringe so I can take her blood." He orders the Maid and she does as he says, reaching for a sterile syringe from the equipment on the table. The Doctor thanks her before he carefully inserts the needle into Allisara's elbow, drawing blood. With the syringe half full, he walks towards the table and inserts the needle into a machine, depositing the blood inside it. I recognize it as a poison analysis, like the one used at the Ball her Grandparents hosted where she was poisoned. Worry gnaws at me as we wait for results, Millia working on removing Allisara's shoes as Clarice moves to her closet, coming out with a night gown. They will need to change her from her ballgown soon if an I.V. drip is needed.

Finally a small ding sounds from the machine, the results quickly being printed out within seconds. Doctor Tomas rips it from the machine, bringing the paper closer to his eyes. Another minute passes as he reads the results. He sighs with relief, collapsing into a chair as he holds the results out for me to take.

"She will be fine." He states with a grin as I take the results from his grasp and read them.

"It is a strong sedative that will leave her unconscious for a few days. Her body will have to work it out of her system naturally." I collapsed where I stand, tears falling from my eyes as relief fills me. She will be alright.

"Thank you." I whisper, looking into the old Doctor's eyes.

"For what? I just did my job." He chuckles out, thanking Millia as she hands him a water bottle.

"You saved her fourteen years ago and you were hear to save her again." I answer, fist clenching the results.

"I did that because Juden needed to be stopped. He is a vile man and I hate that he used the safety of my wife over my head to do is bidding." Doctor Tomas admits. My eyes widen as I look at him, seeing a coldness in his eyes that I have only seen on battle hardened Soldiers.

"Why come forward now?" I ask, realizing that this Doctor could have hidden away for the rest of his life as we had not been able to find him no matter how hard we tried till now.

"My wife died of cancer the same day Allisara took that DNA test. I swore that I would come and save her if anything happened that day. Now if you'll excuse me, that Guard Alice wants to interrogate me and I have years of dirt Juden gave me on a USB thinking I was loyal to him to give to Alice." With that, the Doctor packs up his equipment, Clarice helping him. I realize that she is familiar with the man and I give her a questioning gaze.

"Doctor Tomas is our Uncle. He trained Millia and I in medicine. We did not know he was the one to help the Princess." Her eyes stayed glued to mine and I can sense nothing but honesty in her words. I nod, asking the two to change Allisara into some clean clothes before climbing to my feet and making my way to my own room. I take a quick shower, changing into a fresh pair of pajamas and grabbing my gun before returning to Allisara's side. Ellisia is watching over her, her face filled with worry as she uses a damp cloth to wipe at Allisara's brow.

"You can head to bed." I tell her, Ellisia giving me a soft smile as I climb into bed and lay beside Allisara.

"I was just waiting for you to join her. I will be here in the morning with Adam to watch over her as she sleeps as I have a feeling you will be busy the next few days." I thank Ellisia, telling her to have a good night. She leaves the room, turning off the lights as she does. Exhausted from tonight's events, I carefully wrap my arms around Allisara and place a gentle kiss on top of her head. I don't know how long she will be asleep and as worried as I am about this, I am just grateful that she is still alive and in my arms.

Chapter 53

Pouting beside my cake, I watch as Demitrias talks to all those girls that surround him, my cousin being one of them. My mother just announced that I am to marry him before my fifth birthday party began and I am not happy. Not once has he wished me a happy birthday or come my way.

The girls are called away and finally he is alone. I do my best to march towards him, wanting to talk to my friend and see why he is being so mean to me.

"Allisara get out of my way." He sighs out, annoyed by me.

"No." I cross my arms over my chest and stomp my foot. He is my fiancé now; he needs to talk to me.

"Move or I will make you." He grounds out, glaring at me.

"Why are you being so mean to me?" I nearly shout, tears filling my eyes.

"Because I don't like you. You're just a dumb girl I have to marry." With that he pushes me to the side, nearly knocking me onto the ground. A pair of arms catch me and the scent of pine fills my nose. Before I can say anything to the person, he gently pulls me into a quiet corner and I find myself crying into his shoulder.

"Are you okay Allisara?" The boyish voice asks, patting my back. I shake my head no, hearing him sigh.

"Wanna tell me what's wrong?" His voice is slow and caring, opposite on how Demitrias treated me. Why couldn't my parents betroth me to him?

"Demi called me a dumb girl who he has to marry. That he doesn't like me." I whimper out, hating that I have to be stuck with such a mean person.

"You're not dumb, and Demitrias only wants to be King. But you can break the engagement when you are older." The voice reasons with me and I look up. The boy smiles at me, his emerald eyes twinkling in the light as he wipes away my tears.

"Anyone would be happy to marry some one as smart as you." He reassures me, pulling me into his arms once again.

"I wish it was you I was marrying." I admit, my fist clenching his shirt. But he is a gardener's son and a Knight in training. My parents wouldn't allow it.

"Me too Allisara. Me too." My eyes shut as his voice fades away and I feel my little body falling

♔[1]

I am crying again, my wrists sore from being tied in front of me. A man has me thrown over his shoulder, handling me the way the cooks do to a sack of potatoes.

"Let me go." I sniffle, my little voice filled with terror as I try to kick my feet out, but they too are tied together. The last thing I remembered was arguing with my cousin Lillith. How she and her friends laughed and pulled me away from the adults view towards the open door that leads to the garden. They told me they were going to tell me a secret about Demitrias, but as soon as we were just in front of the door, Lillith pushed me outside, her friends laughing as they shut and lock the door. I knocked onto the glass, screaming for help in the cold May rain. That's when the men grabbed me, chuckling about how easy kidnapping me had been.

"Sorry Princess but our boss has ordered us to keep you with us." The man laughs out and I get a full view of his rotten teeth.

"You're going to make us very rich whether you live or die." His friend states right away, the men laughing at this. They became too preoccupied talking about how they will spend their riches and I realize I am still wearing the bead necklace Sky gave to me. I smile, carefully pulling the necklace over my head. Pretending to struggle. I break the necklace and slowly drop a bead after counting to one hundred. I know Sky will find me; he always does. Even when we are training together he always finds me. I keep quiet as the men carry me to where ever their hideout is, the beads beginning to run out. I am soaked from the rain, shivering from being cold.

"Ah, home sweet home!" The one holding me states, making me drop the empty string.

---

1. https://coolsymbol.com/copy/White_Chess_King_Symbol_%E2%99%94

"We camp here, put the Princess in her new room." A door opens and I am carried into a small shack. Scared for what they will do to me, I try to fight but am thrown onto the floor, a hand connecting with my cheek.

"You will behave or I will make you!" My captor growls out, his rancid breath washing over my face. I nod in fear, not trying to fight back any more and he roughly picks me up, throwing me into a cage by an open window. He locks the cage door, giving me a scoff before walking towards the small fire set in the middle of the room where his partner waits. It was cold where the cage is set but the roof thankfully stops the rain.

'I'll find you' those words goes through my head as I look through the bars at the night sky, wondering when my Sky would get here. He promised he would find and protect me no matter what. That he was chosen to be my Knight in the future.

"Find me, please." I whimper out. My eyes grow heavy and I huddle in the middle of the cage trying to stay warm. I can't sleep now but I am so, so tired...

♔[2]

The sounds of battle outside the shack wakes me up, but the sounds of the cage lock rattling is what causes me to bolt upright.

"Allisara?" Someone whispers, someone I had been praying would find me.

"Sky?" I see his emerald eyes and try my best to crawl towards him. The door opens and he crawls inside, taking in my bound wrists.

"Hold still." He warns, taking out a switch blade and cutting the ropes first from my wrists, then my ankles. After putting the switch blade away, the ten year old pulls me into his arms and hugs me tight.

"I told you that I would find you." He whispers, his hands smoothing out my wet hair. I nod, too exhausted to say anything and so relieved to be saved. He helps me out of the cage but my legs give out as soon as I stand. Tears well in my eyes and I am close to crying when he scoops me into his arms, racing out of the shack. I catch three Palace Guards capture the two men that kidnapped me as Sky races to a black Arabian colt, his yearling Noir. I am helped into the saddle first before he climbs up behind me, wrapping his arm around my waist and covering me with his cloak. The heat from his cloak

2. https://coolsymbol.com/copy/White_Chess_King_Symbol_%E2%99%94

and body warms me up, causing my shivering to slow as he rushes Noir into a gallop. It takes me a moment to realize we are in the Northern forest so close to the Palace and I wonder when my kidnapping was discovered.

"We are almost home Allisara." Sky mutters as we break past the treeline onto open grassland. The rain continues to fall around us, soaking both Sky and I but the Palace lights grow closer. We emerge in the back gardens of the Palace, Sky navigating Noir through the paths until we come to the back of the Ballroom. The cold rushes to me when Sky climbs off but he quickly helps me down before scooping me into his arms, his body heat warming me again. A tent had been propped up just outside the doors to the Ballroom and Sky calls out to the Guards there, one rushing inside while another holds the door open. We barely make it inside when I notice my mother and father rushing towards us. Sky carefully sets me on my feet, helping me stand as my mother comes to stand in front of us.

"Allisara, why would you go out side, you know its dangerous." Instead of asking if I was okay, she begins yelling at me, reaching out to grab me but Sky backs away and pulling me behind him, protecting me from her. I can see anger in his emerald eyes as he glares at my mother.

"Lilith and her friends pushed me outside. They told me they had a secret." I answer back, standing straight.

"Allisara don't lie." My father joins my mother, his own glare directed to Sky and me.

"Lilith said you wanted to go for a walk and she tried to stop you." My father states. I frown, getting ready to argue back when the Ballroom doors slam open.

"Allisara isn't lying. I have proof right here." The Captain of the Guards – Sir Carlos - announces as he walks into the room with a tablet. He comes to stand before my parents, blocking them from me and I silently thank him for it. Sir Carlos has always been protective of me, especially since he has watched Lillith and her friends bully me on many occasions. Passing the tablet to my parents, I watch their faces go from angry at me, to disbelief, then anger again. I can tell they saw the truth and are ready to yell.

"Get my brother, his daughter and all of her friends in the Throne Room now!" My father booms to a Guard that stands by the door. He bows before vanishing and my mother tries to step past Sir Carlos to grab me. I swat her hand away glaring at her as I cling to Sky. She didn't believe me so why should I be nice to her.

"Allisara-"

"No! You yelled at me and didn't believe me. I hate you!" I yell back, taking Sky's hand and marching out of the Ballroom. I know the way to the Throne Room and don't need to follow them.

"Princess!" Hearing Ellisia's voice, I stop and turn to face her. She and Rainnah are carrying blankets in their hands and are quick to wrap them around Sky and I, Rainnah taking Sky's soaked cloak and passing it off to a Butler.

"I am so glad you are safe." Ellisia cries out, pulling me in for a hug. My tears finally fall as I cling to her, finally feeling safe with someone that actually believes me. Her and Rainnah comfort me, telling me not to cry and that a hot bath is waiting once we deal with Lillith and her friends. They lead Sky and I to the Throne Room and we find a spot on top of the dais steps to sit, with Rainnah and Ellisia sitting on either side of us.

My parents and Sir Carlos enter moments later, my mother trying to talk to me but I ignored her. She always believed Lillith over me and its only after Ellisia, Rainnah or Sir Carlos has showed proof of the truth that she tries to talk to me. She slumps in her Throne and my father comforts her before the Throne Room doors are opened and my Uncle enters the room, Lillith and her friends as well as the parents of her friends following after him.

"You found her." My Uncle's first words echo through the room as he comes to stand just before the dais steps, a smile of relief on his face, but I can see the anger in his eyes.

"No, Skylard found her." Sir Carlos corrects him. My Uncle goes to argue but My father cuts him off, glaring at his younger cousin.

"If it weren't for your daughter and her friends, mine might have been dead by now." My father states angrily. The parents of Lillith's friends call out in protest, stating that their daughters would never harm me, but Guards enter the room, pointing their swords at them and silencing their protest.

"My daughter did no such thing!" My Uncle protests once the room quiets down. My father says nothing but nods to Sir Carlos and the Captain of the Guard presses onto the tablet screen. The television slowly descends behind the Thrones and soon the security video of what happened is played.

"Allisara, we have a secret to tell you!" Lillith calls out as she rushes to my side, taking my hand in hers. Her friends giggle as they begin to lead me through the Ballroom and I have a happy smile on my face. They were including me for once. I beg for them to tell me what the secret is but they reassure me that as soon as we are out of sight from our parents, they will tell me. We soon reach the open door and I face them, my back towards the doors.

"So what is the secret?" I ask, hopping slightly in place.

"Demitrias hates you and will marry me instead." Lillith states, her smiling face dropping as she glares at me. Before I can say anything I am pushed outside, falling on the wet ground as rain pelts me. Her friends are quick to close and lock the door as I rush to my feet. They laugh and mock me, saying I will never be Queen because Lillith deserves it as I pound at the glass, crying and begging them to let me back in. Lillith closes the curtains and the view of the camera changes to the one outside. I am still crying and begging for help when two men sneak into view. One grabs me as the other bounds my hands and feet before I am thrown over the shoulders of the one that grabbed me. After that we disappear from view and the screen goes black.

"If it weren't for Skylard noticing that Allisara was missing and tracking her down, I would have no heir." My father bellows, the girls cowering behind their parents. I scoff at their fear, knowing that what ever punishment my father hands out, they deserve. The parents of the girls stay silent, their anger and guilt towards their daughter clear as day.

"So now the punishment." My mother calls out, her voice so cold I shiver from it.

"Prince Leonard, you and your family will be stripped of your title and exiled to the borders. You are no longer part of the Royal Family." My father states. Five Guards step forward, ready to usher my Uncle and cousin out of the room but the doors to the Throne Room slam open and three Guards walk in drenched in water and dragging my kidnappers behind them.

"Your Majesties, these men are ready to confess something to you." The first Guard calls out, kneeling before my parents. My father waves his hand and the two Guards holding my kidnappers push them forward. They fall to their knees trembling as they begin to talk.

"We are sorry your Majesties!" They cry out, tears falling from their swollen eyes as they shiver with fear.

"Prince Leonard hired us to kidnap the Princess. He said whether she lives or dies, we would be paid so that his family could inherit the Throne."

"Liars!" My Uncle shouts, but two Guards work quick in cuffing his hands behind his back and gagging him.

"It's true. We searched through these men's belonging and found a letter with the Prince's seal on it." The kneeling Guard stands and passes a letter to Sir Carlos who confirms the seal is from my Uncle. My father stands from his Throne, marches towards my Uncle and takes a Guards sword, stabbing my Uncle through the heart.

"Your family will still be demoted, but for trying to kill my daughter, you will die." The other girls scream in fear, begging their parents not to let my father kill them. Their parents do not console them as my Uncles body drops to the floor. Sky wraps his arms around me, pulling me close as Ellisia does her best to shield be from the sight.

"Take these men to the dungeon and execute them." My father orders, the Guards complying and taking my kidnappers away. Another two step forward, each taking one of Lillith's arms as they drag her away from her father's body, my cousin screaming and crying hysterically for him. With them gone, the room slowly becomes quiet as my father returns to his Throne.

"As for you all." My mother speaks, addressing the Nobles that pull their daughters in front of them.

"Your families will be stripped of you titles as you have all clearly failed at raising your daughters properly. Everyone in your homes will be sent into the outer Provinces and away from the Capitol. Guards will escort you out and the army will help relocate your families." She continues, glaring at the scared little girls that try to hide behind their parents again.

"We will be seizing half of your assets as payment for the hardships my daughter faced." With that, they too are escorted from the Throne Room. Rainnah and Ellisia are quick to escort Sky and I after, my mother tries to talk to me but Sir Carlos tells her there is paperwork to be done and that I must be freezing being soaking wet from the cold rain. She stops trying, her sad eyes following me until I leave her sight. I am taken to my room, Sky taken to the room across from mine, and given a hot bath before being dressed in warm clothing and my hair dried.

After a mug of hot apple cider, I am forced into bed. Rainnah returns with Sky, helping my friend into bed with me and telling us to keep this a secret. We promise and the two Maids leave my room after checking that a fire was lit in my fireplace and turning off the lights.

"Thank you." I whisper sleepily, my head resting on Sky's shoulder.

"For what?" He asks, playing with my soft curls.

"For being there and finding me." I reply with, smiling as my eyes close.

"I'll always find you and I will always be there for you."

Chapter 54

Gasping awake from my dream, I look around the room and realize that I am safe and sound in my own bed. A fire roars in my fireplace, dimly lighting the room and keeping it warm and my body feels so sore and weak.

"Allisara?" I shiver at the sound of his deep voice, my head turning towards my bedroom door. There Sky stands, his emerald eyes locked onto my violet ones.

"Hi." I croak out, tears falling down my face. He rushes to my side, pulling me into his arms as soon as he sits on the edge of the bed and I begin to sob. How did I forget him, my Sky?

"What's wrong? are you hurting?" He asks, rubbing my back and doing his best to soothe me.

"I'm sorry I forgot about you." I sob out, my arms snaking around his neck. He pulls away in shock, his eyes wide as his hands move to cup my face.

"You...you remember me?" He whispers, his own tears falling down his face.

"Yes!" I manage to say before his lips slam against mine, claiming them in a heated kiss. I melt into his embrace, parting my lips as his tongue dives into mine, claiming me. I moan, my body heating just from the kiss alone.

"I wish it was you I was marrying."

"Me too Allisara. Me too."

Those words echo in my mind as I kiss Sky just as passionately as he kisses me. I am in love with my best friend. The one that promised to always find me no matter where I am. The one who protected me and held me when I needed to cry. Sky is the one who has always there for me.

The kiss ends all to soon, leaving me gasping for breath as Sky reaches for something on my bedside table, holding a glass full of water out.

"Drink, you've been asleep for three days." He whispers, his own eyes filled with emotions. I comply, drinking all of it and asking for more. He refills the glass, telling me to take it easy on the water before calling someone on his phone, letting them know I am awake and to bring me some porridge.

"It will take a while for the porridge to get here, do you want to shower?" He asks after I finish my third glass of water.

"No, I just want to cuddle and hear what happened after I was kidnapped." I answer, taking his hand in mine. Sky smiles and kicks off his shoes before climbing in beside me. His arms wrap around me, pulling me tightly against him.

"Do you want to tell me what you remember first?" He asks instead, pressing a kiss to my forehead.

"Where do you want to start?"

"The night of the Ball, you said three dances." He carefully pulls the blanket around us and I start explaining what happened with Cedirc, how he came to find a girlfriend and fall in love. Sky laughs, cutting me off and explaining that I had punch Cedric in the nose but hadn't broken it. I feel a little bad about this, realizing Cedric was trying to protect me.

"I wanted to introduce him to my cousin Annalise since she has given up on falling in love after her fiancé cheated on her." I admit, shrugging. Sky laughs again, brushing his fingers through my hair.

"Why does that not surprise me." I shrug, giving myself a mental reminder to apologize to Cedric and invite him to the Blanchard Estate to meet my cousin.

"Also, there is no need in setting them up. Annalise helped Cedric with his bloodied nose and those two have already gone on their first date. Your uncle told me this yesterday." Shocked, I pull away from Sky before I burst out laughing. I know Annalise had gone to medical school out of boredom from the talk we had and to know that she had come to Cedric's rescue makes this even better. I guess I did end up introducing her to him in a way.

"Anyways, a group of men grabbed me and they injected something into me. I could hear you calling my name and I wanted to shout back but before I could, I passed out. Next thing I know I am waking up here." I lie back down against his chest as silence settles between us. Sky closes his eyes, his arms tightening around me.

"Do you really remember me?" His voice is small, as if afraid of my answer. I smile, turning my head and pressing a kiss to his collar bone. He shivers under me, his fingers clenching in my hair. The next moment I find myself underneath him, his lips on mine once more as another heated kiss ensues. My fingers find their way into his hair, pulling and tugging at it. He groans into the kiss, his body pressing closer to mine as my legs wrap around his waist. After a while we pull away trying to regain our breath.

"I remember you." I muse, my left hand moving to cup his cheek. His stubble brush against my skin and I finally can see the exhaustion in his eyes.

"I remember my best friend who always cuddled with me as a child. Who saved me from bandits and wild dogs. Who let me cry as you and the Knight carried me to the apple farm. The person I did everything with." My eyes fill with tears again and I gently pull him towards me for another kiss, this one slow and sweet. Something wet falls onto my cheek and as I pull away I open my eyes to fid Sky crying.

"I am so sorry I couldn't protect you Allisara." He chokes out, His head falling onto the crook of my neck. I hold him as he cries, telling him he did everything he could at eleven years old. That without him taking me to the apple farm, I would have died with Rainnah and my parents. Through his sobs I learn that he had been looking for me for the last fourteen years. How he did everything from searching Zalaris to running my DNA through the system while climbing the ranks of the Guards so that he had easier access to resources. He knew I ended up in Lady Pricilla's Prison for Troubled Women before I even told him but didn't say anything because I hadn't regained my memory of him. He was on his way to find me when Demitrias walked into the lab and took the glory of finding me himself.

"You have no idea how happy I was the first time I saw you when you opened the door and kicked that bastard out of your room. How shocked I was when you cussed him out. That was definitely a surprise." I laugh, thinking back to how I woke up in this very bed weeks ago. How Sky held a sword to Demitrias' neck.

"You wanted to kill him, didn't you?" I ask. Sky just shrugs, his face buried once again in my shoulder and I smile. For a moment we lay in bed in silence, the truth between us out in the open. I have my memories back and my best friend as my boyfriend. Nothing could get better than this.

"I love you Allisara" He whispers into my neck, placing a kiss against it. I shiver, deciding that I wanted more, wanted him. I spent fourteen years without him. Fourteen years without my Sky. I didn't want to spend another moment longer.

"I love you too Sky." I whisper back, getting a breathtaking kiss from him once again. A knock on the door has us pulling apart and Sky groans.

"Looks like lunch is here." He sighs out, sounding defeated. I laugh as he climbs off of me and pads towards the door, letting in our intruder that interrupted our moment. A cart is pushed through and as I sit up I catch sight of Ellisia.

"Sia!" I call out, using the nickname I used to use as a child. She stops. Her head whipping towards me as a look of shock and love crosses her face.

"You...you." She stutters as tears fall from her eyes.

"I remember everything." I admit just as Ellisia runs to my side and pulls me into a hug. I smile, Feeling her motherly love towards me and grin. She was always there for me as a child, always on my side when my parents were lied to by Lillith. Her, Sir Carlos and Rainnah were the ones who truly raised me.

"How did I get stuck pushing the cart!" Sky calls out as he joins us, the cart full of food in front of him.

"Oh hush up Sky, I am hugging my Princess. Do you know how hard it was to not say anything to her all these weeks." Ellisia chides him, making me laugh.

"More than you at this point Ell." Shy grumbles, scooping a portion of porridge into a bowl. Ellisia takes it from him before handing it to me, telling me to be careful as its hot. I humor her, blowing on a spoonful before taking a bite. Apple and cinnamon dance on my tongue and I close my eyes. I always loved this taste. The bowl is gone in no time and I ask for another serving as Ellisia explains that she was the one to keep my mother's jewelry in my room. That no one else was allowed inside it after Rainnah's death and Juden allowed it, stating that everything will belong to his grand daughter when Demitrias gives him grandchildren. I scoff at that as I finish my second bowl, handing it to Sky now that I am full.

I start asking about what happened in the Palace while I was gone and she tells me it's a long story to be told later. Right now we have more important things to deal with.

Sky is the one to talk this time, explaining that the ones who kidnapped me were Guards that still worked in the Palace, one being Derik whom I met before the Ball. I wished I could be shocked, but I am not. Juden has men all over the Kingdom. Of course he would have men in my Palace still. Sky then goes on to explain how the Doctor that saved me had helped with interrogating Derik. He had managed to create a truth serum with the money Juden gave him to fund his research and Derik "squealed like a pig" according to Sky. Arian and Kolten led a crusade, cleaning out more than half my Guards, including a few female Recruits.

"So our home is safe now?" I ask, clutching his hand.

"Our home is safe now." He reassures me.

"I think we have done enough talking. You need to rest." Ellisia states, standing from beside me. Sky agrees, helping Ellisia to clear the dishes before she leaves, telling Sky to take care of me.

"I don't want to rest." I admit as Sky closes the bedroom door.

"Then what do you want to do?" I blush as he takes my hand, unsure if I am brave enough to voice what I want to say. Taking a deep breath, I look into his eyes and smile. I want to be with him. Even made him a duke so it would be easier to marry him.

"I want to take a bath. Take one with me." His smile fades for a moment, his eyes searching my face as if to see I am joking. He must have concluded that I am not as he bends down and scoops me into his arm, carrying me into the bathroom. I squeak in surprise as he does this, my arms wrapping around him so that he doesn't drop me. He makes a stop at the bathroom vanity, setting me down on the counter before he turns to the bathtub and runs a bubble bath. He comes back as the water runs, his lips crashing onto mine for a moment.

"Allisara." He groans my name, his hands helping me to undress from the nightgown I wear. Millia and Clarice must have changed me.

"Are you sure you want me with you?" He asks as our clothes fall to the ground.

"Yes." Our eyes meet and for a second I see a slight hesitation in them before I am scooped into his arms and carried into the bathtub. Sky turns the water off after we slide in, the warm water relaxing my sore body. I snuggle close to him, resting my head over the spot above his heart and listen to the steady heart beat. But it seems Sky has other plans. He places a wet finger under my chin, gently lifting it and bringing his lips to mine. The kiss is slow at first, our lips moving against each others, but then his hands position me so that I am straddling his lap, my hands on his shoulders steadying me while his find their way to my waist.

I moan when I feel something hard rub against me, Sky letting out a groan into the kiss that my lips muffle and I blush as I realize just what it was. Sky pulls away first, his eyes dark with lust as he stares at me, his gaze captivating me.

"We can stop any time you want." He whispers, dipping his head to nip at the sensitive skin of my neck.

"I don't want to stop at all." I admit, smirking as I slowly move my hips and watch as Sky hiss in a breath. His hands move to cup my ass, his lips claiming mine more forcefully this time as his tongue pushes through. Our kiss grows heated and desire for the man I love builds inside me.

"We should get you cleaned first." He mumbles as he pulls away again. I try to protest but am met with a pointed look, one that suggests I don't argue. My obedience earns me a quick peck on the lips as one hand leaves my body and Sky reaches to the shelf behind him to grab a bottle of vanilla scented shower gel. The other hand leaves my body as he squirts a lightly tinted glob of it onto his palm, the bottle being returned to the shelf before he rubs the scented gen between his palms.

"Close your eyes, Allisara." His voice is low and husky as he gives me an order, one I comply with. Suddenly his hands are on my body, my breasts to be exact, and he massages the gel against my skin. I moan, the feeling of him squeezing and grabbing at me intensified with my eyes close and I nearly gasp when his finger pinch a hard nipple.

His hands move from there, going along my side and stomach even though the water covers me. Sky is thorough as he washes me, the squirting sound of the gel being added to his hand when he pulls away until I am sure almost every inch of skin as been explored by his touch. His hard appendage twitches when I moan, colliding with my heated skin and making me wonder what he would feel like inside me. Part of me is scared to find out but the other part wants to know right away. His fingers never move to touch me *there* but they do make a habit of grabbing my ass and my breast. Finally his hands find their way to my golden locks and Sky takes his time cleaning my hair, using first shampoo and then conditioner just by the feel of it against my scalp.

"I am just going to rinse you off, then you can clean me." His lips are pressed to my ear lobe and I shiver at the sound of his voice. He is holding himself back and I really wished he would take me here and now. True to his words, the small shower attachment to the clawfoot tub is flicked on and the warm spray hits my scalp. He cleans away the soap and shampoo, his free hand helping alongside the attachment. It doesn't take long and soon the shower spray stops.

"Your turn to clean me." His lips are next to my ear, his voice a throaty whisper. I shiver, feeling myself grind against him involuntarily making him groan. Opening my eyes, I see Sky staring at me patiently, a smirk on his lips. In his hand is a bottle of shower gel, one that I have seen in his bathroom before. My lips match his own smirk as I take the bottle from him. I am careful when I pour the gel into my left hand, finding a spot to rest the bottle on the tub before rubbing my palms together. Sky closes his eyes as I massage the shower gel into his skin, starting with his neck and shoulders and slowly moving lower. I hesitate when I reach *that* area, my face heating up as I think about how I will clean him. I haven't given myself away to anyone and I can tell just by how hard he has grown that Sky is big.

Taking a deep breath, I slowly move my left hand from his thigh to his shaft, my fingers unable to curl fully around him. Sky takes a shuddering breath, his hand moving from my waist to my wrist.

"You don't have to do anything if you don't want to." He groans out as my fingers move slightly.

"Who says I don't want to?" I ask coyly, feeling some sense of bravery. His eyes open in shock, his mouth slightly open as he stares at me. Keeping my eyes locked on his, I slowly move my hand up and down, the water moving with each movement of my arm. He groans again, his head leaning back against the tub. I smile as I feel a sense of control over Sky, his grip on my wrist loosening. He twitches in my hand when I reach the base and then once more as soon as my fingers brush against his tip. My free hand reaches for the shower head and as my hand works on his shaft, I use the shower to clean off and soap left on his exposed skin.

"Allisara." He moans my name, his hand moving to my wrist once more and stopping me from moving.

"If you keep this up, I won't be able to hold back any longer." His gaze locks onto mine once more as I set the shower attachment back on its hook.

"Then don't hold back." Once again I leave Sky speechless but it doesn't last for long. His lips are on mine as his hands move to cup my ass. I squeal into the kiss when he rises from the bath tub, the cold air nipping at my skin. Sky sloshes the as he climbs out with me in his arms, the sound of water dripping onto the floor making me pull away and laugh.

"Clarice is going to kill you for making a mess." I mumble out, placing light kisses along his jawline.

"She will be happy and forgive me when she finds out we were making a little royal." He counters, making me laugh again. Sky is right though. If everyone finds out that we created a little royal, then any mess we make will be forgiven. Sky returns to kissing me, his tongue sliding along the seam of my lips demanding entry, entry that I playfully deny. A sharp slap to my ass causes me to jump in his grasp, my lips opening with a gasps and his tongue slide in claiming me.

Soon my body is placed on my bed and Sky is hovering over me, the kiss ending abruptly as he pulls away, his swollen lips forming into a grin.

"Last chance to back down Allisara." He warns, his right hand trailing from my side down to my thigh.

"I already told you." I chuckle out, my hand clenching his wrist and moving his hand from my thigh to just above the one place that demands his attention.

"Don't hold back." Sky's smirk grows with my provocation and his fingers move, caressing my lower lips. I gasp, my hips bucking from the sensation as my legs spread wider and his finger slips inside me.

"Sk-Skylard!" I moan his name as he moves his finger gently inside me, hooking slightly.

"Tell me what you want Allisara." He whispers, his lips pressing along my neck down to my collar bone.

"I want you!" I cry out, my hands snaking around his shoulder and into his damp hair. His finger leaves me and I let out a sound of protest but soon I realize why. He nudges my legs apart and with his free hand, guides them to wrap around his waist.

"This might hurt Allisara, but only for a moment." He mumbles against my skin, rubbing the tip of himself into me.

"Will...will it feel good in the end?" I whimper out, tugging at Sky's hair and pulling his head back. A see a playful smile on his face as his lust filled eyes twinkle in the dim light of the room.

"I hope so. I've been saving myself for you." With that, he pushes inside me, stretching me. I whimper, the pain something I expected, but not like this. Tears fill my eyes but Sky is quick to wipe them away as he waits fully inside me for me to be ready.

"It's okay." I gasp out as I feel him twitch. He says nothing but claims my lips in a kiss before moving, the ebbing pain turning into pleasure. Pleasure that lasts through the night.

Chapter 55

Exiting my carriage with the help of Sky, I wince slightly from the discomfort caused by waking up in Sky's arms this morning. Last night he and I had fully committed to one another and this morning when we woke up, he made sure to show me how much he loves me.

"Did I over do it?" Sky asks as I link my arm through his.

"Yes." I pout as he leads me towards the stage where I will sit during the execution. I can already hear the crowd demanding bloodshed for all the heinous acts Juden and his men have committed and I will gladly give it to them. My Grandparents, Kolten and Arian are already seated on stage, each one wearing a black suit. Taylor and her own unit are spread out in the crowd, listening in for information in case any of Juden's men are mixed with the crowd waiting to free their leader.

Sky helps me climb the stairs to the stage, escorting me to the microphone that sits to the right corner of the stage we will be sitting on. Below me is another platform, one that houses eleven kneeling men and women. Only one has his head covered with a black burlap sack. These are the Nobles that sided with Juden as well as the man himself. Moving my gaze from them, I look into the crowd and see Demitrias and his family standing there no longer as elegantly dressed as they used to be. My eyes meet my ex-fiancé's and he glares at me. I ignore him as Sky presses a kiss to my forehead before he backs away, taking the seat next to the temporary throne meant for me to use. One day he and I will rule this Kingdom together and he will have his own throne.

"Good morning people of Nimairene." I call into the mic, the crowds chanting for blood quieting down.

"I am sorry that we all have to meet under these unfortunate circumstances but todays event will be a warning to any and all Traitors under Juden Trilavantas' influence." I continue, turning my gaze towards the camera. I had been reassured that today's execution will be broadcasted for the Kingdom to see and I am grateful for it. No one will be able to say that I did something underhanded at today's execution.

"The men and women before us will each say their final words one at a time before their execution. It will be quick for them as we are not monsters like they are. Executioner, you may begin." With that I make my way to my seat, Sky taking my hand in his and giving it a light squeeze. One by one the Executioner brought a prisoner forward, giving them their chance to speak. Some begged for their lives, admitting their guilt and wishing for a second chance but I know better. If you give a Traitor any chance, they will turn around and stab you in the back without hesitation. Only three admitted they would do everything all over again if it meant gaining power and wealth once again. Their words are the ones cut short as a bullet to their heart takes their lives. I wince with each gun shot, my hand clenching Sky's as I think about whether or not this is the right choice. Then I think back to how I was kidnapped in my own Palace, how I was poisoned, threatened, and conclude that executing those who are irredeemable is the right choice.

Finally it is Juden's turn and the Executioner forces him to his feet. I watch their movement, something inside me saying this is wrong. Sky had informed me yesterday after making love to me that Max suggested using a bag to cover Juden's face and he had agreed to it. Make it a way to show he means nothing to us, that he will not be remembered.

"Juden Trilavantas. For the crimes of treason and murdering King Alexander Nimair and Queen Evelyne Nimair, you are sentenced to death. As your confession has been said, we will consider them your last words." The Executioner raises his gun, the barrel pressed to the kneeling man's chest. The safety is released but the sinking feeling inside me won't leave.

"Stop!" I shout before the gun can be fired. Standing to my feet I make my way down the stage and onto the platform, not caring about the blood that covers the temporary stage.

"Remove his hood." I order.

"Yeah!"

"Remove his hood!"

"Show us that bastard's face!"

The crowd shouts their agreeance with removing Juden's hood. I want to yell at them to quiet down as the feeling of dread fills me.

"Are you sure, Princess?" The Executioner asks and I glare at him. He backs away for a moment, turning the safety back on his gun and holstering it before the hood is removed. Kneeling before me is not Juden but Max, his face swollen black and blue. Dried blood covers the cuts that are still healing and I gasp in shock.

"Someone get a medic!" Sky orders, coming to kneel beside Max and removing the shackles around his wrists. Max slumps into Sky's arms, tears falling down his face. Turning to the crowd, I notice Demitrias and his family missing, my bewildered expression being the only thing that greets me on the screens around the execution square while I look around the crowd for the Traitor and his family.

"Where is he!" I shout, turning to face the Guards that brought the prisoners in.

"And why the hell is Max the one injured?" The Guards fall to their knees, explaining that the Guards in the dungeon handed the Prisoners to them. I shake with rage, taking out my phone and calling Alice.

"Go to the Dungeon with a group of Guards you trust. Tell me if the men that were stationed there are still where they should be." As soon as Alice answers the phone, I cut off her greeting and give her the order. She tells me to she will call me back as soon as she can before the line goes dead.

Suddenly a loud gasps courses through the crowd. I look to see what the commotion is and my rage grows. The screens around the Execution stage has changed from the broadcasting that is aired throughout the Kingdom to one filled with none other than Juden sitting in a chair smugly grinning.

"Hello Princess, I do hope you liked my surprise." His voice comes through the speaker, that smug grin growing as I glare into the camera. I know he can see and hear me, know that he is watching everything unfold.

"Unfortunately you are smarter than I thought and your precious friend here lived through the execution. I was so hoping he would have been shot and killed before the hood was removed." He sighs dramatically, taunting me into responding but I know better. If I play into his hand, I will look like the bad guy in front of my people.

"I now know you are a troublesome one, your years in the Slums hardening you into a cunning woman with the perception of a cunning cat and this excites me. Thanks to the people I placed into the Palace, I was able to escape a few days ago and make my way to a safe place. We are now at war my dear and it will end with me reclaiming the Throne I took fourteen years ago." The medics arrived as Juden continues his monologue, Sky helping them to place Max onto a gurney and telling Arian to go with them to the Palace. With Max secured and on his way to being helped, Sky comes to stand beside me, his own gaze locked on the screens.

"Ah, Skylard. How does it feel to know you took my son's bride?" Juden asks as soon as he notices Sky.

"I was never Demitrias' to begin with. He made that known when he impregnated three Palace Maids." I call out, watching Juden's face contort with rage.

"You lie!" He growls out and I chuckle.

"DNA tests do not lie. I have your three grandchildren in my control." I call back. Taking out my phone, I send my failsafe to the broadcasting company with the caption to spread this information. Minutes later a man walks into view of the screen and whispers something into Juden's ear. His face continues to contort further and I realize the company made quick work of what I gave them.

"Believe me now?" I taunt back, Juden snapping his head to me.

"If you do so much as harm my grandchildren even if they are bastards, I will-"

"You will what Juden? You have already declared war, have already planned to kill me for my Throne. Just know I hold three of your kin captive now." I cut him off. Juden stands from his chair, punching the poor man that gave him the news for all to see. I smirk knowing that I have gotten under his skin once more.

"You are right Allisara." He states, his chest heaving as he breathes heavily while trying to calm his own rage.

"We are at war and sooner or later I will be the one to cut down your own family tree. Until then, adieu." The screen turns black as his broadcast ends and I turn to Sky who looks at me with both fear and anger in his eyes.

"Allisara, we need to return to the Palace." He takes my hand and leads me away but I stop him, needing to reassure my people. Kolten is the one to take charge, his men forbidding the crowd from leaving until a background check can be conducted. Some people try to run away but are quickly captured by Taylor's squadron, the all female unit quick to bringing them to their knees and cuffing them while Kolten's men search their bodies and finding Juden's insignia on them. I watch in horror at just how close the rebels were to me today and allow Sky to take me to the carriage without a fight. Once safely inside, my phone rings and I answer it putting it on speaker.

"Alli, the men are gone. The dungeons are empty and only a few prisoners remain claiming they no longer wanted to be a part of Juden's plan." I shake from the rage I feel, Sky taking my phone and telling Alice to lock the Place down. She tells her to have Lia and Mia wait at the front entrance as an ambulance will be arriving soon with Max followed by my Grandparents in their own carriage. After promising to do just that, Alice hangs up.

"What do we do now?" I ask Sky as he pulls me into his lap.

"We make sure Max is okay, then we prepare for war." He answers, hos lips set into a grim line as his eyes stare into mine.

Chapter 56

Sitting in the waiting room of the hospital wing, my left leg bounces as anxiety and worry courses through me. Kian is pacing the floor, his eyes full of anger while Lia and Mia mumble prayers. Alice is sitting beside me, staring at the doors as we all way for a nurse to confirm whether or not we can visit our friend. Sky had gone for a coffee run with Arian and Adam; the two guards having rushed here as soon as they got the news.

"Princess." A small voice calls out causing me to jump to my feet and march towards the Nurse that came through the heavy doors.

"How is he?" I ask right away, taking the Nurse's hands in mine.

"He is resting now. The surgery was a success." A collective sigh goes through all of us, the tension and worry in the room breaking as we all visibly relax. Max had been in surgery the moment he was sent back to the Palace. As soon as we all managed to return home, we had made our way to the hospital wing. The nurse typing on the laptop in the corner was the one to explain how severe his injuries were to us and that until we were told otherwise, we would have to wait here in the waiting room.

Juden's men had done too much to poor Max from two fractured ribs to breaking his leg in four places. His nose had been broken this morning by the sounds of it, the injury being the newest while the other injuries were in various states of healing. Had I not gotten that feeling, Max would have either been accidentally executed or died from his injuries.

"When can we see him?" Lia asks from beside me, her bright eyes filled with unshed tears.

"You can all wait in his room as he should wake soon but remember, he is resting. Please keep your voices down." The Nurse smiles, freeing one hand from my grasp and patting Lia on the shoulder. I hesitate for a moment before letting the Nurse go and asking her to lead the way. She nods, giving us all a reassuring smile before turning and opening one of the heavy doors, Alice sends a message to Adam letting him and the others know where we will be before she trails behind us.

Max's room isn't far and after passing three doors, we are told that the fourth door leads to his room. Everyone watches me, waiting for me to turn the handle and enter first but guilt seeps into me. It is because of me that Max was injured and nearly killed. Had I killed Juden after the first interrogation, Max would be safe and healthy right now. A hand gently wipes across my cheek and I turn to see Mia watching me with a soft smile.

"What if he hates me for this?" I ask in a choked voice, feeling the tears on my skin.

"He won't. No one blames you for what Juden and his men did." She reassures me. I turn to see the others agreeing, Alice coming to give me a tight hug. With their reassurance, I pull away from my friend and face the door once more, pushing it open and stepping into the room.

The first thing to hit me is the sterile smell of peroxide mixed with anti-bacterial hand soap. The second thing is the sounds of machinery helping to monitor Max's condition. He lays so still on the hospital bed, his chest thankfully rising and falling with each breath. Even with the sounds of the machines the room is quiet. Too quiet.

Slowly walking towards the bed, my eyes scan the bandages and casts covering Max's body. His face is swollen and the small amount of ebony skin I can see has grown darker from the bruises.

"I'm sorry." I find my self saying, a tear slipping down my cheek as I take a seat on the chair closest to me, taking Max's hand in mine and closing my eyes.

"Don't be." A hoarse voice whispers. Opening my eyes, I find myself staring into Max's eyes, the right one barely opening from how swollen it is.

"You're okay!" A sob of relief fills me seeing Max awake. Lia rushes to the other side, gingerly sitting on the edge of the bed and taking Max's free hand in hers. He turns to look at her, a smile on his split lips before he turns back to look at me, guilt replacing his smile.

"I'm sorry Alli." He chokes out, squeezing my hand gently.

"Why are you saying sorry to her?" Sky's voice sounds from behind me, his hand coming to rest on my shoulder.

"Because I couldn't stop them." Max closes his eyes, tears slipping past them.

"They were there with me the whole time and a few days before the execution, they attacked me and stole my tablet."

"You were doing your job, Max. This is not your fault." Squeezing his hand, I try my best to reassure Max. His tense body relaxes, the tears flowing freely now. Lia does her best to wipe them away, whispering into his ear that he did his job and no one is mad at him. She places a gentle kiss on Max's lips, making me smile and turning to look up at Sky who smiles down at me. It seems we aren't the only couple in the group.

"Seriously?! Sky gets a girl, and now Max?!" Kian groans, causing the tension in the room to melt and all of us to laugh.

"Don't worry Kian, there is someone out there for you." Arian states with a chuckle, elbowing him.

"Get some rest Max, Lia stay with him." They both looked at me and I smiled, squeezing their hands. Kian just scoffs, turning to look at Mia who fake gags before grabbing a coffee from the tray and bringing it to me. I thank her, taking a sip of the much needed caffeine. With Max being so injured, we stay for an hour before the pain medicine kick in causing Max to slowly nod off. Smiling softly, I tell Max to get rest and order everyone out of the room but Lia, telling her to take care of her boyfriend and giggling when her face turns a shade of crimson. Sky tells to take the time off until Max is healed and given clearance to return to work before we leave, shutting the door behind us.

"You okay Allisara?" Sky asks, pulling me into his arms as I take a deep breath. My body is shaking as I think about Max in the room behind us. Of all the innocent people killed. Of my parents buried in the Royal Cemetery.

"We need to hold a meeting with the Cabinet Members and the Military Generals." I state, looking into Sky's eyes.

"Already planned for tomorrow." He states, making me smile.

"Good. I want that bastard dead." I ground out. Sky's gaze hardens as he nods in agreement, the both of us filled with anger. Juden has gone too far hurting one of my friends – one of my family. I should have known that a vile man like him would not rest until he sat on the Throne again.

Sky leads me away from the hospital wing, taking me directly to my bedroom and pulling me towards the bathroom where a hot bubble bath waits. I protest, claiming that I have war to prepare for but he counters with it being a long day and I need to rest before I do something rash. I sigh, giving in and find myself curled on his lap in the bath, the stress of the day finally washing over me as I cry my heart out.

Epilogue

Pacing her room, the Princess wonders if now is the right time. Plans were made to hold her Coronation next Saturday as this Sunday she will turn twenty-one. She knows with the small fights and skirmishes caused by that Traitor and his rebels that her people need a distraction, but deep down this nagging feeling tells her something bad is going to happen.

The door to her room opens causing the Princess to jump in fright. Her boyfriend, realizing he startled her, takes quick strides and pulls her into his arms.

"Are you okay Allisara?" He asks, pressing a soft kiss on her cheek.

"I am worried about next week. The Princess admits, wrapping her arms around him and pressing her body as close to his as possible.

"Next week you will be crowned Queen-"

"And the Rebellion could be in full swing by then." She cuts in, worry etched into her voice. The man sighs, pulling away from her slightly to look into those violet eyes that melts his heart, giving her a reassuring smile.

"Nothing will go wrong. Everyone is ready for what Juden has planned. We will win." He states, his voice holding the reassurance and conviction she needs.

Feeling a bit better, she takes his hand and leads him to their bed. What she needs right now is a moment to forget, to feel like a normal woman in love.

♔[1]

Sitting at his desk, eyes on his monitor, the man in the shadows smiles. Her Coronation is only a week away. It is the perfect place to set his plan into motion. If he plays his cards right, his men might be able to kill that thorn

---

1. https://coolsymbol.com/copy/White_Chess_King_Symbol_%E2%99%94

in his side. With a grin, he turns to look at his son, the man he was always disappointed in proving to be an asset he never thought possible.

"Did they confirm that they will be attending?" He asks his son, getting a firm nod.

"Yes. If he does what is told, then I promised to marry his daughter and make her my Princess Consort when the time is right." His son answers, a smirk on his face. The man's grin grows and soon he lets out an amused laugh.

He has seven days to wait patiently. When Allisara walks into that room to take a crown that should rightfully be his, the war will begin.

Acknowledgement

Honestly, I just want to thank all my friends on the Wolf Pack Writing Community. Without them keeping me sane during the 2 months writing process while recovering from surgery and the pneumonia I would have never gotten this book out.

About the Author

BORN AND RAISED IN Brampton Ontario - also known at "The Flower City"- Alana Dyer started her relationship with books on a "Hate/Hate" relationship as a child that quickly became a passion for reading as she found that novels can bring you places never seen before.

From finding her love of reading, Alana Dyer soon began writing little stories as a child, and in 2015 with the discovery of Wattpad, Alana started writing seriously with the hopes of one day publishing. Five years later after writing for a loyal fanbase, Alana debuted August 30th, 2020, on Amazon with her first full length novel "The Runaway Breeder".

Now in 2023, Alana Dyer has published 6 novels and two Novelettes under the pen name A. Dyer and spends her days writing, playing with her many pets and planning to expand the distributions of her books.

Rejection Series

Three she-wolves learn that life can take a turn for the worst and those who are supposed to love you can become your worst enemies. When the Moon Goddess and fate play a cruel card that shatters each of their hearts and a budding war is on the horizon can each one find their true strength that lie within and figure out just who is the mastermind in the war that will change the fate of the werewolf race?

Follow Amberle and her Full Moon Rejection in "Rejection on the Full Moon"

See if Geminie's soul mate regrets "Rejecting the Future Moon Goddess"

Can "Rejection to the Alpha King's Daughter" bring out the true Werewolf Queen in Crystalline

And will these girls be able to piece together the true Soulless Evil that hides behind his War?

Rejection on the Full Moon
Book 1

SOULLESS - WEREWOLVES who have turned rogue with no humanity left, giving in to their beastly urges.

Rejection - an act in which your soulmate rejects the mate bond, causing immense pain to the rejected.

These are the challenges Amberle Crest must overcome after becoming an outcast amongst the wolves her age due to an event outside of her control.

When her mate rejects her on her eighteenth birthday, Amberle realizes that living in a pack where the majority would rather use her as a slave than treat her as an equal is not worth the pain. She becomes the notorious wolf, Fire Foot, vowing that everyone would regret how they treated her, as she leaves her pack in the past.

Now a ghost forgotten by those that tormented her, Amberle does whatever it takes to survive as a lone wolf. A fateful day changes her lonely life to one full of happiness and hope—until ghosts from her own past call for aid in ridding their pack of the Soulless who threatens all wolf kind.

Faced with new friends, old foes, and the threat of a building army, will Amberle be able to fight the ghosts of her past to cherish the pack she has found or will an old mate claim her before a second chance mate can show her what being treasured by someone is all about?

Rejecting the Future Moon Goddess
Book 2

Soulless - werewolves who have turned rogue with no humanity left, giving in to their beastly urges.

Rejection - an act in which your soulmate rejects the mate bond, causing immense pain to the rejected.

Moon Goddess - the deity that created the werewolf race whom her creation worship

Omega - The lowest ranked wolf in the pack sometimes treated as nothing more than a slave or an object

These are the things Geminie Blake learns after being blamed for the tragic Deaths of her Alpha and Luna. With the pack turned against her and failing to shift as a wolf, Geminie faces challenges every day with the hope of one day gaining freedom or her mate saving her. But when her fated soul mate ends up being her ex-best friend and the son to the late Alpha and Luna rejects her, Geminie's life changes drastically.

Learning that she is not Geminie Blake - daughter to the Beta couple - but Geminie Starlite - daughter to the Moon Goddess and Future Moon Goddess herself - Geminie quickly faces the new challenges thrown her way as she navigates her wolf form and Goddess powers, creating a pack that rivals that of Blood Moon and building her life from scratch to one day take up the mantel as Moon Goddess becomes her priority.

Now, thriving and loving herself for who she is, Geminie forces the past behind her as she waits for her second chance at love. When her first mate requests help and aid from a threat created by Soulless and a potential Leader of the wolves that have lost their Humanity, Geminie is forced to face the wounds left unhealed and return to the place she called hell for eleven years of her life.

Will Geminie be able to overcome the scars left by years of abuse and find love once and for all, or will the panful wounds of her past and threat from the Leader of the army of Soulless ready to kill at a moments notice take the last bit of happiness this young Goddess has left.

Rejection to the Alpha King's Daughter
Book 3

Soulless - werewolves who have turned rogue with no humanity left, giving in to their beastly urges.

Rejection - an act in which your soulmate rejects the mate bond, causing immense pain to the rejected.

Moon Goddess - the deity that created the werewolf race whom her creation worship

Omega - The lowest ranked wolf in the pack sometimes treated as nothing more than a slave or an object

Alpha King/Queen - The rulers of the werewolf nation

Runt - The smallest of the wolf pack, usually ignored or bullied for being the smallest

Crystalline Thorn grows under the abuse by her father as she trains to take the throne one day and become the Alpha Queen, leader of every wolf in the werewolf nation. She dreams of the day when she meets her mate and be accepted as a strong Queen, especially since she is a runt.

But her dream is soon shattered when on the day of an Alliance her mate discovers her "weak" form and rejects her promptly leading to her father disowning her and her hopes to inherit the throne is dashed. But that is the least of her worries. Soon, with the help of Geminie and Amberle, Crystalline learns of a war that has been brewing for thousands of years, of a destiny that has been written in the stars by the original Moon Goddess - Luna - and the Goddess of Destiny - Morai - have placed upon her and her connection to the Lost Princess.

Will Crystalline be able to retrieve her throne?

Will she accept the mate that rejected her or chose the second chance mate?

Or will the weight of responsibility handed to her crush her entirely?

"THE CAGE DOORS ARE released and I open my sapphire coloured eyes, dashing out of the prison and into the forest.

Seven days for the full moon to be blue.

Seven days from the starting line to the finish

Seven days, that's how long I had to make it to the lodge as an unmated female."

Legends of werewolves have gone back centuries. Always including the Moon Goddess and her blessing of soulmates to the beings she created. But the ugly truth is there is no such thing as soulmates. There is only The Run.

An event created centuries ago held twice a year during a blue moon where she-wolves run from their male counter parts. If they are captured, they are mated and marked, claimed by whoever captures them first.

No one is exempted from this event - not even Grace Harvest.

After being able to avoid attending the event since turning eighteen, Grace finds herself unable to find an excuse not to participate this time. With her last hope of remaining unmated until she can fall in love, she makes a bet with her Alpha. If she wins, he can no longer force wolves of his pack to participate in The Run and allow them to find love. If he wins, Grace will be mated, and her pack mates are forced to go no matter what.

But what will happen when she meets a golden haired wolf by the name Caden Wolfrain, who instantly captures her attention. Will she do all she can to win the bet, will Caden win her heart or will the secrets Caden keeps force her to cut ties with this golden haired wolf without a second thought no matter the heart break.

Books by the Author

CONTACT THE AUTHOR

 alana.dyer.author@
hotmail.com

 author.alana.dyer

 alana.dyer

 Alana Dyer
@alana.dyer.author

E-BOOK | PAPERBACK | HARDCOVERS
available where books are sold

Don't miss out!

Visit the website below and you can sign up to receive emails whenever Alana Dyer publishes a new book. There's no charge and no obligation.

https://books2read.com/r/B-A-LXGX-TAXXC

BOOKS 2 READ

Connecting independent readers to independent writers.